Scattering Stars

Scattering Stars

a novel by

Wendy C. Jorgensen

Printed in the United States of America

First Printing, 2016

ISBN 978-1530301041

Cover design by Walking Stick Books

Layout design by Emily H. Bates

To my husband

Chapter 1

Clues to our future are intertwined throughout our lives. Often, they are barely noticeable, like a double stitch in a piece of fabric or a chance meeting with a stranger. But sometimes, they slam into us with such ferocity they demand to be noticed.

One of these clues came to light shortly after a reckless driver raced down our quiet street, oblivious to the consequences of his behavior. Tons of steel collided with my happy-go-lucky retriever. The horrific impact shook the ground along with the precarious grip I had on my sanity.

Dad and I had been loading our Chevy Tahoe, making one trip after another between the house and the vehicle with our stuff. I'd turned sixteen a few months earlier, and my dad was trying to destroy my life by moving me to the middle of nowhere.

My golden retriever, Quazimodo, lay on the grass watching our every move, probably afraid he'd be left behind. When a rabbit darted across the lawn and into the street, Quaz took off after him. Seconds later, I heard screeching brakes and a terrible thud. The impact reverberated through my body as if I'd been struck myself.

I dropped the box of books I'd been carrying and ran into the road. "No! No!" I screamed, falling to my knees next to my dog's motionless form. Despair and denial battled within me. The driver jumped out of his car, apologizing over and over, but I couldn't even look at him.

Quaz lay still, whimpering softly. His front legs were twisted at an odd angle, and blood seeped out from under his mangled body. My dad rushed over and knelt beside us, his eyes brimming with tears. After a cursory examination, he got to his feet.

"Eve, we need to get Quaz to the vet. I'll put him in the Tahoe." Dad reached down to pick up Quaz, but my hands clamped down on my dog, pinning him to the ground.

"Don't move him!" I shrieked. I felt compelled to do something, but I couldn't figure out what. Despair enveloped me. I couldn't imagine life without my constant companion.

Instinctively, I pressed my hands into the body of my beloved dog, willing him to live and be whole. He was my best friend, and I refused to let him die. I closed my eyes, blocking out everything around me and concentrating all my strength into his body. He would not die. Not today. I needed him too much.

Warm waves of energy welled up inside of me, infusing my body and his with an otherworldly strength. I felt energized and powerful, like something had awakened inside of me. Opening my eyes, I saw Quaz try to lift his head. Choking back my sobs, I whispered, "Dad! He's moving!"

"Thank God," the driver said, crying right along with us. "I'm terribly sorry." I glared at him, even as my dad reassured him that it was an accident. A newly animated Quaz struggled to get to his feet.

"Easy boy. Easy," Dad said, picking him up and placing him in the back seat of our SUV. Climbing in next to my furry friend, I leaned over, wrapping my arms around him. He should've been shaky and whimpering after his ordeal, but something strange was happening to Quaz.

When we arrived at the vet fifteen minutes later, Quazimodo was sitting up in his seat as if nothing had happened. Throughout the drive, he'd looked out the window and whined, expecting it to open so he could plunge his face into the wind. Although blood covered his side, his head and legs had no visible damage. Dad and I could only stare at him in wonder. After a thorough examination, the vet pronounced him free from serious injury and fit to travel.

Within a few hours, the three of us were packed and on the road to Ridgway, Colorado, with Denver disappearing rapidly behind us.

My name is Eve Hunter. My dog's miraculous recovery is only a small part of what I want to share. Like all mortals, my story actually began before I was born, but of course, I have no memory of that part. I'll begin on my sixth birthday because that's when everything changed. It was the last day I would spend with my mom.

It was a perfect summer day in Visitor Canyon, warm with a light breeze. Butter yellow sunshine bathed the earth in iridescent light. Wildflowers dotted the landscape, which glistened, unbelievably green for the end of the summer. A foaming river cascaded through the canyon bordering the meadow. It was a magical place near our home in Ridgway, Colorado, nestled in the foothills of the San Juan Mountains. Mom and I sat along the river enjoying a picnic in this magnificent setting. We had a strong connection and seemed to be able to communicate without saying a word.

Suddenly, we heard a loud rushing sound which evolved into waves of angry, swirling water. The waves originated from above our heads, as if a heavenly dam had given way. Upon hearing the strange sound, mom froze, overcome with fear and confusion, but her expression changed as the liquid tornado descended. Despite the chaos, I remember hearing her voice above the thunderous tumult, "I love you, and I will come back for you." The roaring water engulfed us and within minutes she was gone.

I never saw her again. Later, my dad told me a flash flood had stormed through the canyon and swept her away. But even as a small child I knew there was more to the story. Besides, they never found a body.

After mom's death, Dad and I left Ridgway and moved east to Denver. For the last ten years, Dad has buried himself in his scientific research, bouncing from one company to another. He's a quantum physicist, who specializes in the manipulation of energy, but the stars are his first love. For as long as I can remember, he has entertained me with the possibilities of wormholes and space travel. His fascination with outer space soon became mine. I've spent hours pondering the heavens and imagining life on other planets.

My dad often worked late so I had a lot of time to myself. Sometimes

I was lonely, but mostly, I was just alone. Reading, running, and studying kept me busy. Memories of Mom although ever present, weren't painful; instead, they comforted me like the soft folds of a familiar blanket. Life was good in Denver, and our tragic past was far behind us. It never occurred to me that we would return to the home of my childhood.

My comfortable existence came crashing down in early September, when Dad walked in the front door, dropped some files on an end table, and announced we were moving back to Ridgway. As his tall, lanky frame entered the living room, I knew something was up because he avoided looking at me.

"Eve, I need to talk to you about something." Without waiting for a response, he continued, "I've been offered a job back in Ridgway," he said, trying to sound casual as he straightened his files, first vertical then horizontal.

"You've what?" I asked, unable to believe I'd heard him correctly.

"Your grandfather has invited me to come back to Terra Dyne. He wants me to continue the work I was involved in when you were a child."

I stalked across the living room, stopping inches away from him. "Terra Dyne? Are you serious? Grandfather's company where you used to work with *Mom*? I can't believe you're even considering going back there."

My maternal grandparents, Jarak and Lillian Sorensen, had travelled to Denver in August to celebrate my sixteenth birthday. My grandfather had insisted on the trip, claiming sixteen was a huge milestone in my life. Had the true purpose of the visit been to convince my dad to rejoin his company? I was furious.

Dad went into the bedroom attempting to escape my fury, but I was not going to let him get away. I stormed into his room, glaring at him as he emptied the change from his pockets. Realizing I was not going to leave him in peace, he attempted to calm me down.

"Eve, the truth is I need to be back in Ridgway. I feel like I'm wasting my abilities. Besides, your grandparents and I agree that the family should be together. This will be good for us," he ended, running his hand through his wavy, dark hair. It was a lame explanation, and we both knew it. Something was up.

"But Dad, I'm happy in Denver. This is my home. After all this time, the three of you have decided the family should be together? What about school? My junior year has already started. Have you thought about what this will mean to me? My life will be ruined if you make me move to the end of the earth."

"Come on, Eve. Ridgway is not the sticks. The high school has college-prep classes and plenty of electives. You make friends easily. If you're not happy, you can always return to Denver after graduation. But I know you'll love it there. You can ski Telluride in the winter and hang out at the Reservoir in the summer. Plus, it's a runner's paradise. Hundreds of trails wind through the forest. Think of it—a different running trail every day."

I fought to keep my anger under control, desperate to make him understand that he was ruining my life. "Seriously Dad?" I said, my voice shaking with emotion, "I really don't think I want to be running around in the forest, especially not in Ridgway. I seem to remember that hanging out in the woods didn't turn out so well for Mom."

He stared at me in disbelief that I had dared to play the mom-died-in-the-woods card, and then left the room without a word.

I'd crossed the line, but I didn't care. My emotions cycled between overwhelming anger and paralyzing despair. My life was falling apart. What was I going to do? I needed to get out of the house before I exploded.

Grabbing my running shoes and Quaz, I left the house, slamming the door to announce my frustration to the world. Why did this have to happen now? Why couldn't Dad wait until I finished high school? As my feet pounded the pavement, I sought relief from the turbulence inside me. Running usually helped to calm my inner demons, but today, the physical exertion failed to bring any peace. Passing familiar landmarks, my misery only increased.

When I finally returned to our street, darkness had fallen. Quaz ambled along beside me for the final block, grateful we'd finally slowed to a walk. We lived in a quiet neighborhood, and many people were sitting down to dinner by this time. At least they were free to enjoy themselves because their lives weren't about to be destroyed. I knew I was wallowing in self-pity, but I didn't care.

Not bothering to check in with my dad, I grabbed a sports drink from the refrigerator and went straight to my room. I turned the situation over and over in my mind, but I could see no way out. By all indications we were moving. Not only was I leaving the familiarity of Denver, but I was also plunging into a past I would rather forget.

I read until midnight, struggling to focus on an assigned novel for English class. I knew if I turned out the light, it would take me forever to fall asleep. Exhaustion finally won out over mental turmoil, and as I wrestled with sleep, a familiar nightmare returned.

Mom and I were blinded by a disorienting whirlpool that descended from above. We were quickly separated as rushing water stormed over us. Enveloped by the thick soup, I felt the air being crushed out of my lungs. The relentless force refused to let up, tossing me violently. My mouth filled with the cold, slippery liquid as I screamed, frantically trying to grab my mom as she slipped away from me in the voracious current.

Something strange was happening. Instead of sinking as drowning people usually do, we were rising rapidly. Mom disappeared from view above my head. We were being sucked up as if by some celestial vacuum, inexplicably drowning in a watery vortex deep in the mountains.

I awoke in terror, my heart pounding. Tears of frustration flowed down my cheeks despite my efforts to contain them. My fear of returning to Ridgway had dredged up disturbing memories. Mom's disappearance in Visitor Canyon didn't make any sense. What had really happened? Had she actually drowned? How had I survived?

Any possibility of sleep had evaporated. Slipping my arms into the sleeves of my robe, I wandered through the rooms of our house. My dad could sleep through a passing freight train, so I didn't have to worry about waking him up. I grabbed a kitchen chair, set it up in the dimly lit hallway, and began searching the coat closet for a box of old photos Dad had stashed away on the top shelf. After moving several items, I discovered the dusty box, which looked like it hadn't been touched for years.

Taking the box back to my room, I put it on my bed and removed a stack of photos. All of them had been taken before we left Ridgway. Dad generally acted as the photographer, so it was Mom's face that beamed along with mine from nearly every picture. There were also several with my grandparents and a few other people who resembled my mom.

Gradually throughout that long night in the quiet darkness, a strange but comforting thought enveloped me: these were my people. Along with this thought came a strong yearning to reunite with them, to return where I belonged.

By the time light began to appear through my sea green bedroom curtains, my perspective had begun to change. Somehow I knew leaving Denver was the best thing for us. The moment I allowed myself to consider the possibility of moving, a wave of peace and confidence engulfed me. I even felt a twinge of anticipation.

After mulling my decision over for several days, I gathered the courage to speak to my dad one morning. He looked up warily as I approached, no doubt expecting another angry tirade. His clothes looked like he had slept in them and deep lines etched his weary face. Apparently he'd had a rough week too. I decided to jump right in before I changed my mind.

"Uh Dad, I've been thinking, and I'm good with it. I'm ready to move to Ridgway." Dad held his juice glass in midair and stared back at me as if I'd said I was running away to join the circus. I crossed the kitchen, got the orange juice from the refrigerator, and waited in the awkward silence.

Finding his voice, he managed to ask, "Are you sure?"

"No, not really, but somehow it feels like the right thing to do. You should be happy. Don't make this any tougher than it already is."

"How does it feel like the right thing?" he asked.

"I just have a feeling I belong there," I tried to explain, flustered at my inability to understand my own decision.

"Interesting," he said. "Have you had these kinds of thoughts before?"

"What *kind* of thoughts? No. I mean I never even considered returning to Ridgway. But yeah, sometimes I know that certain things are right for me. It's no big deal—must be a women's intuition thing," I said.

"You're sixteen."

"So? I'm mature for my age." I cracked a half smile.

"I'm surprised you're not fighting this," Dad said, eyeing me suspiciously. "And I'm having a hard time accepting your sudden change of heart."

"Look, I'm sure this is what I want, okay?" I lied. This move wasn't what I wanted, even though I knew it was right.

As we prepared to leave Denver, my resolve wavered, making me question my sanity. Then I remembered other times in my life when I'd felt a guiding influence to act. This was one of those times when the voice in my head was undeniable, but I was still conflicted.

I felt like Luke Skywalker from Star Wars, seeking courage to embrace The Force—that great power of the universe which could be tapped into by those who allowed themselves to be guided by it. Some inexplicable force seemed to be drawing us back to the mountains. Who was I to fight against it?

Chapter 2

Near the end of October, we drove past the bright blue waters of Ridgway State Park Reservoir, north of town. Ridgway was developed in 1891 and named after one of the founders of the Rio Grande Southern Railroad. It straddles the Uncompahgre River and is surrounded by the Cimarron and San Juan Mountains. The town, with a population of a thousand or so, has the only stoplight in Ouray County. Did I mention it was small?

In my mind, Ridgway was the perfect place to hide out and disappear. Denver seemed as far away as another planet. The peace and confidence I had experienced earlier was crumbling. How on earth was I going to survive?

But Dad was happier than I'd ever seen him. Jarak's job offer had changed him. His face glowed with excitement as he talked nonstop about returning to his childhood home in Ridgway. Gone was the brooding man who often stared into space as if he was trying to figure something out. I tried not to destroy his enthusiasm.

With hours of driving behind us, I gazed out the window at the tranquil waters of Ridgway Reservoir, glistening in the bright sun and surrounded by the rapidly fading fall colors. At seven-thousand feet, autumn departed early in this area of Colorado.

The San Juan Mountains were incredibly beautiful that afternoon. As I inhaled the crisp October air, I pictured the steep slopes of Telluride with anticipation. My dark mood lifted with each subsequent view of the awe-inspiring landscape and startlingly blue skies.

Despite what I'd said to my dad about not wanting to run the forest trails, I was looking forward to exploring the woods. I glanced into the backseat of our Chevy Tahoe and smiled at Quazimodo, who smiled back and flopped his tail. When I ran my hand through his thick, reddish-brown fur, he wiggled with pleasure. Quaz and I shared a cosmic human-canine connection. I frowned, remembering that morning's accident. Either he led a charmed life or his injuries had not been as severe as we thought.

Dad had named him Quazimodo—spelled with a "z" per Dad's instructions—because he ran with a funny, lopsided gait. Although we were often met with questioning stares whenever we revealed his name, it fit him perfectly. He was a gentle, happy soul, like Disney's character from *The Hunchback of Notre Dame*, minus the hump but shaped a little crooked. Looking around at the endless miles of wilderness, I anticipated many adventures in our future.

I stole a look over at my dad, trying to discern his thoughts. What could he possibly be thinking, returning to Ridgway? It had to be strange to revisit the places he and mom had been together. I didn't remember much from my childhood—aside from that one terrible day. I wondered if he asked himself the same question I asked myself over and over—what really happened in Visitor Canyon?

"Weren't you surprised that Jarak would ask you to return to Terra Dyne after all these years?" I asked.

Dad frowned at my use of Grandfather's name but decided not to correct me. "Not really. Jarak said they wanted to expand their facility, and it's difficult for him to find physicists he can trust. He thought enough time had gone by since your mom—disappeared—and that I might be interested in coming back to work. This works out for everyone."

Yeah, except for me, I grumbled to myself. "Why even expand here in the middle of nowhere? Why don't they move Terra Dyne closer to Denver? They'd have greater access to supplies, transportation, and other scientists. It doesn't make any sense," I argued.

"It is beneficial for the company to be in the middle of nowhere. Your grandfather prefers it to be away from prying eyes. Some types of research require a great deal of privacy."

"Okay Dad, so are you building a time machine or what? Fess up!" I joked. "What is going on there that's such a big secret?"

Dad opened his eyes wide and whispered dramatically, "I could tell you, but then I'd have to kill you."

"Oh brother. Well don't quit your day job, *Maverick*," I teased. Dad and I had watched the movie *Top Gun* many times. He loved to quote Tom Cruise's character, the hot shot naval pilot. Dad laughed, and it seemed like a strange sound coming from someone who until recently had spent much of his time in brooding silence. "Seriously Dad, what type of research will you be doing up there?" I asked.

"Come on *Evelyn*," he said, watching me grimace at his use of my given name. "You know I can't talk about my work. Don't worry, it's nothing to contact Homeland Security over. We just have to be careful due to trade secrets, patent issues, that sort of thing. It's no big deal," he said, but something about his explanation made me think that it was a very big deal.

Had he purposely used my given name to divert my attention? The more he tried to downplay his job, the more convinced I became that Terra Dyne had big secrets. Homeland Security probably would be interested in whatever was going on out there. I decided to keep my suspicions to myself and responded with the answer that Dad expected me to give.

"Okay Dad, if you promise not to call me Evelyn, I promise not to ask you to reveal Terra Dyne secrets. Deal?"

"Deal," he agreed. I might have been imagining things, but he sure seemed relieved.

We pulled off Highway 550 in Ridgway and made a few turns before taking a dirt road that continued into the forest. Soon a large cabin appeared, encircled by tall evergreens and numerous blue spruce. Sunlight filtered through the trees, spotlighting the cabin and making it glow in the waning afternoon sun.

Even though I considered myself a hard-core city girl, I appreciated the beauty and unmistakable lure of my surroundings. It wasn't hard to imagine that we were standing in an enchanted forest, about to enter a witches' domain. I half-expected to see Hansel and Gretel, the Big Bad Wolf, or a few dwarves enter the clearing from the thick circle of trees.

I opened the back door to let Quaz out of the SUV, and he raced crazily around the house, stopping every few feet to explore the scent of unfamiliar forest creatures. He forgets he's eight-years-old—fifty-six in people years. With Quaz around, I'm pretty sure we'd have early warning of any ravenous wolves or disgruntled dwarves.

Dad interrupted my daydreaming. "I rented the cabin from a guy who moved to Montana several years ago. He visits occasionally, but has no interest in staying in the area. Seems the town got a little too crowded for him. Hard to imagine that. Quite a setting, huh? Peaceful and quiet."

"Dad, everything around here is quiet. We don't have to worry too much about noise pollution or overcrowding in Ridgway," I observed dryly.

He ignored my sarcasm and surprised me by saying, "I thought we'd look into finding a dependable four-wheel drive so you won't have to worry about getting stuck in the snow this winter. Your grandfather knows a guy who has a used Subaru Outback for sale."

"Wow, really? That would be awesome. Thanks! When can we look at it?" Since my sixteenth birthday in August, I was anxious to get my own car. I guessed my dad had saved this little surprise probably expecting me to fall into a funk after the move.

He chuckled. "I'll give the guy a call, and maybe we can look at the car tomorrow. I thought I'd take a couple days to show you around before heading to Terra Dyne on Monday." He paused briefly before adding, "I don't imagine you remember much from when you were here last."

I bit my lip, not willing to discuss our past in Ridgway. "Uh, I'm sure I'll find my way around town. It's not like I could get lost here." Realizing the words had come out harsher than I had intended, I tried to explain "I mean the town seems easy enough to navigate. No biggie." Geesh, Dad offered to buy my first car, and I was being difficult.

We walked toward the front door of the house, and Dad produced a couple of keys from his pocket, handing me one of them. Entering the cabin, we encountered a strong woodsy odor mixed with the familiar scent of Pine Sol. Someone had cleaned recently.

The owner, John Meyer, had left his furniture behind when he moved to Montana. An overstuffed rust-colored couch, a couple of outdoorsman-patterned upholstered chairs, and a walnut coffee table were arranged in front of the fireplace in the living room. He had obviously taken good care of the place. The cabin was immaculate and not at all rustic as I had imagined.

We stood in a large foyer, complete with the mountain home decorating essential—an antler chandelier. The living room was straight ahead, and an open kitchen was off to the left. Upon further exploration, we discovered a large bedroom to the right of the entrance way and a smaller bedroom to the left, tucked away behind the kitchen. Much to my surprise and I must admit, relief, I noticed that each bedroom had its own bathroom. Thank goodness I wouldn't have to share a bathroom with my dad. That would've been awkward.

In addition to the bedrooms, an incongruous semi-circular space resembling a sunroom or observation room occupied the rear of the cabin. The walls were crammed with windows, as if someone had tried to ensure that as much of the surrounding forest was visible as possible.

"Wow Dad, check this out. What a strange room to find stuck in the middle of the woods," I commented, staring out one of the tall windows.

"Maybe Montana wanted to observe the wildlife," he shrugged, brushing off the existence of the odd room.

"Well yeah, but it seems more like *Mr. Meyer*," I emphasized, ignoring dad's nickname for the absentee owner, "wanted to make sure he didn't miss a thing that might pass by. Like he was spying on the forest or searching for something."

"Eve, your imagination is working overtime. I'm sure Montana just liked the view."

I was not convinced. "Maybe, but it seems like he built this mini-observatory for more than just a nice view," I said, resolving to spend time in the mysterious room.

We walked back outside to unload the SUV, while Quazimodo continued to investigate every tree and rock surrounding the house. Most of our furniture had been shipped to a storage unit in Denver, but we also had a small moving truck coming on Saturday. The Tahoe was packed with computers, clothes, lots of books, and a bunch of food. The truth is Dad and I could've survived pretty well for a while with those things.

After unloading our stuff, Dad suggested that we go into town and find a place to eat. I laughed to myself. Had we ever even left town? We couldn't have been more than five minutes from the main road. We locked up and called for Quaz to jump in the Tahoe. As we left, I looked behind me, contemplating John Meyer's cabin—my new home, hidden in the forest.

Chapter 3

When we came to the main road, Dad suggested we drive up to Terra Dyne. "Let's take a look around the perimeter before it gets too dark. You'll be surprised at its size. In addition, there's an adjacent residential area where most of the employees live."

He continued, but with a shift in his voice I couldn't quite figure out. "Your grandfather brought several scientists with him when he started the company. When we left Ridgway, everyone lived in this residential development, but the scientists I worked with were brilliant, and they've probably been recruited by other firms. Even so, I don't think any of them would ever leave Terra Dyne permanently."

"Why not? I would think this town would become terribly claustrophobic after so many years. Talk about a bad case of mountain fever."

"The research Terra Dyne conducts is exclusive to this facility. There is no comparison, no competition anywhere. Still, I thought Jarak was eager to share his knowledge with the world," he ended thoughtfully.

"*Share his knowledge with the world?* Really dad, has my grandfather discovered something earthshattering? You're talking about him as if he's the next Stephen Hawking."

"Eve, your grandfather has exceptional abilities that are far beyond my comprehension. This place—Terra Dyne—is like nowhere else on earth."

My dad had never shared these feelings about my grandfather. It was obvious he idolized Jarak. Why hadn't I picked up on that before?

"So you left because of Mom?"

"I loved my work, but your mom's presence haunted me. I needed to escape—to start over and pretend this place never existed. But I should've known I'd come back. After working for Jarak, nothing else could ever measure up."

I searched for a response to his startling admission. Whatever was going on here, my dad was obsessed. One way or another, I would find out what Jarak was doing.

Abruptly, he declared, "It's good to be back. I shouldn't have waited so long to return."

"Well, at least you won't feel like the awkward new guy. Being back will be more like a reunion. After a few weeks, you'll probably feel like you never left..." my voice trailed off. It could never be the same. Mom wasn't here.

My dad was still puzzling over the fact that all his former colleagues remained at Terra Dyne. "After twenty-three years, I thought at least some of my coworkers would have left to share their technology with other companies. Jarak said everyone has returned. I must've had the wrong idea about what he was trying to accomplish. I suppose he has other plans for them," he said quietly, as if talking to himself.

"Other plans for them? You make grandfather sound more like a dictator than a boss. I would think his employees get to decide for themselves what they want."

Dad made no reply, staring into the gathering darkness.

"It does seem strange that no one has moved on," I continued. "Twenty-three years is a long time to stay in one place, but people in small towns don't move as much as people in the city. Maybe everyone else is as captivated by this stuff as you seem to be. What on earth would be exciting enough to entice a bunch of scientists to remain hidden in the wilderness for more than twenty years?"

Dad remained silent. Something was bothering him.

The skies continued to darken as we turned off the highway at a barely visible sign announcing "Terra Dyne Industries." Traveling down a well-maintained road for several minutes, we arrived abruptly at a massive black gate lined with cameras and motion detectors. Dad jumped out and inserted a key card into the appropriate slot. As he got back in the SUV, the gate swung slowly open.

"Wow, I feel like we've just been granted permission to enter Willy Wonka's Chocolate Factory," I joked. "Is this place for real? Are you sure I shouldn't contact Homeland Security?"

Dad responded with a faint smile. "Terra Dyne has always been security-conscious. Because of its sensitive research, the company has taken extensive precautions. There are people who would do anything to get their hands on our technology."

That sounded rather ominous to me, but I decided not to ask questions. I always pictured Dad as a quiet, intellectual man who was a tad boring. I also assumed he worked in one of the safest professions that existed. Surveying my current surroundings, I began to have serious doubts about that theory.

The road curved to the right, and Terra Dyne loomed in the approaching darkness. The rising full moon provided a clear view of the hilltop. An enormous collection of glass and metal buildings sat at the top of the rise. My grandfather's research complex was huge and space-age modern. I had expected a building the size of a grocery store or maybe even a Wal-Mart, but this monstrosity rivaled the Denver Broncos' football stadium.

"Dad, why didn't you tell me about this place? It's unbelievable! Hiding out here in the woods is this humongous airplane hangar—or several airplane hangars joined together."

He looked at me with that same inscrutable expression I had noticed earlier. "I never thought of it quite that way, but it does resemble a series of airplane hangars. One of Terra Dyne's major projects is the search for alternative fuel sources, particularly for aircraft."

Dad's comments practically begged me to ask questions, but my mind fixated on Mom. It felt like she was accompanying us on this journey. Dad had to be thinking of her too.

"Is it hard being back here, Dad? Won't there be reminders of Mom everywhere?"

"Eve, your mom has been gone for ten years. Being at Terra Dyne doesn't make it hurt any more or any less. I don't need to be here to be reminded of your mom. Every time I look at you, I see her face," he said quietly. "You are the special gift she left for me."

Awkward. We loved each other fiercely, but didn't often express how we felt. I struggled with how to respond. It was both wonderful and painful to hear him say that I reminded him of Mom, but Dad must be delusional if he thought I resembled her.

Fathers really are blind when it comes to their daughters. I was a junk-yard daisy compared to my mom, a perfect greenhouse rose. My mother, Kara, had been an extraordinarily beautiful woman. Maybe all daughters think their mothers are beautiful, but my mom had been positively strik-ing. Even as a young child, I had sensed the atmosphere change when she entered a room.

She'd been tall and slender, with translucent skin and long, blonde hair. People on the street would turn around and stare at her; apparently for-getting that staring was rude. But what really captivated everyone were my mom's incredible blue-green eyes. They were mesmerizing, the color of warm Caribbean waters accented by flecks of gold.

The only physical feature I inherited from Mom was her astonishing eyes. But whereas this feature made my mom look exotic and enchanting; in my pale, ordinary face, the eyes looked strange and out of place.

Mom's classic beauty and ethereal figure had majorly passed me by. I was five feet, six inches tall—not short, but certainly not tall. I've always wanted to be tall since I'm a runner, and logically or not, I equate taller with faster. I'm a decent runner, just not particularly fast. I want to be fast.

Although my hair is long and blonde, it's not corn silk blonde like my mother's hair. Mine is the color of a haystack, sort of a dirty-blonde mixture of ten or twenty shades. Mom's poise and grace were also not passed down to me. I had cuts and bruises to spare from colliding with things. It wasn't likely anyone would ever use the word graceful to describe me.

Dad reached over and patted my arm clumsily, then put the Tahoe in gear and drove around the side of Terra Dyne, where we encountered an-other gate. Getting out of the SUV to look around, Dad explained, "This is The Colony, where most of the scientists and their families live. Your grandparents live here, and your mom and I brought you here many times."

We stared silently through the black metal bars at the homes beyond the gate. I had hazy memories of playing in my grandparents' backyard, but I hadn't been to Ridgway since Mom died so this place was only vaguely familiar. A peculiar surge of energy disturbed the silence, as if the ground were vibrating.

"Can you feel that?" I asked my dad.

"Can I feel what?"

"It's like the streets are humming or vibrating with energy," I said.

"I don't feel anything. Maybe you're feeling the buzzing of the electrical generators."

"No, it's something else—intense, like we're sitting on top of a generator. You can't feel that?" I asked again. He shook his head. In spite of my irritation, I believed he had no idea what I was talking about. For some reason, he couldn't feel the vibrating. And it was intensifying.

Suddenly, a voice came out of the darkness from beyond the gate, "Can I help you with something?" Though not angry or demanding, it was a commanding voice. A large man in jeans and a dark sweater approached us from the other side of the gate. The voice fit the character.

Before Dad could say anything, the man's demeanor changed. "Tom! Tom Hunter! I heard you were coming back to Terra Dyne." The man opened the gate, then grasped Dad's hand and shook it with obvious pleasure. "It's great to see you. We've been waiting for you to return."

We've been waiting for you to return? Was it my imagination or was he referring to more than just a former colleague anticipating an old friend's return to work?

My dad didn't seem bothered by the remark. "Hello Jakob. It's nice to see you too. And it's good to be back, but a little strange. It might take some time to adjust." Dad seemed a bit nervous upon encountering this blast from the past. He pulled me closer and introduced me. "This is my daughter, Evelyn. I mean Eve. Don't call her Evelyn—she hates it. Eve, this is Jakob Andersen."

Mr. Andersen stared at me for a moment as if he were seeing a ghost. "Incredible. You truly are Kara's daughter. What a beautiful young woman you are." His words would have been disconcerting enough, but his blue-green eyes were even more unsettling. They were mirror images of mine.

"Thanks," I managed to say, tearing my eyes away from his. "Guess I'd better get used to a place where everyone knows everyone else."

"Terra Dyne is a small community," he agreed, "and Ridgway isn't a whole lot bigger." Mr. Andersen's light banter didn't jive with his commanding character or my increasing uneasiness. Plus, the pervasive vibrations were driving me crazy.

"Hey Jakob," Dad said, a touch of weariness in his voice, "Eve and I just got into town this afternoon. We stopped by so I could show Eve where I'll be working, but we're on our way to dinner. Can you recommend a place to eat? Things are a bit different from ten years ago."

"Sure, we'll catch up on Monday. There's a new little café—Carol's—past the main intersection on Highway 62. The food is decent, and the service is always good."

"Perfect. Hey, it really is good to see you. We'll talk on Monday." We waved goodbye and got back into the Tahoe. Mr. Andersen closed the gate, checking to see that it had locked.

"*We've been waiting for you to return?* What's that about?" I asked.

"Eve, these people are like family. They keep track of each other and hate to see anyone leave. I'm sort of the Prodigal Son returning to the fold."

"That's too weird and a little creepy. Is Mr. Andersen related to Mom?" I asked.

"Not that I am aware of. Why would you ask?"

"His eyes are identical to mine—blue-green with a touch of gold. Other than Mom and her parents, I've never seen anyone else with those eyes."

Dad looked at me thoughtfully, as if he were deciding what to say. When he finally spoke, he seemed to choose his words carefully.

"Eve, you're going to meet several people around here with similar characteristics. The people of The Colony look alike. Perhaps they are more closely related than I thought."

"So the blue-green eyes are some sort of dominant gene thing with this bunch?" I persisted. "Really Dad, that doesn't make any sense. I'm not a geneticist but even I know that blue eyes are recessive."

"The older you get, the more you'll realize that many things in this world don't make sense."

With that enigmatic remark, we lapsed into silence. What a strange evening it had been. Terra Dyne was not what I had been expecting, and Mr. Andersen seemed more like a security guard than a scientist. What was my dad getting himself into? All sorts of conspiracy theories raced through my head, but then I remembered that my grandparents owned the company and my parents had both worked there. The people I knew couldn't be a threat to national security.

The recommended cafe was easy to find. A cheery green and white sign announcing Carol's Mountain Café gleamed in the moonlight. Four cars occupied the parking lot. Business probably dropped in the off season. Summer visitors had left and winter visitors had yet to arrive. As we entered the café, a smiling, curly-haired woman called out from behind a cash register, "Welcome folks! Have a seat anywhere you'd like." I assumed this was Carol.

My eyes were drawn to a solitary man in a gray hoodie hunched over a cup of coffee. I sensed a darkness about him, but before I could follow my thoughts, a stunning couple stood up and smiled in recognition. My first thought was that a couple of movie stars had suddenly materialized in a nondescript café in Ridgway, Colorado.

"Hello Roger, Devin. It's been quite a while," my dad said, returning their joyful smiles with one of his own. Nearly gasping aloud, I could only stare as two sets of stunning blue-green eyes looked back at us. Holy cow! This town had been invaded by the aquamarine-eyed people. And the eerie vibrations were back.

"Tom! Welcome home!" Roger responded. Something about the way he greeted us made me wonder if he'd known we'd show up at the café. "And this lovely lady must be Evelyn, all grown up," Roger smiled at me. "Jarak informed us you were headed back this way. It has been far too long. We've missed you."

Dad introduced his friends. "Eve, this is Roger Winter and his wife, Devin. We worked together on several projects years ago."

"Eve, it's wonderful to meet you. We're so happy to have you both here with us," Mrs. Winter said warmly. "I imagine you're not thrilled to leave Denver behind, but I'll know you'll grow to love it here," she said confidently. Either she'd read my mind or had a clear understanding of teenagers.

I managed to mutter some sort of greeting, trying not to stare. Despite the fact that the clone-like eyes of everyone were a little unnerving, the Terra Dyne bunch was certainly friendly. I wouldn't have any trouble getting to know people in this town. Besides, they all seemed to know me already.

"Have dinner with us. Devin and I haven't ordered yet," Mr. Winter said. His movements were smooth and effortless, and his jet black hair gleamed in the soft café light. Mrs. Winter reminded me of a jungle cat, lithe and ready-to-pounce on unsuspecting prey. She was impeccably dressed, and her hair glistened like spun gold. As a mere mortal, I hesitated to occupy the same space as these two. Dad was not similarly affected and sat down without a thought. It was all I could do not to gawk at our companions. I surveyed my surroundings, trying my best to ignore the dynamic couple and the incessant vibrations.

Landscape shots by local photographers adorned the walls, interspersed with several wooden plaques filled with folksy words of wisdom. The plaque closest to our table read, "If you're not the lead dog, the view never changes." I immediately thought of Quazimodo. He always had to be at the front of the pack, eager to see what's up ahead or around the corner. This was definitely his motto. I could learn a few things from Quaz. Although I wasn't a follower, I preferred staying in the background to being in charge.

As my attention returned to the Winters and the conversation at our table, I noticed the man in the hoodie pick up his check and head behind me toward the cash register. Suddenly, I heard the loud crash of breaking glass and turned to see the man pointing a gun at the cashier. Carol looked terrified, as she frantically stuffed money from the cash register into a bag. A large jar lay shattered on the floor, striped sticks of brightly-colored candy scattered everywhere.

Mr. Winter lunged toward the gunman. The assailant was less than ten feet away from him when he fired. I screamed as he fired again. But Mr. Winter didn't fall back from the impact of the bullets. Instead, he charged the shooter as if nothing had happened, tackling him and grabbing the gun. My dad knocked over his chair as he sprinted to help restrain the prisoner.

"Get off me! Who the hell are you, Superman?" the man shouted.

"Carol, call the police. We've got him. Everything's okay," Mr. Winter said calmly.

Carol didn't look like she could pick up the phone, much less push any buttons. Mrs. Winter walked over to help Carol make the call. The man cursed and struggled to free himself. I sat frozen to my seat, unable to move.

I nodded slowly when Dad asked if I was okay. How could everyone be so calm? This guy shot Mr. Winter in the chest. What happened to the bullets? I turned toward the wall and saw two holes where the wood had splintered, about seven feet above the floor. The bullet holes were too high.

The man had been standing in front of Mr. Winter, aiming directly at his chest when he pulled the trigger. The bullets could not possibly have struck the wall at that height. And yet the evidence said otherwise. I could see that Mr. Winter was unharmed. He and Dad talked softly as they held the shooter pinned to the floor. I studied the two bullet holes adorning the wall.

The police responded quickly to the scene. I had yet to move from the table when they barged in the door, guns drawn. Two policemen rushed over to the gunman, motioning for Dad and Mr. Winter to step aside. Another policeman asked if anyone was hurt, acknowledging the Winters with a friendly nod.

"We're all in one piece," Mr. Winter said to a husky police officer with short blonde hair. "Thanks for getting here so fast, Martin."

"No problem. Luckily, we were just down the road," he said. He turned his attention to the rest of us. "You girls sure you're okay?"

We assured him that we were fine, just a bit shaken. A fourth policeman took a seat beside Carol, who had collapsed at a table with Mrs. Winter after calling 911.

As the police clamped the handcuffs on, the man began babbling. "You should have seen this guy. He's like a super hero or something. I shot him twice—twice! And he didn't even flinch! He just kept coming at me."

One of the officers eyed the gunman curiously, paying close attention to his ramblings, but his partner merely rolled his eyes. "Okay, pal. Calm down. So you're telling us you tried to shoot someone. Guess that means we'll have to add attempted murder to the armed robbery charges," he said wryly. He began reading the prisoner his Miranda rights. "You have the right to remain silent…"

But the man refused to listen. Highly agitated, he became insistent. "Stop it! Listen to me! You gotta take this guy in and check him out. I tell you he's not human. He's got some sort of supernatural powers. I saw it myself. These people did too. Didn't you guys see what happened?" he demanded, twisting his head around and glaring at us.

There was a deafening silence. Carol looked up and briefly made eye contact. Mr. Winter glanced at me, and then, apparently confident that I was not going to say anything, he shook his head with a bemused expression.

"Martin, this guy is completely off his rocker. He panicked and fired two shots into the wall," Mr. Winter said. To corroborate his story, he pointed to the fresh bullet holes in the wood behind our table. I was amazed at how incredibly convincing he was. If I hadn't been there myself, I'd certainly have believed him. Mr. Winter had complete control of the situation. Although utterly baffled, I had to admit, I was also impressed.

Martin nodded at Mr. Winter in agreement. "Looks like another twenty-first century wack job—probably a junkie who won't even remember what he did by tomorrow."

More emergency vehicles raced into the parking lot, their flashing red lights visible through the sheer dotted-print curtains. "Let the circus begin," Martin said, as the café filled with investigators.

Two officers escorted the protesting gunman outside to a waiting police car, while Martin and his partner remained to get statements from all of us. When it was my turn to give a statement, what else could I say? No visible evidence existed that would indicate Mr. Winter had been shot. The only evidence that bullets had been fired at all was firmly planted in two holes a couple of feet above my head. I gave the same story as everyone else.

Chapter 4

Dad and I were at the café for a couple of hours Thursday night answering the same questions over and over. On Friday, we both slept in, exhausted from our ordeal. My sleep was haunted with swarms of bullets disintegrating in midair.

The next morning I was too tired to go for a run, so I recruited Quaz to accompany me on an exploration of the surrounding forest. Quaz trotted happily through the woods with reckless abandon. Half the time, I had to jog to keep up with him. In spite of my troubled state, I smiled at his antics. Canine therapy has no competition.

After an hour of wandering the forest trails, we returned to the cabin to find Dad seated in the observation room, staring out the many windows.

"Shouldn't we talk about what happened last night?" I suggested.

"Okay. Let's talk about it. You start," he said, sighing heavily.

"You saw the same thing I did. That man shot Mr. Winter point blank."

"Eve, the bullets hit the wall. Somehow Roger dodged out of the way in time to avoid being shot."

"Yeah, but *how* exactly did he get out of the way? The shooter was right in front of him."

Dad stood up, placing his back to the windows. "I can't really explain to you what happened, so you should let it drop."

"Let it drop? Dad, for heaven's sake, we witnessed a shooting!"

"But nobody was hurt, Eve," my dad insisted. "Besides, Roger has no intention of pressing charges. This incident will have to remain a mystery."

"That sure doesn't sound like the tenacious scientist I've lived with for the last sixteen years," I said, leaving the room and conceding defeat— temporarily.

On Friday afternoon, Dad and I checked out the Subaru my grandfather had mentioned. The car's owner, Peter, opened the door of his house as we walked up the driveway. His voice came out deep and gravelly, like the voice of actor Sam Elliott from the movie *Tombstone*. Dad's got a thing for Westerns, so I've seen a bunch of them.

"Hi, I'm Peter. You must be Tom and Eve," he said. "Jarak told me you'd probably stop by today." Peter had auburn-colored hair, a full beard, and a weathered face that testified to his outdoor lifestyle. A long-time local, he told us he did odd jobs at Terra Dyne and part-time auto repair from his home garage.

"Nice to meet you," Dad said. "We arrived in town yesterday, and we're looking for a dependable little car for Eve."

"The Subaru's parked in the garage," Peter said, leading us around the side of the house. "Heard you had some excitement at the café last night."

"Uh, yeah," dad said, giving me a warning look. "Some guy tried to rob Carol and shot up the place."

"The way I hear it, you and Roger wrestled the guy to the ground," Peter said.

"Roger did most of the wrestling, but I suppose I helped hold him down," Dad said.

"Roger's quite a guy, isn't he?" Peter mused. "Can't say I've ever seen anyone react as quickly as he does. I'm glad to hear no one was shot."

Thankfully he didn't ask me directly about last night. There's a fine line between truth and fiction.

We took the silver Subaru Outback for a test drive, and then returned to Peter's house.It was a perfect mountain car, and besides, it had space in the back for Quaz. Not that he usually sat in the back. Quaz preferred sitting in the passenger seat, like a person. Dad and Peter agreed on a price, and I became the grateful owner of my first car.

After telling Dad I wanted to take my new car for a drive, I headed south on Highway 550, before turning towards Telluride. Despite what I'd told my dad, I had an actual destination in mind. Before long, I pulled into the parking lot of Carol's Mountain Café. Since it was between lunch and dinner, there weren't any customers. I refused to heed my dad's advice and let the incident at the café drop. Maybe Carol could give me some answers.

I found Carol putting dishes away in the kitchen. She looked up with surprise when she saw me, straightening her apron and brushing her curly blonde hair out of her face.

"Eve, honey," she said as she walked over and gave me a hug. "How are you doing? I certainly didn't expect to see you back so soon. Everything okay?"

"Oh I guess I'm fine, Carol, but I have lots of questions." I sat down on one of the bar stools she'd set up in the kitchen. "How about you? You're the one who had a gun pointed at you. Are you as confused as I am about the shooting?"

"Well, maybe I am a bit shell-shocked. Like you said, it's not every day that you have a gun in your face. But that's not what you're asking is it?" She took a seat next to me. "Am I disturbed about the bullets missing Roger? Not in the least. It was a miracle, honey. Simple as that. Now I'm not saying I can explain them—miracles—but I've seen them before."

"Sorry Carol, my dad's a physicist. We don't believe in miracles." I paused for a few seconds before asking, "I feel silly even saying this, but do you think Mr. Winter has some sort of special powers like the gunman was raving about?"

"Honestly, I don't know if he does or not. I suppose it's possible, but he seems like a regular guy to me. But I'll tell you this much, I'm not going to waste any time stewing over why the bullets missed him. I am just happy that they did."

This wasn't getting me anywhere. With a heavy sigh, I confessed, "I wish I could be more like you. I always have to know everything. Just between us though, I do think there's something special about Mr. Winter. I can feel it."

"Well, I'm not gonna argue with anybody's gut feelings, Eve. You could be right about him. There are lots of things we don't understand. And don't be surprised if you meet a lot of special people in this town. It's quite a place." Carol gave me another hug then told me to come by the café any time.

My visit with Carol hadn't yielded any answers, and my frustration was mounting. Needing time alone to sort things out, I headed west along Highway 62.

A few miles from Ridgway, the road began climbing up a sharp incline, rapidly increasing in elevation. Nearing Dallas Creek Pass, I gasped as a majestic panorama of mountains came into view. Prominent among this mountain range stands one of Colorado's famous Fourteeners, the massive Mount Sneffels, a fourteen thousand one hundred and fifty foot goliath. I had seen photographs of these jagged and powerful giants, but seeing them up close was awe-inspiring. Snow capped the tops of these mountains for much of the year, showcasing the unparalleled beauty of this wild and rugged part of the state.

Although eager to leave the Subaru and explore on foot, I was not too thrilled about hiking in unfamiliar territory without my four-legged companion. Dad had taken Quaz to the cabin, so I was on my own. In the end, curiosity won out over caution.

Promising myself that I wouldn't go far, I pulled over to the side of the road and grabbed my water bottle and my driver's license. Dad and I always carried our driver's licenses with us when we hiked. Every time we packed for a hike, he slipped his license into his pocket with the same morbid comment: "At least that way, they can identify the body."

I climbed down the steep hillside, being careful to keep my footing. Thick trees lined the road, and I was soon navigating through dense forest. My cautious self was telling me to go back, but my adventurous self argued that I should go a little further. And that's how I saw them.

Well actually, I heard them first. I was surprised to hear voices in the middle of the forest, mainly because there hadn't been any other cars parked along the road. Through a clearing in the trees, I saw a small group playing what looked like dodgeball.

The four of them were standing about twenty-five feet apart from each other. A man, a woman, and two adolescent boys were tossing around a soccer ball. The man pulled his arm back and threw the ball with full force toward the taller boy, obviously trying to hit him. As I braced for the impact, the ball veered off to the left, missing the boy by a wide margin.

"Missed me, Dad!" he called out. With a wicked grin, he picked up the ball and hurled it directly at the other boy, who stood completely still as if taunting his attacker, then smiled triumphantly as the ball veered off to the right.

I couldn't believe what I was seeing. Without realizing it, I had moved forward into the clearing to get a better look. Catching sight of me, one of the boys shouted, "Stop!" The others froze and looked over at me. Guilty expressions covered their faces.

"Uh—hi," I said. "Sorry to interrupt your game. Don't stop on my account. I was…um, going for a hike," I finished lamely.

Glancing over at the woman, the man spoke up. "No worries. We're the Swensens from Ridgway. Great weather for this time of year, isn't it?"

"Yeah, it's awesome. Can't believe its October. I'm Eve. I just moved to Ridgway with my dad." This was beyond awkward. It was time to make an escape.

"It's wonderful to meet you, Eve," the woman said.

"Well, I really should be going. My dad's probably wondering where I went. Nice to meet you guys. Have fun." With a small wave, I backed into the woods as fast as possible. My heart hammered in my chest as I crashed through the trees, anxious to get back to my car.

Those boys had altered the path of the ball without making contact. Somehow they managed to use their minds to change its course. But that was impossible. And yet, I had seen it with my own eyes. Twice. A flash of understanding hit me. That's exactly what happened at the café. Without question, Mr. Winter had altered the path of those bullets.

On Saturday, the moving truck arrived, and we spent all day unpacking our stuff. I declined to mention the family I had encountered on Dallas Creek Pass. I was not ready to face my dad's skepticism.

The shooter's voice echoed again and again in my head. He told the police he'd shot Mr. Winter and insisted that something extraordinary had occurred, even suggesting that he was not human. That accusation was ridiculous; he was obviously human. But something extraordinary *had* happened. There was no way those bullets could've missed Mr. Winter and embedded themselves in the wall behind his head. Had we all witnessed a miracle like Carol claimed?

I had a little trouble with the whole miracles thing. Although I believed in God as a general sort of benevolent, omniscient being, I guess I'd always figured he was too busy to interfere in people's everyday lives. Was God responsible for what happened in the café?

It's troublesome to come face-to-face with questions about what we truly believe. People take great comfort in knowing that the physical universe follows certain guidelines. When those lines are crossed, it rocks our world. Although I was still hopeful for a logical explanation, I could only concede that we must've been witnesses to some sort of miracle.

I considered a second possibility. What if it wasn't a miracle of the celestial type? Maybe the shooter was on to something. Perhaps Mr. Winter really was some sort of enhanced human with super powers. I nearly laughed out loud at the path my thoughts had taken.

Super powers only existed in fantasy. But then I remembered the Swensen family on the Pass. Was it a coincidence that they exhibited similar abilities? Had something happened to change them? Try as I might, I couldn't come up with any rational theories.

Assuming there was something extraordinary about Mr. Winter, it was entirely plausible that my dad was unaware of his powers. He hadn't seen him for ten years. But suppose he did know about his abilities, would he confide in me? And if he didn't know about them, why was he so anxious for me to forget the whole thing? I had always thought Dad and I told each other everything. Now I wasn't so sure. After the last couple days, everything was suspect, even him.

As the hours passed, I became more convinced that my dad was hiding something. It was not like him to brush off an experience like this. The stubborn scientist I knew would be obsessed with finding an explanation for what had occurred at the cafe.

When the movers left, we grilled some mesquite-marinated chicken outside, despite the chilly October air. Although I'd planned to talk to Dad about the shooting at dinner, my suspicions kept me silent. After finishing the dishes, I shared a couple bites of chicken with Quaz before telling Dad we were going for a walk. He mumbled a distracted *be careful* as we left.

Though it was two days later, the remnants of Thursday's full moon illuminated the forest. I had no fears of wild animals or going out alone at night. Besides, I had great faith in Quaz, who was rather large for a golden retriever and a vigilant guardian. His presence would cause most any nocturnal creature to question the wisdom of bothering us.

Quaz and I made a wide circle around the cabin, returning through the backyard. Our only animal encounter was a magnificent pair of hunting owls. As we emerged from the clearing, I saw my dad silhouetted in the windows of the cabin's semi-circular room. His arms were braced against the wall like he carried the weight of the world. Perhaps our night at the café was bothering him more than he wanted to admit.

Once again, I wondered why John Meyer had installed all those windows. Turning my back to the cabin, I studied the forest, scanning the trees for answers. Had Mr. Meyer been searching for something, or had he been afraid of something sneaking up on him? Looking back at the windows, I decided it must've been the latter. He'd been trying to protect himself from something he thought was out here.

I slept in Sunday morning, but still managed to take Quaz for a quick run before my dad got up. As I took off my running shoes, he entered the kitchen, his body groggy with sleep and his hair sticking up in all directions.

"Wow Dad, you look like you've been hit by a truck," I said, trying to coax a smile out of him. I hated the uneasiness that had sprung up between us.

"I didn't sleep well, Eve. I'm getting old. My whole body hurts." He walked over to the coffee maker and began measuring out some coffee. Dad stubbornly refused to buy a new coffee maker. His decrepit Mr. Coffee machine had been around as long as I could remember.

I laughed and teased him about his advanced age and rapidly declining body.

"Yeah, you can laugh all you want, but someday, you'll feel just like me."

"Well, at forty-one, I think you have a few good years left," I said.

"I'm almost forty-two," he grumbled, then added, "I think I'll grab some toast and get started on my computer. I've got a few things I need to look into."

"Sure Dad, no problem. I planned on having cereal anyway. What time are we heading over to Jarak's house?"

"You mean your Grandfather's house?" he asked, raising his right eyebrow, a gesture I'd tried to mimic without success. A raised eyebrow meant he was questioning one of my choices.

"Okay, okay, the grandparents' house. Jarak—*my grandfather*—seems like some sort of emperor or tsar. Grandparents are supposed to be easygoing and comfortable, like Wilford Brimley's character from that movie *Cocoon*. Grandfather reminds me of a grand monarch. I totally expect him to show up one day dressed in robes and carrying a jeweled scepter. Sometimes I feel the urge to bow when I see him. I'm more at ease around Grandmother, but I swear it's like Jarak and Lillian are from a different world."

Dad coughed and nearly spit out his coffee. "What did you say?"

"I enjoy the time we spend together, but it's awkward. When they came to Denver for my birthday, I felt like they were examining me to see if I had some sort of disease. Grandmother even asked me if I'd been experiencing any strange dreams or having any disturbing thoughts."

"What did you tell her?" Dad asked, suddenly as keenly interested in my mental state as my grandmother had been.

"At first I was embarrassed because I thought she was trying to have the birds-and-the-bees discussion. When I asked if that was what concerned her, she laughed and assured me she felt confident that you'd handled that subject already."

"But how did you answer her question?" Dad asked insistently.

"I told her I've always had vivid dreams and odd thoughts and nothing had changed. Anyway you know what she told me? She said I come from a long line of ancestors with special gifts. I played along with the weirdness, denying any special gifts and admitting my lack of noteworthy talents."

"Don't sell yourself short, Eve. A major part of life is finding out who we are and where our strengths lie. I promise you have many undiscovered talents."

"Thanks, but you're my dad, so you have to say things like that." I looked at him thoughtfully, deciding whether or not I should share what had happened next.

"Dad, do you think Grandmother might be getting senile?"

"Lillian?" he laughed. "Not hardly. She's the sanest woman I know. Did something happen to make you think she's losing her mind?"

"She asked me if there were moments when I could tell what people were thinking—essentially if I could read minds. Not knowing what to say to her absurd question, I simply said no. When I asked her if she could read minds, she admitted that she hadn't been blessed with that particular gift. The whole conversation was weird, Dad. *Beyond* weird."

The worried expression I had glimpsed on Dad's face through the back windows last night returned. I immediately regretted bringing up my conversation with Lillian. Putting his hand on my shoulder he said, "Talk to your grandmother tonight, maybe she will be able to clarify things for you. For now, I have work to do."

Sunday night we drove over to The Colony to have dinner with my grandparents. I couldn't wait to go inside the gated compound. There's something cool about having access to places that are forbidden to most people. The peculiar vibrations hit me with a vengeance as soon as we neared the gates. I made a mental note to ask my grandparents about it. I couldn't be the only one who could feel the throbbing energy.

My grandparents opened the front door as we pulled in the driveway. Their imposing ranch-style house was tan stucco with dark wood shingles and stone accents. All the nearby homes were fairly large, leading me to believe that there was a profit to be made from whatever kind of research these people were engaged in.

"Tom and Eve, welcome! We're so happy you're here," Lillian exclaimed, clasping my hand with obvious pleasure. My grandmother wasn't much of a hugger, which was one thing we had in common. I had tried to identify other characteristics we shared, but so far had been unsuccessful. In fact, I found it hard to imagine even being related to this elegant, dignified woman.

Grandmother's pale silvery hair and blue-green eyes reminded me of my mother. She was slim and graceful, but not quite as tall as mom. Lillian wore tan wool slacks and a powder blue ribbed turtleneck that perfectly accented her coloring. She radiated an inner joy and confidence I couldn't help but envy. I bet she'd passed right by the awkward teenager stage.

Jarak could only be described as a distinguished-looking gentleman, with thick, white hair and a kind, intelligent face. Casually dressed in navy slacks and a beige sweater, he was immaculate as always and undeniably handsome. He pulled me toward him, gave me a big hug, and kissed me on the top of the head. "Eve, what a great blessing to finally have you here in Ridgway with us," he said.

"Well, I'm sure you know it wasn't my first choice," I admitted, giving him a half-hearted smile. His enthusiastic display of affection had me rattled. He seemed much more at ease than he had ever been on his visits to Denver.

Jarak chuckled at my bluntness. "We'll have to see what we can do to change your mind about that. I'm sure you'll grow to love it here as much as we do."

Although I knew he was pleased to see us, my cynical self thought I detected a hint of victory in his eyes that he had lured us back to Ridgway. I quickly scolded myself. Of course he would want his only granddaughter to live closer so he could have a stronger relationship with her. I needed to lighten up and quit being so defensive.

"Come on, Eve. Let's go into the kitchen and get some lemonade," Lillian suggested, despite the cold October air. My grandmother operated under her own set of rules and wasn't particularly concerned with the conventions typically observed for the weather or the seasons. She was just as likely to serve lemonade in January as she was to offer hot chocolate in July.

Tall cherry cabinets with elaborate crown molding lined the walls of Lillian's kitchen, accompanied by gleaming stainless steel appliances and a massive tawny gold and cream-colored granite island.

"Wow, this is some kitchen!" I exclaimed, running my hand along the smooth polished stone of the island.

"Thank you very much. I designed it myself. We love our home in The Colony, and we hope you'll spend a lot of time with us here. I can hardly believe the two of you came back." Lillian said, her voice cracking.

Momentarily flustered, she quickly reined in her emotions and began removing tall, etched glasses from the cabinet closest to the refrigerator.

"I'm definitely looking forward to visiting. I am fascinated by this place. Dad drove me out to Terra Dyne our first night in town. What's up with the weird vibrations that I feel around here? There's some sort of pulsing electrical charge in the air. Dad said he didn't notice anything, but for me it's *intense*."

Lillian turned to me, her face a mixture of surprise and pleasure. "Eve, what you are feeling is the combined energy of The Colony's inhabitants. The energy is magnified since so many of us are concentrated in one place. It is actually quite strong here, so I'd expect you to be aware of it. However, I'm not at all surprised that your dad is unable to feel it."

She pulled a pitcher of lemonade from the refrigerator and resumed her preparations. I didn't know what to think of her answer and fought to come up with an appropriate question to clarify the bizarre information she'd shared with me. Since Lillian had always seemed sort of spiritual, I wondered if she subscribed to the New Age belief that people possessed auras, giving off varying amounts of energy.

"Grandmother, why do you suppose the inhabitants of The Colony emit so much energy? What makes them different from other people? And why doesn't my dad feel it like I do?"

"Because you also carry a great deal of energy within you, my dear," she said, ignoring my first two questions. "And that makes you sensitive to the energy in others. Now, let's take this lemonade into the boys," she said, changing the subject. "I've got a roast in the oven which should be almost ready. Meanwhile, can you grab that tray of cheese and crackers on the counter?" Lillian chattered away about dinner as we exited the kitchen through the butler's pantry leading to the great room.

As we entered, I heard my dad say, "For heaven's sake Jarak, she just arrived. Give her some time to adjust." Dad and Jarak were seated in two large upholstered chairs in front of a massive stone fireplace.

"Adjust to what?" I asked, since it was obvious they had been discussing me.

My dad looked annoyed. "Your grandfather wants to introduce you to some people, and I think it's a good idea to wait until you settle in a bit."

My grandfather nodded in agreement, but I knew there was more to the story. I put the cheese and cracker tray on the heavy Mediterranean-style coffee table, and then joined my grandmother on a mahogany leather couch across from Dad and Jarak.

"And just how long do you think it will take me to settle in?" I asked.

"We'll have to see how things go. We've only been here four days. There's plenty of time for you to meet everyone."

Jarak next words brought an immediate end to my probing. "We heard you had quite a scare on Thursday night," he said.

Oh boy, here we go, I thought, looking over at my dad, whose expression had darkened. Was there no safe subject we could talk about?

"Yes we did," I agreed. With a twinge of irritation, I wondered what exactly I was allowed to say. I wasn't accustomed to hiding things. Sending a defiant glare in my dad's direction, I decided to find out what my grandparents knew about the night at the café.

"Did you talk to the Winters?" I asked.

It was Grandmother who answered, "Yes, we see them often since they only live a couple houses down from us. We've known them for many years."

"What did Mr. Winter say about it?" I wanted to learn the truth and could see no reason not to be honest about what happened.

Jarak and Lillian exchanged glances before my grandfather said, "Roger told us someone tried to rob Carol, but he was able to stop the robbery with your dad's help."

"Well, did Mr. Winter tell you the part about being shot? The gunman fired two shots directly into his chest, but somehow missed him. The bullets ended up lodged in the wall a foot or so above Mr. Winter's head." My voice rose with pent-up emotions. In contrast, my grandparents calmly nodded their heads, accepting everything I said without question.

"Don't you see?" I insisted. "What happened was impossible. Carol believes it was a miracle, but I think Mr. Winter altered the path of those bullets." There! I'd said it. My theory was out in the open. The room was strangely quiet, and no one seemed eager to offer an alternative explanation.

"So, what do you guys think? Could Mr. Winter have altered the path of the bullets?" I demanded, frustrated by the lack of response.

Instead of offering any theories, Jarak asked my dad, "What do you think about all this, Tom?"

My dad scowled, clearly unhappy to be put on the spot. "Eve, I honestly don't know for sure why those bullets missed Roger and hit the wall. Maybe he did alter the path of the bullets."

"But Dad, if that's true, how is it possible?" I persisted.

He said nothing, but instead bowed his head, as if he carried a heavy burden.

My grandmother's soft voice broke the silence. "Eve, remember our conversation in Denver, when we talked about special gifts? These gifts actually do exist. Sometimes people who seem quite ordinary possess extraordinary abilities."

"Are you saying Mr. Winter is one of those people with special gifts?" I asked.

"You witnessed his wonderful gift yourself. The power of the brain can be quite remarkable."

"Dad, you've known Mr. Winter a long time. Were you aware of his—um, *special gifts*?" I asked, hardly able to believe we were having this conversation. Lillian had acknowledged Mr. Winter's ability to move objects with his *mind* as if she were discussing the weather. What alternative universe were we living in?

"I always knew there was something unusual about Roger," my dad confessed. "But I've never seen his abilities in action. I was as stunned as you were in the café."

I struggled to accept this confirmation of what I already knew to be true. Mr. Winter possessed powers beyond those of a normal human being. Even though my dad and my grandparents seemed fine with the existence of special gifts, I couldn't wrap my mind around the idea. And I couldn't help but think a piece of the puzzle was missing.

Lilian asked me to help her with the food, and I followed her to the kitchen. She placed the roast on a serving platter, then asked me to grab the potatoes and the salad. Dad and Jarak were not speaking when we entered the dining room. I knew something was being debated between the two of them, and I had the distinct impression whatever it was involved me.

Dinner lasted forever. Everyone tried to pretend that nothing was wrong. My grandparents filled me in on the town and the school, and Dad listened politely to the conversation, throwing in an occasional comment. Just when I thought the tension had begun to dissipate, Lillian mentioned that two of Mr. Winter's sons attended the high school.

"Have Mr. Winter's sons inherited these special gifts?" I asked, assuming this was the logical question after our fireplace discussion.

Dad let out an exasperated sigh. "Honestly, Eve. Can't you give this thing a rest?"

"I don't understand what's wrong with talking about the miraculous. I would think you would be thrilled by the existence of paranormal powers."

"Eve, of course I understand your curiosity, but I'm not ready for all this right now." Addressing Jarak and Lillian he said, "Thank you both so much for dinner. Please excuse us."

Dad stood to leave, and I did the same, feeling self-conscious and embarrassed. His behavior was completely out of character. My grandmother put her arm around my shoulders, assuring me that all would be well. Jarak walked us to the door and shook Dad's hand with what seemed like disappointment, then stood in the doorway and watched as we drove away.

Halfway home, I realized Lillian hadn't said whether Mr. Winter's sons had inherited his gifts. I actually had something to look forward to at school tomorrow.

Chapter 5

Half an hour before school started Monday morning, I entered the parking lot. Being early for school was not normal for me, and I didn't anticipate it happening very often. My plan was to pick up my schedule and slip into class quietly. I hated being the new kid.

A prominent sign announced "Ridgway High School, Home of the Demons." Since we were in the mountains, I expected the school mascot to be a wolf or a cougar, maybe even a bear, but not a demon. I wondered what inspired the whole demon thing. Despite the bright sunshine and the brilliant blue sky, I shivered, feeling the hair rise on my arms. My vivid imagination must be working overtime again.

Several cars already occupied the parking lot. I chose a spot close to the exit so I could make a quick getaway when school got out. Dad thought I made friends easily, but the fact is I'd been around the same group of kids for most of my life so I never really had to make friends. They were just always there. Grabbing my backpack, I took a deep breath and headed for the entrance, following the sign that directed visitors to the front office.

"Good morning! You're here early!" the red-headed woman behind the desk exclaimed. She was cheerfully round and rosy-cheeked—a dead ringer for Mrs. Claus.

"Yeah, well, it's my first day. I'm from Denver," I mumbled, overwhelmed by her enthusiasm. "My name's Eve Hunter."

"Wonderful!" she responded, snatching a folder from her desk. "Your schedule is right here along with your locker number and combination. Do you need someone to give you a tour?" she asked hopefully.

"I don't think so," I declined. "I'm pretty good at finding my way around. If you could point me in the direction of the lockers, I'll check things out and find my classrooms before the halls get too crowded."

"Well, okay dear. Suit yourself. Lockers aren't too far. Take a left outside the door, then straight down the hallway," red-hair said, her disappointment at my declining the tour obvious. They probably didn't get many new students in Ridgway. Thinking it wasn't a good idea to upset the office staff on the first day, I tried to salvage things.

"Thank you very much for your help, uh…." I struggled with what to call the woman. I finally settled on "ma'am," hoping she thought I was at least polite.

"Oh how rude of me! I was so excited to meet you I forgot to introduce myself. I'm Mrs. Walters. Maggie Walters."

"Nice to meet you Mrs. Walters," I said, then still feeling guilty added, "I'll be sure to let you know if I need anything. Thanks again."

I left the office, relieved to have escaped an excruciating tour filled with Mrs. Walters's early-morning exuberance. It was positively abnormal for a human being to be so cheery at seven-thirty in the morning. I let Quaz get away with it, him being a canine and all, but humans—no way. I needed a few hours in the morning before I turned into a halfway decent human.

As I headed down the hallway, I removed the slip of paper with my locker number and combination from the folder. Arriving at my assigned locker, I successfully dialed the combination on my first attempt and decided to take that as a good sign. It was going to be a good day. Think positive, I counseled myself.

I opened the file, examined my schedule, and immediately groaned when I saw Pre-Calculus first hour. How could anyone negotiate math class at eight in the morning? So much for positive thinking. I sighed heavily, slammed my locker, and backed up, colliding with someone walking down the hall.

"Oh crap. I'm sorry. I didn't know anyone was behind me," I stammered, turning red with embarrassment. Then I looked up into the most gorgeous green eyes I'd ever seen. Those exceptional eyes shimmered with the tiniest hint of blue and a touch of gold. I felt utterly lost in them, mesmerized as if struck by sunlight reflecting off the deep hues of Caribbean seas. "Um, wow—I'm really sorry. I didn't see you," I said, sounding like a complete dope. I seemed to have had lost most of my vocabulary.

Green eyes spoke to me with a rich, mellow voice. "No worries. I wasn't looking where I was going. These halls are always empty until just before class. Sorry, I was texting my little brother," he explained, his voice trailing off as something about me captured his attention.

I froze, spellbound. The marvelous green eyes belonged to a tall, dark-haired, striking young man. I knew I was staring but I couldn't help myself. And I was not the only one staring. His hypnotic gaze trapped me like a laboratory specimen as he examined me closely. Despite my muddled state, I became aware of the same odd vibrations I'd experienced at The Colony.

The enchanting creature in front of me spoke after several moments of intense scrutiny. His perplexed expression evaporated, replaced by a friendly, overly casual smile. Something weird had transpired between us, but I couldn't figure out what exactly. Although he was a stranger, he seemed hauntingly familiar.

"Hey, I know who you are. You're Tom's daughter, Eve, from Denver." This proclamation brought me to my senses, and thankfully, I regained my voice.

"Yes. How do you know who I am?" I asked, desperately trying to determine why he seemed so familiar. The quick shift in his demeanor made my head spin, but if he wanted to act like nothing had happened, so could I.

He laughed as if amused by an inside joke. "Ridgway is a very small town. You met my parents at Carol's place—Roger and Devin Winter."

"Please don't remind me of the café," I groaned. "I mean, I'm not referring to the meeting-your-parents part—they seem like great people—but being trapped in a restaurant with a man waving a gun is not exactly how I planned on spending my first night in town."

Surprisingly, he brushed off the whole incident. "Yeah, I heard about that. We don't get many robberies around here." It was immediately apparent that he wanted to change the subject. I felt like we were playing some sort of game, and I hadn't been told the rules. I also had the distinct impression that he knew something that I didn't—some knowledge about what happened at the café or maybe even some information about me. But what secrets could he possibly know about me? My imagination really was a pain sometimes.

He introduced himself, forcing me to refocus. "I'm Daniel—Daniel Winter. I'm from Ridgway. Lived here all my life," he said. "Boring, huh?" Amusing, but not convincing.

It was my turn to laugh. "It's okay. I won't hold it against you. As they say, there are worse places to be from."

"Actually, I'm pretty attached to this place," he replied. "I wouldn't mind visiting other places but I'd probably return to Ridgway. Bet it was hard for you to leave Denver though," he added, as if he could relate to how I felt.

"Truthfully, I'm hating life right now. The last thing I wanted to do was move here," I confessed, surprising myself for being so honest. I don't usually share my inner most feelings with people I've just met. But I felt an immediate connection with Daniel, like I already knew him. It was thrilling and terrifying at the same time. Daniel's next words struck me as completely out of place and eerily prophetic.

"Eve, I believe I can make you a promise. It won't take long before this town will become the only place on earth you want to live. You won't have any desire to return to Denver."

"Is that right? What are you, a psychic?" I teased, studying his dazzling face.

"Something like that," he answered, regaining his earlier inscrutable expression. We were interrupted by an impatient, high-pitched squeal which echoed down the hallway.

"Daniel! I've been looking all over for you!" The voice belonged to a pouting, voluptuous blonde, who bounced over and kissed Daniel on the cheek. She wore a short, white skirt and a green and white sweater, appliquéd with the letters RHS. "Who's this?" she said, eyeing me suspiciously, like a cat taking stock of a mouse.

"Hey Natalie, this is Eve. She just moved here from Denver," Daniel said, sounding oddly deflated.

"How nice," Natalie said, although it was obvious she thought just the opposite. She turned her back to me and tugged on his arm. "Come *on*, Danny boy. Let's go. The team's already gathered in the gym."

For the second time in five minutes, I was rendered speechless. The whole Natalie thing made me cringe, like a bucket of ice water had been dumped on my head. She continued to ignore me while Daniel shot me an apologetic look. "Hey, well, nice to meet you, Eve. Gotta go. Basketball. See you later."

My attraction turned to disgust. I couldn't believe Daniel was one of those stereotypical brainless jocks with the ditzy cheerleader girlfriend. Somehow he didn't seem to fit the profile. Okay, so maybe he wasn't actually brainless, but he was clearly a jock, and his transformation into a submissive sheep when his bouncy girlfriend showed up made me want to vomit. I had totally embarrassed myself and was positively mortified.

It's not that I hate jocks, or cheerleaders for that matter. As a runner, I suppose I am an athlete, but I've never really considered myself a jock, and by that I mean a member of the in-crowd—the beautiful people. Most of the jocks I knew were primarily concerned with trying to look cool. The whole high school social hierarchy thing bothered me. I couldn't believe I had actually been flirting with one of *them*. I wanted to crawl away and hide.

Pretend it never happened, I told myself as I searched for my classes. By the time I entered the Pre-Calculus classroom, a few kids were already seated. I purposely avoided eye contact so I didn't have to talk to anyone. My encounter with Daniel and Natalie had erased any morsel of sociability I might have possessed that morning. I wanted to find a seat in the back of the class and blend into the walls. Of course, since I was not only the new kid but had also showed up mid-semester, the teacher had to make a big deal of my presence.

He spotted me hiding in the back the minute he entered the classroom. "Miss Evelyn Hunter? Mr. Dale Ayers," he said, walking down the row of desks and handing me a textbook. "Good to have you. Hope that Denver high school has you well prepared because we kick butt in this class. No tolerance for stragglers," he said, returning to the front of the room without waiting for a response.

The bell rang, signaling the start of class, and I relaxed a little, opening my math book. Loud voices sounded in the hall seconds before the door opened and three tall dark-haired guys entered, jostling each other. Their similarity was startling. The three of them could've been brothers.

"Gentlemen, so nice of you to join us," Mr. Ayers said.

"Sorry, Mr. A," the first guy to enter apologized with a disarming smile. "Coach kept the team in the gym past the bell."

"Of course he did, Erik," the teacher muttered, clearly perturbed. "Take your seats."

Daniel followed his teammate into the room, and a scowling third member of the team walked in behind him. I put my head down, now more than ever wishing I could render myself invisible. The day was continuing its downhill slide. Luckily, my math class in Denver had already covered the section Mr. Ayers was teaching that day, so I could let my mind wander and not miss much. My plan to forget what had happened earlier this morning had evaporated when Daniel came in.

When the boys arrived, I experienced the same strange vibrations I'd felt earlier that morning. Was it connected with Daniel? The atmosphere in the room felt charged with electricity. There was a compelling hypnotic quality to it that kept me from focusing on anything else—except Daniel, of course. The vibrating hum had a familiar feel to it, like an unremitting deja-vu experience.

Since Daniel was taking Pre-Calculus, I was forced to admit that he was probably not a brainless jock. Even more surprising was the presence of three members of the basketball team in the advanced math class. Okay, so my jocks and brains theory needed to be revised. However, I did note Natalie's absence with some satisfaction.

Stealing a glance in Daniel's direction, I discovered he was watching me also. As he caught my eye, he self-consciously turned his gaze toward the blackboard, pretending to pay attention. Was it even possible he felt the same weirdness I did? Not likely, I concluded. Yet another part of me was absolutely certain *something* had happened between us in the hallway.

Moments later, I convinced myself that I'd completely lost my mind. Somehow I had managed to conjure up a cosmic connection after only talking to some guy for five minutes—some drop-dead gorgeous guy who turned out to have a blonde bombshell girlfriend, no less. Get a grip Eve, I chastised myself. Besides, Daniel was probably an ego-maniac who thought he was God's gift to women, I thought maliciously.

Throughout the class, I observed Daniel and his friends. After seeing Erik interact with Mr. Ayers, I pegged him as the kind of person who liked to smooth things over, putting everyone at ease. The third guy never seemed to lose his scowl completely, listening to the teacher with alternating expressions of boredom and intensity. All three of them would attract attention wherever they went. Again, I wondered if they were related.

My exasperating attraction to Daniel went beyond his obvious good looks. He was like a magnetic field that relentlessly drew me in. It was driving me crazy. I contemplated transferring to another class, even though this was the only Pre-Calculus class offered. Just as the excruciating hour was nearing the end, Daniel jumped out of his seat in alarm.

"Mr. A, I smell smoke! We need to evacuate!"

"Everybody get out! There's a fire!" Erik echoed Daniel's alarm.

No one questioned the boys; the students reacted instinctively. Before Mr. Ayers could protest, the entire class ran for the door. All three boys raced down the hallway, throwing open doors, and screaming for everyone to evacuate. People began streaming from the classrooms, fleeing in terror. Everyone was in a complete panic, but I didn't get it. There was no sign of a fire, and I still couldn't smell smoke. I became part of the desperate crowd trying to escape.

As I made it to the exit, the fire alarm shrieked, and students pushed to get out the doors. Sprinting across the parking lot, I questioned the absurdity of our actions until I heard a huge explosion. Realizing I was far enough away from the building, I stopped and turned back to see fire and smoke billowing from the school.

Within minutes, fire engines roared into the parking lot with their sirens blaring. The firemen leaped off their trucks and moved everyone further away from the flames. I shook my head in amazement. This was unbelievable.

We stood back behind the barrier for at least half an hour, watching in horror as the firemen fought to put out the flames. Our class had gathered together so Mr. Ayers could account for all of his students. Word was being passed around that no one had been injured in the explosion. Everyone had been evacuated in time. Relief was apparent on the surrounding faces, as we realized how lucky we were to have escaped the fire.

Next to me, I noticed an athletic-looking girl with an emerald green braid interwoven into long, kinky blonde hair. Eyeing me with an expression of disbelief, she said, "This is beyond bizarre."

"Tell me about it. I can't believe I'm actually watching the school burn. I've been in town five days and have already witnessed a robbery and now a fiery explosion. And I thought this place would be dull."

The girl grinned. "Ha! Don't underestimate us. This place—as you call it—is full of surprises. You must be talking about the attempted robbery at Carol's?"

"Yeah. My dad and I stopped there for dinner the day we drove into town, and the next thing I know someone started shooting."

"Good thing no one was shot. Were you freaking out or what?" she asked eagerly, making it sound as if she would've traded places in a heartbeat.

I thought about contradicting her first comment, and then decided to ignore it. "A little, I guess. It was over so quickly."

"Cool," she commented, an excited gleam in her eye. I had no doubt that she found the robbery fascinating, in a morbid sort of way.

Apparently deciding I was someone she found interesting, she stuck out her hand. "I'm Sarah. Nice to meet you."

Gesturing to a petite girl standing beside her with a blunt pixie cut and huge brown eyes, she said, "This is Emily. We saw you in Pre-Calculus. Don't worry, Mr. A is not as much of a slave driver as he thinks he is." She contemplated the now smoldering building with a wry grin, "Well, looks like we might get a vay-cay."

"Not likely," the girl named Emily responded gloomily. "They'll figure out some way to keep us in school. Last winter we had two feet of snow overnight, and the district refused to give us a snow day. "

I introduced myself to the two girls. "Hey, I'm Eve. I was actually born in Ridgway, but we moved to Denver when I was six."

"Great to have you here, Eve," Emily said.

"Yeah, we need some new blood," Sarah agreed.

I immediately felt comfortable with both of these girls, who appeared to be close friends even though they were polar opposites. I pegged Sarah as brash and adventurous, whereas Emily was soft-spoken and cautious. Sarah probably dragged Emily into trouble on a regular basis.

Most of the students were bunched in small groups discussing the fire and trying to decide whether they should wait for the official word or just go home. Several cars were already exiting the parking lot.

"Ladies, are we good?" a flirtatious voice called out. The basketball player that Mr. Ayers called Erik sauntered over to us, smiling like the Cheshire Cat. Where on earth did so many tall, dark and handsome guys come from?

I couldn't resist returning his contagious smile. As he approached, the air once again became charged with electricity. I swear he carried his own atmosphere around with him. He was impossible to ignore. I was transfixed, just as I'd been with Daniel. What was going on around here?

"Erik, have you heard what happened?" Sarah asked.

"Daniel's little brother, Mikey, said some dude's Biology experiment backfired. Looks like a couple of the classrooms might have burned."

"That's awful!" Emily exclaimed. "People could've been killed. I can't believe everyone got out of there before the explosion. Thank goodness no one was hurt."

"Guess that kid will fail the class," Sarah quipped, dismissing the near disaster. She motioned toward me. "Erik, this is Eve. She's a new student from Denver."

"Pleasure," he said. To borrow a phrase from an ESPN-junkie friend of mine, this guy was cool as the other side of the pillow. His genuine, almost courtly air might have seemed fake coming from someone else. Blue-green eyes twinkled beneath thick brown hair that fell just below his ears and curled slightly at the ends. He had a strong, honest and open face, unlike Daniel's closed, secretive one. I couldn't help comparing the two boys.

"Lucky you guys smelled smoke," Emily interjected quietly. Sarah and I looked at her, instantly remembering that it was Daniel and Erik who told us to evacuate. How did they smell smoke when no one else did?

"Pre-Calculus is only a couple of classes down from the Bio lab," Erik explained. "We must've been sitting under a vent or something."

"Well I sure didn't notice anything," I persisted, staring him square in the eyes. "Not even in the hallway. You guys must have a keen sense of smell."

Erik put his head down and shifted his feet awkwardly. Although I had just met him, I knew I had made him uncomfortable.

"Hey Erik! Today would be nice!" a female voice hollered from across the parking lot.

We turned toward the voice, and I saw Daniel and the other basketball player from our class. Next to Daniel was a younger, light-haired version of him, whom I assumed was Mikey. A tall, beautiful girl with long black hair stood with them, glaring at us. Without a doubt, this group could take Hollywood by storm. They put the Twilight vampires to shame.

"Gotta go. My evil twin summoneth," Erik joked, winking at Sarah. "Ladies, we'll talk soon."

"See ya later," Sarah answered, pulling on her braid while watching his every move. He went directly to his sister and her scowl quickly disintegrated. It would be difficult to stay mad at Erik for long. He reminded me of Quaz, always smiling and eager to please.

"Is he beyond gorgeous or what?" Sarah gushed. Apparently she was as enthusiastic about boys as she was about everything else. Or maybe her enthusiasm just extended to Erik.

"He's a doll," Emily murmured. It was clear we already had one thing we all agreed on. Even as I contemplated this charismatic new friend, I felt Daniel watching me closely. Although I didn't see Natalie, I assumed it wouldn't be long before she made an appearance. I was still puzzling over their relationship. Somehow it didn't seem to fit.

"Tara is Erik's evil twin, and she is one wicked customer. You don't want to get on her bad side." Sarah made a face as she pointed out the tall girl as Erik's sister. "Next to Tara is Daniel, and next to him is Daniel's little brother, Mikey. The other guy is Brad. He's a cool guy, but tends toward the cranky side—hence the scowl. They're all on the basketball team as you've probably guessed. But not Tara, of course," she giggled. "She might break a nail." She and Emily exchanged glances and rolled their eyes. "We think Tara belongs in a totally separate universe, apart from us mere mortals. She's a goddess. Who can compete with that?"

"Lucky for you, you don't have to since she and Erik are related," I teased.

"Thankfully, she is one competitor out of the way," Sarah sighed dramatically.

"So what's Daniel's story? We met in the hall this morning," I explained, trying to sound as nonchalant as possible.

"Emily and I honestly can't figure out why Daniel hasn't fallen for Tara. Maybe he doesn't want to date his best friend's sister. But it's obvious she worships him, and she despises his girlfriend, Natalie. Tara won't even acknowledge she exists."

"Okay, got the thing about Tara, but what's the deal with him?" I asked again. Then, realizing I was pursuing the subject a bit too vigorously, I added, "Just curious since I met his parents in the café on the night of the shooting."

"Uh-huh. It sounds like Eve has set her eyes on Daniel," Emily said. I had already figured out that Emily didn't miss much.

"I don't usually go for jocks," I protested. "I can't compete with the confidence factor."

"Yeah, right," Emily said. "Personally though, I think he's a tough one. He's a great friend, but as a boyfriend, I don't know. Daniel is not like other people. There's something different about him—like he can see right through you. Both Daniel and Erik grew up in Ridgway, and their families were founding members of The Colony."

"My dad and I drove out to The Colony the other night to have dinner with my grandparents," I said. "It seems a strange that the Terra Dyne people have lived there so long. And from what I hear, no one's in any hurry to leave. Dad said the families emigrated from Norway over twenty years ago," I said.

"That's the story," Emily said, "but I've always wondered why the colonists aren't all Nordic-looking blondes." Then as if something had just occurred to her, she looked at me a little closer. "Oh I nearly forgot. Your grandparents live in The Colony."

I wondered why she thought my connection to The Colony was so interesting, but before I could ask her what she meant by her comment, Sarah jumped in, defending the colonists' story. "They're probably descended from a separate sect that settled in Norway hundreds of years ago or something. Obviously, not all Norwegians are blonde," she declared.

Turning to me she said, "The truth is, Em thinks it's a bogus story."

"But why would they lie about where they came from?" I asked, addressing Emily. "I mean, what difference does it make?" Then conjuring up a wicked grin, I suggested, "Unless they're fugitives, or maybe they're in witness protection and hiding from the mob." Emily flashed a fake smile but offered no explanation for her suspicions.

"Who knows?" Sarah answered for her friend. "Like I told Em, most of the colonists are scientists, and scientists *are* different from the rest of us. We should expect them to be strange." I wondered if Sarah's interest in Erik had anything to do with her defensive behavior.

"Anyway, here's the scoop on the boys. Daniel and Erik are inseparable," she continued. "Daniel is the serious and bossy one, while Erik is the fun-loving and easy-going one. Daniel has two younger brothers, Mikey, a freshman, and Sean, who is in junior high. He and his girlfriend, Natalie, have been dating a few months. We think he's with her because she pursued him until he gave in. Natalie usually gets what she wants. We can't imagine what he sees in her—aside from the voluptuous body thing. Maybe Daniel likes the arm candy." Sarah obviously had no problem saying exactly what she was thinking.

"My boyfriend, Augustine, has known Daniel, Erik, and Brad since kindergarten," Emily contributed. "They're pretty tight. Augustine and his family are vacationing in Florida this week. They've got the big bucks. Augustine's dad owns a few car dealerships all over western Colorado, but he actually likes living in Ridgway. Go figure."

"Emily's got the hots for Augustine," Sarah added wickedly.

"Okay. Got the message loud and clear, girls. Augustine is off limits. What about Brad?" I asked, looking over at him and noticing that the hostile scowl had been replaced with an expression I couldn't decipher. He appeared to be examining me, as he might an exotic animal.

"Brad has the proverbial chip on his shoulder. Life is all about competition for him, like he's always trying to prove he's good enough. Despite the fact he's a great basketball player—in fact, the best on the team next to Augustine, of course," she said, shooting Emily a grin.

"Brad struggles like Em and I do in math class, whereas Daniel and Erik are the class brains. He skis and hangs out at the Reservoir with us, but he never seems to be able to let loose and enjoy himself. He dated Natalie's friend, Rachel, for most of the summer, but it's over now," Sarah said, making sure to clarify his relationship status.

"He looks like he's angry most of the time," I said.

"He's intense and serious like Daniel—probably because his mom died when he was little. He lives with his dad south of town."

"So he doesn't live in The Colony?" I asked.

"No, but it's funny you should ask, because I think his parents used to live there, before his mom died," Emily responded. I was about to ask what had happened to Brad's mom, when an angry shout erupted from the direction of Daniel's group.

"Listen Winter, where do you get off asking me if I was in the Bio lab? Did Jarak tell you to spy on me? I'm warning you to back off. What I do is none of your business!"

We moved closer along with several other students to see what was going on. I was surprised to see Daniel grab an irate guy in a skin-tight muscle shirt by the shoulder and command him to control himself.

"Relax Mack. Think about what you're doing," he hissed in a barely audible, lethal tone. "This isn't a game. It's not all about you. We're supposed to be keeping a low profile."

"You have no authority over me," Mack said, hatred blazing in his fiery light-colored eyes. "I don't care who you are. Get your hands off me." He shoved Daniel away from him and stalked off. Daniel definitely had an enemy—a dangerous one. The intensity of his rage nearly took my breath away.

Seeing my shocked expression, Emily whispered, "Mack is bad news. I swear he'll end up in jail someday—or worse. Good thing he's a senior so he'll be out of here at the end of the year."

"What's his beef with Daniel?" I asked.

"Who knows? It's hard to find anyone he doesn't have a problem with, but he despises Daniel and his friends."

This clearly was no ordinary high school rivalry. I got the impression that Daniel really felt some authority over Mack, whether real or imagined, and Mack hated him for it. What had he said to Daniel, *I don't care who you are?* What was he talking about, and why would my grandfather have asked Daniel to spy on Mack? *Who* was supposed to be keeping a low profile? My head was spinning with everything that had happened. It was time to exit.

"Hey girls, I've had enough fun for my first day at a new school. I'm going to head back to the cabin and finish unpacking. Either of you need a ride?"

"No thanks," Sarah said. "Emily and I rode to school together in her car. I guess Mrs. Walters will let us know the plan for tomorrow. It was great to meet you, Eve. Give me your number, and I'll text you later. Oh and try to stay away from trouble. It seems to be following you," she added with a lopsided grin.

"You're hilarious," I grimaced. "But I'll do what I can. I think I'll go home and hide."

We exchanged cell numbers and waved goodbye. Walking to my Subaru, I stole one last look at Daniel. His face was animated as he spoke to Erik, but I swear his eyes followed me to my car. I wondered what the confrontation with Mack was about. It suddenly occurred to me that Daniel was Mr. Winter's son—the Mr. Winter of the special powers. Had his ability to manipulate objects with his mind been passed on to his son?

Chapter 6

Despite Emily's prediction, school was cancelled for the rest of the week. Two classrooms had been severely damaged, and school inspectors had to ensure that the building was safe. My dad grilled me with questions about the fire, paying close attention when I told him how Mr. Winter's son, Daniel, and his friend, Erik had smelled smoke before the explosion but no one else had.

"The rest of us had no idea there was a fire, but somehow they knew before anyone else. They definitely saved a bunch of people. Who knows what might have happened?"

Dad studied me thoughtfully, and then said something totally unexpected. "Eve, it wouldn't be a bad idea for you to get to know Daniel. His parents are wonderful people, and the word at Terra Dyne is that he's a great kid. He can look out for you, and besides, you might find the two of you have a great deal in common."

I rolled my eyes dramatically. "Are you seriously giving me dating advice? Please. And since when have I needed someone to look out for me?"

"I know you can take care of yourself, but you're in a new town, and Daniel would be a good person to get to know."

"Even if I wanted to get to know him—which I don't—his clingy girl-friend is never far from his side. I already met both of them, and I can tell you, she's not crazy about me and Daniel's pretty much off limits."

Dad walked over and gave me an uncharacteristic hug. "Circumstances can change. I have no doubt you shook him up the first time he saw you. You're an awesome, beautiful young woman. Try to be open to new experiences."

I hugged him back, feeling awkward at the turn the conversation had taken. We weren't demonstrative wear-your-emotions-on-your-sleeve types, even though Dad was empathetic and kind to everyone. It was easy to see why my mom had fallen for him. It would be impossible for me to find anyone that could measure up.

Despite my dad's advice, I couldn't picture myself spending much time around Daniel. Although ever since I'd met him, he had never been far from my thoughts. Could it only have been this morning that we'd met? Hopefully my obsession would fade with time.

On Friday night, Sarah and Emily invited me to hang out with them at The Well, a local bar with a separate area for the under-twenty-one crowd to eat and socialize. Sarah's car pulled in to the parking lot right behind me with Emily riding shot gun. Both girls were dressed for the chilly fall evening in long sleeve tees, jeans, and parkas. Sarah looked like a cat burglar, outfitted in black from head to toe. Emily wore a retro eggplant purple jacket, which shimmered in the moonlight.

"Awesome jacket, Emily," I complimented her.

"Thanks," she responded, pleased that I'd noticed. "I've got a thing for purple."

"Well, I've got a thing for being warm, and your jacket looks toasty." Lots of teenagers thought they were being cool by dressing in t-shirts and flip flops all winter and pretending they weren't freezing. I didn't get it. The most important aspect of mountain fashion was staying warm, and I imagined my parka would become my constant companion.

The three of us entered the dimly-lit club and slid into a sage green booth. Neon signs adorned the adobe-colored walls, plants were scattered between the tables, and a retro jukebox flashed assorted colors in time to the beat. I noted with satisfaction the absence of any dead animal heads.

Being an animal lover, I didn't understand stuffing a dead animal and hanging him or his head on the wall. In fact, the whole hunting thing made me uncomfortable, unless someone hunted to feed their family. There weren't many mountain-dwellers who shared my ideology.

I glanced around the dimly-lit room, spotting a couple of teenagers playing pool, and four others engaged in an intense game of foosball. Every so often a shout rang out as someone scored a goal. An impatient-looking waitress came to our table, and we ordered burgers and diet cokes. Tips were undoubtedly better in the regular bar versus the teen room.

Sarah pointed out the club's owner, Sid, who was standing at the teen bar talking to some kids. Despite his baggy flak jacket and cargo pants, he moved like a panther and was obviously in good shape. Watching his weathered face as he kept a vigilant eye on the room, I sensed that this man with the short-cropped, military haircut had seen a lot in his fifty or so years. Sarah also surveyed the room, but for entirely different reasons.

Emily groaned. "Oh for heaven's sake, Sarah. Erik's not here. Get a grip."

"Listen, Juliet. Just because you've already bagged your Romeo, doesn't mean the rest of us are as fortunate," Sarah countered, twisting her emerald green braid in anticipation.

"Are you expecting Erik to show up?" I asked Sarah.

"He usually drops by The Well on Friday nights at least until basketball season starts. As of November, the only place we hang out is the school gym. We're pretty much groupies once the games start. Even squeezing in a ski day can get tricky. Hope you like basketball."

"I like basketball, but like I told you girls, the whole jock mentality ticks me off. Sorry, I'll try to get over it."

"Something tells me Daniel Winter might help you get over it," Emily teased.

Emily had struck a nerve. "I only met Daniel a few days ago. How can you possibly have us pegged as soul mates?"

Sarah chuckled and patted my shoulder consolingly. "It's no use, Eve. Em's good at reading people. It's impossible to keep a secret from her."

"I'm beginning to think the Ridgway motto is: 'Everyone has secrets, and this town knows them *all*'," I grumbled. "Okay, Emily, we're done talking about me. When does Augustine get back from Florida?"

"Sunday night," she sighed. "It feels like he's been gone forever. We've been texting and talking on the phone every day though. I told him about the fire. Too bad he was already on vacation when we got a bonus week off school."

"At least he won't have a bunch of work to make up since school's been out," I said. "How long have you two been going out?"

"Seems like forever!" Sarah testified. "Actually, they started seeing each other a year ago in January. Right, Em?" She looked at Emily, who nodded her head in confirmation. "Augustine and Emily are the real deal. He's crazy about her."

Emily blushed and shook her head at Sarah. "She is a bit dramatic, isn't she?"

I didn't have a chance to respond because Sarah whispered a victorious *Yes!* as the door to the club swung open and Erik entered, followed by Daniel and Brad. The increasingly familiar jolt of energy hit me moments before Daniel's eyes connected with mine, and I felt certain he'd known I was here before he'd entered the room.

Had he recognized my Subaru in the parking lot? Surely Daniel didn't know what my car looked like. Or did he? Was he already keeping an eye on me, as my dad had suggested? This was too weird and contributing to the weirdness were the distinct vibrations that had started when the three guys came in the door.

Erik followed Daniel's gaze and strolled over to our table, smiling as usual. "Ladies! Looking good as always."

This time it was Sarah who blushed, obviously thrilled with the compliment, but she didn't miss a beat. "You know it. We're the most foxy chicks in the club." I stifled a laugh as I noted that we were in fact, the only girls in the club.

Daniel gave Sarah a wry grin. "That's what I like about you, Sarah—nothing ever escapes your attention." Sarah aimed a wicked punch at his arm, but he dodged the assault in time. She patted the spot next to her in the booth and said to Erik, "Have a seat." Then turning to Daniel and Brad she said, "You boys can grab a couple of chairs."

Losing his forbidding scowl, Brad stretched out his hand to me. "Hi, I'm Brad Spencer, and you must be Eve—the hot topic in town. We don't get many new people around here." The smile transformed his face, and his beautiful dark blue eyes revealed flecks of gold. The boys' physical similarities made me wonder yet again about the relationship between these three.

It was the first time I'd seen Brad up close and was stunned to realize how handsome he was—over six feet tall, but more rugged and muscular than Daniel and Erik. His smooth, coordinated movements spoke of natural athletic ability. I remembered Sarah's comment about him and Augustine being the best basketball players on the team. She had also mentioned his competitive nature. My intuition told me Sarah was right: Brad thought he had something to prove to the world.

It was odd, the strong impressions I received from these three guys. I had known them less than a week, and yet they were strangely familiar. This familiarity was deeply disturbing and something for which I had no explanation.

When we'd first arrived, Emily had moved over to the inside of the booth, with me on the outside edge. Brad had remained standing as he and I talked, and Daniel took the opportunity to pull a chair right up next to me. My heart began to race erratically, and it took all my concentration to focus on what Brad was saying. Daniel seemed to take satisfaction in my discomfort and scooted his chair even closer. He could be incredibly annoying and dangerously attractive at the same time. I turned my face away from him.

"So, how was your first week in Ridgway?" Brad asked.

"You mean other than the shooting and the fire?"

"Well, yeah, other than those two things," he said. The unexpected softness of his tone caught me off guard. All of a sudden, I felt like I was being a jerk. Brad was trying to be friendly, and I was taking my irritation at Daniel out on him.

"After such a crazy start, I've had a real quiet week. Quaz and I—he's my golden retriever, Quazimodo—have been exploring the woods. I've been running the trails around our place. It's an amazing spot."

"Oh that's right, you and your dad moved into John Meyer's cabin," Brad said.

I shook my head in utter disbelief. "Does everyone around here know *everything* about me?" I demanded in frustration.

Daniel interrupted with a chuckle and a bemused expression. "Pretty much," he admitted.

Giving him a look of total exasperation, I said, "Guess I'd better get used to it then. I surrender. You guys win."

Although Daniel sat only a few feet away, he moved his face closer, obviously trying to make a point. "I'm disappointed in you. The fact that you're giving in so easily seems out of character." His tone was entirely too smug and condescending. "Let me try to make all this a little easier. The bad news is that we know all about you, but that's also the good news. That knowledge will help us watch over and protect you."

"Protect me from what?" I asked, unable to keep the anger from creeping into my voice, "Grizzly bears and mountain lions?"

Daniel couldn't help but smile at my indignation. "Actually, I believe the last grizzly bear sighting in western Colorado was about thirty years ago. We do have black bears though—and mountain lions."

Although he spoke teasingly, he was dead serious. Daniel was declaring his intentions to watch out for me and protect me from whatever dangers hid in the shadows. Brad and Emily listened, but said nothing. Daniel had taken center stage, and his friends had obediently faded into the background. The whole situation was surreal. I had moved to a sleepy little mountain town, safe and secluded from the prevalent crime of city life. What did I have to fear? The conversation was so bizarre I didn't even know where to start with my questions.

Lowering my voice to a whisper, I demanded answers. "What's with this obsession about my safety? First my dad says you can look out for me, and now you're talking about protecting me. And what about Monday when you and Mack were arguing? Are you watching him too? Did my grandfather really ask you to spy on him?"

Daniel grimaced. "I figured you heard what Mack said." He studied me for a few seconds, saying nothing. I glanced over at Erik and Sarah, trying to determine if they were also following the conversation, but I couldn't tell for sure. Erik looked up when I did, but then turned back to Sarah. They appeared to be having their own intense discussion.

"Well?" I asked, glaring at Daniel.

"Eve, Mack isn't like the rest of us. He's angry and confused, and to be perfectly honest, destructive. Jarak suggested that I try to keep him out of trouble. His actions could cause problems for us. We're all part of The Colony and like I said, we look out for each other."

"Mack isn't like the rest of *who*? The colonists? Okay, suppose I accept that the colonists all think the same and look out for each other, but why you? What did Mack mean when he said 'I don't care who you are?' Have you been appointed as some sort of watchman?"

Daniel exchanged knowing looks with Brad, who shrugged as if to say: This one's all yours, buddy. I'm staying out of it.

"Eve, I'm sort of, that is—I'm…" he stopped, clearly frustrated. "Sorry. You need to ask your grandfather these questions."

"Why ask him? Does he run The Colony? Is he your boss or something?"

"Not exactly," Daniel replied. "We have simply chosen to follow him, because we have great respect for his wisdom."

"Follow him? What are you guys, some kind of Norwegian tribal group? It almost sounds like some sort of cult."

Daniel shook his head, indicating that he'd said all he was going to say about the matter.

As I was digesting this last piece of information, I heard a voice that definitely signaled the end of our little chat.

"Daniel! There you are! How come every time I come searching for you I find you hanging out with this city girl? Getting bored with the mountain women?"

Wonderful. The blonde bimbo was back. How could Daniel stand her? Natalie sashayed over to our table in skin-tight white jeans and a fur-trimmed jacket. A short, blonde girl followed close behind her, wearing a turtleneck, plaid mini skirt and tan Uggs. Brad glanced approvingly at the little blonde, but she ignored him. He shook his head and scowled.

That must be Rachel, I surmised. I wonder who had dumped whom? Brad seemed eager to be friendly, but she was having nothing to do with him. I'm sure Sarah and Emily would fill me in. I was suddenly quite interested in Brad's love life.

"Let's head over to Rachel's. This place is boring," Natalie whined, pulling on Daniel.

Daniel looked annoyed and not at all pleased that Natalie had shown up. "We just walked in the door, and I want to grab something to eat first."

"Fine. Enjoy yourself. We'll be at Rachel's," Natalie hissed furiously and then stomped off with Rachel close behind.

58

"Man, you've done it now," Erik cracked. "The princess will be sulking for a week."

"Drop it, Erik," Daniel warned.

Erik held up his hands in mock surrender. "Okay. Relax. I'm just messing with you."

"So, Erik," Sarah chimed in, eager to change the subject. "Where's Tara?"

"My evil twin went shopping with my mom. Apparently, she thinks she can squeeze at least one more pair of shoes into her closet. What is it with girls and shoes?" he asked.

"Definitely one of life's great mysteries," Sarah humored him.

The waitress returned, and the boys ordered burgers and fries. The six of us talked about the upcoming basketball season, buying season ski passes at Telluride, and our classes at school. I discovered that Brad and I shared Pre-Calculus and Spanish. After our brief discussion, I looked forward to getting to know him better. Ridgway High School had suddenly become a great deal more interesting.

My feelings toward Daniel were complicated. Although he was a puzzle I felt compelled to solve, my emotions alternated between attraction and annoyance. He was arrogant and seemed to think I needed his protection. Avoiding him would be difficult though since he'd revealed we had three other classes together, in addition to Pre-Calculus. The fact that he'd scarcely left my thoughts since we'd met also complicated matters.

We proceeded to have a normal conversation, despite the underlying tension between Daniel and me, and the ever-present vibrating atmosphere. It was Sarah who finally brought up the fire. Judging by the looks on the boys' faces, I suspected they'd agreed not to discuss the subject.

"Come on Daniel, tell us what you really think. Do you believe Mack had anything to do with the fire? We heard what you said to him."

"Maybe," Daniel sighed heavily. "I don't know Sarah, but I'm hoping it was an accident. Tons of chemicals are stored in the Bio lab. It's entirely possible that some destructive combination was accidentally thrown together. Mack was in the lab, but I don't really believe he would try to blow up the school."

"I wouldn't put it past him," Emily said.

"Me neither," Sarah agreed. "But didn't Mikey say someone's lab experiment backfired?

"Yeah, Mikey did notice some kids hanging out in the back of the lab. I'd like to believe the whole thing was just someone being stupid."

Erik offered no comments, but grabbed Sarah's arm and suggested a game of pool with a little too much enthusiasm. He obviously wanted to avoid talking about the fire.

"Come on Sarah. Let me demonstrate my expert pool-playing skills."

"I seem to remember I kicked your butt the last three times we've played."

Erik shook his head in mock shame. "No reveling in the past, my sweet. You had some lucky shots. Tonight's the night I'll show you who's got the skills!"

He slid from the booth, reached for Sarah's hand, and the two of them headed toward the pool table. As they left the table, Sarah glowed with pleasure. She raised her eyebrows at us, mouthed the words "Can you believe this?" and practically floated across the floor after Erik.

Mercifully, Daniel stood up and put on his jacket. "I guess I'm going over to Rachel's. Are you coming Brad?"

"No, I'm not Rachel's favorite person right now. I think she needs a few more months to cool off."

"No kidding. See you tomorrow at practice. Bye Em," Daniel said. Then he turned his mesmerizing green eyes on me, destroying my plans to dismiss him with a disinterested nod. "Take care of yourself, Eve and watch out for those grizzly bears," he advised, grinning wickedly. "We'll talk more soon." Daniel walked away, waving to Erik and Sarah as he exited the club.

We'll talk more soon? Was that an invitation or a promise? More like a threat. I couldn't figure out if he was merely playing the protective big brother, or if he was showing me who was in charge. I didn't know whether to be annoyed or flattered. Why was he so secretive and bossy, as if he had some kind of authority over me?

It only took me a few seconds to realize the vibrations had diminished. I had grown accustomed to the intensity of the electrical hum while Daniel was here, but after he left I felt almost deflated, like my energy had been zapped. Grandmother's explanation of the colonists' energy hadn't been very enlightening.

Daniel radiated what I could only describe as a powerful magnetic field, and Erik possessed a similar charged presence, but not as intense. Daniel's energy was invasive and unnerving, whereas Erik's felt somehow protective and calming. And the vibrations hadn't completely disappeared, so there must be a small amount of this strange energy emanating from Brad. According to the girls, Brad didn't live in The Colony, but Emily said he used to live there. I'd already decided something in The Colony was the source of this mysterious energy.

After Daniel left, Emily excused herself and went to the ladies' room. I gazed over at Brad, feeling more comfortable with him now that Daniel was gone. My attraction to Brad had nothing to do with any sort of energy field. He belonged on the cover of a romance novel. His cream-colored shirt outlined his upper body, hinting at his powerful arms and chest. I would definitely enjoy watching him play basketball.

Anxious to find out more about him, I opened my mouth to ask him what he liked to do besides play basketball. But before I could speak, Brad hopped into the booth vacated by Erik and Sarah and leaned toward me. "Why are you really here, Eve?" Shocked by his accusative tone, I had no idea how to reply.

Too late, he must've realized his brusque manner had offended me. He touched my arm, and I recoiled from his touch. "I'm sorry," he said. "That didn't come out so well. What I mean is why did your dad come back to Terra Dyne? I thought he'd left Ridgway behind and moved on. Or maybe I wanted to believe he'd found a new life because sometimes I wish I could."

I still had no idea what Brad was talking about. "What do you mean you thought my dad had moved on? We're here because my grandfather offered my dad a job. I don't know of any other reason. Why do *you* think we're here? Do you think we have some kind of secret agenda?"

Brad looked around the room to see if anyone was listening before speaking. "Just between us, I think Jarak is gathering his people. Since you're his granddaughter, I thought maybe you'd know something."

"Brad, I don't know anything. I don't even know what *people* you're referring to."

He stared at me in disbelief. "You really don't know anything about us, do you? Well, here's my theory: Jarak is gathering the colonists."

My confusion must have been obvious. "My dad said the colonists never left," I insisted, choosing to ignore his insinuation that I was ignorant.

"Most of them stayed in Ridgway, but the few who left are trickling back into town, like you and your dad. Something's coming. I can feel it."

"Brad, you seem like a great guy, but honestly, you're freaking me out. I don't know anything about the colonists or why Jarak might be gathering them. I only see my grandfather a few times a year, and he certainly doesn't confide in me."

Just when I thought things couldn't get any weirder, Brad's next words took my breath away. "I bet you also didn't know that my mom disappeared the same day as your mom."

"What? Oh my gosh, Brad, I'm sorry. I didn't know. No one told me someone else died that day. So your mom drowned in Visitor Canyon too?"

Brad's blue eyes widened. "Yeah, something like that."

"But I was there, and I don't remember seeing anyone else," I protested. "Why hasn't anyone told me this before?" My surprise had evolved into anger. What was going on around here? How many more secrets were buried in this town? I was suddenly furious with my dad. What else was he hiding from me?

Oblivious to my anger, Brad continued, slowly shaking his head and ignoring my questions. "You really don't know who you are. How is that possible?"

"Brad, for heaven's sake, who do you think I am?"

"You're one of us," he replied softly.

Sarah, Erik, and Emily chose that precise moment to arrive at the table. "You two look way too serious. What's up?" Sarah asked.

Neither of us uttered a word. I felt betrayed by my dad, my grandparents, everyone. Why had this information been kept from me? And what did Brad mean when he said I was 'one of us?' I looked at him for further explanation, but he ignored me.

"Uh, is everything okay?" Sarah asked again, anxious for someone to say something.

"We're good," Brad responded, getting up from his seat. Speak for yourself, I thought.

"Brad, you can't just leave without explaining yourself," I said.

Erik shot a questioning look at Brad, who shrugged as if it was no big deal.

"It's not my job to explain things to you. You'll figure it out soon enough," he said. "I gotta go. See you guys later."

Brad left the table and headed out the door before I could even think about moving.

"Is he for real?" I blurted out. It was all I could do to keep from screaming in frustration.

"What do you mean?" Sarah asked.

"I mean is he the kind of person who likes to exaggerate or make up stories?"

"Brad? No way. He's usually on the level. If you can get him to have a serious conversation, you can believe it's straight up." Emily nodded her head in agreement. Erik merely shrugged as if he wanted to stay out of the conversation.

Somehow I managed to come up with a flimsy excuse so I could get out of there. "Hey guys, I need to take off. Dad's got some stuff he wants to do around the cabin tomorrow and wants to start early. Thanks for inviting me."

Emily surprised me with a hug. "Eve, you can come out with us anytime. Don't let Brad get to you. He's fighting a lot of demons, and sometimes he gets carried away. Don't take it personally."

I plastered on a smile. "I'll keep that in mind. See you all on Monday. Great seeing you again, Erik." His expression was friendly, but revealed something else. Pity, maybe, like he felt sorry for me. Perhaps he too was aware of something I wasn't.

Chapter 7

The lights were out, and Dad was sleeping when I returned to the cabin. Quaz greeted me at the door, and I stooped down to scratch his floppy ears. Sleep was out of the question. I was half tempted to wake up my dad and demand an explanation. I tried to remember all the conversations we'd had about the day mom disappeared. It had been ten years; surely the subject of another woman's death in the canyon on the very same day would've come up. For some reason, he'd decided to keep the information to himself. But why? Since Dad was the only one who could answer that question, I'd have to wait until morning.

Retiring to my bedroom, I pulled out my laptop and began researching auras. I'd been thinking about what Grandmother told me at dinner on Sunday. She hadn't used the word "aura" specifically, but I assumed this was what she'd meant. One website defined an aura as a form of psychic energy, whose existence was debated by mainstream scientists. Proponents of the aura theory described it as a field of light surrounding a person, often associated with someone who possessed great powers or spiritual holiness.

My research didn't shed much light on the issues I was experiencing. Even if I bought into the whole aura thing, the stuff I read referred to visual or emotional perceptions of the aura. Nowhere did I find anything about experiencing a physical sensation of a person's aura as a disturbing vibration in the air. Grandmother and I definitely needed to talk.

On a hunch, I decided to google Terra Dyne Industries and find out what type of research the company focused on. Surprisingly, there was little information online. I couldn't find any history on the company or bios of its employees. Google had a few other references to Terra Dyne, most notably where Jarak was quoted in a *Time* magazine article on experimental fuels and jet propulsion. In another instance, he'd been interviewed by a neurological journal on the possibility of manipulating electrical impulses in the brain to create thought-controlled wheelchairs. I couldn't make a connection between jet propulsion and brain research.

Searching for Jarak Sorensen brought no additional information. I expected to find highlights of his career or some sort of scientific recognition. It hardly seemed possible that Terra Dyne could operate so far under the radar. Either Jarak's company was not the cutting-edge research firm Dad said it was, or somebody was taking great pains to conceal what was really happening in Terra Dyne's massive mountain hideaway.

I finally fell asleep around two a.m. and awakened to bright sun streaming in my window. It was after nine, and despite my foggy state, it occurred to me that Dad must've taken Quaz out already. To add to my irritability, my mind filled with a compelling vision of Daniel's handsome face and vivid green eyes. I rolled over and groaned. So much for my determination to erase Daniel from my thoughts.

Squashing the treacherous image, I moved on to recreating last night's disturbing conversation with Brad. Dad had some explaining to do. I dragged myself out of bed, reluctant to face the day, but anxious to get some answers. I pulled on a pair of navy sweats and a long sleeved t-shirt, brushed my hair and my teeth, and set out to find my dad. We'd planned on clearing some of the brush away from the cabin this morning. I only felt a little guilty as I realized he'd probably started without me.

He wasn't in the kitchen, so I headed to his bedroom to see if he was still in the house. "Dad, are you in there?" I called, knocking softly. Receiving no response, I wandered into the observation room at the back of the cabin. The walls of glass made me feel exposed, like a guppy in a fishbowl. Seeing in was as easy as seeing out. Apparently, John Meyer hadn't worried too much about someone spying on him.

I could see Dad working in the backyard, surrounded by several large garbage bags which appeared to be full. I grabbed a light jacket and my shoes and hurried outside.

"Good morning. Sorry I slept so late."

"No big deal. I figured you were tired and decided to let you sleep."

I wasted no time getting right to the point. "I found out last night that another woman disappeared in Visitor Canyon the same day as mom. Why didn't you tell me?"

The world-weary expression I had seen so often on Dad's face in the last few days reappeared. "Eve, for goodness sake, you were six. What good could it possibly have done to tell you there were others who had died that day?"

"Others? You mean more than Brad Spencer's mom? Are you kidding? Don't you think you could have shared this with me some time in the last ten years?"

"There were three women: your mom, Lauren Spencer and Jakob's wife, Anika Andersen. Your mom and Lauren were in the Canyon, and Anika disappeared not far from the cabin."

"This cabin? It flooded out here?"

"The water rose out here too, and well, all I know is that they're gone."

"I still don't understand why you didn't tell me before," I said.

"I'm sorry I didn't tell you. It never seemed like the right time. Besides, there isn't much I could tell you. I don't really know what happened myself."

"Come on, Dad. There's got to be more to the story. You didn't *want* to tell me. All of a sudden, I feel like you've been hiding things from me. Not just about Mom, but about Ridgway and Terra Dyne and Mr. Winter. It's like I don't even know who you are anymore."

Dad exhaled slowly. "Eve, all this is more complicated than you think. I am in way over my head here. I knew this day would come, but I can't believe you're already sixteen. It's time you understood some things about your mom."

"What things?" I demanded.

"Lots of things. As strange as this may sound, your grandfather is the one with the answers to your questions, not me."

"What does Jarak have to do with Mom's drowning? Does he know what really happened? What can he tell me that you can't?"

Dad stared directly into my eyes, willing me to accept what he was saying. "He can tell you everything. Unfortunately, your grandparents are out of town for a couple weeks, but they will want to discuss this with you themselves. I promise we'll meet with them as soon as they get back. Please, Eve. Trust me on this one. Talking to Jarak is the only way to handle this."

"Handle what…" I started to say.

Dad interrupted, "Eve, I promise—you'll have all your answers soon. Wait for Jarak."

What could I do? Dad pulled me to him and hugged me fiercely, as if he were afraid I would disappear like my mom. His desperate hug drew the anger right out of me. It was startling, and more than a little scary. It was then I realized my dad was afraid of something. I'd received more hugs from him since I'd arrived in Ridgway than I'd received in the past several years. Something was definitely not right.

I briefly flashed back to Brad's solemn declaration that Jarak was gathering his people. Since Dad was also insisting Jarak had all the answers, maybe Brad was right. Maybe my grandfather was planning something—something big.

"Can't you at least give me some idea of what we're talking about? You must know something," I persisted.

"Even the things I know, I can't explain. So what good would it do?"

"Okay, I'll wait until Jarak gets home," I said finally. I didn't see what choice I had in the matter; Dad was not budging. "You need to answer one question, though. Are we in some kind of danger, and if we are, why did we come back?"

He considered me carefully. I could tell he was trying to decide how much to reveal. "Are we in danger? I don't think so. But if we are, if *you* are, we came back so Jarak could protect you."

There it was again—the protection thing. More riddles. More questions. I was not afraid, only curious. For some reason, I believed Dad when he said my grandfather could answer my questions, but I was also convinced my dad knew more than he was telling me. Protect us? That was a whole different animal. I couldn't quite figure out how Jarak would be able to protect us.

How could I possibly wait a couple weeks? But what else could I do? I walked over to the pile of trash bags, chose one, and began stuffing handfuls of pine needles inside.

The next day was Sunday and I got up early, taking Quaz for a run through the woods. Clearing my mind seemed futile, so I purposefully allowed everything I'd seen and heard since I'd come to Ridgway to flow through it. What Brad said about Jarak gathering the colonists echoed over and over in my head. I wondered if we actually were part of some proposed gathering and if we were, to what end? It hadn't escaped me that since my mom had been one of the colonists, then I must have some connection to them. I also had no idea what being one of them really meant.

I was so engrossed in my thoughts that Quaz started barking at some-one coming through the trees before I saw anything. Great. It was Daniel—perfectly gorgeous, even at seven-thirty in the morning. He didn't look at all surprised to see us. As he got closer, Quaz stopped barking and went right to him, putting his paw up. So much for my loyal watchdog.

"Found any grizzly bears yet, Miss *Hunter*?" Daniel asked.

"Just when I thought you couldn't get any more irritating, I discover that you're an aspiring comedian," I retorted, a bit surprised at the mean-ness in my own voice.

"Well, excuse me for trying to coax a smile out of you," he said. He actually seemed hurt by my sarcasm. I immediately felt guilty and decided to go a little easier on him.

"I suppose if I had found a grizzly, you'd at least feel like your protection was needed, and I would be grateful for your help," I conceded.

He bowed gallantly. "My lady, I am forever in your service, no matter what lurks in the forest."

"Wow, I'm flattered, um, I think," I smirked. "So, what brings you to our lovely forest so early in the morning?"

"I suppose I should be honest with you. Besides the fact that this is a particularly beautiful area, I thought there was a chance you might be here, and I came looking for you."

"On protection detail, are we?"

"Always," he smiled crookedly. "But I'm also here because I felt bad about Friday night. I know I upset you, and I want us to be friends."

"Okay Daniel, we're friends. Mission accomplished," I said flatly, wondering if my blatant lie was obvious. He wanted to be friends? It wasn't that simple. Being around him drove me crazy. The part of me that couldn't resist his magnetic appeal and the part of me that wanted to smack him were constantly at war. There was no chance of peace.

"Why do I irritate you so much?" he asked in exasperation. Gold sparkled in his beautiful green eyes as they searched mine, trying to see right through me.

I sighed. "I don't know Daniel. I suppose you're too domineering and overprotective for me. It grates on my nerves. I'll tell you what, let's call a truce. You try not to be so bossy, and I'll try not to get so irritated." Actually, I had only revealed part of my problem. I found his irresistible attraction and distracting good looks irritating too.

Daniel reached down and began scratching Quaz's ears. "I'll give it my best shot, but Eve, seriously, if you ever need me, I'm not far away."

For heaven's sake, he was a hopeless case. I couldn't imagine what I'd ever need him for, but in an effort to be nice, I thanked him for his offer.

"So how do you like John Meyer's cabin?" he asked, changing the subject.

"It's great—nicer than I expected. The observation room is really cool."

"The *what* room?"

"Mr. Meyer built a fishbowl room at the back of the house. He has panoramic views of the surrounding forest." Since Daniel seemed to be in a revealing mood, I decided to take advantage of the situation and get some information out of him.

"Okay, Daniel, since you seem to know everything that happens in this town, why do you think he might have put in all those windows?"

Daniel spoke carefully. "Ten years ago, Mr. Meyer saw Anika Andersen swallowed up by the water that swept through here. It must've freaked him out."

"I'm sure it was scary, but why would a flash flood cause him to build an observation room?"

"I guess he wanted to make sure he could always see what was coming. Besides, it wasn't exactly a flash flood," he said, searching for a more accurate description. "It was more like a waterspout—a mountain tornado."

"You mean like a waterspout that forms over the ocean? I've never heard of those in the mountains. When Mom and I were in the Canyon, this tornado thing you're talking about came down out of nowhere. Do these storms happen often around here?"

"No, I'm pretty sure that storm was one of a kind," he said, biting his lip. "Hopefully, we'll never see another one."

"I found out a couple days ago that my mom wasn't the only one who drowned ten years ago. When we were at The Well, Brad told me about his mom. I felt horrible for him, and I got pretty angry that my dad never told me."

"Are you still upset with your dad?"

"I don't know—yes and no. Yes, because I feel like he's hiding something from me. But on the other hand, no, I was only six at the time, and I can understand why he didn't mention it. We talked yesterday, and it didn't seem like he understood what happened to Mom any better than I did. Dad wants me to talk to Jarak." Once again, I found myself telling Daniel everything. I seemed to have this compulsion to bare my soul to him.

"Your dad wants you to go to Jarak? That's awesome, Eve. Jarak has the answers," he insisted. I eyed him warily.

"You know, when you talk about my grandfather as if he's the Dali Lama, it kind of creeps me out. It sounds like you'd follow him blindly into a raging fire or a den of lions."

Daniel laughed. "He's definitely not the Dali Lama, but I might follow him into a den of lions—I've always been partial to lions. It's a Biblical thing." He winked at me, turning up the charm full blast. I felt sure he could charm the Queen of England.

"I'm glad I found you today, but I need to get back to the house or I'll be late for church. I snuck out the back door without telling my parents," Daniel admitted.

I must've had a questioning look on my face because he added, "Don't look so shocked. Most of the colonists go to church in Montrose, same as your grandparents. You know how we like to stick together," he smirked.

Now I was the one who felt the need to explain my dubious expression. "I'm okay with it—the church thing. I guess I'm just surprised. I don't know many people who go to church. We used to go when Mom was still alive. Do you actually enjoy going, or do you go along to make your parents happy?"

"Honestly, both. Sometimes it's boring, but mostly it's not so bad. We go to church to show God our gratitude for all he has done for us. After all, God is the reason we are here."

"Here? As in 'here on earth' or as in 'exist'?"

"Exactly," Daniel said, not really answering the question.

"Well, it must be nice to have absolute faith. Me, I'm not so certain about the whole God thing. I don't know if someone can know for sure."

"Oh you can know for sure, but there is a catch." Daniel paused, knowing he had my complete attention. "You have to want to know more than anything else." He flashed his captivating green eyes leaving me no doubt he was serious. "I'll see you at school tomorrow." He started to walk off then turned back with a disarming smile.

"Don't forget our truce. I'll try not to be pushy, and you'll try to be nice to me."

"Okay. I'll be on my best behavior," I agreed, rolling my eyes at his boyish appeal. This new side of Daniel confused me. What happened to the secretive, arrogant guy from The Well?

"Awesome! Bye!" he hollered as he disappeared down the trail into the woods.

Chapter 8

Quaz and I finished our run and returned to the cabin. During dinner, I told my dad I'd met up with Daniel while running, and he was pleased Daniel had sought me out. I decided not to mention the church thing because I didn't want to have *that* conversation. When I told him Mr. Meyer had witnessed Anika's disappearance, he didn't offer any comments.

"Why haven't you kept in touch with Jakob Andersen?" I asked. "I mean you guys seem like you're friends, and you both lost your wives in the flooding—or as Daniel says, the water spout. It seems logical that you would have some sort of bond."

"I suppose I wanted to sever all ties when I left Ridgway," he explained. "Your grandparents were the only ones I kept in touch with." He got up to grab the milk from the refrigerator. "Actually, Jakob has a daughter a year younger than you. Her name is Ruth."

This piece of news intrigued me. "So all three of the women who died had children. How sad. I wonder why I haven't met her."

"Jarak said she's never recovered from losing her mom. You probably haven't met her because she keeps to herself. Apparently she's deathly afraid of the woods and the water. Many lives changed that day," he finished, talking more to himself than me.

"I'll have to look for her at school. Maybe she'll come out of her shell and talk to me, since we have something in common."

"Speaking of school, I know you don't want to hear this again, but it wouldn't be a bad idea to stay close to Daniel and his friends."

"Oh Dad, please. I'll be fine. However, my new friends Sarah and Emily hang with Daniel's group, so I'll be hanging around him whether I want to or not."

"Wonderful. That gives me one less thing to worry about," he said.

Somewhat smugly, I shared Daniel's theory about John Meyer's observation room. "See Dad, I was right," I said, barely containing my triumph. "Mr. Meyer did build the room to watch the forest. He wanted to know what was coming before it hit him."

"If only it were that easy, and we could all see what was coming before it hit us," he replied, making no attempt to hide the deep regret in his voice.

I imagined he referred to not having any advance warning of what had happened to Mom. But I had long since determined there was nothing I could have done to save her, and I refused to wonder what might have been. I cleaned up the kitchen, said goodnight, and went to my room to finish a science fiction novel I'd started the day before.

Monday morning, I drove into the school parking lot, pulling the Subaru under the spruce trees. As I reached over to the passenger seat to grab my backpack, I heard the driver's door open behind my left shoulder. To my surprise, it was Brad Spencer.

"Good morning, Eve. Sorry if I scared you." Words began tumbling out of his mouth. "It's just, well, I acted like such a creep on Friday night, and I wanted to show you I am capable of some manners. That is if you're not too mad at me. I'd really like to be your friend."

I could only stare at him in amazement. Could this be the same psycho guy I talked to on Friday? Something strange was going on around here. First, Daniel sought me out yesterday to apologize, and today, Brad comes looking for me wanting to be friends. Either everyone around here suffered from schizophrenia, or I had suddenly become everybody's pet project. In my grouchy morning mood, my first instinct was to brush him off completely. However, I am only human, and my female side simply couldn't resist those magnificent blue eyes.

"Look, Brad. I'm not exactly mad at you—a little freaked out maybe. You *were* acting weird, but I'm beginning to realize everything around here is a little bizarre. I figured out that when you said I was 'one of us,' you meant I was one of the colonists since my mom belonged to The Colony. I don't exactly know what that means, but I'm getting the idea there's something extraordinary about Jarak's people—as you called them."

As I took a breath, a smile broke out on Brad's face. "Great! Honestly, Eve, I'm sorry about all that conspiracy theory stuff. Sometimes all this secrecy gets to me too. I know your grandfather would never do anything to jeopardize The Colony..." He paused briefly. "I was a little nervous to come over to your car, but I hoped you would at least talk to me." He stuck his hand out eagerly. "Friends?"

"Sure," I replied, feeling a little foolish but shaking his hand anyway. He really was adorable when he wanted to be. "One thing though," I said with only a hint of a smile. "Lose the scowl when you're around me. I like you much better when you're smiling." My audacity surprised me, but hey, he was asking for forgiveness, and I had the upper hand.

Brad broke out into a huge grin, but I could tell he was dead serious when he said softly, "Eve, it's not hard to smile when I'm around you."

It was my turn to be embarrassed. "Okay, let's not be laying on the charm too thick, or I'll start believing whatever you say," I joked, trying to lighten things up.

He laughed, and we started walking to Pre-Calculus, accompanied by mild vibrations in the air. Being with Brad—at least in this incarnation— was nice, comfortable, and easy. He didn't irritate me like Daniel did. I could hardly believe he was the same person I had spoken with at The Well. My attention shifted as I noticed part of the school was blocked off where the fire had damaged the building. Pointing it out to Brad, I mentioned how disturbing my first day had been, and not only that first day of school but my whole first week in Ridgway. A dark look passed across his face as he expressed his relief that the damage from the explosion had been minimal.

"It looks pretty bad to me. A couple of classrooms are gone."

"It could've been a whole lot worse. We were really lucky that no one was hurt," he insisted. I looked at him with surprise. I pegged him as a glass-half-empty kind of guy, but this time, he chose to look on the bright side and be grateful for what hadn't happened. Brad was turning out to be a person of many contradictions.

As we neared the front entrance, Natalie and Rachel brushed passed us without a word.

"Rachel doesn't like you too much, does she?" I asked, still feeling brave.

"That's an understatement," Brad admitted. "You know what the saying is—if looks could kill. And Natalie goes along with whatever Rachel wants her to do. They've been best friends since elementary school."

"Yeah, well, I don't think Natalie likes me too much either," I admitted.

We entered the classroom behind Sarah and Emily. Daniel and Erik were seated close to the door, and I saw Erik give Sarah a huge smile and a wink as she walked by. For a moment I thought the new desperately-trying-to-be-friends Brad might invite me to sit next to him, but when he saw his friends, he said he'd catch up with me later and took a chair next to them.

The minute we'd entered, I'd felt an immediate electrical surge in the air, so I knew Daniel was there before I caught sight of him. I wondered why his energy field was more intense than the slight vibrations I'd felt around Brad. I waved to the boys and followed my girls to the other side of the room, noting with some satisfaction the look of dismay on Daniel's face when he'd seen me with Brad.

"Wow, you sure are getting a lot of attention," Sarah said, raising her eyebrows.

"I could say the same thing about you. I caught that wink. Looks like things are going well with Erik."

Sarah's deep blush confirmed my suspicions. "Things are good. But hey, I couldn't help but notice Daniel's face when you walked in with Brad. What's up with you and Brad? After the other night, I thought you'd go out of your way to avoid him."

"It's nothing. Brad ambushed me as I was getting out of my car this morning. He wanted to apologize for acting so weird on Friday night."

"Really? What did happen on Friday?" Sarah asked.

I opened my mouth to respond but found myself reluctant to tell her what Brad and I had talked about. I searched for something to say. "He told me his mom died in Visitor Canyon the same day as my mom. That alone was enough to freak me out."

"I'm surprised he told you about her. He never talks about his mom."

"He was trying to make some sort of connection between us."

"And?" she persisted.

"He said some crazy stuff and insisted I was one of *them*. I guess he meant since I'm Jarak's granddaughter, I'm one of the colonists. It felt like he was accusing me of something."

"Maybe you misunderstood what he was saying. I don't see why he would resent your connection to The Colony. Brad's mom was one of *them*, so by that logic, he's also a colonist. But I do think he has a love-hate relationship with Jarak because of what happened with his mom. He seems to hold him responsible," Sarah said.

"Why would he blame Jarak for her death?" I asked, confused by her revelation.

Emily spoke up, her voice barely above a whisper. "Because Jarak is supposed to protect the colonists, and he failed them."

I was stunned. As I started to protest, questioning how anyone could possibly expect Jarak to stop what Daniel had called a freak of nature, Mr. Ayers interrupted our conversation.

"Ladies and gentlemen, I trust you had a nice week off and are ready to get back to work. Turn to page sixty-five and pay attention. There's a quiz on Friday. Oh and by the way, you'll be happy to know that all science labs have been cancelled until further notice."

Nervous laughter erupted throughout the classroom. No one was happy about the fire, but everyone seemed relieved to forego lab experiments and write ups. We opened our textbooks as Mr. Ayers began writing on the board. Before he finished, the door opened and a striking, olive-skinned young man entered, flashing sparkling white teeth in an apologetic grin.

"Welcome back, Mr. Salas," Mr. Ayers said, momentarily pausing at the chalkboard. Looks like you missed all the excitement. I'm sure everyone will fill you in on the details *after* class. Hope you enjoyed those sunny Florida beaches."

The newcomer glanced around the room, nodding briefly to the basketball boys before his eyes connected with Emily. His face beamed with pleasure as he crossed the room, touching Em's shoulder as he took the empty seat beside her. I could feel the emotion between them from two seats away.

So this was the infamous Augustine. I couldn't imagine how she could focus on anything else with him next to her. Lucky for her, the feeling was obviously mutual. Sarah had been right on. Em's relationship was the real deal.

Aside from several glances at Daniel and Brad, the remainder of Pre-Calculus was uneventful. Mr. Ayers started where he'd left off last Monday before the fire, once again renewing familiar material. My mind was free to wander, and I puzzled over Daniel, Brad, and Erik. Something was peculiar about them. Originally, I'd assumed they were close because they'd known each other for years and played basketball together. But, as I watched them interact, I felt certain it was more than that. Something undefinable connected them. They seemed to know one another's thoughts and anticipate each other's actions.

The bell rang, and we collected our stuff. Emily introduced me to Augustine, who was as charming as he was attractive—a rare combination.

"Hello, Eve. It's great to meet you. Emily tells me you're Jarak's granddaughter." For a minute, I thought he might take my hand and kiss it, like a courtly gentleman. Augustine had high cheekbones, soft brown eyes, and piercing gaze. His voice was smooth, and he moved with the natural grace of an athlete. I could hardly wait to see him on the basketball court.

"Yep. I never realized he was a local celebrity until I moved to town. I'm not used to being in the spotlight. It's really nice to meet you, Augustine."

The four of us walked toward the door, and Brad waved distractedly as he left for his next class. I was almost relieved to see the return of the quiet, more reserved Brad.

Erik grabbed Sarah's arm, pulling her close. "Hey Sarah, save me a seat at lunch."

She awarded him with a flirtatious smile. "I suppose I could do that."

"Unless you two want to be alone, we'll all join you," Daniel said. He glanced over at me to indicate "we" included me.

"Oh yeah, I imagine Natalie will *love* that arrangement," I said, keeping my voice low for his ears only. I was at it again. Taunting him. Daniel brought out the worst in me. He made a face to show his irritation at my comment. I pasted a cheeky smile on my face and waved goodbye.

Sarah and I headed to AP English—my favorite subject—while Augustine and Em went down the hall in the opposite direction. I knew Daniel was in my English class but I had no intention of walking to class with him.

Besides, the bimbo might be joining him any minute.

The minute we were alone, I blurted out, "Sarah, I don't know what I expected when Em told me about Augustine, but he's magnificent. He's so aristocratic or something, like he's descended from royalty."

"Aren't you the perceptive one, girlfriend. Believe it or not, you're exactly right. He is descended from royalty, at least according to Augustine's dad. His family is from Mexico, and their ancestors were Mayan kings."

"How cool is that? One look at him, and I'm a believer."

"Yeah, well wait until you meet his dad. He looks like a king, and the whole town loves him. He should probably run for mayor."

"If he's anything like his son, he's already got my vote, when I'm eighteen that is."

Sarah introduced me to the English teacher, a petite, bookish woman, with short gray hair and a bright red cardigan. "Mrs. Murphy, this is Eve Hunter. She moved here from Denver."

With a kind, intellectual voice, Mrs. Murphy welcomed me to class and handed me a thick short story anthology and a syllabus. I sat next to Sarah and breathed a sigh of relief. Since I loved to read, English class had always been my happy place. Less than two minutes later, my newfound comfort zone was shattered.

Daniel and Natalie entered first, with Natalie simultaneously glaring at me and hanging all over Daniel. I turned away in disgust, but not before Daniel saw my expression. I'd been hoping Natalie wasn't in this class. Thankfully, they took seats on the opposite end of the room from us. It wouldn't have been so bad if sharing the class with the two of them had been the only issue. Erik's evil twin, Tara, walked in seconds after the happy couple.

Even the bored, disdainful look she wore so well couldn't detract from her stunning beauty. She passed by Daniel and Natalie as if they were invisible. I hated to admit it, but Sarah was right; she was a goddess. Her sinuous arms and legs moved gracefully as her silky black hair brushed her shoulders. She strolled into class like a runway model, fully aware every eye was on her. To add to my misery, she chose a seat directly behind me, sending out angry waves of pervasive, nauseating vibrations.

"Well, look who it is—the prodigal granddaughter returned to the fold," she sneered.

"Excuse me?" I said, mainly because I didn't know what to else to say.

"Oh, you know, the elect, the Chosen One, the one Jarak's been waiting for all these years. Surely, you've figured it out by now, haven't you?" She raised her eyebrows before lowering her icy blue-green eyes and examining her manicure.

"Figured what out?" I asked.

With a sickly sweet smile, she replied. "Why, who you are and what you're doing here, of course. You can't really be as naïve as everyone says. But I could be mistaken, maybe you are a little dense after all."

"Come on, Tara. Give Eve a break," Sarah said, coming to my defense. "Save your nasty little games for someone else."

"Oh, but Sarah, I'm not playing games. This is dead serious." She abandoned her nail inspection and eyed me maliciously. "I'm not sure I'm buying Eve's gullible little girl act, although she does seem a bit clueless. As for you Sarah, don't get your hopes up. You're nothing more than a temporary distraction for my brother."

She focused her cold eyes on me. "You shouldn't have come back to Ridgway, no matter what stories your grandfather tells you. Despite what most people think, Jarak is not infallible. Sometimes he makes mistakes—costly ones. Oh, but I guess you and your dad know all about that, don't you?"

After my discussion with Emily in Pre-Calculus, I instantly grasped her meaning and felt like I'd been punched in the stomach. For the second time that morning, someone brought up Jarak's failure to stop the disaster in Visitor Canyon. Why did everyone seem to hold him responsible? How could he possibly have prevented a natural disaster? My questions consumed me with an overwhelming torment. I desperately needed answers.

The bell rang and Mrs. Murphy began speaking. In distress, I laid my head down on the desk, nauseous and light-headed, memories of the day my mom drowned enveloping me in great waves.

"Miss Hunter, are you okay?"

I heard Mrs. Murphy's voice from a long way off, but my memories of the past were so vivid I couldn't connect to the present. Suddenly I felt a light touch on my shoulder. "Are you okay, dear?"

I raised my head, feeling disoriented. Muffled voices came at me from all directions. I couldn't determine if they spoke to me from the past or the present. What was happening? My mind cleared enough for me to be aware of the whole class staring at me. I mumbled something about not feeling well and asked to be excused. I stood up, giving Sarah a weak smile to let her know I was okay. Mrs. Murphy gave me a pass for the office, and I stumbled out the door. Daniel watched me leave. With grim satisfaction, I realized he wouldn't be able to follow me.

I couldn't possibly go to the office, so I went to the parking lot and sat in my car. The cold air felt wonderful. I needed to sort out the conflicting voices. Something was happening to me. My life-long sense of intuition, something I'd always viewed as a gift, had evolved into a jumbled torrent of impressions. My frequencies jammed as I received glimpses of people and situations I struggled to understand.

My mom's words echoed in my head. She said she'd come back for me. Come back from where? Where did she think she was going? She drowned. Did she plan to come back from the dead? How creepy. But here's the thing: I believed her, and as crazy as it sounds, I still expected her to come back.

Then there was the problem with Jarak. Everyone seemed to think Jarak had failed to protect her—his own daughter—from the mysterious storm. They accused him of failing his people, as if he could've stopped it from happening. And then it hit me with startling clarity. Mr. Winter and the bullets. The family on Dallas Creek Pass. Lillian and her chatter about special gifts. Of course, how could I have been so dense? Grandmother hadn't been talking solely about Mr. Winter. She'd been trying to tell me that Jarak also possessed gifts. Maybe Grandfather could move objects with his mind too.

But even if he did have this special gift, he could only have stopped the water spout if he'd been in the Canyon when it occurred, or if he'd known it was coming. How could the colonists blame him for not preventing something that he had no idea would happen? Once again, my mind expanded with a clarity I could scarcely fathom. There was only one way—only one reason they could have for holding him responsible. The colonists blamed Jarak because they had expected him to know the tornado was coming.

Chapter 9

I spent the entire class period sitting in my Subaru, thinking about my mom, my grandparents, Brad, and Daniel. We were connected in ways I couldn't understand. The colonists were hiding something, and instinctively, I knew my dad was right: Jarak had the answers. Somehow I had to keep myself together until his return.

A glance at my watch reminded me English class was almost over. I shivered, pulling on my jacket as I walked toward the school's entrance. It had grown colder since I'd walked out to the car. The looming clouds and the feel of the air signaled the approach of a snow storm. Hopefully, Quaz and I would get a run in before the weather turned bad.

The hallway suffocated me after the brisk fall air. I stopped by the office to get a pass and had to endure the sympathetic clucks of an excessively cheery Mrs. Walters as I explained where I'd been the last hour. Claiming I had to rush to class, I escaped to Spanish, looking forward to seeing Augustine and Emily and of course, my new best friend, Brad.

I walked to class lost in my thoughts, trying to figure out what to do about the latest piece to the Ridgway puzzle. My grandfather had some sort of premonitions about the future, or at least people thought he did. Glancing up, I was startled by the purposeful approach of a dark-haired girl in a chunky beige sweater, long paisley skirt, and pumpkin-colored leg warmers.

"Hey, you must be Eve," she said. "I'm Misty Meyer."

"I'm Eve." The admission escaped with a sigh. "I don't mean to be rude, but I can't seem to adjust to the small town thing where everyone knows you."

"No worries. You and your dad rented my uncle's cabin, so I knew you were coming. I also know you're Jarak's granddaughter. Plus my dad went to school with your dad," Misty explained. She examined me closely. After two weeks in Ridgway, I suppose I should've been used to this sort of treatment. Everyone stared at me.

But this time I stared back. Misty had five or six beaded necklaces wrapped around her neck, gold hoop earrings, and milky-white stone rings on both hands. Her long, silky black hair and almond eyes reminded me of a bohemian gypsy, someone more at ease gazing into a crystal ball, reading palms, or telling fortunes. I've always wondered if people with names like Misty, Summer, or Rainbow developed free spirit, unconventional personalities because of their earthy names, or if the person who named them had a sixth sense about how they'd turn out. Whichever the case, whoever had been responsible for naming this girl had nailed it.

I struggled to find something conversational to say. "Your uncle did a wonderful job building the cabin. We really like it, and his observation room is totally cool."

Misty gave a strangled laugh. "Why am I not surprised you already figured out what that room is for? Uncle John was obsessed with what he saw in the forest. He spent hours staring out those windows. I can't believe he'd abandon Ridgway and move to Montana."

"Daniel told me your uncle witnessed a drowning not far from his place. I can see why that might make someone a little crazy."

"That's the official story, but lots of odd things happen around here, especially since the colonists came. My ancestors, the Utes, have lived in the Uncompahgre Valley for hundreds of years. Many changes have come to this quiet little valley."

"So if our parents are friends, your dad must know the colonists pretty well. Does the rest of your family still live here?"

"No one in our tribe has any plans to leave. This area is sacred. My grandfather actually saw the arrival of the colonists in a vision. For years, he tried to tell our people these Visitors would come and change everything. Grandfather encouraged us to be prepared for them. As time passed and no group of strangers arrived, some members of the tribe began to ridicule him."

I frowned and Misty paused, but I encouraged her to continue. "The tribe's lack of faith frustrated him so he moved up into the Canyon, receiving many visions and developing a clear understanding of the Visitors. He shared stories about them with me and spoke of a terrible storm in the Canyon which would endanger the Visitors' purpose. Grandfather often wondered why only he had been entrusted with this foreknowledge, but he was a deeply spiritual man and a seeker of wisdom. You know my grandfather is responsible for naming Visitor Canyon."

"Wow, what a fantastic story. Do you believe your grandfather saw these colonists in a vision? Is that even possible? I'm not sure I believe anyone can see the future."

"I'd probably think the same thing but my grandfather had too many details correct—a small group of intelligent strangers, a dynamic white-haired leader, a horrific storm in the Canyon, even the disappearance of three blonde women with blue-green eyes. No one doubts Grandfather's visions now."

I gasped involuntarily. "He saw my mom in his visions?"

"Along with Ruth's mom and Brad's mom. There are too many coincidences to dismiss his visions. Lucky for him, Grandfather lived long enough to meet Jarak and some of the other colonists. Before he died, he called me to his bedside insisting that the people of his visions had arrived. I was only ten, but I'll never forget the look of absolute wonder and peace he had."

"What else did he see? Did he tell you more of his visions?"

Misty was silent. Fearing she might not tell me anymore, I grabbed her waif-like frame and nearly shook her in my eagerness to get information.

"Misty, what else did he tell you?" I demanded.

She spoke so low I had to lean forward to hear her response. "More of them are coming."

"Coming from where? Norway?"

"Grandfather never discovered where they came from." She shifted her eyes as if she were hiding something. "The truth is the colonists are not what they appear to be, Eve."

"What do you mean? Do you think they're some kind of spies or criminals?"

"No! That's not what I meant. I've got nothing against the colonists.

I feel a strong bond with them since my people have awaited their arrival for so long. But I should warn you, not everyone feels the same way. Some people fear them—then and now. The fear mongers are most likely the ones responsible for creating our mascot—the Ridgway High School demon."

I felt a chill as I remembered my reaction that first day of school when I'd seen the entranceway sign *Ridgway High School—Home of the Demons.* "People *fear* the colonists? They associate them with demons? But why? They don't seem dangerous to me."

"People always fear those who are different from them. It's human nature. A few hundred years ago, they might have been burned at the stake as witches." At my horrified expression, Misty patted my arm. "Ignore the gossip. I'm sure you'll hear it soon enough if you haven't already. Jarak's people are good people. They're here to do good things. I'm certain of it."

Misty grinned as she turned to leave. "Oh, one more thing, I'm pretty sure they came here from some place far beyond Norway. Take it easy, Eve. Nice meeting you." She nudged my shoulder as if we were old pals, and Misty Meyer disappeared down the hallway.

My eyes followed her until she was out of sight. *Jarak's people are here to do good things. I'm pretty sure they came here from a place far beyond Norway.* Where? The South Pacific? Australia? I pondered her words, wondering what sort of rabbit hole I'd fallen into.

When the bell rang to signal the end of second period, I jumped so violently I hit my head on the glass fire extinguisher box I'd been leaning against.

Brad walked up at the perfect time to see my little collision. My face flamed with embarrassment, but instead of the smirk I expected, his face showed only concern. The worried look in his eyes dissolved my irritation instantly. He took my arm, turning me around to face him. "Are you okay? I heard you were sick in English."

"I'm fine. I got a little dizzy that's all. It must be the altitude up here. You know us lowlanders." I didn't ask how he could possibly have known what happened when he'd been several classes away. I liked this kinder, gentler Brad. Even though his behavior was a bit like Forrest Gump's box of chocolates—I never knew what I was gonna get—I was relieved to see him. He'd said I was one of them, which meant I belonged here and had nothing to fear.

"Come on dizzy girl. Let's go to Spanish. I'll sit next to you and make sure you don't fall over. *Habla espanol?*"

"*Un poco,*" I replied, holding two fingers an inch apart. Spanish came fairly easy to me, but I didn't want to seem conceited. "For a second year student, I should know more than I do."

"Good. Sounds like we'll have to help each other."

On the way to class, I asked Brad about Misty.

"Misty is cool, but definitely Ridgway's token hippie chick. She designs jewelry, plays the guitar, likes to dance. Her grandfather and Jarak were close. People say he had visions."

I moved out of the hallway and pulled him over to the wall. "That's what she said—visions of the colonists and the disappearance of our moms."

"I've heard that rumor. The Utes claim he foretold many things about our arrival in the Uncompahgre Valley. Pretty weird, huh?"

"Weird, yes. But true? How could he have known about the storm in the Canyon?"

He brushed it off. "The world is full of strange stuff, Eve. Let's go to Spanish."

We got to class and grabbed desks by the window. Sitting next to Brad felt oddly normal, like we'd known each other all our lives. I stifled a laugh when Augustine followed Emily into the class. I knew he spoke Spanish from talking to Emily. As they sat down next to us, Augustine took note of my expression.

"Hey don't give me that look," he said. "My dad says I need to work on my Spanish grammar. Besides, it's an easy A, and I get to spend more time with my girl."

I rolled my eyes at them. "You two are killing me. Just make sure you keep your hands to yourselves during class. And since you're here, you can help the rest of us."

"No problemo." Augustine smiled naughtily at Emily. "At least not with the last part."

Brad held up his hand for a high five, and Augustine smacked it. Emily shook her head and blushed. "He'd better behave. I need to pay attention even if he doesn't."

My three companions calmed my anxiety, and Spanish passed quickly. When class was over, I was sorry to see Brad leave. Although I enjoyed his company, my disappointment at his departure was something more. With Brad around, I felt safe and protected. Geesh, there's that loaded word again. As much as I tried to keep the traitorous thought out of my mind, the feeling persisted. I wondered what Daniel would think if he could read my thoughts. Thankfully, he was nowhere in sight.

Phys Ed was bearable despite my discovery that we were in the middle of a volleyball unit. I hated volleyball. The ball always seemed to be aimed straight for my head. Since it was my first day, I stayed in my street clothes, but the P.E. teacher made it clear she expected me to dress out tomorrow. Her short blond hair and muscular frame reminded me of the girls' basketball coach from my Denver high school. No slouches and no excuses.

It was during lunch that I first saw Ruth. Our seating arrangement worked out better than I expected since Daniel and Natalie were at the far end of the table, and Tara was nowhere in sight. When Brad came into the cafeteria and sat down next to me, it occurred to me I had become part of the in-crowd in less than a week.

Normal-looking, unassuming Eve Hunter had transformed into a popular girl. No one could've been more surprised than me. Since I hadn't changed, I knew the people surrounding me made all the difference. In the midst of the cafeteria chatter, an overwhelming impression came to mind: *This is where you belong here. These are your people.*

I carefully observed those around me, trying to determine how they were different from my friends in Denver. Sarah and Emily made sense to me. They reminded me of friends from my old high school. But I was having trouble understanding my instant connection to Daniel, Erik and Brad. These were the popular boys—the jocks everyone fawned over. It almost felt as if they had been prepared for my arrival—like we were long-lost cousins or something. Our friendship seemed inevitable.

As I expanded my observations to include the rest of the cafeteria, I noticed a small blonde girl sitting in the corner. She hunched over her lunch and a book in a protective posture. I immediately thought if she raised her eyes to mine I would be looking into a pair of blue-green orbs. Some intangible quality about her drew my attention. Brad saw me watching her.

"That's Ruth, Jakob Andersen's daughter," he said. The sadness in his voice was unmistakable. "She's fragile, like a piece of blown glass that could shatter any minute." I waited for him to continue, but he only stared at her in silence.

"I met her dad at The Colony. He seemed like a nice guy, not a lot of baggage," I offered.

"Maybe he's accepted his wife's disappearance, but Ruth still suffers. We used to talk sometimes, but now she has withdrawn from even me. I guess I feel sorry for her because I get it, you know what I mean? Everyone wants us to pretend it never happened—to accept our loss like what happened to our mothers was destiny or something. I refuse to buy into that garbage."

His eyes begged me to grasp what he was feeling. I wrapped my hands around his arm to console him, pulling him closer. His gaze burned into mine. My heartbeat quickened as I realized what I had done. For a several seconds, it was only the two of us in the room.

Breaking the spell, Brad moved away shrugging indifferently, ashamed at the exposure of his raw pain. His bitterness was undeniable.

I hung my head and clasped my hands in my lap, too embarrassed to meet his eyes. "Sorry about that," I said. "You seemed so sad. I just wanted to make you feel better."

He pasted on a cheesy grin, changing his demeanor in an instant. "Hey, you can grab me anytime you want."

I'd uncovered clues to the mystery of Brad's persistent scowl. He'd bared his soul to me for a brief moment before burying his emotions under a practiced expression. He carried his hostility around like a shield to keep the pain from breaking through. He refused to accept the loss of his mom because he couldn't make sense of it. I wondered if he was drawn to me because we shared the same tragedy and confusion.

I looked over at Ruth, wondering why I had escaped the emotional pain she bore. Perhaps my dad had been wise to leave Ridgway. Brad and Ruth had been surrounded by haunting memories all their lives, but we'd escaped the painful people and places who reminded us of my mother. Plus, my dad and I bonded immediately. Maybe Jakob hadn't known how to relate to Ruth. And then there was Brad. How had his dad reacted to his wife's death? Were he and Brad close? That was a question I would soon have answered.

Brad walked me to my next class, informing me he had basketball practice every day after school, so he'd catch up with me later. Since I knew

Daniel had AP History next, I braced myself for the encounter. With some relief, I realized I'd hardly thought about him at all during lunch. With any luck, my obsession with him was passing.

"You and Brad seem pretty friendly," Daniel said as I entered History class. I bristled at his disapproving tone. Why should he care?

Remembering my promise to be nice, I fumbled with an explanation. "He feels guilty about some things he said Friday night. Besides, I'm sure you know we have a lot in common."

"I suppose you two do have a lot in common. Well, at least he can be trusted. You should be safe with him around."

Despite my promise, I couldn't hold back the sarcasm. "Oh Daniel, I'm so happy you approve of my choice of friends." I stalked to the back of the class, fuming. Who I hung out with was none of his business. I'm sure he wouldn't appreciate me telling him what I thought of his blonde bimbo. It took the entire class period for me to calm down.

Remembering Daniel also had last period Chemistry, I hurried out of History, trying to latch on to Sarah and Emily in the hall so I could avoid him. The vibrations refused to dissipate. Suddenly I felt cold, as if a door had opened to let in the chill from the approaching storm. Turning to look for the source, I passed directly in front of Mack. His icy blue-gray eyes bore into mine. He moved toward me and seemed about to speak, but Sarah intervened, barreling into me and grabbing my arm.

"Come on, Eve. We'll be late," she said loudly. Then whispered, "Stay away from him. I get the feeling he's got something against you."

"She's right," a second voice whispered, making both of us jump.

"Holy cow, Daniel! You scared us to death," Sarah scolded.

"Yeah? Well, you should be scared. Keep Eve away from Mack," he ordered, walking away without another word.

"Sarah, what the…" I started to ask when Erik came up behind us.

She cut me off. "Sometimes you just have to follow your gut." Then smiling sweetly at Erik, she said, "Hey guy, what took you so long? You missed your chance to save two damsels in distress." I observed her wryly as she told him about Mack's menacing advance and Daniel's orders. He didn't seem surprised.

"I'm not too worried about you though, Sarah," Erik teased. "In fact, I pity the poor guy who tries to take you down. He has no idea what he's in for." We all laughed, perhaps a bit too enthusiastically.

Mack resurfaced in Chemistry. He had taken a seat in the far back by the time we got to class. The intensity of his glare pummeled me like a wave of evil, and I suppressed a shudder. I chose a seat close to the front, but I felt his eyes boring holes in the back of my head.

Halfway through class, I noticed something odd about the seating arrangement. Daniel, Erik, Sarah, and Emily had formed a tight circle around me, creating a protective barrier as if by some mutual agreement.

Chapter 10

For the next couple weeks, Brad and I fell into a routine. We met at my car in the morning, sat beside each other in class, and shared lunch. We'd rapidly become close friends. He was the big brother I'd never had, although I must admit, a mighty fine-looking big brother. We laughed at each other's jokes, texted back and forth, and studied together. I should've figured it was too easy. Our safe, uncomplicated friendship hit a snag by the end of the second week. On the Friday before my meeting with Jarak, Brad's life began to unravel.

The sun shone brightly that Friday morning, warming my car. I stayed in the parking lot waiting for Brad until the bell rang for first period. When he didn't respond to my texts, I gave up and went to class. He probably felt like he needed some space, since we'd been spending a lot of time together.

I walked down the hall lost in my thoughts, responding to Mrs. Walters's enthusiastic wave as I passed by the office. Dad and I were meeting with Jarak on Saturday, and I was preoccupied with what his revelations would be. These two weeks had tested my patience. I felt certain I'd been waiting for answers from Jarak for a very long time.

Brad never made it to Pre-Calculus. Daniel and Erik came into class together, somber and uncharacteristically quiet. I had become so accustomed to the odd vibrations the boys produced that I hardly noticed them anymore.

But on that particular Friday, I sensed a stark change in the magnitude. The normally vibrant energy fields seemed despondent and lifeless, like a balloon that had lost half its helium.

Emily asked Augustine what was up, but he said he had no idea. Erik sat down heavily in between Sarah and Augustine and would only tell us Brad had some trouble at home. Daniel's kept his eyes glued to me for the entire class, so it was impossible to focus on Mr. Ayers. I couldn't help wondering if Daniel thought I was responsible for Brad's absence.

When the bell rang, I raced over to him. "Where's Brad? Did something happen?"

Daniel pulled me aside so we could speak in private. "Brad had a huge fight with his dad. It's not the first time, but this time Mr. Spencer threatened to leave Ridgway."

"Is Brad okay? I mean, his dad doesn't get violent, does he?"

"Not yet, but at some point he will snap. He's been angry at Jarak and the colonists for a long time, and now he's mad at you."

"Me? He doesn't even know me."

"Eve, come on, don't you get it? You're one of us. Guilt by association. He tolerates Brad hanging with me and Erik because of basketball. But the last thing he wants is to see Brad get romantically involved with one of the colonists. You're his worst nightmare come true."

I won't pretend I understood all of what Daniel was saying. After all, I didn't consider myself one of the colonists—except by lineage. All I really knew was I had made an enemy. And once again Daniel's abrasive manner put me on the defensive.

"Brad and I are just friends. We're not 'romantically involved.' Do you think I should avoid Brad altogether?"

"Of course not. This is Brad's deal—his decision. He should be free to choose his own friends. I wouldn't avoid him for the sole purpose of making his home life easier. Besides, if his dad decides to leave Ridgway, Brad can always move in with us." Daniel's face blazed with a steely determination. He was a fighter this one. With dismay, I belatedly realized I had asked Daniel's advice without even thinking.

"You are still meeting with Jarak tomorrow, right?" Daniel asked, abruptly changing the subject. So, he hadn't forgotten my appointment with my grandfather.

"Yes. With all the questions I have, it might take all weekend."

Daniel smiled at my indignation, his green eyes glowing softly. "It might even take longer than that."

Natalie chose that moment to appear, and I made a quick exit, stumbling down the hall to English. Collapsing in a chair next to Sarah, I groaned. "Everything is positively bizarre around here. Mr. Spencer is mad at me because I've been hanging out with Brad."

"You're kidding. Daniel told you that? Does he have something against your dad?" Sarah asked.

"No, like I told you the other day, it's because I'm one of *them*. Apparently, his dad hates the colonists."

"But his wife was one of them," Sarah argued.

"Yeah, I think that's the problem," I said. "Poor Brad. I didn't know things were bad at home. He hasn't said anything about his relationship with his dad."

"You know, I'm beginning to wonder about you, Eve. Wherever you go, bad things happen," Sarah said, shaking her head. I'm not completely sure she was kidding.

Brad showed up next period for Spanish, his scowl back in full force. He kept his eyes on the floor, tossed his textbook on the desk, and dropped into his seat. The energy radiating from him was surprisingly weak. I'd expected it to pulsate violently like a throbbing headache.

"Hey Eve," he finally said. "Sorry I missed you this morning."

"No problem. Anything I can help you with?"

He made an unsuccessful attempt to smile. "Not unless you can change the past."

"I'm afraid I haven't figured out how to do that one yet, but I'll keep you posted." He managed to put on a tight smile though it never reached the bleakness in his eyes.

After Spanish, Brad admitted he'd had a fight with his dad and apologized for his black mood. He looked down at his feet, not so much angry as miserable and discouraged. I tried to find somewhere else to focus my gaze, not only to avoid staring at his misery but also because I couldn't decide if I should tell him how much I knew. Brutal honesty eventually won out.

"Daniel told me about your dad," I blurted out. "He said your dad didn't want you hanging out with me."

"The grapevine in Ridgway operates like nowhere else. I should've figured you already knew." I couldn't determine if he was frustrated that I knew or relieved that he didn't have to be the one to tell me.

"Daniel didn't offer the information. I demanded to know where you were because I was worried." With surprise, I heard myself defending Daniel.

Brad ran his hand through his thick, dark hair. "Its okay, Eve. We're a tight-knit bunch around here. Everyone knows everything. Something you're no doubt catching on to. By the way, are you and your dad still meeting with Jarak tomorrow?"

Funny. That was the same question Daniel had asked me earlier. Maybe Brad was just trying to change the subject, but both boys seemed a bit too interested in the meeting with my grandfather. Daniel even hinted that Jarak could explain the protection thing. Brad must have his own reasons for wanting me to talk to my grandfather.

I told him Dad and I planned to get together with my grandparents and expected to spend the whole day with them. Since he obviously didn't want to talk about the argument with his father, I asked him if he had plans for the weekend.

"Actually, a bunch of the colonists are getting together on Sunday afternoon. Maybe I'll see you there." He paused, watching for my reaction.

"I'm not sure that's a good idea. I mean your dad doesn't seem too thrilled about the colonists, not to mention our friendship. I don't want to cause problems for you."

"My dad won't be there. Besides, he's my problem, not yours. If you chose to get out of my life, *that* would cause problems for me. I hope you'll be there on Sunday. I really like you, Eve, and I want you to know I will be here for you. Do you understand what I'm saying?"

The brooding, scowling Brad had disappeared and the sweet, compassionate one had returned. I would never have believed we could become so close within such a short period of time. But upon learning how he felt, I realized this relationship was already much bigger than I thought. The sudden sharing of his feelings made me uncomfortable, but I enjoyed his company too much to put distance between us. As long as we agreed to keep things the way they were between us, I planned to stick around.

Brad and Daniel agreed we shouldn't end our friendship because of Brad's father, so I figured the matter was resolved. I would soon learn my thinking was incredibly naive. Tara lost no time letting us know she thought otherwise. When she saw us sitting together having lunch as usual, she stormed in our direction, her eyes blazing.

"Are you crazy?" she hissed at Brad. "How can you be so selfish and clueless? We don't know what kind of trouble your dad will cause for us. Don't you think it might be a good idea to keep your distance from Miss Chosen One until your dad calms down?"

She glared at me, but I had no response. Since Brad and Tara had grown up together, I assumed he was familiar with her outbursts and expected him to brush off her assault. I couldn't have been more wrong. Perhaps Brad decided he'd had enough for one day. He stood slowly, possessed by a fury that made me want to dive under the table. His body shook violently as he raised his arm toward Tara, as if to push her away. An intense vibrating energy electrified the atmosphere as Tara shot backwards and slammed into the cafeteria wall.

Erik and Daniel shouted simultaneously, "Brad, stop!" Their shouts echoed throughout the room. Brad examined his hand, clearly stunned. Tara gaped at him, but not in terror as I would've expected. Despite her embarrassment and physical discomfort, her facial expression was eerily smug. She was *pleased* she'd provoked Brad to such overpowering rage.

"Well, Bradley. You surprised us all, didn't you?" Tara said, in a cold, menacing voice. She spun around and fled the room, triumph overcoming disgrace. I refused to believe this evil wench could be related to Erik. He must've inherited the good traits and left her all the bad ones.

Everyone who had witnessed the bizarre incident stared at us. The deadly quiet lingered. Brad stumbled out of the cafeteria, moving in a daze. Daniel and Erik looked around uncomfortably. Natalie and Rachel were so busy gloating over Tara's humiliation, they didn't even question the cause. Emily studied the floor, clinging to Augustine's hand. His clenched jaw and controlled manner made me wonder if he knew something. Sarah finally broke the silence.

"Somebody care to clue me in on what that was all about?" she demanded. Erik shook his head, signaling her to drop it, but she was adamant. "Erik, didn't you see what happened?" She tried to sound belligerent, but her quavering voice gave her away. She was terrified.

Daniel shot Erik a warning look. As if obeying orders, Erik put his arm around Sarah's shoulders and whispered in her ear. The two of them tossed what was left of their lunches in the trash and exited. The rest of us remained glued to our seats.

Daniel studied me, trying to extract my thoughts. I knew he expected me to accept and even understand Brad's actions. But how could I? Admittedly, the spectacle I had just witnessed was not entirely new to me, but the perpetrator was Brad, of all people. My lineage dictated my membership in The Colony, which made me a keeper of some sort of secret. The tricky part was I had no idea what secret I was supposed to be keeping.

My shock disappeared giving way to exasperation. Were the colonists a special group of gifted people who'd formed an alliance? Did these people pass on these gifts to their posterity? In which case, the need for secrecy made sense. After all, the colonists would be corralled like lab rats if word of their abilities got out.

Even as I drew these conclusions, I knew I was missing something. I couldn't help but wonder why these particular people possessed such gifts. What made them different from everyone else, and where did the gifts come from?

I had to find Brad. His unexpected and potentially dangerous power surprised him as much as anyone else. People around me began to talk and move at once, but I felt as if I were encased in a bubble, detached from the chaos. The pandemonium in the cafeteria faded into the background, replaced by vibrant images of Mr. Winter in the café and the Swensens in the meadow. The explanation thrusting itself into my mind couldn't be true. But it had to be. I had seen it for myself. Brad had the gift. Why hadn't he known about it until today?

I looked everywhere for Brad, finally checking the parking lot. His Jeep was gone, and he didn't respond to my calls or text messages. I didn't know him or the area well enough to know where he might have gone.

I considered suffering through my last two classes, but couldn't do it. Even as I slid behind the wheel of the Subaru, I pictured my dad's disapproval. He'd flip out when he discovered I skipped class. Well Dad, I reasoned, it was your idea to move to Ridgway.

Although I didn't know where to look for Brad, his black Jeep was pretty tricked out, so it would be relatively easy to spot. I headed north on Highway 550, letting my instincts guide me. Brad had mentioned Ruth's fear of the water and asked me if I shared this fear. When I told him I loved the water, he admitted he did too, especially the Reservoir. Acting on the hunch, I decided to drive to Ridgway State Park Reservoir.

I found his Jeep parked at the first turnoff. Pulling in behind him, I grabbed my jacket and wandered down towards the water. It was a chilly November day. The numerous aspens stood bare, stripped of their golden leaves. Heavy-scented pines and spruce dominated the forest encircling the Reservoir.

Brad sat on the edge of the cliff overlooking the man-made lake, his elbows resting on his knees. He didn't seem surprised to see me when I walked up beside him. I sat down, assuming the same position, taking comfort from his presence and drawing peace from the magnificent view. We sat in silence, contemplating the beauty of the scene.

When Brad spoke, his voice echoed with unexpected wonder. "The Earth really is beautiful, isn't it? I wonder if the other planets out there are as awesome as this one." He didn't seem to want an answer, so I simply nodded my head in agreement. Several minutes passed before he said anything else.

Finally he said, "Kind of a shock today, huh?"

I nodded again, determined to keep quiet and let him say all he needed to say.

He turned back to the Reservoir, searching the turbulent waves for the right words. "I didn't know I had it in me. By now, you must've figured out that some of us have these powers. You witnessed Mr. Winter's evasion of the shots at the café, and I heard Lillian talked to you about our gifts."

"Who told you about that?"

"Jarak told Daniel's dad that you'd asked about it. Mr. Winter shared it with Daniel who shared it with me. Like you said, nothing is a secret around here."

Oh boy. Although I didn't care that this particular topic of my conversation with the grandparents had been passed around, I made a mental note to be careful what I said. Right now though, I wanted answers from Brad.

"What happened in the cafeteria, Brad? Your little display of power shocked everyone. And you seemed surprised too, as if you didn't know what would happen when you—I don't know what you call it—channeled your energy toward Tara."

"I didn't know, Eve. It had never happened before."

"So this mysterious gift showed up for the first time today? You must be in major shock. Do you think your anger brought it out? Where does this power come from? "

Brad shifted a little, enough for me to know I'd crossed a boundary. He chose to answer the first two questions.

"Today was definitely a first. Maybe anger did bring it out. Rage completely took possession of me, but I didn't really want to hurt Tara, I only wanted to stop her. It's hard to wrap my mind around what I did—what I'm capable of." He lifted his hands and stared at them, as if they belonged to someone else.

To my complete surprise, tears filled his amazing dark blue eyes. "Until today, I didn't believe I had any special gifts. Last year, some of the other Colony kids began exhibiting extraordinary abilities. As the months went by, nothing changed for me, and I assumed I had missed out. You can't imagine what it felt like to be, well, ordinary, without gifts—while all those around you possess incredible abilities."

He looked at me to gage if I understood how he felt. When I shot him a cynical look, his expression changed. After all, I was one of those ordinary humans, and I was okay with it.

"Come on. It's not the same for you, Eve. I've been around these people all my life. I've had to watch them change while I stayed the same. Can't you see how it would be difficult?"

"I do understand; it's a competition thing. I think one of the biggest problems around here is the closeness of everyone. It's suffocating sometimes. Isn't there any way to create some space between the colonists?"

Brad didn't answer, but turned back to gaze at the water. "Space, that's an interesting concept," he murmured. "Most of us don't want space. We want to be connected. Our connection increases our strength. But, there are a few who fight for their own space. Mack for one. He's gonna self-destruct someday. Let's hope he doesn't take anyone with him."

"I would feel the same way he does," I insisted. "All this togetherness is stifling."

To my surprise, Brad put his arm around my shoulders and pulled me closer. "Does this make you feel like you're suffocating?"

I flushed, stammering an embarrassed reply, "Uh, no, but that's not fair

Brad, it's not the same thing."

"The closeness of the colonists is nothing to fear or run away from," he said, removing his arm and wrapping his arms around his knees. "Besides we can always create space when we need to get away. Look at us right now. Together. Alone."

We were headed down a dangerous path I was not prepared to travel. Maybe I would never be. For now, I wanted Brad to be my friend, a buddy to hang around with. His actions led me to believe he had more romantic intentions. I scooted away, pretending I needed to stretch my legs. Determined to steer the conversation to safer ground, I pounced on his comments about Mack.

"If Mack hates it so much, why doesn't he avoid everyone else? Or better yet, he could leave Ridgway. He's a senior, so he must be eighteen or close to it."

Brad sighed. "It's not that simple, Eve. My guess is he will eventually leave, but then he'll return like all the others who've tried to leave. There is power here that can only be found among Jarak's people. It's magnetic and addicting, and once you've felt its pull there is no other place to go. Everything else pales in comparison."

"What's so special about this place? Why is this power you're talking about centered in Ridgway?"

Brad searched me with his eyes. I already knew that look. Before he could get the words out of his mouth, I held up my hand to stop him.

"Wait, wait. Let me take a wild guess as to what you're gonna say. 'Go ask Jarak.' I'm right aren't I, Brad?" My voice rose as my agitation increased.

He turned away from me and stared across the lake at the gathering clouds.

I shook my head in frustration. "Every time I talk to you or Daniel I feel like I get vague explanations and half-truths. At least answer one question. You've been forbidden to tell me any more, haven't you?" I demanded.

Brad nodded reluctantly.

"By Jarak?"

Brad ventured a smile. "Uh, that's two questions." I made a move to punch him in the shoulder, but he dodged my blow. "Okay, okay," he said. "Yes, Jarak forbid it. He is the only one who can tell you about The Colony."

I stood up, brushing the leaves off my jeans. "Actually, I already knew the answer to both my questions, but I wanted to hear you admit it."

"And I knew you already knew. You're one of us, Eve. It's inescapable. There's a reason your grandfather has been waiting for you to return to Ridgway. This may sound lame, but things will work out. Jarak knows what he's doing. Besides, some really smart people have total confidence in him, so that's good enough for me."

"What about your dad? He doesn't seem to have any confidence in Jarak. And what about this newfound power of yours? Can you be sure everything's going to work out for you?"

"Forget about my dad. After my mom died, he allowed his grief to take control of his life. He's blinded himself to Jarak's abilities. Sometimes I get a little crazy and start freaking out about stuff, but I still have confidence in Jarak. I don't know how to explain it exactly, but I don't just *believe* Jarak speaks the truth, I *know* he does. You will come to know too, I promise."

"How can you promise such a thing? You've only known me a few weeks."

Brad chuckled, and then said the most surprising thing. "Well, let's just say I know who your ancestors are, and that's good enough for me."

"Whatever. I'll leave you alone to commune with nature. I'm going to catch my last couple classes, then head home to grab Quaz and go for a run. Are you headed back to school?"

"Yeah, I need to get back. I can't skip all my classes then show up for basketball. Hopefully, coach will buy my story about getting sick at lunch. I need to make the last couple practices before our first game tomorrow night. Coming to the game?"

"Sarah and Emily are forcing me to go," I teased.

"Is that the only reason you're coming?" he prompted.

"Come on Brad, now you're fishing big time. It's shameless," I said, then got serious. "You sure you're going to be okay?"

"Of course, I will. After all, today I finally got my wings. All I have to do now is learn how to fly. What could possibly go wrong?"

I shivered as I listened to his words. "Don't fly too high, or you might lose those wings." Even as Brad rejoiced in his new power, I felt apprehensive about the whole thing. An ominous thought entered my mind: If Brad has been given a special gift; he's going to need it.

"Take care of yourself. I'll fill you in on Jarak's revelations, *if* I live to tell about it," I joked. "Good luck at the game."

"It's not luck, it is pure skill, baby," he said, in a low, sexy voice. "And the support of my adoring fans, of course. See you at the game and hopefully Sunday too."

"I'll text you about the Sunday gathering." I waved goodbye and headed back to my Subaru. Two questions competed for my attention: How would Brad handle his newfound ability, and how would I survive the remaining hours until the meeting with my grandfather?

Chapter 11

Friday night crept by like an endless nightmare. I woke up every hour to stare in frustration at the glowing red numbers on my clock radio. Sometime around three a.m., I finally turned the clock face toward the wall. Dreams of trying to find my mom in a blinding storm alternated with those of running in terror as someone chased me through the woods. The first dream was most likely a flashback; the second one was hopefully not a premonition.

After my tortuous night, I expected to wake up to a stormy, overcast day, but instead the sky reflected a brilliant shade of blue, and the temperature gauge registered a relatively warm day for the middle of November. Thanksgiving was less than two weeks away.

Despite being exhausted, I dragged myself out of bed, determined to take a run. Poor Quaz slept soundly in the corner of the bedroom. Apparently my tossing and turning had ruined his sleep too. I considered going without him but figured we could both use the fresh air.

As I forged a path through the woods, my legs seemed cumbersome and unresponsive. Part of the reason was undoubtedly fatigue, but the other part was an unexplainable sense that all was about to change. I knew this was perhaps the most important day of my life thus far, but I couldn't explain how I knew it. I both anticipated and feared Jarak's revelations. My stomach lurched as the pounding in my head matched the striking of my feet on the ground.

Relax, I chided myself. Jarak is your grandfather, whom you've known all your life. You have no reason to fear him. My dad wouldn't have suggested we go to Jarak if it were a bad thing. Whatever lay ahead must be good and something positive would emerge from our little conference. Perhaps I would receive answers which would be hard to accept, but at least I would know the truth. I repeated these rationalizations over and over, nearly convincing myself I was overreacting. So why couldn't I shake the overwhelming impression that Pandora's Box was about to be opened?

I flashed back to a discussion I'd had with Sarah and Emily after school Friday. When classes got out, Sarah grabbed me in the hallway and insisted we needed to talk.

"What happened between Brad and Tara in the cafeteria?" she demanded.

"Sarah, I don't know any more than you do."

"You left school and tracked him down, didn't you?"

"I found him out at the Reservoir. Brad said his anger took over, and he lost control. He was as shocked as everyone else."

"Yeah, well everyone else isn't capable of throwing someone against a wall without even touching them. Didn't he have an explanation?"

I debated whether to mention my grandmother's comments about special gifts, but decided to wait until I understood why the colonists had these powers. "Not really, Brad seemed pretty vague. What do you guys think?"

Sarah was disgusted that I had no answers. She and Emily exchanged glances.

Emily said quietly, "Even though you're new here, you're also a colonist so you must know there's something different about them. Strange things happen when they're around. Unexplainable things. This might seem crazy, but we think they have certain, uh, capabilities that normal people don't."

I was dumbfounded. Sarah and Emily *knew*. But of course, Ridgway was a small town. Over the years, the townspeople must've seen things. It would be difficult for the colonists to hide their secrets. My friends looked to me for answers because I was Jarak's granddaughter. I managed to escape by telling them I'd noticed strange behaviors too, but had no explanation. I promised to ask my grandfather and let them know what I found out. So why did I feel so certain I'd have to break that promise?

By the time Quaz and I returned from our run, I was ready to face whatever Jarak revealed. What I wasn't expecting was my dad, standing beside the door, staring out the window. He stood still as a statue, wearing a tattered plaid robe, which he'd probably had since college, and holding his usual cup of black coffee. I could tell I wasn't the only one who had suffered through a rough night.

"Dad? You look awful." I pulled off my running shoes and walked over to the window. "Is something wrong?"

Haunted eyes turned to me. "Eve, before we go to your grandfather's house, I need you to understand that every choice I've made has been because I thought it was best for you. I thought leaving here was the answer after your mom died, but I was wrong. Please forgive me."

"Forgive you for what? Dad, please stop it. I'm tired of hearing veiled hints and spooky innuendos from you and the kids at school about who I am and why we're here in Ridgway. How can I even respond when I don't know what you're talking about?"

"I'm sorry, Eve. You're right. You've always been strong and smart and brave. I'm the one who's always running away from things I can't control." He smiled wistfully. "You become more like your mother every day. I'm sure you can handle whatever the future holds for you."

"Thanks for the vote of confidence, and for the record Dad, I think you're great. We make the best choices we can at the time with the information that's available. Let's just wait for the almighty Jarak to reveal whatever it is he's going to reveal and move on."

Dad nodded with relief. "Good idea, let's get this show on the road. One favor though—can you please try to remember to call him Grandfather?"

I grimaced. "I'll work on it. Give me thirty minutes to take a shower and put my face on in preparation for the big event," I said, taking a Power Bar from the cupboard before I headed back to my bedroom.

The hot shower felt so good I didn't want to get out. Anticipation and dread competed for control of my state of mind. I chose a pair of tan slacks and a sweater instead of my normal jeans and hooded sweatshirt since my grandparents tended to be a bit formal. I told my dad I was ready, whistled for Quaz, and grabbed my water bottle. As the three of us jumped in the Tahoe, it felt a bit like we were off to see the Wizard of Oz. I hoped Grandfather didn't disappoint me.

When we reached the gates at Terra Dyne, something had changed. During my first visit—could it have been only a few weeks ago?—the high tech compound seemed foreign and almost hostile. This time, it was different. Instead of threatening, it felt more like a safe haven. Even the mysterious vibrations had taken on a soothing quality, meshing perfectly with the whisperings of the pines. It struck me as odd that such a dramatic change had occurred in a short time period. Especially peculiar was the realization that the transformation had taken place in me not in my surroundings.

Jarak and Lillian both answered the door, welcoming all three of us into their home. Even though my grandparents kept an immaculate home, they were big dog lovers and had encouraged us to bring Quazimodo along with us. Quaz accepted a few scratches around the ears before settling himself in front of a crackling fire in the huge fireplace.

"How are you, dear?" my grandmother asked. "You can't imagine how much we've been anticipating your visit. You look wonderful!"

"Nice try, Grandmother," I protested. "Dad and I were up all night. We look exhausted, and you know it." I smiled wryly, trying to soften the edginess of my words. I hoped we could skip the pleasantries and get on with the purpose of our visit.

"I'm sorry dear, but you always look wonderful to me. Of course, you're anxious to speak with us. I'll grab some hot chocolate from the kitchen, and we'll get started."

"Would you like some help?" I asked, trying to speed up the start of our conversation.

"No, no. I already have the hot chocolate warming in a kettle. You stay here and visit with your Grandfather," she insisted as she hurried toward the kitchen.

I studied my luxurious surroundings, taking note of the dining room with its intricately carved walnut table and the pale green and gold brocade drapes framing the floor-to-ceiling windows. My grandparents' house hugged the mountainside and featured panoramic views. I briefly wondered if I would ever have a home like this in Colorado. Perhaps, I thought, but certainly not in Ridgway.

"It's beautiful isn't it?" Jarak asked, noting my interest in the view. "We found a rare treasure when we happened upon such an incredible spot."

"How exactly did you discover this particular spot? What drew you to Ridgway?"

"All in good time, Eve. Let's wait for your grandmother."

Studying the walls, I examined several photos I'd seen on our previous visit. Each one featured brilliant nebulas, galaxies, and constellations. An enormous, awe-inspiring photo of the planet Earth swirling with vivid greens and blues dominated the only wall without windows. My grandparents were obsessed with the heavens.

When Grandmother returned, we seated ourselves around the fireplace, my grandparents on the leather couch with Dad and me occupying the chairs. My first instinct was to pace the floor, but I forced myself to remain in my chair. Perhaps spontaneous combustion in human beings was not a mere theory.

Jarak gazed at me thoughtfully before he began speaking.

"Eve, I know you have a lot of questions, but let me start at the beginning of our story." He reached over and squeezed Grandmother's hand. "Twenty three years ago, the colonists settled in the Uncompaghre Valley and built Terra Dyne and The Colony. We had arrived in Colorado two years earlier." He paused, and I jumped right in.

"So you didn't come straight here from Norway? You mean your entire group lived somewhere else in Colorado first then dropped everything and moved here?" I asked. Talk about a determination to stay together. But Jarak's surprises were only just beginning.

"Twenty-five colonists to be exact," Jarak said. He had a far-away look as if he were reliving the experience. "Our arrival was the most incredible day of our lives." He paused, taking a sip of hot chocolate. "The truth is Lillian and I, the colonists—we never lived in Norway. We needed a distant place of origin, so we chose a Scandinavian country." Jarak leaned forward, capturing my eyes with a stunning forcefulness.

"Well then, where *did* you come from?" I blurted out the obvious question. Even as the words escaped my mouth, visions of an otherworldly landscape burst into my mind like a panoramic movie sequence. All confusion dissipated and understanding took its place. Amazing. I stared at Jarak in astonishment. Was it truly possible?

Jarak locked his shimmery blue-green eyes with mine. This was the answer I had come seeking. Gripped by an overwhelming sense of epiphany,

I stood on a precipice about to leap into a vast unknown. There could be no turning back. Although I knew what was coming, I waited to hear him speak, hardly daring to breathe.

"Our planet, Karillion, lies on the far reaches of what Earth's astronomers call the Milky Way Galaxy. We are not from your Earth, Eve, but from an equally beautiful planet many light years away." He stopped, watching me closely. "Can you see it?"

"Yes," I whispered, reluctant to break the spell. "I can't believe it, but I have to because I can see it all. The spaceship, your arrival, and the people—uh, I mean the beings. And your planet! It's incredibly beautiful," I said, simultaneously scanning through mental images of lush jungles, towering trees, humongous mountains, and three glowing moons.

"Three moons!" I exclaimed. "I can't imagine looking up at the night sky and seeing three moons. Your planet is amazing! It must have been difficult to leave such a place. But, Grandfather," I asked, tearing my focus away from my mental photo album, "How is it possible that I can see these things? Are you projecting your memories into my mind?"

"Remember our talk about special gifts? This is one of my gifts."

"And you both…Grandmother, you have this gift too? Can you do this—put pictures into my mind?"

Grandmother's face lit up with delight. "Yes, my dear. Isn't it marvelous? And best of all, you can learn how to transfer images too." At my look of confusion, she walked over and knelt in front of me, wrapping her hands around mine. "Your mother came with us on the ship. As her daughter you possess many of the same abilities. You're one of us, Eve."

A dozen thoughts and questions competed for my attention, but doubt never entered my mind. The instant I'd experienced the visions—no other word seemed grand enough— I'd known whatever Jarak was about to tell me was the truth. Not only did I see them, I *recognized* them. Had my mother shared these memory pictures with me when I was a child? Or was this some kind of collective consciousness the colonists possessed?

Grandmother got to her feet, no doubt anticipating my next move. Excitement, confusion, and fear raged within me. Quaz began to whine softly, sensing my distress. I jumped up and began pacing the floor, figuring I was entitled to abandon my attempts at self-control. After all, I'd just been told I was an alien.

I gasped, suddenly remembering my dad and his silence. I turned on him with a vengeance. "You knew!" I shrieked. "You had to know about all this! About Mom. About them. Why didn't you tell me?" I took a breath, then another thought occurred to me.

"Wait. Wait a minute. Are *you* one of them, uh, one of *us*?" I had to sit back down. Dad came over and tried to put his arm around my shoulder, but I pulled away, desperately needing space. I began shaking uncontrollably.

"Calm down, Eve. One thing at a time. We're all going to make it through this." He turned my face to look at him. "First off, I am not an alien. My parents and I were born right here in Ridgway. At least that much about your family is true. As for the rest, well, I didn't know what to do after your mom disappeared. There's so much I couldn't really grasp about Kara and your grandparents. I didn't understand what the implications were for you. Jarak tried to explain that you needed to be around your people, but I resisted. I guess I believed everything your mother told me, but when she was gone, I couldn't hold on to it. I wish I could see the pictures in my mind the way you can."

"That's why we came back to Ridgway? So I could be with my people?" The last two words felt strange coming out of my mouth.

He nodded, his eyes filled with anguish. "I couldn't figure out how to tell you the truth. I knew you'd have hundreds of questions, and I didn't have the answers. Besides, you need your grandparents and the other colonists to teach you about your abilities. It is essential for you to learn how to control them."

I heard echoes of Daniel's prophetic promise in the hallway at school: *It won't be long before this town will become the only place on earth you want to live.* Of course Daniel knew all about me, as well as Brad, Erik, and even the despicable Tara. Who knew how many other alien kids I'd passed in the hall? Did they all have special powers?

I turned back to my grandfather in confusion. "But I don't have any special gifts. Maybe because my dad is a human, I didn't inherit enough alien genetic material."

Grandmother laughed. "We are certain you have, Eve. All the other children of mixed parents have demonstrated extraordinary abilities. Besides, you come from a long line of powerful ancestors, so we expect you to possess great gifts. Now that you are sixteen, these gifts will begin to develop, much as Brad experienced his first appearance yesterday. Some gifts take longer to emerge, and some colonists acquire their abilities at an earlier age. Today, we'd like to bestow upon you telepathic transmission skills."

"Seriously? You mean I will be able to talk to people with my mind? Unbelievable. Can all the colonists do this? Does this mean everyone will know what I'm thinking?" All of a sudden I felt vulnerable and exposed.

Grandmother rushed to ease my fears. "All the colonists communicate telepathically, but it's not the same as reading minds. Thoughts must be projected to you, mentally sent in your direction. Although, we are able to pick up distress messages transmitted by anyone. However, there are a select few who are able to read minds, but this gift develops later in life— approximately mid-thirties in Earth years."

"This is not what I expected when we came here today. I thought maybe the colonists were some sort of genetically-enhanced group since you have these special powers. I mean you are scientists, so maybe you guys discovered a super power formula or you were exposed to high radiation levels. Not in a million years did I expect to find out I was an alien. This is way cool, but it's also terrifying, like the floor has collapsed beneath my feet, and I'm scrambling to find something to hold on to." I was babbling, but I felt powerless to stop myself.

I looked over at my dad who was definitely not enjoying any of this. Despite my own anxiety, I couldn't quite figure it out. Did he feel guilty? "Dad, cheer up. I'm not mad at you. Okay, well maybe a little irritated because you didn't tell me, but this is totally awesome. I seriously don't know how you were able to keep all this from me. I would have exploded with the need to tell somebody. It's crazy, amazing stuff."

My dad allowed the faintest glimmer of a smile. "It is incredible, isn't it? Now we know we are not alone. There is intelligent life on other planets. Aliens do exist, and they're here on Earth. Alien blood runs through your veins. You're right, it's mind-boggling."

I stared at him in confusion. "So—what's the problem?"

"Eve, we haven't discussed the implications of the colonists' presence. As wonderful as all this is, you need to understand why the colonists are here."

My smile disappeared. "All of a sudden, I'm getting the feeling their presence is not a good thing." I turned to address my grandparents. "How can it be a bad thing though? I know you're not here to harm us or take over our planet. And if you had brought alien diseases with you like the explorers did when they spread smallpox to the Indians, then people would have died already. What is it? Did evil aliens follow you here to destroy humanity?"

Chapter 12

My grandfather studied me thoughtfully. "Perhaps your gifts are beginning to reveal themselves. I'm afraid your guess is not far off the mark. It was never our intention to harm the inhabitants of the earth. The truth is we were running for our lives and barely escaped our planet. Just after Lillian and I were joined—uh, married—everything changed on Karillion. Subtle changes occurred years before, but no one noticed what was happening until it was too late."

Grandmother interrupted, her voice filled with an uncharacteristic bitterness. "Some of us noticed, but most people were oblivious and wouldn't listen to the voice of reason. People wanted to believe the lies our leaders were telling us. We were so gullible, so willing to surrender our freedoms."

Jarak explained, "One of our global technology companies developed a microchip which could be implanted beneath the skin to increase the distance of telepathic communication. It seemed harmless at first. This company, The Source, offered to implant the microchip free of charge, claiming their product was a public service which would improve the lives of everyone. Businesses jumped at the new technology, and young people couldn't wait to obtain a microchip. The only negative appeared to be the location of the implantation. The chip had to be implanted at the base of the skull in order to access the brain waves needed for telepathy. We were repeatedly assured of the safety of this procedure."

"There were those of us who suspected something more to this company's alleged good will gesture, but we couldn't pinpoint the reason for our objections," Grandmother added. "The first time I heard the company's announcement, a cold sense of foreboding washed over me. Unfortunately, your grandfather and I worked for the government, and it wasn't long before implantation was required as a condition of employment."

My grandmother shook her head in disgust. "I nearly quit because the thought of having that chip implanted gave me nightmares. Colleagues told me I was overreacting, that the device was perfectly harmless. But in the end, it wouldn't have mattered. Everyone has them now. They forced our children to be implanted as babies. Escape seemed impossible."

"I guess I don't understand. Escape from what? I'm guessing these chips turned out to be some sort of tracking devices, but the aliens keep pretty close tabs on each other anyway. I don't see the problem."

"Lethal tracking devices. The chips worked exactly as advertised, and telepathic communication improved, convincing millions more to be implanted," Jarak said. "What we didn't know was that the ultimate goal of implantation was domination. The Source designed the microchips to set off a deadly electrical current if removed without authorization. Rumors began to emerge as citizens who publicly demanded the removal of the chips started to disappear. Those who tried to take the chips out themselves died instantly. But we didn't know all of this for several years. Within a decade, The Source had gained control of our entire society—indeed, our world."

Jarak took a long swallow of his hot chocolate, and Grandmother continued their story. "After we discovered the chips weren't coming out, I'm ashamed to say we resigned ourselves to being tracked. As you may have noticed, the inhabitants of earth don't have a problem carrying cell phones which allow their movements to be tracked."

"No kidding," I said. "A few months ago, I read about a telecom company who has developed a magnetized tattoo that alerts its host if their cell phone is ringing. Using these tattoos for other purposes wouldn't be a huge leap. We already put tracking chips into our animals. Human tracking implants can't be too far in the future."

"You are dangerously close to embracing the very technology which could be used by those who thirst for power," my grandmother acknowledged. "We're hoping to warn the people of earth and protect them from the same mistakes we made. Our people were blinded by promises of utopia. Many believed the treacherous falsehood that our leaders knew what was best for us, that we couldn't decide for ourselves what we needed or even wanted."

Jarak shook his head, recalling conditions on Karillion. "Governments all over our planet praised The Source for its service to humanity. They promised we were entering a new age of equality and prosperity. It was not unlike the Russian Bolshevik Revolution where equality was assured to all, but this revolution encompassed the globe."

My grandfather's voice became bitter. "Before long, puppet governments established by The Source began assigning jobs and housing. Curfews were imposed and designated perimeters constructed within which we were permitted to move about. Propaganda was distributed promoting a prescribed course of procreation in order to improve the planet. Joining partners were selected for us in order to give birth to 'genetically improved' offspring. Those with physical or mental challenges weren't allowed to reproduce."

"I can't believe thousands didn't stand up and protest," I said. "Isn't rebellion part of being alive?"

"There were small rebellions, but most crumbled as the body counts mounted. Our freedoms disappeared one by one, and we watched them go with little protest. The Source sought total domination. No rivals temporal or spiritual were tolerated. Our freedom to worship was systematically eradicated as religious leaders were imprisoned and churches closed by the hundreds. Governments criticized religion for weakening the people and destroying the unity of society. It wasn't enough to control our actions. The Source wanted to manipulate our consciences. We finally decided it was time for us to escape. Since the madness infected the entire globe, we needed to find a new planet."

"Couldn't you have banded together and found a way to fight?" I asked.

"Taking away the right to choose destroys the soul. And besides, so few actually understood that their very souls were being destroyed one particle at a time. The evidence was staring them in the face, but they couldn't see it. It's been twenty-five years since we escaped Karillion, but the tragedy we brought upon ourselves continues to haunt me."

Jarak stood, brandishing a look of defiance and determination. "The colonists have been given a second chance at freedom on your planet, but we believe we were sent here for much more than self-preservation. We must help Earth's citizens see clearly, to understand the dangers before them. We can't allow the people of Earth to make the same mistakes."

I listened spellbound as my grandparents painted pictures of life on Karillion before and after the emergence of The Source. In some respects, the evil they described seemed unimaginable on our planet. On the other hand, their portrayal of Karillion sounded like some dystopian novels I had read. I suppose if it could be imagined, it could happen. Were all mortal beings doomed to make the same mistakes? Were struggles for domination playing out all over the galaxy?

"I don't understand why the colonists are so *human*," I said. "As an earthling, I consider myself to be human, or at least I used to think I was. Does all this mean other planets exist where more humans like us live? I expected life forms to be different on other planets. What are the chances that all life in the universe evolved to look and act the same?"

Grandmother answered without hesitation. "We are all God's creations, Eve, and his creations are in his image. Even though Earth is the only planet we've visited, we believe human beings exist on many worlds. God scattered his children throughout the universe."

"How can you be so certain?"

"Perhaps I should share with you how we came to earth. We believe we were sent here for a purpose. As we contemplated our options for escape, Jarak received a vision of your planet. He is what we call a Seer on Karillion. One of his gifts is the ability to receive occasional glimpses of the future. Our people believe—or most of them used to believe—God reveals to those who seek him. We departed Karillion uncertain of our path. Although we knew other planets existed with compatible atmospheres, we leaped into the unknown guided solely by faith that God would show us the way to Earth."

"Wow. You mean you just packed up your spaceship and launched? What if you had—I don't know—missed the turn and ended up lost in space? Didn't you have any idea of where you were going?"

Jarak once again captured my eyes with his, drilling into my soul the truthfulness of his next words.

"If God deemed it important to show me a vision of a new planet, I had no doubt he would lead me there. But don't misunderstand me. Besides continuously seeking his guidance, we also studied astronomical charts and referenced journals of space travel, though few existed. Our civilization is not much more advanced than yours when it comes to interstellar travel. The discovery of a potent fuel source in the last century, supplied us with a significant breakthrough. This substance, makar, has enabled us to travel further than we'd ever dreamed. It brought us the great distance to Earth."

"But even if you travelled at the speed of light using this miraculous fuel source, it would still have taken a lifetime for you to get here, Jarak. Uh, I mean Grandfather. I don't see how it's possible," I protested.

"You are quite right, Eve. We were able to make the trip in a few months with the help of a few providentially placed traversable wormholes—tunnels which in essence fold space, creating shortcuts through spacetime. The journey was exhilarating. Traversing the wormholes felt like hurtling through the air on one of your roller coasters."

"A few months? That's incredible. Dad told me about wormholes when I was in sixth grade, but I always assumed they were just a theory. No one has ever positively identified one. How were you able to locate them?"

"While preparing our ship, we installed instruments capable of detecting electromagnetic fields and changes in space density. We were surprised to learn how well these instruments worked. Although I must admit the first dive into a wormhole was a leap of faith. It was terrifying, but we were confident. We believed we had a mission to perform."

Jarak paused briefly before continuing. "It's all about faith, Eve. If you know without a doubt that you have been given a task to accomplish, the means will be provided for you to accomplish that task. Faith is the most powerful force in the universe. Through faith, numerous worlds and great multitudes have been created. The universe has been organized according to faith in the principles that govern it."

"Honestly Grandfather, all that faith stuff is a lot to take in right now along with everything else. Give me a chance to process all the rest and I'll deal with the faith part later. How were you able to remove the implants and escape Karillion?"

"A few inhabitants of our planet possess exceptional abilities, even by our standards. Years before The Source sought control through technological manipulation, our people looked to a particular group of gifted individuals for guidance when faced with serious threats. The wisdom and gifts of the Khalaheem, or Wise Ones, have guided our civilization from the beginning."

"Are you saying your planet has its own group of beings with powers like the Jedi Knights in *Star Wars*? It's incredible to imagine they actually exist somewhere out there. So George Lucas envisioned your Khalaheem," I marveled.

"The creator of *Star Wars* possesses great insight and appears to have pondered much on the universe. The Khalaheem are similar to the Jedi with the same capability of passing this legacy to their offspring. They are a spiritual group who seek wisdom and peace rather than wealth or power. They exist to strengthen and uplift, not control and destroy. They initiated our escape plan and offered their assistance."

My grandmother interrupted, asking if anyone was hungry or needed to take a break.

"Grandmother, we're talking about the literal existence of Jedi Knights. How could I even think about eating at a time like this?"

She chuckled at my enthusiasm. "Of course, our revelations are astonishing. As your grandfather was explaining, we needed the Khalaheem to help us escape. Karillions possess the capability to transmit thoughts, as well as images of actual memories. Most of us do not have the capacity to project falsified visions."

"However, some of the Wise Ones are exceptional. They possess the ability to transfer fabricated mental images, altering perceptions and creating false realities in other people's minds. In addition to employing the talents of these gifted individuals, we also utilized skilled computer technicians—hackers, in Earth speak. Our implants were removed while The Source's computers continued to report they were fully functioning and firmly in place. In addition, our ship embarked while our planet's tracking systems recorded clear skies."

"That sounds like mind control. So this Khalaheem bunch can make people believe whatever they want to like the Emperor of the Dark Side?"

Grandmother smiled at my comparison. "Yes, but there are limitations. This type of mind control, as you call it, has a short duration; ultimately, the will of the individual prevails."

"Those who've defected over to the Dark Side on your planet must have this power also. That's scary. But The Source must have known about these Wise Ones. Why weren't they imprisoned or executed before they could help the rebels?"

"About fifty years before The Source emerged, belief in the prophetic powers and extraordinary gifts of the Khalaheem began to diminish. Members and their families dropped out of the public eye and blended in with the rest of society. This proved to be beneficial for them when The Source gained control, because otherwise they'd have been exterminated. Fortunately, our rulers dismissed their powers as superstitious traditions and foolish myths."

Sadness engulfed Grandmother's elegant face as she continued, "I never understood how so many lost sight of their heritage. Only a few remembered—and believed. The Khalaheem Elders maintained their values and honed their abilities in secret, remaining safe. Unfortunately, The Source and their charismatic leader, Zaran, were successful in recruiting some of their children."

Grandmother exhaled heavily. "One particularly powerful being, Zorak, joined forces with The Source and convinced many to follow him. His gifts allowed him to rise quickly in the dictatorial hierarchy. By the time we left, he was second in command of Zaran's forces. Some descendants of the Khalaheem joined The Source. Others made the journey to Earth."

"Members of the Khalaheem are here?" Wow—actual Jedi Knights in our midst! I glanced over at my dad, who'd remained quiet, refusing to meet my eyes.

For the first time, my grandparents looked uncomfortable, almost guilty. A deep melancholy had enveloped Grandmother when she began speaking of Zorak. Jarak resumed their story where Grandmother left off.

"Several Wise Ones and their children traveled with us. The Source probably discovered our escape within days. Although Commander Zorak dismissed the spiritual roots of the Khalaheem's gifts, experiences from his childhood convinced him of the existence of extraordinary powers. The loss of those with such immense power had to infuriate him. I suppose it was inevitable that someone would try to follow us." Before I could digest the implications of his last statement, Jarak dropped another bombshell.

"Roger and Devin Winter are Khalaheem, along with Leka Spencer, Brad's mother, and Jakob and Anika Andersen, Ruth's parents. Your mother, Kara, is also one of them." This last sentence emerged as a whisper.

"What? Wait a minute. My mother *isn't* anything," I shrieked. "My mother is dead in case you've forgotten. Why would you talk about her like she's still alive? What you mean is these dead women *were* members of the Khalaheem." A staggering notion about Mom's disappearance wormed its way into my consciousness, but I couldn't quite grasp it in my agitated state. This impression hovered on the edge of my understanding.

"So Mr. Andersen and the Winters are the only ones left, except for their children...oh my gosh, Daniel! And of course, there's Brad and Ruth, and *me*? No, that's not possible. I'm not anything special. I can't dodge bullets or read people's minds. This is crazy!" I paced the room, talking furiously to myself, while my dad and grandparents waited for me to vent the agitation that threatened to engulf me.

Understanding dawned once again, accompanied by confusion mixed with escalating anger. "But if Mom was Khalaheem then at least one of you must be too, right? Imagine that, my grandparents are all-powerful alien beings."

I took a quick breath to continue my tirade. "Explain something to me—if my mom was so powerful, why did she drown? Why couldn't she save herself? Why didn't *you* save her?" I sank into my chair shaking my head and sobbing, completely spent. "There is no way I am possibly going to survive this day."

"Maybe we should take a break," Dad said, knowing I'd reached my limit. "Eve, let's go outside and get some air." From the minute I'd begun my agitated pacing, Quaz had assumed an anxious, protective post by my side. At the mention of going outside, he whined and wagged his tail vigorously indicating his vote.

"Sure. Come on, boy, let's go for a walk," I said, dragging my hand through his soft, russet-colored fur. Turning to my grandparents, I managed a lame apology before heading outside with Quaz and my dad. Hopefully they understood how being told you were an alien would turn your world upside down.

Fifteen minutes in the cold November air cleared my head as much as could be expected. Dad walked briskly beside me with his hands in his pockets but didn't say much. What was there to say? The most bizarre revelation I could have imagined had been dumped on me. Who was I really and what was I capable of? Somehow I had to find a way to accept a new reality.

After watching Quaz romp in the snow and throwing a stick a few times for him, we returned to the house. The tension I'd felt before we'd left seemed to have disappeared. My grandparents waited at the door and both of them hugged me fiercely. We'd reached a huge turning point in our relationship. The distance I'd always felt had narrowed. We were co-conspirators now. All the secrets were out in the open—except for one very big one.

Chapter 13

"Let me answer some of your questions, Eve," Grandmother said, her voice soft and soothing like the caress of thick velvet. Her attempt to calm me down worked. I suspected her ability to soothe my frazzled mind must be one of her gifts.

"Your grandfather and I are members of the Khalaheem. We are blessed with extraordinary abilities, but we are not infallible. If we were, the mortal experience would be useless to us. We have to suffer, grow, and endure along with all other mortals. Your mother did not possess the ability to save herself. And Jarak and I could not prevent what happened to Kara either, but we are immensely grateful we saved you."

"*You* saved me? That means you were there, in Visitor Canyon. You must have seen everything. Tell me what happened to my mother," I demanded, glaring at my dad for neglecting to share another key point of the day Mom disappeared. I'd always believed the sheriff had found me unconscious by the river, and my grandparents had shown up later. I shot a withering look his direction, informing him he had some explaining to do.

"We witnessed some of what happened," Grandmother admitted. "Jarak didn't know where you and your mom were headed that day, but sometime around mid-morning he insisted we leave for the Canyon. He could hardly wait for me to get in the car. By the time we arrived, a Karillion

119

ship was taking off from the meadow. As the treacherous water spout receded, we discovered your body. You lay face down by the river, not breathing. We thought you were dead. Thank God I was able to revive you." Tears slipped down Grandmother's cheeks as she relived the awful scene.

I ignored the part about my near death, but the rest of her story intrigued me. "A spaceship generated the water spout?" I asked, trying to reconcile this information with my memories from ten years ago. "What was a ship from your planet doing in the Canyon?" But suddenly it was clear. "Your enemies came after you!"

"Somehow they traced our path. We have no idea why they waited so long to pursue us. Perhaps navigational tools had improved since we left Karillion. You see, many years ago, Jarak shared his vision of planet Earth with those close to us. Some of those individuals later rose to positions of power in The Source. They must've suspected Earth was our destination. Once Commander Zorak arrived on your planet, he could have quickly located the colonists using makar-tracking instruments. Our planet's fuel source leaves behind a distinctive residue."

"But why would they travel so far for a handful of people? What did they want?"

"What they wanted was Kara," Grandmother sobbed. "We were caught off guard and weren't able to protect her."

"Are you saying the bad aliens took my mom?"

"Yes, we believe they came specifically for Kara, and perhaps Leka and Anika also."

"So she's still alive?" I whispered. It came out as a question, but it was more of a statement. My mother *was* alive. Somewhere deep inside I'd always known it. It was like someone revealed you were adopted, and you're not surprised because somehow you always felt it to be true.

Grandmother grabbed a tissue from a cleverly disguised pinecone-shaped dispenser. Add that silly object to the list of things in my life that weren't what they appeared to be. My world continued to spin out of control as I observed the distraught, emotional woman who used to be my grandmother. Her raw grief rattled me.

Jarak rubbed her shoulders, attempting to soothe her. She managed a fleeting smile, and he picked up where she'd left off. "Zorak knew Kara and the other women were Khalaheem. Most likely, he and some of his soldiers travelled to Earth to find them in order to harness their powers. They were the only ones taken."

"I was right next to my mother. Why didn't they take me too?"

"We don't know the answer to your question," my grandfather said. "I can only guess they didn't know about you."

"She told me something that day," I said quietly. "She said, 'I love you and I will come back for you.' I believed her but as the years passed, it became harder and harder to keep believing."

"I'm sure she intended to return, Eve. She must've realized Zorak had come for her. She probably felt our presence in the Canyon and knew we would rescue you. We believe she wanted you to stay on Earth with your dad, so she gave herself up, hoping you would be overlooked. Your mother has an exceptional ability. She's a gifted mind reader."

"My mother is alive, and she can read minds. Wow, what a concept." I wanted to block the barrage of information and take some time to contemplate what all this meant. But Jarak didn't allow me the luxury.

"Eve, we'd all like to believe she's okay, but we can't be certain she's still alive. Certainly it's illogical for Zorak to travel across the galaxy to capture Kara if he intended to kill her. Kara's gifts should keep her alive."

I ignored his caution not to get my hopes up, because all my doubts had vanished. My mother was alive. "Why didn't you go after them and try to save her?"

"We had no way to stop them. Besides, we didn't have a source of fuel at that time for interstellar travel. Much of our research has been toward developing an energy substitute for makar capable of transporting a spaceship over long distances."

"At that time? Does that mean you've found one since then? Can you power the ship?"

"We searched the globe for years and believe we've finally found a fuel source at Lone Cone actually. How ironic that we've discovered what we needed right in our own backyard after years of searching elsewhere. The tests we've conducted these past few months show great promise. We're fairly certain this fuel will be an adequate alternative, but there are a few problems to work out. It's highly combustible and difficult to store."

I brushed aside any reservations Jarak presented in his explanation. "Supposing this fuel source works, are you preparing to go to Karillion?

Aren't you anxious to rescue your own daughter? We have to go get her."

My grandparents looked at each other as if trying to come to an agreement. I glanced at my dad to see if he knew anything but he shook his head.

"Well? What's the holdup?" I questioned when no one spoke up.

Jarak spoke softly. "We're not sure exactly how to proceed because the situation has changed."

"What does that mean 'the situation has changed'? We're wasting time!"

"Eve, we wanted to wait until the colonists' gathering to tell you this, but perhaps this is an appropriate time to share our news." Jarak paused. "A Karillion ship is on its way here."

My dad and I gasped simultaneously.

"Holy cow! Is it a good ship or a bad ship?" I asked. Feeling slightly hysterical from mind-blowing information overload, I nearly laughed as my words reminded me of Glenda the Good Witch from *The Wizard of Oz* when she asked Dorothy, "Are you a good witch or a bad witch?"

After a slight hesitation, my grandfather responded, "This next ship brings good people."

"Thank goodness," I exhaled. "How exactly do you know this ship is coming? Do you have some sort of spaceship-sensing device?"

Grandmother laughed, her sobs forgotten. "Our ship's radar devices only function during space travel. We know the ship is coming because Jarak is a Seer. He's had a vision."

She spoke with absolute conviction, as if his visions left no room for doubt. For her, if Grandfather saw a ship coming, then a ship would show up any day. I had no experience trusting in paranormal prophecies. They sounded so, well, biblical. Watching my dad's face, I knew the two of us were on the same page—the proverbial Doubting Thomases.

Jarak stood up abruptly. "Someone's coming," he said, heading for the front door. We all trailed after him as if drawn by a cord. He opened the door and stepped out on the porch as a fluorescent green Jeep screeched to a stop nearly jumping the sidewalk. It was Daniel.

"Brad called. We need to get over to the ski swap at Town Park," Daniel exclaimed. "Brad gave his dad a demonstration of his new powers, and Mr. Spencer completely flipped out and left the house. Brad followed him to Town Park where he's screaming to the crowd about aliens. Every time Brad tries to get near him, Mr. Spencer accuses him of being an alien freak."

Daniel drew a quick breath, preparing to continue when he noticed me. His intense green eyes glowed with pleasure. "Hey Eve, how are you holding up? Guess we'll have a lot to talk about later. Sorry for interrupting, but Brad's in trouble. Come on!"

We all piled into our Tahoe and sped down the road, screeching through the gate. My grandfather grilled Daniel with questions about the situation with Brad. I had more than a few questions myself, but Jarak's interrogation kept him busy. Daniel sat next to Quaz, studying me and probably trying to gage how I was dealing with the whole alien thing. Our eyes connected, and his gaze smoldered with something I couldn't quite identify.

For a moment, I was so buried in the intensity of our connection that I completely forgot about Brad. Conflicting emotions tumbled through my mind as my heart pounded. Get a grip, Eve, I chastened myself. Brad needs you to focus right now.

In less than ten minutes, we arrived at Town Park. The scene resembled my worst nightmare. Police cars surrounded the park. People huddled in small groups, close enough to satisfy their curiosity, but far enough away to make a quick escape if something went horribly wrong. We jumped from the SUV in time to see Brad's dad wrestled to the ground and handcuffed. Brad shouted at the police to take it easy while Mr. Spencer screamed non-stop about alien invaders.

My grandparents crossed the park to the police without hesitation. I trailed behind my dad and Daniel, wondering how we—the aliens—were going to get out of this one. With some relief, I recognized the husky blond officer and his partner from the café. One good thing about small towns, at least the police knew everyone. And as long as you stayed on their good side, they usually had your back.

"Martin, let me talk to Chris, please," my grandfather asked.

"Jarak. Glad you're here. Think you can talk some sense into him?"

"I hope so. Give me a minute."

"You got it," the cop named Martin agreed. He and his partner stepped back a few feet.

The three of us held back as my grandparents approached Mr. Spencer. He spotted them and started to protest. "Don't let them come any closer," he yelled. "These are the alien leaders. You can't trust them. They'll hijack your mind. Keep them away from me!"

My grandparents kept moving forward. I expected Mr. Spencer's screams to escalate, but as they neared him, his distress melted away. Martin motioned for his deputies to give the prisoner some space.

Grandmother advanced like a lion tamer entering a lion's den. She knelt at Mr. Spencer's side and placed her hand on his shoulder. I couldn't believe he allowed her to touch him. This must be the power of the Khalaheem. The wild-eyed, crazy person had disappeared, replaced by a quiet, almost docile man. The crowd watched in silence.

Brad approached us warily from behind a police car. "Is he okay?"

Daniel and I shook our heads in unison. "Listen!" Daniel said.

The three of us moved closer, placing ourselves between the policemen and Mr. Spencer. I expected the police to stop us and tell us to move back, but they said nothing.

"Chris? What's wrong? Tell us what we can do," we heard my grandfather say.

"Jarak, I can't do this anymore. I'm losing my mind. Every day I ask, 'Will this be the day Leka comes home?' And then I realize how crazy this whole mess is. How can I actually believe my wife is still alive? I don't know what's real anymore. I can't even tell if I'm managing to regain some self-control, or if Lillian's using her power to make me think I am." He shot Grandmother a suspicious look.

"Why you're no longer agitated doesn't matter. You seem to be in control of yourself for now. Focus on remaining calm. Here's what's going to happen: the police will take you in and probably charge you with disturbing the peace. They might test you for drugs to try to determine what triggered this breakdown. Most likely, they'll keep you under observation for twenty-four hours. People are going to ask you a lot of questions, Chris. Please, for Leka's sake and the sake of your son, stop this madness. You've got to realize the danger you've put us in. Think of what could happen to Brad."

Mr. Spencer did not reply. I didn't trust him. I had a bad feeling this was far from over. Martin and his partner approached and gripped their prisoner's arms, lifting him to his feet. "Come on, Chris. Let's go down to the station." Martin turned to my grandfather, "Thanks, Jarak. We owe you one. We'll take it from here."

Everyone watched as the police led Mr. Spencer away. Martin returned to speak to us after putting him in the squad car. "Strange stuff's happening all over. First, that lunatic starts shooting at Carol's, and now Chris Spencer goes off the deep end. I've known that guy for years." He shook his head. "I don't know what's up. Must be something in the water."

After the police left the scene, Brad surprised me with a light kiss on the top of my head before getting in his Jeep and mumbling some excuse about needing to practice his lay ups. Brad's exit triggered whispered conversations all around us. I heard snatches of "He's totally lost it. He called Jarak an alien" and "What makes him think little green men have landed?" Fortunately, I didn't hear anyone admit to believing his ravings, at least out loud. I don't know if it was my overactive imagination—or my newfound identity as an alien—but I swear there were some who surveyed us with suspicion. Maybe Brad's dad had succeeded in planting a few seeds of doubt.

Chapter 14

On the drive back to my grandparents' house, the mood was somber. Exposing the colonists would be disastrous. Horrific visions of armed government agents swarming Terra Dyne filled my head. Would Brad's dad risk his son's safety? I asked my grandfather if he thought Mr. Spencer posed a threat.

"I have no way of knowing how far he'll take this. As Chris suspected, Lillian did calm him down with her healing power, but it won't last. Her powers are only effective if the person truly wants to be helped. I'm not sure Chris wants to be healed. Pain has become his identity and his closest companion. He's not going to give that up easily."

No one seemed to know what to say after Jarak's disturbing conclusion. I glanced back at Daniel several times, anxious to know his thoughts, but he ignored me and stared out the window. I couldn't help but wonder if his attitude had anything to do with the kiss Brad had given me at Town Park. The minute that thought entered my mind, I dismissed it. There was no way Daniel was jealous, after all he had a girlfriend. Whatever passed between us before must've stemmed from the intensity of the moment. Despite this rationalization, warmth flowed through me as I remembered his smoldering gaze on the drive to the park. If pain was Mr. Spencer's constant companion, confusion appeared to be mine.

Daniel offered a preoccupied *see you later* when we reached the house, jumping out of the back of the SUV before my feet touched the pavement. What was his problem? Was he worried about Brad, or was I missing something? Either way, his rudeness irritated me.

Once inside, Jarak officially invited us to the colonists' gathering on Sunday afternoon. He planned to introduce us and tell the others about the ship headed our way.

"Are you really going to tell them a ship is coming based only on some dream you had?" I asked.

"Yes, I am," he said with a confident raise of his eyebrows. "Don't worry. My visions no longer surprise our people. The colonists have become accustomed to me revealing things of this nature. Remember many of them agreed to follow me across an unknown universe based on my visions. However, please don't say anything to anyone before tomorrow. I want to observe everyone's reaction first hand."

"Why? Everyone should be thrilled to have contact with other aliens and news from your planet. Are you expecting a problem?"

"I expect some excitement and anticipation, maybe even some fear. Of course, all will welcome a friendly ship, but there may be some among us who hope to use the ship's arrival for selfish purposes. Not all the colonists feel the same way we do about our Earth mission, especially the younger generation who were born here."

"The young people will be stoked about a spaceship. I can hardly wait myself. Think about it Grandfather! This ship brings others who can help us rescue my mom. We can go get her and bring her back to Earth. Or—oh my gosh—maybe she's on the ship!"

"Don't get your hopes up. Most likely she's not on board. I believe I would sense her presence if she were returning. Anyway, we won't know anything definitive until the ship arrives. We don't know why it's coming, or what message it may bring. You must be patient. It may be awhile before anyone travels to Karillion."

My dad frowned. "Your grandfather is right, Eve. There's no reason to hope for a miracle. We aren't any closer to getting Kara back than we were before. Don't forget she's been gone for ten years. I don't want you to be hurt all over again."

Maybe Dad thought he was trying to convince me, but it was obvious he was trying to convince himself. With a shot of clarity, I realized how often I focused on my pain over the loss of my mother and dismissed his. More than anything, I wanted to liberate both of us. I vowed silently that I would find a way to bring her back.

Grandmother patted my dad's shoulder. "All we can do is hope and pray. Now, I want to start putting together some lunch. But first, Eve, your grandfather and I would like to transfer the ability to communicate with your mind. Are you ready?"

I gulped. Was I ready to begin using telepathic communication? Is anyone ever ready? "Uh, sure. Beam me up Scotty," I joked to cover my nervousness. "What do I have to do?"

"Relax while Jarak and I place our hands on your head. You may feel some energy transference just prior to hearing thoughts projected into your mind. When you receive our messages, try to send a thought to both of us, one at a time."

I started to shake. "Grandmother, what if it doesn't work? What if I can't do it—like I have a blocked mind or something?"

"Eve, you possess the gifts of the Khalaheem. Your mind is incredibly powerful. There is nothing to fear. It's simple. Formulate your thought, visualize its receiver, and then mentally press the send button."

"Okay, I guess I'm ready." Once again, an overwhelming sense of jumping off a cliff enveloped me. When I left this house, I would be a changed being.

"Before we begin," Grandfather said, "I'd like to warn you to exercise caution in two areas while using this ability. The first caution exists to protect all the colonists, including yourself. Because mental telepathy will be unfamiliar, you might have the tendency to treat it like a new toy, obsessively playing with it and becoming overly absorbed with its capabilities. Don't indulge in frivolous telepathy in the presence of Earth's humans. Be extra careful to communicate out loud with the colonists in public as much as possible. Don't answer telepathic questions with the spoken word as it will raise suspicions. All this sounds easier than it is because mind speech will soon become second nature."

"Becoming too accustomed to telepathy is something I hadn't considered," I admitted. "What's the second warning?

"The second aims to protect you personally. Sending out telepathic waves operates much as a radio station broadcasts along a particular frequency. Your thoughts travel along a specific pathway you've created to another person. For the most part, the other colonists can't intercept the waves you're sending to another. However, you still need to exercise caution. Remember your thoughts are actual speech. Like spoken words, once they are sent out, you can't bring them back. Don't transmit rash thoughts. Control your emotions."

"Gotcha," I said, shooting my dad an uneasy glance then moving over to sit on the leather couch. My grandparents intertwined their hands, placing them firmly on my head. Silence enveloped the room. The now-familiar vibrations filled my head as I strained to hear something.

Jarak's words began softly, faint whisperings of comfort and peace followed closely by my grandmother's velvety voice. "We've connected you to The Colony, Eve. You have joined your brain waves with ours. This ability will never leave you but will be linked with your mind and soul throughout eternity."

In my fascination with their voices in my head, I couldn't think of anything to say. For the second time that day, pure knowledge entered my head without words being spoken aloud.

"Eve?" my grandmother prompted me, whether in my mind or aloud I wasn't sure.

"Oh, okay," I giggled at my awkwardness. *Thanks for sharing this gift*, I thought enthusiastically, focusing on Grandmother. Simultaneously, I forcefully hit my imaginary send button as she'd instructed, squeezing my eyes shut.

"Oompf," Grandmother expelled as if I'd knocked the wind out of her. "Take it easy," she laughed. "You don't need to put so much energy into it. I heard you loud and clear."

I grinned. "Sorry. Guess I need to work on my forwarding." Focusing on my grandfather, I sent him a similar message of gratitude. *We're happy to share everything we have with you*, he messaged me in reply.

Dad walked over to the three of us in amazement. For the first time that day, he looked pleased with something. "What's it like, Eve? Can you describe what you're experiencing?"

"Well, it's like having headphones on and listening to recorded speech. What's really cool is how an individual's thoughts sound like his or her spoken voice. Because their voices are familiar, I know immediately who's sending a message. Unless of course I receive a message from someone I don't know, then I guess they'll have to identify themselves. I totally understand how someone might mess up and answer a telepathic question with a spoken aloud answer because I do 'hear' the communication."

"Jarak, I can't believe I never asked Kara, but is it possible to turn it off? Can someone block messages from being sent?" Dad asked.

"Yes, Tom. If Eve desires, she can turn off her reception, the same as you would turn off a phone or the television. Most communication does not get through while we are sleeping. The one drawback is all telepathic messages sent while the mind is blocked simply dissipate, as if they never existed. They are not stored like voicemail. Thought waves are not as pervasive as you might think since telepathic communication operates only over short distances, say within a few hundred yards. Again, the only exception lies with emergency pleas for help. You can imagine why our people jumped at the opportunity The Source offered to increase telepathy's range."

"It's good to know I can turn it off. Grandfather, what about my dad and other non-aliens? Can you give them this gift too?" I asked.

"All our attempts to do so have failed. There seems to be a genetic difference in the neurological makeup of the brain. Perhaps someday we will find a way to transfer telepathy to Earth's people."

"Well, Eve," my dad said, his voice tinged with disappointment. "You'll just have to keep me in the loop and be my mind-message translator."

I gave him an apologetic smile even as something huge struck me. This new knowledge and my ability separated us. We were no longer connected in the same way. I felt a sense of loss, similar to leaving for college and realizing my place at home would never be the same.

We sat down to lunch, and I practiced sending a few messages to my grandparents. I quickly realized I must've been born with this ability because it came as naturally as breathing.

"Grandmother, I remember I had a different sort of connection with Mom that I've tried to identify throughout the years. Do you think we communicated telepathically?"

"I'm sure you did. We begin using telepathy with our children as soon as they can distinguish language. The message your mom gave you before she disappeared, can you remember if she used telepathy? It's unlikely you could have heard her words over the rushing water, especially if her tone was calm and determined."

"Maybe. Your explanation makes sense, but I can't remember for sure. What about Brad? After he lost his mom, how did he figure it out? It's not like he could practice with his dad. He must've felt abandoned and out of place."

"We have instructed and protected Brad from the beginning. There's no doubt he's struggled, but he has always been embraced by The Colony."

"Oh my gosh, Brad knows about his mom! He's always known his mom didn't drown. What a bizarre secret to carry around your whole childhood. I can imagine his frustration when kids would ask, 'What happened to your mom, Brad?' He probably thought he'd run out of patience at some point and blurt out, 'Well to tell you the truth, she was abducted by aliens.'"

My grandfather eyed me thoughtfully. "Eve, the loss of his mom is Brad's cross to bear. Who's to say which is better: to know your mom is missing and have some hope of her return, or to believe your mom is dead and have no hope of ever seeing her again? I don't have the answer, but you and Brad both adapted to the realities you possessed. We don't get to choose what life throws at us. All we can do is endure and hopefully, learn and grow stronger through our trials. No one escapes pain."

"I understand what you're saying, but you are wrong about one thing. Growing up, Brad and I were not as far apart as you might think because deep down, I hoped. No, it was much more than hope. I *believed* my mom would come back to me just like he did."

Jarak did not respond, contemplating what I'd shared. Throughout lunch, my grandparents answered question after question. The years of secrecy had ended, and they seemed as relieved as I was to get everything out into the open. Every so often, Dad threw in an explanation or suggestion, enough so that it became obvious he knew far more than he let on. We finished eating and carried our dishes to the kitchen.

"You're very quiet," Grandmother said as we loaded the dishwasher.

"I can't help but think I am no longer the same person who showed up on your doorstep this morning. I need some time to figure out what happens next. Who is this new Eve Hunter? What should I do, and what do I want? How do I even act? I feel like Jim Carrey's character in *The Truman Show*. Everything I thought was real was a fantasy or worse, a total lie."

"Well at least you picked a movie reference I'm familiar with, but it's not a valid comparison, Eve. Truman's life was a pure fabrication. Calling your whole life a lie invalidates all you've become and experienced up to this point. You know that's not true. Your journey has been completely real. Today, we've simply opened your eyes to new possibilities."

I gave her a skeptical look, and she tried a different tact. "Try to view all this as if you've discovered a hidden talent within yourself, like someone who picks up a paint brush and suddenly realizes she's a gifted artist. Your dad has done a wonderful job of teaching you strong moral values of honesty and integrity. He's taught you responsibility and perseverance. So you didn't grow up knowing you were the child of an extraterrestrial parent. That doesn't change who you are as a person or negate the qualities and skills you've acquired thus far."

"I guess you're right, but I still need to get a grip on all this and figure out how to act. This is way out of my comfort zone. I *like* being normal and flying under the radar. I'm not used to having special gifts. I'll probably jump out of my skin the first time someone mind messages me in class. Knowing those guys, they'll make me suffer through telepathy hazing," I grinned as a signal to my grandmother that everything was fine. Too bad I didn't feel so sure myself.

We finished in the kitchen and headed back to the living room to join Dad and Jarak. Despite that day's revelations, I couldn't stop thinking of my grandfather by his given name. If he'd seemed larger than life before, his newly-revealed position as the leader of a group of ultra-wise and gifted aliens only cemented his supremacy. Lillian's role as a grandmother was easier to accept, although her gifts were equally impressive. I had witnessed her healing abilities, and she'd revealed that she could also move objects with her mind, like Mr. Winter and Brad. What a trip to think I was related to these two. It was totally mind-boggling.

"Do you have any other questions for today?" Jarak asked. "As time goes on, you will have more. We want you to feel like you can ask anything. One of the reasons we pleaded with your dad to bring you back to Ridgway was to draw you closer to your people. The Colony needs the intelligence and skills of all its members."

"I do have one question about something disturbing I heard at school," I said. "One of the kids referred to me as the Chosen One. She said I'm the one you've been waiting for all these years. What does that mean?"

"I'm surprised someone would say something like that to you, knowing you weren't aware of your extraterrestrial lineage. I instructed the colonists to keep your identity a secret until you and I were able to talk."

"It was Erik's sister, Tara, taunting me. She didn't believe I had no idea of my heritage. From what I've seen so far, she's positively ghastly. I'm pretty sure she hates me."

Jarak erupted with laughter. "Ghastly? That's quite a description. I'd be surprised if she hates you. Maybe she resents the competition."

"Competition for what?" I asked.

"Maybe she's jealous because you're the new star attraction in town, the prodigal alien returned to the fold—and a beautiful alien too. Tara insists the spotlight shine only in her direction. Or, maybe she hates the attention you've drawn from Daniel because she's had a crush on him since she was five years old. It's also possible she believes the prophecy."

Tara had a crush on Daniel? That information explained a few things. I seemed to remember Sarah saying something about Tara's feelings for him, but I hadn't noticed anything.

I decided to ignore the obvious exaggeration in my grandfather's comment on my looks. All grandparents think their grandchildren are beautiful. His last comment intrigued me. "What prophecy is that?"

"Many years ago, one of the Khalaheem shared a vision he'd had about a descendant of the Wise Ones, a pale blonde girl with great gifts who would save our people. This was long before The Source took over our planet, and we were living under the most prosperous and peaceful conditions we'd ever experienced. No one paid much attention to the prophecy. What could we possibly need saving from? Times soon changed. After people began to recognize the evil intentions of The Source, followers of the Khalaheem remembered the prophecy and looked for its fulfillment. Our people referred to this young woman as the Chosen One."

"Okay…so what does some old prophecy have to do with me?" I asked warily. After everything I'd been told today, I naively assumed nothing Jarak said from here on out would surprise me. His next words dispelled that theory.

"Before members of the Khalaheem left Karillion and traveled to Earth, the Elders reminded us of the prophecy. Most of those left behind were past the years of child-bearing, with a couple of key exceptions. However, many of the colonists thought the Chosen One would be born on Earth. There are those who believe that young woman could be you."

"The two of you can't honestly believe I am this chosen person who will save your world. It could be anyone. Maybe Mom or Anika or Leka are busy saving Karillion as we speak. Or maybe Ruth? She's blonde, and unlike me, both of her parents are aliens. Doesn't that give her double alien powers? Besides, how am I supposed to save your planet if I'm not even there?" I shook my head at the weirdness of this conversation. "Do the colonists really buy into all this prophecy stuff?"

"The gift of prophecy is very real. Please don't mock something you cannot yet comprehend. Are you our Chosen One? Perhaps. I do not know for certain, but I feel impressed to caution you not to underestimate yourself. God has a plan for you which will be revealed in time. Prepare and be ready."

"You are speaking in riddles. What does that mean 'be ready'? And how am I supposed to prepare?" Confusion reared its ugly head once again.

"Seek to learn all you can and develop the talents you've been given. You can't be expected to know what's coming, but you can acquire the strength and faith to overcome whatever may be placed in your path."

My dad stood up and stretched his arms over his head, his customary method of indicating we should be leaving. He might not be an alien mind reader, but he could read me like a book. I'd had more than enough for one day. We said our goodbyes and promised to be at the colonist gathering the following afternoon.

Chapter 15

As we exited the tall, black metal gates, I realized my entire perspective had changed. Terra Dyne no longer seemed forbidding and secretive. The brilliant blue sky, the snow-capped mountains, the thick pine forest, even the winding road appeared enchanted. Ridgway and the Uncompahgre Valley promised unimaginable opportunities. When we'd raced down the hill to Town Park, I'd been too caught up in the urgency of the moment—and Daniel's proximity—to notice my surroundings. But now I was mesmerized.

I tried to imagine seeing the rugged landscape of Colorado and the beautiful vistas of planet Earth for the first time. Thoughts of the colonists' arrival led me to wonder how my mom felt when she spotted her new home from the space ship. Was she excited? Terrified? There was so much I wanted to know about her.

"Dad, all these years you knew mom might be alive and never said a word. How did you live with such a huge secret? Didn't you want to tell me?"

He stared through the windshield as if gazing back in time. "For what purpose? Even if she's alive, we don't know if she'll ever come back. I didn't want you living your life as I lived mine—always waiting, expecting her to return, never able to move on or be content with the life we'd created for ourselves. After Jarak told us about the ship, a spark of hope burned within me that she might come home. But it's been ten years, and

I refuse to allow myself to hope."

My dad's vulnerability made me uncomfortable. He'd never talked about his pain. "I'm sorry. I never realized how much you suffered."

"I didn't want you to know what I was feeling. It was my job to protect you."

"There's that word again. Everyone's always trying to protect me," I grumbled. "Tell me the stuff mom told you about her childhood. She must've shared memories of her planet and what it was like to travel through space. Did she miss her home? Was she happy here? I have so many questions."

"Your mom was a teenager when the colonists landed. She missed Karillion—especially its three distinctive moons—but she accepted our world as her home. Being here made her happy. Her parents managed to shield her from many of the horrors happening on her planet. They escaped before Kara could be taken from them by The Source. Your mother showed signs of great gifts early in her life, and your grandparents wanted to protect her from evil influences that might hinder her potential. Who would have thought that evil would travel millions of miles to find her?"

"I can't believe you knew all this alien stuff and kept it from me. More important, you knew Mom might be alive and let me believe she was dead. It's going to take me awhile to come to terms with all that."

"Like I said, I didn't want to give you false hope. What good would it have done for you to believe she might return? Besides, telling you would've made it seem like a real possibility."

"Didn't you think I had a right to know about my alien heritage, especially considering the colonists' bizarre prophecy and the chance that I'd develop some unearthly super power?"

"Kara never mentioned the prophecy. And it wasn't until August, when Jarak told me you had reached the age when you should be developing gifts that I even knew you'd possess extraordinary abilities. I knew the Karillions were—different—but you were half human. Your mom and I never talked about a genetic predisposition for special gifts."

"I want to be angry because you hid all this from me, but I kind of understand why. I don't think I would've handled the truth about my alien identity the same way you did."

"Probably not. You face your problems straight on. There have been times I've worried because you're fearless. It's one of your basic *human* gifts," he raised his right eyebrow meaningfully so I'd recognize his attempt at humor.

"Me? Fearless? Sorry, wrong person. Didn't you ever wonder if I might show telltale signs that I was the daughter of an alien? Weren't you afraid that I might contract a weird medical condition or some other extraterrestrial problem?"

"Of course not. I have always viewed you as my beloved daughter, never as someone alien. As for the disease issue, that's easy. You were never sick. Other than your mom, you're the healthiest person I know. Remember that time your foot swelled up and we thought you sprained your ankle? You were back at the track the next day as if nothing had happened."

I remembered the ankle incident. And there had been others. Memories of rapid healing from cuts and bruises came to mind. I had a sneaky suspicion something remarkable governed my wellbeing. The accident with Quaz on the day we left Denver was fresh in my mind. After the car hit him, I had wrapped my arms around him, willing him to be okay. He'd made a miraculous recovery. A nagging suspicion entered my mind. Was it possible…had I healed him?

"Dad, do you think I can heal animals and maybe people too?"

Dad nodded slowly. "It's possible. You're thinking about the day Quazimodo was hit, aren't you?"

My eyes filled with tears as I reached to pet Quaz in the back seat. "That's exactly what I was thinking about. I didn't say anything at the time, but I felt something weird. When I pressed my hands into his side, strength seemed to leave my body. It's hard to imagine I might be responsible for his miraculous recovery."

The implications overwhelmed me. Could I heal any living thing? What about people or animals dying of old age? Could I keep them alive? Should I? Surely, my grandfather would have something to say on the matter. One more question to add to the list.

As we travelled down the dark highway, I thought of something I'd forgotten to ask. "Dad, where did the colonists land their spaceship? It must've been difficult to find a place where they could land undetected."

"Jarak's ship landed out by Lone Cone Peak, an extinct volcano west of Telluride. The surrounding area is isolated and accessible in the winter only by snowmobile or snowcat. There's a State Wildlife Refuge out there, some ranch land, and a few cabins. The elevation of the landing site is around nine thousand feet, so this season's snowfall has probably already blocked the roads."

"But wouldn't a ship have been spotted coming into Earth's atmosphere or picked up on radar?"

"You'll love this part. The colonists possessed a cloaking device which made the ship invisible to radar and the naked eye, similar to Romulan technology in *Star Trek*."

"Cool! Where is the ship now?"

"Jarak and Roger scouted the area and found the perfect parcel for Terra Dyne in Ridgway. Once the hangars were completed, they moved the ship in the middle of the night by semi-truck. The ship is scarcely large enough to accommodate all the Karillions. Your mom and her companions travelled in cramped quarters."

"The ship is at Terra Dyne? So you've seen the alien spaceship?"

"I'd been working at the company for over a year before Kara and I were married, but I had no idea anything out of the ordinary existed. Your mom told me everything a couple months before the wedding. I think she wanted to give me an opportunity to back out."

His eyes glistened at the memory. "Shortly afterwards, Jarak granted me access to the restricted areas of Terra Dyne, and Kara took me to the ship. Despite her revelations about coming from a distant planet, I struggled to believe her. I guess I needed proof—something I could see and touch that was not of this Earth. The moment I laid eyes on an actual spacecraft, everything fell into place. The ship looks and feels like it came from another world. You will understand when you see it."

"Definitely. All of this is so hard to take in. My grandparents built a huge complex in the mountains where they're hiding a spaceship and a bunch of aliens. What a perfect setup. But how were the colonists able to buy anything, much less an expensive parcel of land? What did they do for money?"

"Precious metals. The planet Karillion and Earth have gold, silver, platinum and other precious metals in common. The Khalaheem anticipated the travelers would need something to barter with in order to get established. It's amazing how every detail of the expedition was planned and executed. "

"And now? How does Terra Dyne make money? Does it produce anything marketable?"

"The colonists share their planet's knowledge a small piece at a time in order to avoid disrupting earth's technological balance. Imagine the implications of this new fuel source. Releasing the colonists' findings would have huge geopolitical repercussions. If the United States gained total energy independence overnight, it could trigger the economic collapse of the Middle East and other oil producers like Venezuela and Canada."

The colonists' technology could disrupt the entire planet. Jarak's people—my people—had the potential to change the world. I wondered if humanity would even question the origin of these advances. We'd become accustomed to the fast pace of new technology. Scientists would marvel at the colonists' information, but they would never suspect an alien source.

I asked Dad to drive by the high school before heading to the cabin. Tonight was opening night of basketball season for the Ridgway Demons, and I was worried about Brad. I breathed a sigh of relief when I saw his black Jeep parked in front of the gym alongside a familiar fluorescent green one. My extraterrestrial buddies had made it to pre-game practice. Not even the threat of being exposed as aliens could interfere with basketball for those guys.

Later that night, Sarah and Emily picked me up so we could ride to the game together. Both girls were decked out in green and white Ridgway Demon t-shirts. Sarah had woven a glittering gold ribbon through her emerald green braid. Assorted noisemakers and pompoms laid on the backseat.

"Hey girls, thanks for the ride," I said.

"Cool cabin," Emily said. "Mr. Meyer has a great spot out here."

"Yeah, I've become attached to the cabin already, aside from the fact it's buried so deep in the forest I keep waiting for the three bears to show up looking for porridge."

"No way, they're all hibernating by now," Emily said. "But you can bet those three bears will show up in the spring, and they won't be looking for porridge. Watch out for Quazimodo."

"I plan on it. I don't want him tangling with any bears no matter how tough he thinks he is. What's with all the stuff in the back?" I asked.

"Sarah likes to make noise so she can draw attention to herself," Emily said with a smirk.

"Hey, what's wrong with a little school spirit? I want everyone to know I'm enthusiastic about my boys—especially one in particular." Sarah raised her eyebrows provocatively. "Besides, basketball games give me the perfect opportunity to scream my head off in a socially acceptable way."

"Since when did you ever care about being socially acceptable?" Emily asked.

"Quit your hating, Emily. You know you love me," Sarah said.

"Should I grab a suitcase so we can lug all this stuff into the gym, Sarah?" I teased.

"Hey! I thought you were on my side, Eve. What a couple of party poopers!"

We bantered back and forth on the way to the high school as if we'd been friends for years. Three average American girls headed to a high school basketball game. It felt so ordinary that I managed to escape the whole alien identity thing for a time. But when we pulled into the parking lot, I experienced the first of several reality checks I'd receive before the night was over.

Since it was nearly Thanksgiving, the sun disappeared behind the mountains before six o'clock. The dark, cloudless sky sparkled with thousands of stars, and a bright moon bathed the school in cold winter light. Thirty minutes before game time and forty or fifty cars filled the blacktop. I heard a car door slam as we got out but didn't see anyone nearby.

Stop it! Let go of me! Desperate words burst into my head. One of the colonists had transmitted a telepathic plea for help. Recognizing the obnoxious voice immediately, I gasped and spun around, scanning the cars for Tara.

"What is it? What are you looking for?" Emily asked.

"Uh, I don't know. I thought I heard someone yell," I said. Geesh, I needed a few ready excuses for when I screwed up the telepathy thing. I searched between the rows of cars with the girls following close behind.

Voices erupted near the edge of the parking lot. Tara and Mack were arguing. I ducked out of sight and motioned for the girls to do the same.

"Yikes! It's Mr. and Mrs. Nasty. There's a match made in Heaven," Sarah whispered.

"Shhh! Listen!" Emily scolded. We concealed ourselves behind a truck with big tires.

"Keep your creepy hands off me. What's your problem?" Tara demanded. Unlike the rest of us, it was obvious she had no fear of Mack.

"You, your gullible twin brother, Mr. Self-Appointed Authority, and now Miss Chosen One—all of you are my problem. You're like a bunch of sheep. No one can make a decision unless they ask for permission first. I'm the only one who can see Jarak for who he really is—a control freak and a manipulator. Well, I'm sick of bowing to him and the rest of the Elders."

I began to get nervous that one of them would say the "alien" word, and I'd be stuck with questions I couldn't answer. "Let's go!" I pleaded, desperate for Sarah and Emily to relocate.

Sarah shook her head vigorously. I silently begged Tara and Mack to watch their words. It should be a no brainer. They'd had years of practice being cautious and blending in. Tara's next words floored me, but not because she used the "A" word.

"Okay. I get it, but I'm on your side." Tara said, surprising all three of us. "I feel the same way about our situation, but there's nothing we can do about it. Jarak leads the colonists whether we like it or not. Where are we going to find another…?" Her last few words were unintelligible. Then Tara said, "This place isn't secure. Too many people might hear us. Let's meet somewhere after the game."

Emily nudged us, and we crept away, hiding behind cars until we felt safe.

"Now there's an unholy alliance if I've ever seen one," Sarah muttered. "Tara's not my favorite person, but if that girl gets messed up with Mack, she's going to end up in the Lost and Found—permanently."

Emily nodded in agreement. "What a weird conversation. We know her twin, Erik, and it's pretty easy to figure out who Mr. Self-Appointed Authority is—Daniel, of course—but who is Miss Chosen One? Who are the Elders? And what's Mack got against Jarak?"

I froze, unable to formulate any sort of answer. Suddenly, Emily gasped as she remembered my connection to the colonists.

"Oh my gosh. Sorry, Eve. I forgot that's your grandfather they're talking about. You don't think they'd harm him do you? I can't believe Tara listened to Mack and didn't shut him down. Do you have any idea what they were talking about?"

Here we go, I thought. At least when I'd been clueless myself, I hadn't had to lie to my friends. I chose my words carefully.

"I don't think they'd physically hurt Jarak. Besides, he can take care of himself. Mack resents my grandfather because the colonists look to him for guidance. He wants to be the boss, and in the world according to Mack, there can only be one boss. I wish he would leave Ridgway, and take Mrs. Nasty with him."

"Wouldn't that be sweet?" Sarah mused. "However, it's not going to happen, so forget about it. We're stuck with her and probably him too for the rest of the year. Come on! Let's go get a good seat, and we'll try to figure out what those two are up to."

I breathed a sigh of relief at the plausible explanation I'd come up with, then issued myself a stern reminder: You are an alien. As of this morning, your life will never again be anything remotely related to normal.

We entered the gym to the screeching of basketball shoes on hardwood. Daniel and Erik stood by the home team bench talking to the coach. My eyes sought Daniel almost against my will. I swear he knew the minute I walked in the door, and I blamed him for managing to harness my attention. I wondered if his ability to draw me to him was part of whatever gift he possessed. Magnetism, perhaps?

As we took our seats, Brad dribbled the ball down the court, making a quick pass to Augustine who threw it up for a long three-pointer. Emily squealed with delight.

"Show off!" Sarah yelled. Augustine flashed a plastered-on smile to Sarah, exchanging it for a genuine look of pleasure as he caught Emily's eye. The emotion passing between those two never failed to take my breath away. How incredible to have someone look at you the way Augustine looked at Emily. Lucky girl.

I waved at Brad and simultaneously formulated the thought, *Glad you made it despite your crazy day*, then pressed an imaginary button to send my first telepathic message to someone other than my grandparents.

His face transformed with a huge smile as he sent back, *Back at ya, my fellow alien.*

Yeah, about that, I've got a million questions. Have you heard anything about your dad?

Nope. But don't worry, I'm good.

Brad's response was exactly what I expected him to say, but I wasn't buying it for a minute. *Sure you are. You can talk to me about your dad, you know. Don't be a tough guy.*

Can't help myself. You know me—the man of steel. But I'll take any excuse to talk to you.

Be serious, Brad. I mean it. Don't shut me out.

No way that will ever happen, Eve.

My grandparents warning that telepathy was not a toy echoed in my head as I responded, *Enough mind chatter, Superman. You need to concentrate on this game. We have lots to talk about later. I'm hanging up now.*

I giggled at his brief reply, *Yes ma'am!*

Emily and I went to buy popcorn and sodas while Sarah saved our seats. Tara and Mack entered the school through different doors, obviously trying to conceal that they'd been together. Tara's eyes connected with mine, her look of loathing forcing me to take a step back. Did she really hate me because of some stupid prophecy about a Chosen One? There was no way she viewed me as competition for Daniel, as my grandfather had suggested. I didn't believe Tara or Mack would actually hurt me. Nevertheless, my self-preservation instinct kicked into high gear whenever I encountered either one of them.

When we returned to our seats, the boys were having pre-game shooting drills. Their interactions on the court played out like a well-choreographed ballet—not that I would ever share that comparison with them. The players wove in and out, spinning and twisting, making basket after basket. Could the magic be attributed to years of practice or did the aliens use telepathy to gain an advantage?

No sooner had I formulated the thought than I heard a message in my mind. *In case you're wondering, we never use telepathy on the court. We agreed it would give us an unfair advantage.*

It was Daniel's voice. I gasped in shock as he grinned at me from across the court. *Nice mind invasion. You scared me to death. What happened to minimal telepathy in public?* I scolded.

This is minimal. Sorry I made you jump. Just making sure all connections are working, he replied, his soft, husky voice ringing in my head.

Oh boy. Please, oh please, don't let him be an actual mind reader. Then I remembered Grandmother telling me those aliens who could read minds acquired their gift later in life. Leave it to Daniel to be an exception to that rule. Was it possible he shared the same mind-reading gift as my mom? I refused to consider the possibilities.

My thoughts bounced off in another direction as I focused on my mom. I marveled at the thought that I might actually see her again. Could my grandfather bring her back to earth?

A loud buzzer sounded, indicating the start of the game. Thoughts of Mom fled as the teams took the court, and the crowd began to roar. Daniel played point guard, which didn't surprise me since he liked to control everything. His style of play matched his personality—calm, calculating and confident. Augustine was also a guard, while Brad and Erik played forward. It was easy to tell they'd spent years playing together.

Natalie and Rachel took their places with the other cheerleaders facing the crowd, but fortunately they weren't directly in front of us. Otherwise, I would've had to change my seat. Several times I felt Natalie glaring at me, and once, I saw Rachel whisper something in her ear as she glanced in my direction. I'd been in town less than a month and had managed to make more than my fair share of enemies.

The game progressed quickly with Daniel, Brad, Erik, and Augustine dominating the court. Watching their tightly coordinated movements was riveting. At times, I felt oddly connected as if I played alongside them. Maybe they didn't use telepathy, but they'd developed the ability to antic-ipate one another's next move. By halftime, I was hooked and knew I'd be joining my girls every weekend as a basketball groupie.

Ridgway tied it up then defeated Ouray by three in the last twenty seconds, and the crowd stormed the court to congratulate the team. The cheerleaders gathered around the players, and Natalie ran over to Daniel and leaped into his arms. Sarah, Emily and I were pushed along in the tide of excited fans. Raucous cheers thundered throughout the gym, celebrating the victory.

As the euphoria subsided, Augustine broke away from the team and planted a big kiss on Emily's lips. Erik found Sarah and grabbed her hand, grinning at fans and teammates who clapped him on the back. Brad was busy giving high fives to everyone within reach, turning every so often to smile in my direction. Slowly our little group of aliens and friends congregated, including Tara and her entourage, all of whom displayed a similar air of superiority.

"Well done gentleman. It looked like you knew what you were doing out there," Tara said. This was a supreme compliment coming from Miss Perfect.

Augustine was not nearly so reserved. "Man, Brad that was awesome! I thought Jimmer was on the court when I saw you hit that last three-point shot from the outside!"

"Who's Jimmer?" I asked, the words out of my mouth before I could consider how dumb they might sound. Tara rolled her eyes in exasperation, her expression screaming, "Really?"

Sarah jumped on my question with typical gusto. "Who's Jimmer? You've seriously never heard of Jimmer Fredette? What planet are you from?"

She might as well have dropped a bomb in our midst. No one said anything for at least five seconds, which felt like forever. My face flamed with embarrassment mingled with horror. Of course, it was Daniel who recovered first and offered an explanation.

"Jimmer Fredette is a fantastic three-point shooter who played guard at BYU. He was named the 2011 college basketball Player of the Year. He became so popular during his senior year at BYU that his name became a verb, like when another team lost to BYU, people started saying, "You got jimmered!""

I could only nod, still trying to breathe. I didn't know how the other colonists handled comments which came too close for comfort, but I felt like I'd been caught skinny dipping. Brad noticed my discomfort and tried to make a joke of the whole thing.

"Yeah, Eve. What planet are you from?" Brad laughed and I elbowed him in the ribs—hard. The other colonists probably enjoyed these inside jokes, but I was new at this.

Are you okay? I heard a voice echo in my head. Without thinking I opened my mouth to tell Brad I was fine, when I suddenly realized the words had come from Daniel. Turning to find him, I sent a quick *Nice recovery!* My smiled faded as Natalie came up and snuggled under his arm, but Daniel's eyes remained fixated on me. The fierce scowl Natalie sent my direction indicated that his gaze hadn't escaped her attention. Whatever. Her suspicions were completely unfounded since I had no intention of getting involved with him.

Ugh! How can he stand her? I thought, accidentally transmitting the message to Daniel. Mortified, I cringed, dreading his reaction. He wouldn't need to be a mind reader if I tossed my innermost thoughts out with such abandon. My telepathy skills needed some fine tuning.

The corner of Daniel's mouth twitched, accompanied by an odd reply. *Guess you have to love the one you're with.* He shrugged and gave Natalie his full attention.

Sarah interrupted our inner dialogue. "I'm sorry, Eve. I didn't mean to set you up like that with the Jimmer thing. You know me, I never think before I open my mouth."

"No worries, Sarah. I guess you'd better fill me in on all the basketball facts I need to know. Meanwhile, I'll try not to look like a complete idiot."

"You know how small towns are. There's not a lot to do so we're all basketball geeks," Sarah explained.

"It's not rocket science," Brad said with a smirk. "Our girls love us, and we love basketball. Besides, we need something to keep us off the streets."

"Not so fast, Mr. Smooth. What makes you think we're in love with the likes of you guys? Maybe we just like to watch you run around in those sexy basketball shorts."

Hearing Sarah's comment, Erik pulled his long shorts out on both sides, strutting like a rooster. "You think these baggy things are sexy? Girl, you need to get out more."

Sarah whacked him playfully on the butt. "This is true. Maybe you could help me with that," she suggested with a wicked gleam in her eye.

Wow. Those two had come a long way in a very short time. Tara must be completely clueless if she couldn't tell her brother was smitten with Sarah.

A couple other guys came over to our group and told the cheerleaders about a party up on Dallas Creek Pass. Several people said they'd meet up there later, but when Natalie asked Daniel if he wanted to go, he declined.

"It's November. It will be freezing up on the Pass. Besides, you know I'd be kicked off the team if I'm caught at one of those parties," he said.

"I'm sure there will be a bonfire, plus you'll have me to keep you warm," she coaxed him. "Come on, have some fun for a change. Some of the other players are going. Take a risk."

"Sorry, Nat. I'm not interested in watching a bunch of kids get drunk and puke all over themselves. But hey, I don't mind if you go with your friends. The boys want to head over to The Well and get some food."

"That place is a total dive. Can't we go somewhere else?"

"I like hanging out at Sid's place. The food tastes good, and Sid takes good care of us. What's not to like?"

She grabbed his arm, her whiny voice getting louder. "It's so boring. Why can't we do something different? Sometimes you're a little dull, Danny Boy."

Daniel grimaced, and they moved away so I didn't hear his response. Emily, Sarah and I shared knowing glances, while the other kids pretended they hadn't heard the awkward exchange. All was not well with Ridgway High's model couple.

"Guess you all heard we're meeting up at The Well," Erik said. "I'm going to say hi to my mom and dad, then grab a quick shower. Better warn Sid I'm on my way, and I'm starving!"

As Erik galloped toward a group of parents gathered at the gym entrance, Sarah sighed dramatically. "Does it get any better than that? Not only is Erik a gorgeous hunk but he's nice to his parents too. Hold me back!"

"Easy there, girlfriend. Take a breath. We totally agree but let's not have any swooning in the gym," I said.

"Swooning? I don't know what swooning is, but I just might do it," Sarah giggled.

"Uh that would be, you know, fainting, passing out from sheer joy— that kind of thing," Emily offered.

"Then that man's definitely swooning material. What a prince," Sarah said. Emily and I rolled our eyes at each other. Sarah watched as Erik talked to his parents, pure adoration written all over her face. Forcing herself to avert her gaze, she turned to us. "Ready to go ladies?"

"In a minute," I said. "I want to make sure Brad's coming to The Well. He shouldn't be alone tonight. Be right back." On the way to the game, I'd shared with the girls what had happened with Brad and his dad that afternoon, being careful to emphasize Mr. Spencer's craziness and down-play the alien comments.

Brad was discussing the game with Augustine. His voice rose enthusiastically as he shared a play-by-play account of his efforts leading up to the final few seconds, but the moment I began walking in his direction, he shifted his focus to me. Again I wondered if the colonists somehow sensed the presence of another alien. Perhaps the odd vibrations had something to do with this constant awareness.

"Quick question," I whispered, after we said goodbye to Augustine. "You knew when I headed your direction. Can you guys feel it when another colonist is nearby? I notice some sort of weird humming when I'm around you and the others. Is this like an individualized aura thing? Is it possible that I emit some sort of vibrations too?"

Brad laughed. "I suppose I could flatter you and say that my radar is only locked on you, but the truth is you are right. We do have an awareness of each other. It has something to do with the strong energy fields we produce which enable telepathic communication. I suppose they are like auras. Everyone has their own distinct vibrations and some are stronger than others. I hardly notice the energy fields of people I've grown up with, but the vibes you radiate are powerful stuff. I can sense you a mile away."

"Come on, now you're messing with me."

"No, I'm serious, Eve. Your energy field could stop a train."

"Like you said, you've become accustomed to the familiar ones; my vibrations only stand out because they are unfamiliar. After a while, I'll blend in and you won't even notice me."

"Believe what you want to believe, but I don't think so," Brad said.

I smiled to show confidence in my theory, but I found this news disturbing. Was my energy field stronger than the other kids? I quickly dismissed the idea.

Brad surveyed the gym catching sight of the other players greeting their families and being congratulated. As he turned his back to them, I glimpsed the desolation in his face.

"You're going to get through this, Brad. I promise. Someday what happened today with your dad will seem relatively minor."

"And you know this how exactly?" he asked.

"Well you see…I've got these special gifts," I teased.

"Yeah, I've heard about those. But you'd better be careful, those gifts have unintended consequences."

I smiled at his attempt to make light of his disastrous afternoon. "You're coming to The Well, aren't you?" I asked.

Brad grimaced. "I don't know if I can face people asking questions. I'm sure what my dad did is all over town by now. Everyone's going to want an explanation. What do I tell them?"

"Give them the my-dad's-been-under-a-lot-of-stress-lately excuse. It's perfect, especially since your dad lost his job recently. That line always ends the discussion."

"Eve, you always have an answer for everything. Okay, I'll go, but only because you asked me. I'll meet you there, and Eve…" He reached out, touching my shoulder.

Brad stood inches from me, his deep blue eyes luminous. I looked up at him, studying his face, the two of us locked in place.

After a moment, he averted his eyes, embarrassed. "Thanks."

"Thanks for what?"

"For being here. For being you."

Now it was my turn to be flustered. I tried to hide my confused feelings with something flippant. "Hey, no problem. I've always got your back."

Brad headed toward the locker room, and I sent a desperate signal to the girls that it was time to go.

"Girl, that was some intense stuff," Sarah said, watching me curiously.

"You're telling me. Brad's upset and vulnerable right now, so he's making our relationship out to be more than it is."

"Oh really?" Emily said. "It didn't look that way to me. Serious sparks were flying between you two. All that heat could start a forest fire."

"Someone's been hanging around Sarah too long. I'm afraid she's wearing off on you."

"I'm just saying what it looked like from here. Don't shoot the messenger," she batted her eyes in mock innocence.

"Let's go. One of Sid's Oreo milkshakes is screaming my name."

Sarah and Emily exchanged knowing glances. Ignoring them, I collected the rest of Sarah's game time paraphernalia and headed for the parking lot.

Chapter 16

On the drive to The Well, we talked about Mack and Tara's conversation. I told the girls that 'the Elders' was a slang term Mack called the older colonists. His accusations stemmed from his own personal power trip, I explained, and he targeted anyone who stood in his way. Sarah accepted my power trip theory completely, but Emily had reservations. I could only hope seeing Augustine would divert her attention.

The Well was already packed when we arrived. It seemed like the whole town wanted to celebrate Ridgway's victory. A couple of tables were filled with cheerleaders, and though we tried to attract as little attention as possible as we passed by, Natalie spotted us and pounced like a hawk hunting field mice.

"Look who it is girls, the three musketeers—or should I say, the three stooges?"

The other cheerleaders snickered at Natalie's catty comment. I refused to dignify her remark with a response but Sarah couldn't contain herself.

"Who's the Stooge? Seems to me I heard someone's taking Algebra—for the second time—while the three of us smart gals chill out in Pre- Calculus with your darling boyfriend."

"Yeah, well if you had any hint of a social life you might have something else to do besides math homework," Natalie retorted.

"Don't worry your empty little head about me, Natalie. I'm sure Erik will think of something the two of us can do to keep ourselves busy this winter."

"Whatever. I have no idea what he sees in you, but it won't last. Trust me."

"Ha! That will never happen," Sarah said, then turning to Natalie's companions she added, "Ciao ladies. Try not to let her wear off on you."

We grabbed the last empty table and ordered milkshakes. Sid came over to say hi, so we shared Daniel's comments about his place and told him the boys were on their way.

Sid massaged his scraggly beard thoughtfully. "I really like those boys," he said. "But there's something different about them. All of them—Daniel, Erik, Brad and even Augustine—are wise beyond their years. I can't put my finger on it. They remind me of some of my Army buddies from Desert Storm—courageous but cautious. Go figure."

So there were people who recognized the colonists were different. Sid had been a soldier in Iraq and Afghanistan. Being an accurate judge of character had probably kept him alive. Like Sid, the boys could immerse themselves in a crowd with ease, even while remaining a step apart from others. Maybe he sensed kindred spirits in the colonists and Augustine, who had probably inherited a strong sense of self from his Mayan ancestors.

"Anyway, I gotta get back to the kitchen. Enjoy yourselves girls. Let me know if you need anything." We watched as Sid made his way through the crowd.

"What do you suppose that was all about?" Emily asked.

Sarah and I shrugged simultaneously—Sarah had no answers and I had too many. The noise level rose as the door opened and the team entered. People cheered and clapped the boys on the back. It was hard not to get caught up in the excitement. The players grinned widely, enjoying the momentary fame. Small towns were great at supporting local athletes.

"Is this seat taken?" Brad said, sneaking up beside me in all the confusion.

I jumped and scolded him silently. *What's with sneaking up on me, Mister? I think I've had enough trauma for one day.*

"Sorry. Didn't mean to scare you," he said out loud, not sounding the least bit sorry.

"Why is it guys think it's so funny to scare girls?" Sarah complained.

"Because when you're scared we can act all macho and pretend to save you," Erik said, appearing on cue and nuzzling up to Sarah. "Deep down our greatest desire is to be your fearless protectors. I think it must be a species survival thing—like a cave man protecting his woman."

"Oh brother, what a load of crap. I think I'm going to be sick," Sarah said.

"Now that would be attractive," Erik said.

"Watch it smart guy," she said.

Erik pretended his feelings were hurt and mimed zipping up his lips.

Augustine and Daniel walked over to our table. "Ladies, I see these two clowns are already bothering you," Augustine said.

"It's a heavy burden we must bear," Emily said. "Grab a chair and join us."

Augustine sat down as Daniel motioned toward the group of cheerleaders. "I have to check in with the boss lady first and see what her plans are. Could someone order me a cheeseburger and onion rings?"

Erik said he'd order the food, but instead of Daniel leaving to join Natalie and her friends, he remained at the table as if undecided about something. His hesitation persisted until everyone at the table stopped talking and stared, waiting for him to speak.

"Uh, you want a milkshake or a soda, Daniel?" Erik finally asked.

"Yeah, order me a Dr. Pepper." Simultaneously, a message shot into my head. *Make sure you find me later. We need to talk!*

That might be a little tough with your boss lady around, I shot back.

I'll take care of her. Just find me.

Yes, Daniel-san.

He ignored the sarcasm of my *Karate Kid* remark and walked away. When the food arrived, we ate like we were starving. Nail-biting basketball games worked up an appetite in the players and the fans. Daniel stopped over to grab his stuff when the food was delivered, thanked Erik for ordering, and glared as he sent me another mind message. *Don't forget. This is serious.* His demanding attitude had returned with a vengeance.

The six of us hung out discussing the game and entertaining each other with comments about the people we were watching. Considering the fact that we were teenagers, the jokes and observations were surprisingly tame and not mean-spirited. My new friends were the best, and despite knowing them less than a month, I trusted them completely. I felt momentarily overwhelmed with the good things and great people I had in my life. The move to Ridgway had not turned out the way I expected.

My warm fuzzy feelings of comfort and security faded as I remembered what my grandfather had revealed. The alien ship rocketing its way through space on a path to Earth was sure to change our lives.

After we grew tired of people-watching, Sarah, Erik, Emily, and Augustine took off for the pool table, so Brad and I finally had a chance to talk.

"So tell me, how was it yesterday? Did you freak out when Jarak told you about us?"

"A little. Jarak did his memory transfer thing and pictures of Karillion appeared in my mind. I recognized the images as a place I'd seen before. Maybe my mom shared them with me before she left. Whatever the reason, I knew immediately what he was telling me was true."

"I can't imagine what it would be like to find out you're an alien. I've always known, so it's not the same. Okay, so you knew it was true, but how did you *feel*?"

"It was what, twelve hours ago? I'm still in shock. It's thrilling and inspiring to find out my family came from outer space; but at the same time, I feel unhinged, like I don't know who I am. I thought I had a pretty good grip on who I was and what I wanted, but now? I have no idea what I might do next. Plus, it's a little creepy to think that other people might know you better than you know yourself."

"I hear you. Jarak and the Elders always make me feel that way. I can't tell you how many lectures I've had about my great potential because my mom's some gifted healer. When my powers showed up yesterday in the cafeteria, I wanted to tell the world. After all the years of feeling different from the other aliens, I finally had absolute proof I belonged."

"How could you have doubted you were a colonist?"

"My dad stopped believing what my mom told him several years ago. I guess without mom's presence, doubt crept in and eventually won him over. When I was twelve, he started feeding me lies about the colonists, telling me Jarak was part of a government conspiracy and had invented the whole alien thing as a cover up. I never believed what he said. How could I with Daniel and Erik around, not to mention my own telepathic ability? But I was afraid I'd never develop any gifts. Maybe my dad and I have more in common that I thought. "

"What do you mean?"

Brad looked at me with a profound sadness. "You know the hardest thing about this morning? My dad's absolute refusal to accept what was right in front of his eyes. I couldn't wait to show off my gift. I thought once he realized what I could do then he'd have to believe that everything Mom told him was true. I began slowly, moving a couple small objects without touching them, and then finished by levitating our couch. I even impressed myself," he said, attempting a tiny smile.

"You're such a show off," I teased.

Brad ignored my ribbing. "I kept waiting for him to apologize for doubting me, to be happy for me. But instead, he blew a gasket, denying the proof and accusing me of somehow tricking him. Why do some people refuse to believe?"

"Oh Brad, I don't know. Maybe he doesn't want to believe because if he does then everything your mom told him has to be real. Acceptance would force him to find a way to move forward and deal with the pain. Or maybe, he's just one of those people who've hardened their hearts to anything they can't explain. They don't want to believe anything miraculous. What are you going to do?"

"Jarak thinks they'll release him tomorrow afternoon so I'll probably see him at home after the gathering. By the way, you have to go to the gathering since you're practically the guest of honor. Jarak's been waiting years to flaunt his granddaughter. There's supposed to be some big announcement."

"I wouldn't miss it," I said, feeling a twinge of guilt for keeping my grandfather's secret. My alien friends were sure to be shocked about the ship. How would its arrival affect Brad and the others? Maybe one of our mothers would be on board.

As much as I wanted to discuss this possibility with Brad, I squashed the thought and steered the conversation into safer territory. Tomorrow would be soon enough to speculate about who or what the ship might bring. "It must have been totally weird for you when you first met me and found out I didn't know I was one of you guys. I thought you were certifiably nuts."

"Even though Jarak told us all knowledge of your heritage had been kept from you, I still couldn't believe you didn't know *anything*. Sorry I acted like such a lunatic, but I had to find out what you knew, and I also felt like I had to warn you. I meant what I said. Jarak *is* gathering the colonists. Something is coming."

Back on that subject again. What was I supposed to say? Thank goodness I only had to keep the secret for one more day. I struggled to reply, but in the end, I didn't have to say anything. Once again, Daniel saved me.

He appeared at our table, looking agitated. "Hey Brad, I need to talk to you. It's important."

"Can it wait buddy? Eve and I are in the middle of something."

"Not really, Brad. It won't take long I promise. You don't mind if I borrow him for a few minutes, do you Eve?"

I shook my head. When Daniel wanted something, resistance was useless.

Brad sighed. "Okay. Hold that thought, Eve. Back in a few."

Daniel and Brad walked to the corner of the room. I tried not to watch, but when I noticed Brad getting angry, I began to monitor the situation closely. The two boys were inches from each other, arguing. Brad took a step back, standing with his hands on his hips and his head tilted slightly to the side, his expression incredulous. Daniel seemed to be pleading with him. Brad shook his head in disgust and stalked over to our table. As he sat down, his energetic vibrations nearly shook the table from its mountings.

"Uh oh. I'm not a mind reader, but I know whatever he said wasn't good," I said.

Brad's trademark scowl returned. He clamped his lips together, trying to control his temper. Finally he blurted out, "I swear, if Daniel wasn't one of my best friends, I'd deck him. I've known him all my life, but the last couple years he's developed this thing—like he's got this mission in life to watch over and protect everyone. He's obsessed, and he's way out of line. And as if that's not bad enough, now he's got some crazy idea he can see the future."

My mouth opened and shut. I agreed with him about the annoying protection detail, but Brad's comment about Daniel seeing the future stopped me cold.

Trying not to add fuel to the fire, I asked carefully, "Do you think it's possible? I mean, the colonists believe my grandfather has visions and can predict what's going to happen. Maybe Daniel has the same ability."

"Yeah, but Jarak's in his sixties, and he's an Elder. Daniel just celebrated his sixteenth birthday a few months ago. If he is a Seer—and it's a big *if*—his gift for prophecy shouldn't be emerging already."

"What did he tell you?"

"Forget it. It's not worth repeating. He's hallucinating."

"Come on, Brad. What did he say?"

Our glasses slid as the table shook violently. "Nothing, okay. Just drop it. Daniel doesn't know what he's talking about."

I wasn't going to argue, but I felt certain he was wrong. Even though Brad had been around the colonists his entire life and knew more about them than I did, that didn't stop me from wondering what Daniel was truly capable of. Maybe I didn't buy into the whole prophecy thing, but I would at least consider what he said. Looking around nervously, I felt the energy pulsing from Brad and tried to hide the shaking table. Visions of the disastrous scene in the cafeteria added to my uneasiness. I didn't know if Brad had much control over his new powers.

With relief I heard him say, "I have to get out of here before I explode. Do you want to take a ride?"

"Um, sure. But I need to tell Sarah and Emily I'm taking off. Sarah's my ride." I was a bit nervous about riding in the car with him, but at the same time I wanted him out of there.

Brad nodded and slid out of the booth. "Okay, I'll meet you outside."

I walked over to the pool table and told the girls I was leaving with Brad. I'd almost made it to the entrance when Daniel pulled me aside.

"Eve, give me a minute," he said tersely.

I yanked my arm from his grasp. "What's the matter with you? Don't you think Brad has had enough trouble today? Can't you at least let him enjoy Ridgway's victory for a few hours before giving him something else to freak out about?"

"I don't have a choice," he said. "Tell Brad to stay away from his dad. Something bad is going to happen. Please! He'll listen to you."

"How do you know something's going to happen to him?"

"I don't know how or why, but I've seen it. The details aren't clear but it's not safe for Brad to be around his dad. Please talk to him."

"Have you said anything to my grandfather?"

Daniel looked guilty. "Well, no…I guess I should, but well…I thought I'd handle this myself. I've never had a vision as powerful as this one."

My world had gone completely nuts. I glared at him, enraged he had put me in the middle. "Daniel, you are infuriating! I don't know if I believe you or not, but okay, I'll talk to him. That way he can be mad at both of us. Satisfied?"

Instead of responding to my anger, Daniel shot me a look of pure misery. I almost felt sorry for him. But not quite.

The blast of cold November air calmed my frayed nerves as I walked the few yards to Brad's Jeep. He saw my approach and jumped out to open the passenger door. The mountain air seemed to have worked its magic on Brad too.

"At your service, milady," he bowed.

"Thank you, kind sir. I could get used to such service," I responded to his gallantry, breathing a sigh of relief that his personal thunderstorm had dissipated. Brad could do a Dr. Jekyll and Mr. Hyde faster than anyone I'd ever met. Thankfully, I wouldn't need the I-can't-drive-with-you-until-you-calm-down speech I had prepared.

Oblivious to my inner turmoil, he responded, "Anything for you, after all, you're practically royalty—or at least, a lot of people seem to think so."

"Don't tell me you buy into the prophecy too? Whatever you do, don't start bowing in my presence. I don't think I can take any more of that Chosen One stuff tonight."

"Your wish is my command," Brad said, starting the engine.

I giggled, "You do realize you just transformed from a knight in shining armor to a genie in a bottle. How about we skip the fairy tales for a few moments and focus on the here and now. Seriously, are you okay?"

"I guess. Nothing like a shot of freezing cold air to cool me off," he joked.

"I'm grateful you calmed down. That energy transference was a little scary. I thought Sid might have to replace that poor, defenseless table in there. So, where do you want to go?" I asked as he pulled out of the parking lot.

"Let's drive up to Terra Dyne."

"Can you get through the gates? Do you have a key card?"

"Of course. I'm still a colonist even though I don't actually live in The Colony." He paused for a moment, staring quietly through the wind-shield at the dark night. When he spoke again, the turn his thoughts had taken surprised me.

"The Colony. I'm surprised Jarak chose that name. Doesn't it make you think of something foreign? Not that people would actually suspect it's an *alien* colony." He shrugged. "I guess that's what they call hiding in plain sight. Were you suspicious when you first saw it?"

"I knew right away there was something mysterious and maybe even dangerous about the place, but I didn't think aliens—more like top-secret government stuff. My alternate theory was that my grandparents were involved in something underhanded."

Brad raised his eyebrows in disbelief at my cloak-and-dagger suspicions. "Not possible. Jarak and Lillian are as straight-laced as they come. However, since they're extraterrestrials, they do have to practice a little deception to keep their identity secret."

"Speaking of identity, I want to ask you something. I'm new at this whole idea of my ancestors being from another planet, so I'm not sure I understand who or what I am right now, but what about you? Do you view yourself primarily as an alien or an earthling? When you're surrounded by non-aliens do you feel separate, like you're different from everyone else?"

"Sometimes I do feel out of place, but not always. Like tonight when I'm on the court, I'm just another kid playing basketball. It's liberating, those times I can escape all the extraterrestrial lineage crap."

I smiled at his cynical description. "But being an alien is a good thing right? Doesn't it make you feel sort of privileged? I don't mean that you're—or we're—better than other people. But we do have these cool gifts that set us apart."

"You know what Jarak says about having gifts?" Seeing my blank look, Brad continued, "With great gifts comes great responsibility."

"I can see where those expectations might be a heavy load to carry—like Daniel and his determination to protect everybody. His obsession is more than irritating, it's suffocating."

"For him it's much more than a desire to protect everyone. Daniel buries himself under a mountain of self-imposed responsibility. I swear he thinks the future of The Colony rests on his shoulders. Let me share a little secret," he said, with a touch of bitterness in his voice. "You know the difference between Daniel and me?"

I grimaced. "Seriously? Uh, where should I start the list?"

Brad looked amused at my pained expression. "Here's the deal: Daniel wants to save the world, and the honest, brutal truth is I just want to save myself."

If Brad meant to set me straight about him with this admission, he'd failed. I simply didn't believe it. I'd seen enough of his behavior to know he wasn't as self-centered as he claimed to be. I wondered why he couldn't see that about himself.

We reached the huge Terra Dyne entrance gates, and Brad swiped his key card. Heavy clouds had moved in over the last few hours. Snow wasn't expected until the early morning hours, but the skies threatened to unleash the storm any minute. The road wound steeply up the dark mountainside, tall pines casting long shadows wherever a touch of moonlight peeked through the clouds. I kept waiting for security to emerge from the darkness and ask what we were doing wandering around up there at night.

"What are we doing here?" I asked.

"Can't you feel it?" Brad said, with a hint of anticipation.

"Feel what?"

"The power. The potential. Whenever I lose track of who I am, I drive through these gates and up to the top of the hill so I can see Terra Dyne. I look out over the valley and contemplate the millions of miles the colonists travelled through space so we could be here, in this particular place at this particular time. And somehow I know it all matters, that *I* matter."

Brad's words hung in the air, haunting and beautiful. He had spoken as if lost in a trance, his face raised to the heavens. Breaking the spell, he jerked his head toward me to gauge my reaction. "Does that sound stupid?"

"No, it sounds amazing. I had no idea you were so *deep*. Hearing those words coming from someone else might make me wonder, but considering what the colonists have overcome, they make perfect sense. You have extra-terrestrial blood in your veins. The sky's the limit."

"Don't forget, that goes for you too."

"It is crazy, isn't it? It's so fantastic and unbelievable. I keep waiting to wake up and discover this has been a dream. But is sounds like you feel the same. The enormity of our existence still hits you sometimes, even though you've had your entire life to get used to it."

"Come on. Let's walk," he said. Brad got out of the car, opened my door, and took my hand. Daniel's warning troubled me, but I didn't want

Brad to find out that I knew what Daniel had told him. Somehow I had to get Brad to tell me about their conversation and then convince him to heed the warning.

We followed a path behind the massive glass and metal complex to a marble bench perched on the side of a cliff. The bright moon had emerged from thick clouds to illuminate the magnificent valley below. Although transfixed by the incredible view, I couldn't help thinking about the alien spaceship concealed somewhere within the buildings behind us.

We sat in silence for a few minutes, each lost in our own thoughts but both of us transfixed by the majesty of the mountains. Despite my promise to Daniel, I hesitated to spoil the moment with his dire predictions.

Suddenly, a sharp wind hit the ridge and a wintry chill cut through my heavy jacket. I snuggled closer to Brad, instinctively seeking his warmth. Misinterpreting my actions, he put his arm around my shoulders and pulled me toward him. And then he kissed me.

I'd be lying if I said what happened was totally unexpected. Maybe it was the long, traumatic day or the stark contrast between the bitter cold and the welcoming shelter of Brad's arms. Or maybe I needed to feel acceptance for my newly discovered self. Whichever the reason, I surrendered eagerly to his advances, reveling in the experience of my first kiss.

He kissed me slowly, tentatively, as if expecting me to pull away at any moment. Ignoring my conflicting emotions, I gave in to the intoxicating sensations coursing through my body. As he felt me responding, his lips pressed harder onto mine and his muscular arms wrapped around me. The strong masculine scent of his cologne drew me closer. Our energy fields merged, and any misgivings I might have had evaporated. The biting wind and dark night had disappeared. Nothing existed but the two of us.

When we finally separated, I had to struggle to regain my breath and slow my racing heart. Brad leaned back, studying my face in the moonlight. "I've wanted to do that since I first saw you. The day of the fire, when you were standing in the parking lot with Sarah and Emily, my heart skipped a beat. The breeze blew your silky blonde hair off to the side, and your cute little nose wrinkled at the smoke billowing from the school. I was hooked."

My senses slowly returned to normal, and my rational self regained control. I wasn't ready for this abrupt shift in our relationship. As much as I enjoyed the feelings Brad had awakened in me, I had to put on the brakes.

I hadn't moved past viewing him as a good friend and wasn't sure I ever would. Despite the fact that he was a gorgeous hunk and a great kisser, something was missing. The last thing I wanted to do was hurt him. I would have to tread carefully.

"Brad, I—I've only known you a few weeks. I like you and I'm attracted to you—who wouldn't be—but so much has happened today. I'm confused. Let's take it slow."

"How can I take it slow, when I want to put my arms around you every time I see you?"

"Please, Brad. I need some time to work everything out—who I am, who you are—you know, all the trivial stuff," I said, trying to lighten the mood.

"I'll try to control myself. I'm not happy about it, but of course, I want to give you all the time you need to figure things out. But hey, as soon as you're ready, don't waste any time letting me know because I'm dying here. Agreed?"

I smiled and kissed him softly on the cheek. "Agreed."

He released a frustrated sigh. "Is holding your hand off limits too?" he asked sheepishly.

"Absolutely not," I answered. His warm hand enclosed mine perfectly. We stood up and circled around to the front of the immense building, trying to escape the biting wind on the ridge. It was as good a time as any to bring up a bad subject.

Taking a deep breath, I dove in. "Do you want to talk about what happened with Daniel?"

"No, I want to talk about us."

I raised my eyebrows questioningly. "I thought we covered that already."

"You said you wanted to take it slow and I agreed, but how about you let me help you work through your questions about me and the colonists. Are you afraid of me?"

"Of course I'm not afraid of you. That's not the problem. I've never had a boyfriend before, and I don't know if I'm ready for a relationship." Geesh, that sounded like a textbook cliché. I had no idea how I was going to extricate myself from this situation. I tried once again to steer the conversation back to Daniel.

"Brad, if we're setting the foundation for a relationship, we need to be honest and trust each other. Why can't you tell me why you're so mad at Daniel?"

"What does it matter?" Brad demanded.

"Because I know Daniel cares about you and whatever he told you, he did it because he's looking out for you. Don't shut him out."

He glared at me. "What do you know about it? Okay, since you're obviously fixated on earlier this evening, I'll tell you what happened. Daniel said to stay away from my dad because he's dangerous. When I asked him why, he claimed he'd had a vision of my dad attacking me. It's crap though. Daniel's not a Seer."

"Maybe he's not a Seer. Maybe he only *imagined* something awful. There's no harm in being careful around your dad is there?"

"Great, now you sound exactly like Daniel. You two should get together." Belatedly, Brad realized what he'd suggested and scowled. "Let's get back to the Jeep. The snow's going to come down any minute."

It didn't make me feel any better that I'd accurately predicted what would happen if I took Daniel's side in this argument. Brad was now mad at both of us. He drove me to the cabin without a word. Throughout the drive, my own anger steadily rose. Why was he so stubborn? I opened my mouth to say I'd had enough of his inflated ego, but he spoke first.

"Sorry I'm such a total brute. I shouldn't have taken my irritation out on you. This has been an insane and stressful day. I'm exhausted and wound up all at the same time. I'll never be able to sleep. Maybe I'll check out that party on Dallas Creek Pass."

"Do you think that's a good idea?" His face darkened, and I tried to reason with him. "Look, I'm not trying to be your mother, but I care about you. You've had your powers for a little more than twenty four hours. What if someone does something stupid and you react without thinking? What if the police or worse, your coach shows up as the party? Everyone in town must know about it. Besides, I didn't think you were into the party scene."

Brad exhaled. "I'm not into the party scene, but I need to blow off some steam. Don't worry. I'll just check it out and hang out with some of the guys." He shot me a disarming smile. "Please mom, can I go if I promise to behave?"

His little-boy pleading obliterated my cranky attitude. Maybe I shouldn't have given in so easily, but I didn't have enough energy left to be angry. "This has been one of the longest days of my life too. I'm going to collapse the minute I get through the door. Watch your back at the party, Brutus. See you tomorrow."

Brad pulled in front of the cabin, leaned over and kissed my forehead gently, sending a silent reply: *Thanks for coming with me tonight.*

Chapter 17

I awoke the next morning to a layer of fresh snow outside my bedroom window. When I leaned over the side of the bed to see if Quaz was awake, he lifted his head up with a look that said, "It's about time you woke up." I scratched his ears while telling him a run was out this morning so we'd have to settle for a walk. He stretched, arching his back with pleasure, and then eyed me expectantly. If only humans were as easy to please.

I dressed in the cream-colored turtleneck and faded jeans I'd deposited last night on a chair in the corner and traipsed into the living room, Quaz trailing close behind. My dad called good morning from the kitchen table as I pulled on my snow boots and heavy jacket.

"Good morning," I said. "No running today. The snow looks deep; hopefully, I won't need snowshoes."

"It's only a few inches. You definitely won't need snowshoes, but running might be difficult. Are you okay?" Dad asked.

"I'm good. Really. No worries."

"You're sure?" Dad persisted.

"Absolutely. Feel like making pancakes when I get back?" I asked.

"Sure, I'll whip up pancakes for breakfast."

"Okay. Back in a few," I said, slipping through the door behind Quaz.

Sun reflected off the dazzling white blanket of snow which covered everything in sight. The five or six inches of powder made it too deep to run the trails but shallow enough to walk easily. Quaz and I headed off into the woods, stopping every so often for him to investigate and mark his territory. My four-legged companion and I turned simultaneously at the crunching sound of approaching footsteps. My heart started beating faster as Daniel appeared around a bend on the trail, and I realized with chagrin that I'd been anticipating his arrival.

Before he could say a word, I cross-examined him. "How is it that you knew exactly when I'd be here?"

He tapped his finger to the side of his head, with a sardonic grin. "Ha— you thought I was only telepathic. Maybe I'm clairvoyant too."

Better a clairvoyant than a mind reader, I thought. Besides, if his latest fears about Brad proved to be accurate, Daniel probably could see the future. "Actually, a better explanation would be that you have a good memory, and I am a creature of habit. Since I can't imagine you wander aimlessly through the forest in twenty-degree weather, you must be looking for me." When he nodded, I continued, "Because you wanted to find out if I talked to Brad."

At least he had the decency to look a tiny bit guilty when he nodded the second time. A traitorous part of me wanted him to deny it and say that he'd sought me out because he wanted my company. Like that would happen. My inner battle raged as he continued to attract and repel me. Although I couldn't unravel my own feelings, one thing I could be sure of—Daniel's protection instinct took precedence over everything else for him.

"Mission accomplished. Of course Brad got mad at me like I said he would. So that makes two of us who are clairvoyant," I said, punctuating my remark with a nasty look.

"He'll get over it. What's most important is keeping him safe."

"You really think Brad and his dad are headed for disaster don't you?" I asked.

"Without a doubt. If only I could stop it, but what can I do other than follow Brad everywhere he goes? I never thought seeing the future would be such a burden."

"Okay," I said, trying to be open-minded. "Let's say for argument's sake I believe you, and you can see the future. Why do you think you saw the vision instead of Jarak? I thought he was the only one who saw visions and made predictions for the colonists."

"I don't know for sure that I'm a Seer, although lately I've been barraged with disturbing dreams and visions. More likely, I'm a Reader because sometimes it's easy for me to tell what people are thinking." I cringed at the thought that my suspicions might be true.

Daniel continued, oblivious to my panic. "But Jarak is not the only Seer. Karillion has had many gifted Seers throughout the centuries. Although your grandfather is primarily the one who receives revelations for the colonists, visions are not exclusive to him. Others get glimpses of the future for themselves and their families. Maybe I had this vision because I'm the one closest to Brad. He and I are tight, like brothers since we were little kids. However, I am going to talk to Jarak this morning and enlist his help."

"What made you decide to go to my grandfather?"

"Two reasons. First, I no longer have any doubts about what I saw, and second, I'm in way over my head. You're right. This knowledge is too big for me. I wanted to tell you I'd listened to your advice because…well…"

"Spit it out, Daniel."

He eyed me warily. "You don't make things easy do you?" he said.

"Daniel, I have no idea what you're talking about."

"Well, you should. Why is it so hard for you to figure it out?" He glared at me with exasperation. "The truth is I want you to think good things about me. I want you to like me. I'm not such a bad guy," he blurted out.

Awkward. My first instinct was to reassure him that I did like him, but I couldn't. What if I had misinterpreted his words? He couldn't possibly mean *like* as in romantically, after all he had a girlfriend—one he'd been hanging all over last night. He probably felt obligated to secure my friendship and ensure we were allies. After all, aliens were in limited supply on planet Earth. We needed to stick together. Unwilling to risk rejection, I settled for irritability.

"I do like you, Daniel," I said, as if talking to a five-year-old. But then I couldn't resist adding, "Despite the fact that you're incredibly arrogant, bossy, and a bit of a know-it-all." There. I said exactly what I thought, but my words didn't give me half as much pleasure as I expected them to.

Daniel looked dejected. "Yeah, you've already made those things pretty clear. Guilty as charged," he said. "Satisfied?"

Not wanting him to see how guilty I felt, I ignored his question. "Can we change the subject? I've got tons of questions."

"Okay, if that's what you want," he said, but the look on his face indicated he wasn't finished with the subject. "I'll answer your questions. I've got a little bit of time before I have to leave for church."

"I've been thinking about that. It's awesome that you go to church with your family, but I wonder what your fellow parishioners would say if they knew you were aliens."

"After the initial shock wore off, I think they'd be cool with it."

"Really? They'd accept the fact that God created aliens?"

"Why not? He created the heavens and the earth, and since other planets and their inhabitants are part of the heavens, it's actually quite logical."

"Why would God create other worlds?"

Daniel shrugged. "Creating worlds and giving life is what God wants to do. His children bring him joy—well, at least some of them do some of the time. Why do you think humans want to give life and bring children into the world?"

"I don't know. Because it's an instinctive desire to continue the human race so we don't become extinct?"

"And that's it? I think the reason is much bigger than that. I believe mortals have a divinely-instilled desire to create and shape a life and to find joy and purpose in their offspring. Whether we realize it or not, we're mimicking God."

"My grandparents believe there are inhabited planets throughout the universe, even though Karillions have never encountered other aliens," I said.

"I believe there are others out there too. Just because we haven't discovered them yet, doesn't mean they don't exist. God sends his children throughout the universe 'scattering stars like dust.'"

"And we're the stars?"

"Apparently."

"So in addition to your other talents, you moonlight as a poet."

Daniel laughed in a way only he could, sounding both humble and arrogant. "Hardly. That line comes from a poem written by a thirteenth century Persian poet named Rumi. My mom's obsessed."

"Did this Rumi believe in aliens?"

"All I know is he spent a lot of time searching the heavens for answers. Rumi believed his soul originated elsewhere and intended to return to that place. He also said, "If light is in your heart you will find your way home.""

Daniel's voice took on a certain reverence as he quoted the ancient poet. I listened spellbound. "Is that your goal, to find your way home?"

"Absolutely."

"So you believe the same as Jarak, that God directs our paths to accomplish his purposes?"

"Of course, don't you?"

"I've never really thought God checked up on my day-to-day life. I guess I figured he was kind of busy taking care of other things."

"What could possibly be more important than his children? Think about it. If you were a parent, what would be most important to you?" Daniel asked.

"I suppose you're right, but with trillions of children to worry about, I'd imagine quite a few would fall through the cracks."

"God has an extensive tracking system."

"Thanks for sharing, Daniel. I'm not sure what I believe. But one more thing—about this vision of yours—do you believe God sent it to you?"

"God sees the future. Sometimes he gives mortals a glimpse."

"Why would he do that? Why not just stop something bad from happening to Brad?"

"Because ultimately, mortals must be free to choose and experience growth from their choices, otherwise they're merely robots. Revelations serve to forewarn us, but we still must act according to our own judgment. God guides us to make correct choices, but he will not force us to do so. And of course, people make bad choices all the time. Mr. Spencer gets to choose too, even if it doesn't turn out so great for Brad."

"Do you think Brad will listen to your advice?"

"Probably not. He's as stubborn as the rest of us."

"Then someone should shadow him and make sure he's safe. Maybe I should do it."

"Good luck with that. Brad would see right through your plan, especially now he knows both of us are watching him."

I sighed. "Hopefully Jarak can talk some sense into him. Meanwhile, I'll try to stay close."

"Let's talk about you. How are you dealing with everything Jarak told you?"

"Here's what I learned: My mother came to earth with a bunch of extraterrestrials to warn earthlings to protect their freedoms at all cost. Mom was—I mean *is*, because I found out she might be alive—such an exceptionally gifted mind reader, that a rogue alien tracked her millions of miles through space and kidnapped her along with two other women. Hmmm…what else? Oh yeah, even though I thought I was a mere mortal, the reality is I am also an alien, and I've inherited extraterrestrial abilities. These special gifts—as my grandmother calls them—should show up any day now. And on top of that, I can communicate with my fellow aliens without uttering a single, spoken word. Am I leaving anything out?"

Daniel smiled at my wacky narrative. "I suppose that about sums it up, although you make it sound like you're living a Hollywood blockbuster." His next words made me wonder once again if he could read my mind. "Are you sure your gifts haven't showed up already?"

"No, I'm not sure," I admitted. "There was this awful incident with Quaz the day we left Denver. A car slammed into him, and we thought he was dead. I refused to accept his injuries and placed my hands on him, willing him to recover. Not long afterwards he jumped in the Tahoe to start the trip to Ridgway. It was wonderful but kind of disturbing."

"Sounds like you're a Healer. Hopefully, you won't have too many opportunities to find out how much your skills have developed. Did Lillian tell you she is a Healer?"

"No, but I suspected as much after watching her calm people down, especially Mr. Spencer at the park."

"She has other gifts as well, but I'm sure she'll reveal those when she's ready."

"What about your gifts, Daniel?"

"I can't move things with my mind like my dad, Erik, and Brad, so I'm not a Mover. Sometimes I get impressions and seem to know things, like a Seer. It's not an exact science—some of this stuff I seem to know—I'm always second guessing myself. I might turn out to be a Reader in a few years. However, I'm leaning toward the Seer theory. My mom and maternal grandfather are both Seers."

"Maybe heredity plays a part in our powers. Did your grandfather come to Earth?"

"No, he stayed on Karillion with the other Khalaheem." Daniel turned away as his voice wavered. "We couldn't bring everyone. Some people needed to remain on Karillion to continue the resistance against The Source. Many of our group left family members behind." He turned back toward me, catching the look of pity on my face. "I guess it shouldn't be such a big deal for me. I've never met him. Maybe someday I will."

"There's nothing wrong with missing someone you've never met. In fact, I'd say it's a very *human* emotion." I couldn't resist teasing him.

"Miss Hunter, are you insinuating aliens aren't human? I believe one of your planet Earth proverbs states: People who live in glass houses shouldn't throw stones. I suppose you're familiar with that one, my fellow *alien*?"

"Touché. Once again, you win the verbal sparring match."

"You know how much I like to win."

"Yeah, I've figured that part out."

"My parents think this trait might be my downfall, so I'm trying to let other people win occasionally—but not too often." He grinned wickedly.

I ignored his attempt to bait me. "You're hopeless. Another question, do your parents really believe all the stuff Jarak says? Do they accept his visions without question?" I was dying to tell him what my grandfather had revealed and ask him if he believed a ship was really coming. I wanted to know the extent of the colonists' confidence in Jarak. Would everyone accept his announcement without question or would there be doubters?

"I think they believe he's inspired, but we don't follow him blindly. We listen to what Jarak says and then search our own hearts and minds for answers. Our trust in him has built up over time, and he has yet to lead us down a wrong path."

"What if he did though? I mean, what if he told everyone something was going to happen, like something he had a vision of, and it didn't come to pass?"

"I'm not sure what you're getting at, but if it happened as you suggest, of course we'd lose faith in his abilities. But as I said before, it hasn't happened yet." I digested this piece of information, marveling at my grandfather's perfect track record.

"I know you have to go, but something else has been bothering me.

Jarak said he had a vision of planet Earth which he shared with his followers. I assume he meant *only* his followers. So how was Zorak able to track the colonists to Earth and kidnap my mom and the others? It's not like the ship left a trail through space."

Daniel was oddly quiet. "What else did Jarak tell you about Zorak?" he finally asked.

"He said Zorak had joined forces with the dark side and must've been furious that members of the Khalaheem had escaped Karillion."

"Anything else?"

"Not that I can remember. Why?"

"Jarak shared his vision with the Khalaheem and his family."

"Zorak is a member of the Khalaheem?"

"He is Khalaheem, but he is also Jarak's son."

I gasped. "His son? But of course, it makes sense. Zorak knew his father planned to travel to Earth someday. And my mom was…Zorak's sister. Maybe that's why he traveled so far to kidnap her, but how did he know she was a Reader? She was only a teenager when she left Karillon, and her gifts hadn't developed yet."

"Zorak is the only one who can answer that question, but I can give you a partial answer." Daniel hesitated, as if evaluating how I would handle the information he was about to divulge. "Eve, your ancestors are some of the most powerful beings our planet has ever produced. Because Zorak possesses great abilities himself, he had to assume his sister had tremendous potential. Plus, he had additional evidence to support this assumption."

I raised my eyebrows encouraging him to continue. "You have two uncles. Jarak's other son, Ryker, remained on Karillion as the leader of the resistance. When the colonists fled, Ryker and the resistance were gaining ground. He and Zorak were sworn enemies."

"So while the two sons battled each other for control of Karillion, Jarak decided to ditch the planet and escape into outer space with his wife, daughter, and a bunch of Elders."

"Don't forget, Jarak's inspired mission drove him to act. He wanted to save his family, but he also felt compelled to find Earth and warn its inhabitants."

"Sorry, but that's crazy. How did he know he wasn't—I don't know— hallucinating or something? Or maybe he wanted to leave so bad he imagined this mission of his?"

"Eve, think about it. Jarak has a vision of Earth years before he discovers it's his destiny to travel to this previously unknown planet. Somehow, he procures a ship, grabs his family, and convinces some pretty intelligent people to come along for the ride. On top of that, the travelers manage to escape a hostile environment without detection, find an enormously helpful wormhole which drops them amazingly close to Earth, and arrive in a welcoming mountain town, where they set up a wondrously prosperous colony. There were too many coincidences, too many lucky breaks. Doesn't it sound like some powerful forces in the universe are at work?"

I couldn't help but smile at his passionate speech. "Well, since you put it that way, I have to agree with you. It does seem as if otherworldly influences are at work. So where does that leave us? What are the colonists supposed to do?"

"Jarak must have told you the colonists' mission is to save the people of Earth from technological oppression. We must find a way to open their eyes and help them recognize conspiring men who seek to lull them into a false sense of security and enslave them."

"Enslave? That's a strong word. Do you really think we're headed that way?"

"Humans have always sought power. If it happened on Karillon, it can happen here. We're here to save the people of Earth. And in case you haven't figured it out, that's why you're here too."

"What can I do? I'm a sixteen-year-old girl with no special skills," I protested. "How am I supposed to save the world?"

"At the risk of sounding like a Jarak-clone, I can only repeat his mantra: all you need to know will be revealed."

"I wish I had your confidence, but I'm progressing rapidly. Only yesterday, I thought my grandparents were about to be hauled off by one of those alphabet soup government agencies and charged with espionage. What a difference a day makes, or even a few hours. Everything can change in an instant."

"Remember those words," Daniel said, as he took off down the trail.

Oh don't you worry, Daniel. I will remember those words, I thought. And after the gathering this afternoon, so will you.

When Quaz and I returned to the cabin, dad poured circles of pancake batter on the griddle and started breakfast. "What, no bacon?" I asked. "I love your pancakes, but we're missing an essential breakfast ingredient. I can't imagine life without bacon."

"It seems our grocery shopper forgot to buy bacon at the store. Don't blame the chef. I can only make use of the ingredients at hand."

"I guess we'd better trade our grocery shopper in for a new one."

"I suppose we'll have to be satisfied with our existing staff, flawed as it may be."

I rolled my eyes at my dad's droll expression. At least his attitude had improved since yesterday.

After breakfast, I hurried upstairs to check my phone. A text from Brad triggered instant anxiety. *Need to talk ASAP. Overheard Tara and Mack at the party. Watch your back.*

When I dialed his cell, he picked up immediately.

"Eve, I was beginning to worry. What took you so long?"

I was dumbfounded. "Chill out Brad. It's 8:30 on a Sunday morning. I'm surprised you're even up. I forgot to check my phone before I took Quaz out, and then I had pancakes with my dad. Did something happen at the party?"

"You were right, the party consisted of a bunch of kids drinking too much and getting sick. Not my scene at all. Good thing I went though, because I overheard Mack tell Tara they needed to find a way to get rid of you."

"Get rid of me? What's that supposed to mean?"

"I didn't hear the entire conversation. I followed them into the woods, but when they reached the meadow, I had to remain hidden in the trees. Tara said there was no way you'd ever leave voluntarily now that Jarak has his hooks in you, but Mack insisted they'd come up with a plan if they worked together."

"Why does he feel so threatened by me?"

"All I know is you are his new favorite target, and Tara agreed to help him. The last thing we need is those two teaming up. Maybe they think if they got rid of you, your grandparents might leave too. I can't figure out why they're insistent on new leadership. We need to tell Jarak."

"My grandparents would never leave Terra Dyne. What am I supposed to do? I can't share this with my dad because he'd freak out. And if we say something to Jarak, he'll tell my dad, and Daniel will intensify the protection detail. No thanks. I think I'll take my chances."

"Eve, this is not a joke."

It was my turn to scowl. "I didn't say it was. Let me think about this for a few hours. See you at the gathering this afternoon." I hung up the phone before I could say something I'd regret. I wasn't afraid of Mack and Tara's threats. Besides, I could take care of myself.

Chapter 18

Dad and I entered Terra Dyne a few minutes before four o'clock. He led me down several corridors to a central indoor park-like area with floor-to-ceiling windows, towering plants, and a huge retractable dome. Forty or fifty people were scattered around the room in small groups.

"This place rocks!" I exclaimed. "You think you could put in a good word so they'd hire me at Terra Dyne?"

My dad smiled at my attempt to be flippant. "I might be able to arrange something. We'll have to see if you graduate from college first."

So this is what an alien gathering looks like, I thought, attempting to view the room's inhabitants through non-alien eyes. Would others see us as different? Many colonists possessed the tell-tale blue-green eyes, but otherwise this could be an ordinary gathering of people anywhere on Earth. I felt comfortable in their midst, and the ever-present vibrations seemed almost soothing and no more noticeable than chirping crickets on a summer night.

A stage dominated one end of the room, with a long conference table arranged on top. Ordinary metal folding chairs with blue cushions were placed on the blue tile floor, facing the stage. My grandparents stood off to one side talking with Roger and Devin Winter. I zeroed in on Daniel and his beautiful green eyes met mine as I checked out his family. I quickly shifted my gaze, pretending to search for someone else. Erik and Tara sat beside two younger kids and a couple I'd never met. According to Sarah, Erik's parents were Loren and Raina Nielsen, and the kids were Sam and Maddie.

I scanned the room, searching for Brad. He was not there. A twinge of fear seized me. *Please let him be safe* I pleaded with whomever might be listening. I recognized a few others. Ruth Andersen and her dad, Jakob, sat without speaking in one of the back rows. Mack and his parents hovered by one of the tall plants with two blonde girls—freshman twins, Lara and Lisa—more info I'd gained from Sarah. The four Swensens appeared at the entrance and gave me a friendly wave. My face flamed with embarrassment as I recalled my guilty exit when we'd last met on Dallas Creek Pass.

The balance of the group consisted of a few couples my grandparents' age and some young parents with school-age children. From this select group would emerge the beginnings of an alien race on Earth. All future alien inhabitants would descend from them—like a group of otherworldly Adams and Eves. The coincidence of my own given name was not lost on me. Had my mother had these same thoughts when I was born?

Jarak climbed the steps to the stage followed by the Winters and others I didn't know. Standing behind the podium and facing his people, Grandfather looked commanding and regal, like a captain standing on the bow of his ship, directing orders to a deferential crew who obeyed him without question.

Before he could speak, Brad raced into the room, spotted us, and took a seat beside me with a sheepish grin. My dad nodded to greet Brad, not quite able to conceal his frown of disapproval at Brad's late entrance.

"Now that we're all gathered together," Jarak looked pointedly at Brad. "I'd like to welcome everyone and express my gratitude for who you are and what we've accomplished in the past twenty-five years on Earth. We are fortunate to have an exceptional group of colonists. I am going to begin with a couple of announcements. Afterwards, the other members of the Khalaheem and I will try to answer your questions."

He paused, looking straight at me as he continued. "First, I'd like to introduce my granddaughter, Eve, and her father, Tom, whom most of you know. They have rejoined our colony after ten years in Denver. Please welcome them back." He motioned toward us, and I forced a self-conscious smile when the colonists focused on me. My dad grimaced and squirmed in discomfort. He hated the spotlight more than I did.

Nearly everyone clapped and smiled in our direction. Everyone except Mack and Tara, who shot venomous looks at me. Brad noticed and grabbed my hand, as a sign of protection or reassurance. I wasn't sure which.

If looks could kill, I mind messaged him.

Let's hope that's not what they're thinking, he replied.

Jarak waited until all eyes returned to him, then continued, "Our quiet little colony is about to undergo some changes. We've compiled a plan to implement several elements of our mission. The technology of this planet has moved rapidly in the years since we arrived. The inhabitants of Earth have responded to these technological advances much as our people did, with great acceptance and practically no suspicion. Dangerous conditions surround them. A large majority of Earth's inhabitants are already tracked daily through their computers, phones, and even their vehicles. It is time for us to act. This will necessitate some exposure."

There were gasps and murmurings throughout the crowd. When my grandparents and I talked yesterday, I wondered what progress they'd made toward accomplishing their mission since they'd taken precautions to remain under the radar. From the protests around me, I sensed many of the colonists weren't ready to reveal their extraterrestrial identities. Would I be willing to risk exposure? Would I have to?

"Terra Dyne has established a stellar reputation in the scientific and technological communities," Jarak continued. "Some of you have also cultivated valuable political connections. Sufficient time has passed. We believe we are ready to send our people throughout the globe to assist in various facilities and share our knowledge to a much larger degree than we have in the past. Exposure will be limited and carefully monitored."

"Spreading our message through blogs and websites will commence. The younger members of our group can warn of the pitfalls of technological monitoring through school and social networks. The people of Earth need to be awakened to the potential for bondage. We've traveled across the galaxy to perform a specific mission. We must accomplish our goals."

The colonists' plan to reveal themselves was disturbing. Only yesterday, my grandparents warned about the dangers of Mr. Spencer's rant about aliens. Any exposure could be catastrophic. A steady roar filled the room. Although the colonists knew the plan from the beginning, there was noticeable hesitation and understandable fear.

A woman in the front spoke up. "Sharing our knowledge is good, but crusading against technology? We'll be expected to supply evidence and be dismissed as alarmists. Why should the people of Earth listen to the voice of warning any more than the Karillions did?"

Someone else called out, "Will we have to disband The Colony and go into hiding? How can it be safe to remain as a group once we reveal ourselves?"

Jarak chose to answer the second question first. "We plan to continue our current living arrangement for now, keeping a close eye on safety issues." He paused before addressing the first question, measuring his words carefully. "Your choice of the word *crusade* is insightful. We should not forget this is indeed a crusade. Our primary mission on planet Earth is to warn the inhabitants of their propensity for captivity. Whatever the danger this task brings upon us, we have no choice but to proceed."

Jarak's penetrating eyes swept the room, gauging reactions. Mack's parents' expressions matched their son's—unconvinced and angry. Several colonists tossed out more questions. He answered a few of them, and then held up his hand.

"Please hold the rest of your questions until I'm finished. The timetable we've developed has us moving forward by the first of the year. However, there's been a slight change of plans—a complication has arisen." Jarak took a deep breath and for the first time—maybe ever—I saw him hesitate as if uncertain whether or not to continue. His reluctance made me nervous. Was he bothered by the reaction of the colonists, or did he have doubts about his vision?

He exhaled, apparently deciding to roll the dice and let them land where they may. "My fellow colonists...a ship is coming. It should arrive in early December."

The room erupted in chaos. "A ship is headed this way? Is it Zorak?" I heard someone shout. "What should we do? How are we going to defend ourselves?" other colonists demanded.

"Quiet everyone, please. I can only tell you with certainty that this is not a hostile ship, but other than that piece of information, I'm afraid there's not much else we know. All we can do is wait and see who and what the Karillion ship is carrying."

Brad's grip on my hand had tightened when Jarak announced the ship. He was cutting off my circulation. Gently, I loosened his grip. "My mom," he murmured. "My mom could be on that ship."

"Maybe, but don't get your hopes up. Anybody could be on that ship. We don't know anything about it."

He stared at me in disbelief. "You knew," he whispered fiercely. "You knew, and you didn't tell me. I trusted you. Unbelievable."

His resentment surprised me. "Jarak told me yesterday. He asked me not to say anything. One day, what's the big deal?"

"Man, I was so wrong about you. I thought you were this sweet, naïve young girl, but you're just as deceptive and manipulative as everyone else."

"Brad, what was I supposed to do? Jarak told me in confidence."

"Yeah, but this is me we're talking about."

It was all I could do not to lash out at him. "In case you've forgotten, you're the one who kept secrets from me—the big alien secret actually. You're blowing this way out of proportion."

Brad folded his arms and sat back in his seat. The formidable scowl had returned. My dad raised his eyebrow in question, but I shook my head. This was not something I wanted to discuss with him. Voices were raised throughout the room; so thankfully, our little argument didn't get much attention from anyone else.

My grandfather managed to regain the crowd's attention and outlined the plan to infiltrate various organizations that controlled the direction of emerging technology. Despite the dissenters, many of the original colonists nodded and appeared to be on board with the proposal. But among the young people, several voiced protests about the risk involved.

Something my grandfather had said about faith echoed in my head. It wasn't hard to see the difference between the older and the younger generation. The faith of most of the colonists who travelled from Karillion was rock solid. They'd experienced the captivity of their planet. They'd courageously rebelled against dictators and journeyed thousands of light years through space to an unknown world. Their confidence was strong, and they expected success. Their children—and that included me—hadn't been tested. We cared more about how exposure would change our lives than we did about some disastrous hypothetical future that we couldn't imagine.

Brad shifted restlessly in his seat. It was obvious he did not support

Jarak's plan. His vibrations shot into overdrive, and I half expected him to eject from his seat and flee the room. After the meeting broke up, Dad glanced at Brad and raised his right eyebrow, reminding me to keep my head on straight, then left to talk with the other colonists.

Within seconds Brad blurted out, "Sounds like this ship is arriving just in time to stop the madness. I don't get this exposure thing. All my life, we've been told to keep our origins a secret. And what about yesterday? Jarak panicked when my dad started yelling about aliens. Revealing our identity puts us all in danger. We're all going to end up like rats in some covert government lab in Washington."

I defended my grandfather. "It's not like Jarak's going to put an ad in the newspaper saying aliens have landed. He said limited exposure only. What happened to that guy from a couple days ago who thought Jarak knew what he was doing?"

"Yeah, but this? Government agents will converge on Ridgway, rounding up the colonists and shutting down Terra Dyne."

"Exposing ourselves scares me too, but I think you're overreacting. Besides, you must've heard stories about what it was like on Karillion. How can we let that happen here? We have to warn people."

He shook his head in disgust. "I don't believe it. Who knows for certain what will happen? It's possible the people of Earth are smarter and wouldn't make the same choices."

"Seriously? Do you live on the same planet Earth that I do with Honey Boo Boo and the Kardashian sisters? You honestly think most earthlings recognize the dangers?"

Brad ran both of his hands through his thick hair in frustration. "I don't know, but like I told you before, I'm more concerned with saving myself."

"Brad, don't you get it? This *is* about saving yourself. It's about saving all of us."

"I'm telling you, this will not end well. Forget it. I don't want to discuss it anymore. Tell me what Jarak told you about the ship."

"Not much really. His vision wasn't very specific, but he did say it was unlikely my mom was on board. He believed he'd sense her presence if she was coming."

"So all we know is friendly aliens are headed our way. They must've escaped just like our parents did. But their arrival could be a bad thing.

Maybe they're coming to warn us someone not so friendly is close behind."

Suddenly a chill ran down my body, followed by that feeling you get when someone proposes an idea and instinctively, without any rational explanation, you know it's accurate.

Before I could contemplate the implications of Brad's theory, Daniel appeared at my side. He stuck out his hand to Brad, with a tentative smile.

"Still friends?"

Brad rolled his eyes and started to protest, then changed his mind and took Daniel's outstretched hand. "Okay, we're friends; now quit trying to be my babysitter."

"I'm just trying to watch your back. I can't stop the visions."

Brad shook his head with resignation, brushing off Daniel's persistence about visions. "When do you plan to stop this crazy obsession with my safety?"

"Not sure. But if you promise to be careful, I promise not to stalk you."

"What choice do I have?"

Daniel grinned. "Exactly." Then his face became dead serious. "No joke, man."

"Message delivered. Relax, okay?"

Daniel nodded. "Sure as long as we're clear. Come on, let's eat. Jarak's gatherings always have awesome food, and I'm starving."

He led the way to the buffet table, and Brad and I followed. We filled our plates and found a table. Dad had already taken a seat with my grandparents and the Winters. Erik and Tara joined us along with some of the other colonists from school. Thankfully, Tara sat several seats away so I barely noticed her withering looks. Mack and his parents were nowhere in sight.

"What's it like to discover you're an alien—and a Chosen One no less?" Erik asked me.

"Get over it Erik, that Chosen One stuff is so much crap," Tara said.

He shrugged. "I don't think so. I think it's pretty cool. Eve might just save the world."

"If our future depends on her, we're all in trouble," Tara replied.

"Lighten up, Tara. What's your problem with Eve anyway? Jealous because no one thinks you're the Chosen One?" Erik teased.

"Like I said, that prophecy is all a load of crap. Superstitious nonsense."

Don't think for a minute you're anything special," Tara mind messaged me.

Ignoring Tara's taunting, I answered Erik's question. "When Jarak told me about the alien stuff it blew my mind, but his image transfer left no doubt. He showed me Karillion with its mountains and its three moons. It's incredible. Who'd have thought we had aliens in our midst?"

Erik laughed. "Seriously, and we've never even set foot on Area 51."

After we'd finished eating, Brad said he wanted to head back to his house to see if his dad had made it home. I didn't like it. The warning bells going off in my head sounded increasingly like fire alarms. Seeing my troubled look, he reassured me that he'd be fine.

"Look Eve, I'll text you as soon as I get home. Don't worry."

"But what if your dad takes one look at you and goes ballistic?

"Aren't you forgetting something?" he asked.

"What?" I said, impatient with his inability to see he was flirting with disaster.

"My special powers will save me. I may not be able to fly like Superman, but I can leap tall buildings in a single bound."

"Oh really? I didn't know you'd mastered that one yet."

"Okay, I'm exaggerating a bit, but give me a little time, and I'll get the hang of it."

I groaned and followed him to the door. "Brad, don't you see? You haven't learned how to control your powers yet. Maybe I should go with you."

He shook his head in disgust at my lack of faith. "Oh, so you're going to save me? Come on. You're the one who doesn't get it. I expected you to have more confidence in me. Like I said before, your problem is you've been hanging around Danny Boy way too much." And with that, he walked out.

I didn't even have time to recover from his nasty comment before a shadow fell across my path. A claw-like hand gripped my arm forcefully, forming instant bruises. Looking up, I found myself staring into the coldest pair of eyes I'd ever seen. It was Mack.

"Hey Princess. What's the matter, your little puppy dog boyfriend leave you in the lurch? It's pathetic how he follows you around like a devoted slave. "

In that moment, I knew what it felt like to be in the presence of pure evil. Fighting my paralyzing fear, I wrenched my arm away. "What do you want from me Mack?" I demanded.

"What do I want from you?" he hissed like a snake. "What I want is for you to disappear. I'm sure by now Jarak has filled your head with lots of bogus stories and phony revelations. He's lying to you, Eve, and you're too stupid to see it. I want you to leave Ridgway, and if you don't make it happen, I will. Count on it." He released his grip and slipped out of sight.

Unable to move, I stood by the door, watching the colonists pass by, oblivious to the cancerous evil in their midst. I had been wrong. Mack meant exactly what he'd said, and now I knew in the depths of my soul that he was capable of murder.

Eve, what's wrong? Daniel's tension-filled voice echoed in my head as his eyes found me from across the room.

My mind had frozen along with the rest of me, and I couldn't remember how to send a message to him. Luckily, he appeared at my side and steered me behind one of the tall plants.

"It's Mack. Daniel, you were right. He's dangerous. He wants me to leave town."

"Did he threaten you?"

I shuddered. "He said if I didn't leave voluntarily, he'd force me out. It wasn't an empty threat. If he's capable of burning down a school with hundreds of kids inside, getting rid of me won't bother him. He was responsible for the fire, wasn't he?"

"We think so, but we can't prove it. It's possible he was messing around and things got out of hand...but probably not. Mack is smart—scary smart. He's a bad enemy to have."

To my utter shock, Daniel wrapped his arms around me and pulled me close. At first, I didn't know how to respond, but being in his arms felt wonderful. Oh just give in to it, I chided myself. Surrendering to his embrace, I laid my head against his muscular chest and trembled with a combination of pleasure and fear. "What am I going to do?"

Daniel stroked my hair reassuringly. "You don't have to be afraid of him. I promised to protect you, and I will keep you safe."

I snuggled closer before gazing up into his smoldering eyes. For one crazy moment, I thought he was going to kiss me, and I wanted more than anything to kiss him back.

"Daniel! What do you think you're doing?" an all-too-familiar voice shrieked. I pulled away from Daniel so fast I nearly collided with the wall.

Oh great, I thought. My stomach sunk as I realized I'd given Tara ammunition to fuel her jealous suspicions.

"Relax, Tara. Mack threatened Eve. She's freaking out, for heaven's sakes."

Stop! She and Mack are allies! I screamed silently.

Daniel's eyes shifted from Tara to me and back to Tara. He didn't believe me.

Don't! I shrieked in horror, certain he was going to confront her before we had a chance to talk. Furiously sending messages from my mind to his, I tried to warn him. *The girls and I heard Mack and Tara at school. Brad overheard Mack and Tara conspiring at the party Friday night. She wants to get rid of me too. Don't say anything!*

Daniel hesitated. Tara's eyes narrowed as she realized we were mind messaging. "Talking behind my back is rude even if it is telepathic. How can you listen to her? She's obviously lying to get your attention."

She stalked off in a huff, muttering "This entire night has been unbelievable." For once, Tara and I were in complete agreement.

"What's all this about?" Daniel demanded.

His frown deepened as I told him everything that had happened. I could tell he was struggling to believe Tara was involved. He stumbled over to a chair and sat down.

"Why would Tara get involved with somebody like Mack?"

"Who knows? But we need to figure out what they're doing before you confront her."

"I suppose you're right. I can't believe it."

"Can't believe what?" my dad said, making an abrupt appearance.

"Nothing," Daniel and I said simultaneously.

My dad shrugged. "Okay, I get it. It's none of my business. You ready to hit the road?"

"Yeah, I guess I am." I looked around nervously, searching for Mack. Daniel responded to my edginess by rubbing my shoulder gently.

I meant what I said. I'll keep you safe, he messaged me. Then for my dad's benefit he said, "Text me when you get home, okay?"

Warmth flowed through me, and I felt blissfully safe and unafraid. I agreed to let him know when I got home before leaving to say goodbye to my grandparents. Heated discussion surrounded Jarak and the rest of the Khalaheem. They had some daunting obstacles to overcome in order to accomplish their mission.

Chapter 19

On the way home, my dad asked if something was wrong. Instead of answering, I asked him what he knew about Mack's parents.

"The Larsens? They arrived on the ship in their mid-twenties and were already experts in their fields. Although they are not members of the Khala-heem, your mom often spoke about their remarkable intelligence. With a group like the colonists, that's saying something. Mack's dad is a chemist, and his mom is a psychiatrist. She's made ground-breaking discoveries on the power of the mind. Why do you ask?"

"I'm trying to figure out what sort of mutants gave birth to a monster like Mack. He doesn't like me very much, and the feeling is definitely mutual."

"Eve, he's a rebellious teenager. He resents Jarak telling him what to do, and he's transferred his dislike of your grandfather to you."

"Dislike? I think what Mack feels toward Jarak is a little stronger than dislike."

"Give him a few years. He'll get over it."

"What if he wants to leave Ridgway? Could he leave, I mean for good?"

"Of course, but he'd come back. This psychic connection the colonists share has a powerful attraction. Your mom used to say she felt empty and disconnected whenever she travelled, like her mind had gone silent."

I didn't want my dad to worry, so I dropped the subject. I spent the rest of the drive reliving Daniel's embrace. He had pulled me to him so naturally, like he'd been thinking about it for a while. But there was no escaping the problem of his annoying girlfriend. I could only hope Tara wouldn't share our cozy moment with Natalie. Even though they didn't like each other, Tara would do anything to cause trouble for me. I cringed as the thought of having to explain things to Brad. No doubt it would get ugly.

Upon entering my room, I obediently sent a text to Daniel. For once, I didn't resent his protective nature. Mack had really shaken me up, and I'd be looking over my shoulder every time I left the house. But that was only part of it. Daniel's embrace had changed me. Despite our encounter, I was still unsure of his feelings, not to mention my own.

After taking Quaz for a quick walk, I did a load of laundry and some homework. Brad had been in my thoughts since the gathering, but my guilt over Daniel kept me from contacting him. Finally, I bit the bullet and texted him. No response. Twenty minutes later I called him. No answer. Something was up.

The alarm I'd felt earlier returned with a vengeance. I tried to read, then gave up and attempted to watch television with my dad. I was practically pacing the floor when my cell rang, and I raced to pick it up. It was Daniel.

"Eve, Brad's in the hospital. He's been shot, but the doctor says he's out of the woods."

I gasped and nearly dropped the phone. "Oh my gosh. Who shot him?"

"Apparently Mr. Spencer got out of jail, had a few beers, and came home drunk. He decided to use Brad for target practice."

"No! Why didn't he listen to you? I'll be right there!" I hung up and told my dad what happened. He grabbed his keys, and we raced out the door.

The waiting area at the hospital was already packed with colonists. Word travelled fast in alien circles. Daniel and Erik approached us as we crossed to the check-in desk.

"They won't let anyone in to see him except family, although Jarak got an exception for him and Mrs. Sorensen since Brad doesn't exactly have any family at this point. After he regained consciousness in the hospital, Brad called them for help," Daniel informed us.

"How did he get here?" my dad asked.

"Mr. Spencer called 911. When the police arrived at the house along with the ambulance, he was gone. Mr. Spencer's probably halfway to Mexico by now. "

"How could his dad shoot him? Has he completely lost his mind?"

Daniel dropped his head and Erik answered my question, making sure no one else could hear him. "Brad made the mistake of telling his dad a Karillion ship was headed this way. Then he made it worse by suggesting his mom might be on board."

I gasped. "He didn't! Of course his dad flipped out. What was he thinking?"

Erik shrugged and exchanged looks with Daniel. My dad shook his head in exasperation. Then Daniel murmured to no one in particular, "I'll never forgive myself if his shoulder is permanently damaged."

"What about my grandmother's gift? Can't she heal him?"

"That's a problem, at least for now. The doctor has already removed the bullet and seen the extent of Brad's injuries. Your grandmother will have to wait to do any healing until after he leaves here. And even then, she can eliminate the pain, but she'll have to heal him gradually so as not to arouse suspicion. His shoulder might be messed up for good."

Daniel looked terrible. He blamed himself for Brad's injuries.

Hey you did everything you could to prevent this. It's not your fault, I messaged him.

Yeah well I should've done more. He was not in the mood for consoling.

At that moment, Augustine, Emily, and Sarah burst through the hospital's glass doors.

"Where is Brad? Is he going to be okay?" Sarah screeched.

Erik put his arm around her. "He'll be fine, babe. The bullet passed through his upper chest by his left shoulder. He should be fine. Unfortunately, his basketball season is finished."

"Only you would think of basketball at a time like this," she scolded him.

"You know Brad's already thought about it. We're basketball players and the season started two days ago, what do you expect?"

Erik's sheepish expression made me smile. Thank goodness we had him to provide comic relief. Several members of the basketball team trickled in, looking for information. Daniel and the others moved away from the check-in desk to fill them in. My grandparents spotted us as they came down the hallway.

"How's he doing?" my dad asked.

Lillian's face expressed her concern. "Physically, he should recover without any long term effects. But psychologically, he may never heal. I'm not sure he'll be able to forgive his father for shooting him."

"I can't believe Chris is so far gone. Why couldn't he hold on a little longer? If his wife is on that ship, she'll be visiting her husband in prison," Dad said.

"Only if the cops manage to catch up with him. When can we see Brad?" I asked.

"I'm afraid not until tomorrow during visiting hours. Besides, he needs to get some rest."

"Grandmother, Daniel said you'd have to wait to use your healing powers until Brad leaves the hospital. Isn't there anything you can do for him now?"

"I already have, dear. I used my gift to calm his mind. He's going to need all his physical and emotional strength to recover from this terrible tragedy."

The next day, I skipped Pre-Calculus and arrived at the hospital shortly after 8 a.m. My grandparents were already in Brad's room. My entrance coincided with an angry outburst.

"What difference does it make?" Brad wailed. "You said we were all going to be exposed anyway?" He nodded his head dismissively as I entered the room.

"Brad, calm down," my grandfather responded. "I never said we'd run around town telling everyone aliens are in their midst. My intention is for a select few of our scientists to reveal our technological concerns, and only if necessary, to divulge how we know this information. The Elders' plan necessitates controlling the release of all data. Otherwise, we'll have complete chaos, and we will be in danger."

"But the doctor said I'm going to miss the entire basketball season. I'll go crazy sitting on the bench. Come on. It's one stupid shoulder. Why can't you heal me, and let everyone chalk it up to a miraculous recovery?"

Grandmother put her hand on Brad's good shoulder. "We know waiting is difficult, but we don't have a choice. If I heal you, the x-rays will show no damage, and you'll have complete range of motion overnight. How will you explain that to your doctor?"

"That's his problem. I don't have to explain it. Let him think whatever he wants."

"Brad, we have to think of the rest of the colonists. I'm sorry, but the answer is no." Grandfather was firm, and the disappointment in his voice was unmistakable. He clearly thought Brad was being selfish.

"Maybe we'd better go. Take care of yourself," Grandmother said. My grandparents said goodbye to us both and left the room.

"Can you believe this garbage? What's up with them?" Brad said in disgust.

"I'm so sorry. I'm sure they're doing what they think is best, but I totally agree with you. It doesn't seem fair." Thank goodness Brad didn't know anything about my developing gift of healing. It would be impossible to say no to him.

"One lousy game, and I'm out for the season. Yesterday has got to be the worst day of my life." He paused for a minute then reconsidered. "Well, it's tied with the day my mom disappeared. At least I was young then and didn't really understand what it all meant."

"Do you want to talk about what happened with your dad?' I asked.

"It probably wasn't very smart to pounce on him the minute he walked in the door and start crowing about a ship and the possibility of Mom returning to Earth. I knew he'd been drinking, but I was so excited to tell him. I'm a complete idiot."

"Hey, he's the one that shot you, remember?"

"You should've seen him. He listened to me without saying a word, went to his bedroom, and came back with his shotgun. Cripes! I never thought he'd shoot me. He pointed it at me and hollered, "Let's see if your super powers can stop a bullet, alien boy," and then he pulled the trigger. I didn't have time to use my powers. I felt this awful burning in my shoulder, and then I must've gone into shock. I remember my dad calling 911, but everything else is a blur until I woke up in the hospital."

"I can't believe your dad took off. Where do you think he went?"

"Who knows? He has some friends in Cabo, but with the police looking for him I don't think he'd try to cross the border."

I leaned over the bed and kissed him lightly on the forehead, being careful not to put any pressure on his left side.

"That's it? What's a guy have to do to earn a real kiss? I was shot you know," he joked.

"Take it easy, Romeo. I wouldn't want to send that heart monitor racing. Look, I'm sorry about Jarak's decision. I wish there was something I could do to fix this."

"Talk to your grandparents and change their minds."

"In case you haven't noticed, I have no influence with them."

Brad sighed. "You don't have to remind me, I know exactly who runs things."

Squeezing Brad's hand, I said goodbye and told him I'd be back after school.

Mrs. Walters ambushed me when I stopped by the office to get a pass for class. She wanted to know all the details on Brad's condition. Desperate to escape, I shared a few things which seemed to satisfy her curiosity then slipped out, hoping to avoid anyone else.

I made it to English and grabbed a seat next to Sarah before the bell rang. Mrs. Murphy reassured everyone Brad's shooting was an isolated incident and no one was in danger. For some reason instead of making me feel better, her words sent a chill through my body. I was convinced things were about to get much worse.

Hey, how's Brad this morning? Daniel's words interrupted my dark thoughts.

As well as can be expected. He wants my grandmother to heal his shoulder so he can play basketball, and that's not going to happen, I messaged him.

Does he know about your gift for healing?

No, thank goodness. Let's keep it that way.

Of course, but you're going to have to tell him at some point.

I know that, Mr. Voice of Conscience, but now is not a good time. I scowled in Daniel's direction and caught Natalie watching me. It felt weird to have a silent conversation with someone across the room, but I couldn't help myself as I shot a smug look her way.

Returning my attention to Mrs. Murphy, I pondered her lecture on man's search for meaning in Herman Melville's *Moby Dick*. I was unsure of what I believed, but I knew for certain Jarak's revelations had changed me. For the first time, I'd caught a glimpse of the big picture. Maybe life was not some random accident but part of a larger, universal plan. All I needed to do was figure out how I fit into that plan.

A soft telepathic whisper interrupted my reverie. *He's lucky to have you, ya know.* I turned to look at Daniel, but he refused to meet my gaze. Would I ever figure him out?

By the time class ended, I felt energized and ready to tackle the universe. Tara pushed her way between Sarah and me, managing to squash my upbeat mood in an instant. She pulled me toward the wall and told Sarah to give us a minute. I nodded that it was okay. Tara's eyes glittered dangerously as she delivered her message.

"See how much trouble you've caused. Brad is only the beginning. How many other people are going to be hurt because of you?"

"Me? The shooting had nothing to do with me. Mr. Spencer freaked out because Brad told him about the ship," I whispered furiously. I was too mad to be afraid.

"The ship was just the last straw. His collapse started when Brad decided to hang out with you. Don't you get it? You're the problem. Jarak initiated this whole let's-get-out- and-warn-the-humans thing because you showed up. He sees your return as some kind of sign, but a bunch of us think he's losing his mind. If you really care about your grandparents, you'd better convince your dad to move back to Denver before it's too late."

"Look Tara, you don't scare me with your empty threats. Get over it. I'm not leaving."

"We'll see about that, won't we? Your enemies are more powerful than you think."

Daniel and Natalie chose that moment to pass by. "Is there a problem?" Daniel asked.

"Not one I can't handle," Tara said, stalking off down the hall. I shrugged, too angry to respond to his question. "Come on, Sarah. I feel the need to wash off the dirt."

I'd barely closed the bathroom door when Sarah demanded to know what Tara was all riled up about. "What's her problem?"

"She blames me for what happened to Brad."

"Oh come on, even she can't make that leap. Is it because his dad doesn't like you? Something I totally don't understand, by the way."

"It's complicated, Sarah."

She checked the stalls making sure the bathroom was empty then leaned against the door to prevent anyone from entering. "Look, Eve. I'm not stupid. I know something's going on. I've lived here my whole life, and I know the colonists are—different. Besides, I saw what happened in the cafeteria between Brad and Tara. Brad's shooting has something to do with what he did that day, doesn't it?"

I sighed, convinced everything was going to come out but knowing it wasn't my secret to tell. "Yes, but that's all I can say right now. I'm sorry."

"You sound like Erik. We're not blind, you know. People notice things." She left the bathroom without giving me a chance to reply.

I missed Brad in Spanish. Augustine and Emily tried to cheer me up, but my optimistic mood from English had evaporated. Brad lay in the hospital with a bullet wound. His dad was a fugitive. Sarah was mad at me because I couldn't tell her what was going on. My grandparents were in danger, and somehow I had gained enemies that sought my destruction. My life was disintegrating. How could I possibly believe everything was happening for some cosmically arranged reason or that I had some foreordained mission to fulfill? Was my grandfather truly crazy? Was the impending arrival of an alien ship the hallucination of a senile old man?

The more I focused on my doubts, the worse I felt. Darkness invaded my body. I could hardly believe my euphoric mood in English class last hour. I tried to think positive, but from the depths of my black mood, reality stunk.

I ate lunch in my car and stumbled through the rest of the day, hoping to avoid any other disturbing encounters. Hiding is impossible at a small school like Ridgway High, and everyone wanted to know about Brad. Not to mention the fact that the place was crawling with aliens. Aliens in Ridgway. A few short weeks ago, I might have laughed at the absurdity of it all.

I nearly made it through my last class, Chemistry with Mr. Denison, when a new terror reared its ugly head. I'd seen Mack at the back when I came in, but figured he'd ignore me since he'd already accosted me at the gathering. I was wrong.

In the midst of struggling with a chemical equation, a vicious whisper penetrated the silence. *We won't stop harassing you until you get out of town. There's nowhere to hide.* I knew the voice immediately. Mack had invaded my mind.

Startled, my hand flew out and collided with a rack of test tubes sitting on the lab table. The rack crashed to the floor, and the sound of breaking glass sent all eyes in my direction. My face burned with embarrassment even as horror enveloped me. How could I escape him if he used telepathy?

Sweet! So much for your breakage fee refund, Mack's evil voice taunted.

I refused to communicate with Mack. I had not anticipated this particular nightmare. Without making a move to clean up the broken test tubes, I screamed at Daniel with all the telepathic power I possessed. *How do I get Mack out of my head? He's making me crazy!*

Eve, calm down, Daniel replied. *Get out of Mack's transmitting range. Tell the teacher you're sick and need to leave class. I'll deal with him and find you after class.*

Sarah and Emily asked what was wrong, but I shook my head, knowing this would widen the divide between Sarah and I. Telepathy was not a subject we could discuss. Dodging the broken glass, I stumbled to the front of the room, realizing this was the second time in a month I'd had to leave class sick. The aliens weren't proving to be good for my health.

By the time I pleaded my case at Mr. Denison's desk I looked terrible, so it wasn't hard to convince him I was sick. Students whispered all around me. Sarah was right. The colonists' odd behavior was being noticed, and I wasn't helping matters any. The angry looks passing between Daniel and Mack as I left convinced me they were having a telepathic argument. At least they were already enemies so I didn't have Daniel's safety on my conscience too.

After sitting in the Subaru for a few minutes, I drove away from school in a daze. When they transferred the gift of telepathy to me, my grandparents said I could block my mind, but we hadn't discussed how to go about it. Besides I needed someone else to test the effectiveness of any self-imposed block. I hesitated to add to Brad's worries, but I needed answers and waiting wasn't an option.

Brad's face lit up as I entered his hospital room. "You're early!"

I didn't answer but kissed him so forcefully, he pulled away in surprise.

"Whoa! Now that's the kind of kiss I was hoping for this morning, but take it easy on the poor patient here. Like you said, we don't want to set off the heart monitor."

"School was a disaster. Tara threatened me in the hall and blamed me for what happened to you. Sarah witnessed everything and got mad because I wouldn't tell her what's going on. And then Mack invaded my head! How do you people live with secrets like this every day?"

"You probably don't want to hear this Eve, but things were pretty quiet before you showed up. You've stirred up a hornet's nest."

I sat down on the bed with exasperation. "Great. That's exactly what Tara said. So she was right, the chaos is my fault."

"Blaming yourself isn't going to solve anything. Wasn't that your advice to me? You're going to have to block your mind at school. You won't be able to send or receive messages, so none of us will be able to communicate with you, but you don't have a choice. Mack won't stop tormenting you. He's relentless when he wants something."

"How do I block my mind?"

"Simple. Picture an open door or an open curtain in your mind."

"This feels silly," I said, but he urged me to focus and create the picture. I closed my eyes to concentrate. "Okay, I'm in the fishbowl room at the cabin staring out the side window. There's a navy blue curtain."

"Now pull the curtain closed and visualize the room and your mind going dark."

I followed his directions and immediately felt closed off, like a vacuum had sucked the air out of my head. "It must've worked because I feel sort of blank or separated."

"Sounds like it worked. I'll send you a message."

I raised my eyebrows. "Did you send it?"

Brad smiled wickedly. "Yep, and you didn't receive it because if you had, you would've smacked me!"

"Glad to see you still have your sense of humor."

He smiled and reached out for my hand. "Listen Eve, I know you want to take our relationship slow, but you should know I'm crazy about you."

A familiar voice saved me from answering. "Looks like you're feeling better, Brad. Are you lovebirds so wrapped up in each other that you can't answer my texts?"

Daniel was smiling as he bumped fists with Brad, but his eyes revealed something else when he turned to look at me. Hurt? Jealousy?

"Uh, I shut my phone off when I left school. Sarah and Emily want an explanation for Tara's outburst. I didn't feel like answering any more questions today. I figured you'd catch up with me at the hospital right after school. Brad helped me block my telepathy," I babbled.

He glowered at me with such intensity I cringed. I had asked for his help, and then totally blew him off. I felt like a creep. An awkward silence passed between us. Thankfully, Brad didn't appear to notice.

"Great, well, guess you don't need my help. Coach and the rest of the team are coming over for a short visit before practice starts. I wanted to talk to Brad before it got noisy in here."

"What are we going to do about Mack?" Brad asked.

"I told him to back off, but I don't think he's going to listen. It's time to bring Jarak in on this situation. Eve is in danger."

"What about Tara?"

"I'm surprised she's part of Mack's vendetta. I'll talk to Erik and see if he can figure out what she's thinking. But I still don't believe she'd actually hurt Eve."

I swallowed my guilt and finally managed to join the conversation. "Tara said Brad got hurt because of me. She told me others will get hurt if I stay in Ridgway. She insists some of the colonists reject Jarak's prophetic ability and leadership."

"No one has expressed those concerns with me, but they probably wouldn't because they know Jarak and my parents are close friends. Everyone seems to support him."

I shook my head miserably. "Not according to Tara. She made a good point. Trouble started the first night we were in town. I should've never come back here."

Daniel grabbed my arm and locked his eyes onto mine. "You couldn't be more wrong. If you believe Jarak, you must know your return to us was destined. You rejoined The Colony for a purpose. The colonists need you, even if they don't know it."

Even though my mind was blocked, I heard his next thought as clearly as if he'd spoken it aloud. *I need you.*

Oh boy. My life was getting complicated.

Chapter 20

By the end of the week, Brad had left the hospital. The police would not let him stay at his house, so he moved in with Jakob Andersen and his daughter, Ruth. His dad remained a fugitive, and Brad did not expect him to return.

Thanksgiving Day was quiet. The colonists gathered in the morning to express gratitude for the blessings of planet Earth and the freedom of America. Although a few of them had married earthlings like my mother, most of them had no extended family to spend the holiday with. The Winters and the Andersens joined my grandparents for dinner, so I had to juggle Brad and Daniel for a few hours. Ruth seemed anxious around me and spent most of her time talking to Daniel's younger brothers, Mikey and Sean.

By late afternoon large snowflakes began falling, and we happily watched the snow accumulate through the huge windows overlooking the valley.

"Are you skiing with us tomorrow, Eve?" Daniel asked.

"I wouldn't miss it. The snow should be awesome for early season. Sarah said we're meeting at Erik's before driving up to Telluride."

Brad groaned. "Do you people have to rub it in that I'm an invalid?"

"I'm sure you'll be hitting the slopes by the end of December, but we'll make sure to take a few runs in your honor tomorrow," Daniel said.

"Do you ski, Ruth?" I asked, trying to draw her into the conversation.

"Actually I snowboard, but I don't go very often."

"You should come with us," I suggested.

"I don't think so. I'm one of those fair weather riders. Gotta have perfect conditions. Maybe I'll wait until there's more snow on the mountain," Ruth said.

"Well, if you change your mind, meet us at Erik's at eight a.m."

Ruth favored us with one of her rare smiles. A warm feeling flooded my body, and I was indulging in a moment of self-congratulation for pulling her out of her shell when Brad made a surprising offer.

"Ruth, if you're going to stay in town, we could hide out in your dad's basement and watch movies. Someone needs to make sure I don't expire."

"Oh brother. Sounds like we've got a drama queen in our midst." Daniel said, poking Brad in his good shoulder. My thoughts exactly. It was all I could do not to grimace.

"Sure, I guess," Ruth brightened before shooting me a questioning look. "I mean as long as that's okay with Eve, we could hang out." I nodded with perhaps a little too much enthusiasm.

"Of course it's okay with Eve," Brad said, raising his eyebrows in some sort of challenge. Was this his idea of a guilt trip? I'd spent every day after school this past week with him, and I refused to feel guilty. His negativity was getting to me. I needed a break.

"Why would she have a problem with us hanging out?" Brad continued. "And since my other friends don't have a problem abandoning me in my time of need, I'd really like it if you'd keep me company."

Daniel rolled his eyes. "Come on, Brad. If Erik and Augustine were here they'd tell you to quit your whining and get over it. This is opening week at Telluride. You wouldn't think twice about leaving us if we were busted up."

"It's fine. Don't worry about me. Ruth and I will have a good time without you guys."

If this tirade was an attempt to make me jealous, it failed miserably. Too disgusted to reply, I went to the kitchen to help my grandmother with the dishes.

Snow continued to fall through the night, but by the time we jumped on the gondola, the sun was bright and warm, despite temperatures hovering around twenty degrees. For early season, the runs looked decent, and more terrain was open than I'd expected. Erik had borrowed his dad's Suburban so Sarah, Emily and I rode to Telluride with him, Daniel and Augustine.

Earlier that morning as we loaded all our equipment, Sarah made an awkward attempt to be polite. "It's too bad Tara's not coming with us."

Erik laughed heartily. "You're an awful actress, Sarah. I can tell how terribly upset you are that she won't be joining us. Tara said she didn't feel like going even though she loves snowboarding," he shrugged. "I give up trying to figure out women."

Sarah slugged him playfully. "Contrary to popular belief Mister, we are not all alike."

"Whew! Thank goodness!" he replied with a mock sense of relief.

Sarah rode up front with Erik, I shared the second row of seats with Emily and Augustine, and Daniel reclined in the far back. It was cozy, but no one wanted to take two vehicles. Feeling brave, I turned to ask Daniel if Natalie liked to ski or snowboard.

"She snowboards. Natalie and Rachel plan to meet us on the mountain in a couple hours."

"Great," I replied, sounding as convincing as Sarah had moments before. I had hoped getting out of Ridgway would offer me a brief escape from the ever-present small town drama.

The Thanksgiving weekend crowds weren't too bad. Snow conditions were surprisingly good, and we managed to find powder in a few places. Snowboards ruled the slopes, but lucky for me, Augustine had brought his skis so I wasn't the only skier in the group.

Emily carved her way perfectly down the mountain, while Sarah's haphazard turns matched her personality. She sped downhill confidently then stopped abruptly the second something caught her eye. I learned quickly not to follow her too closely. The girls had no problems keeping up with the boys. Everything went smoothly for the first hour or so. Then, without warning a near catastrophe struck and changed everything.

We got off at the top of the chairlift, and everyone buckled in before following Sarah as she rode her snowboard behind some trees. We emerged into a clearing and found her, perched at the edge of a steep cliff, staring out at an incredible snow-covered panorama.

Daniel frowned seconds before Erik called out a shrill warning. "Sarah, don't get so close to the edge. The mountain got a lot of snow last night, and it hasn't had time to pack down."

Sarah brushed off his warning. "Relax, Erik. Nothing's going to happen."

But something did happen. Erik must've heard a crack or sensed a shift in the snow bank because he shouted "Get back!" at the precise moment a section of the cliff gave way.

Emily and I screamed, expecting to see Sarah tumble over the cliff with the plummeting snow. But instead of falling, she did something nearly as terrifying. Her body froze, suspended in mid-air, then shot forward, speeding directly toward Erik as if she'd been ejected from a canon. White-faced, he captured her and pulled her into his arms.

"What the...?" she yelled, pushing away from him. "Erik, what happened? How did you do that?"

Erik was speechless. He stared at Daniel begging him for help, but his friend's stony expression revealed nothing. From the look of incredulity on Erik's face, I guessed that they'd mind messaged and Daniel refused to step in. Glancing over at me, Erik sent a frantic mind message. *Eve, what do I do? What should I say?*

I shook my head while sending him my thoughts. *It's up to you, Erik. You need to decide this one for yourself.* Several seconds passed in silence.

"I've had enough of these secrets," Sarah said, looking around at the three of us—the colonists. Shock over her narrow escape from almost certain death hit her, and tears of relief mingled with frustration erupted. "I thought we had something special, Erik. Please tell me—tell us what's going on," she begged. Her naked vulnerability was heart wrenching. "The three of us have known you guys since we were little kids. Don't you trust us?" She moved over to stand beside Augustine and Emily who stood silently, watching the scene unfold.

"I promise we'll keep your secret safe," she continued. "We've known for a long time that something's unusual about all of you. But we've tried to respect your privacy and figured you'd tell us the truth when the time was right. The colonists obviously possess some kind of powers. Our suspicions were confirmed when we saw Brad and Tara in the cafeteria."

Erik gazed at her with a mixture of adoration and pain. "Okay, Sarah. I'll explain everything." In some bizarre, unscripted show of allegiance, Daniel and I moved at the same time to stand by him. Maybe we both knew this moment would come.

Erik beckoned to Augustine and Emily. "Let's find a spot in the lodge and get some hot chocolate." Once more he looked to Daniel and me, no longer seeking confirmation, but instead showing his determination. He wanted to reveal everything.

My eyes met Daniel's as I mind messaged him. *We're really going to do this? Shouldn't we ask Jarak first?*

A tiny smirk broke out on his enigmatic face. *Careful, Eve,* he replied. *You sound like you've adopted the colonist party line. I'd hate to think we've indoctrinated you so easily.*

I barely refrained from kicking him in the shin with my ski boot. *Be serious, Daniel. Sharing our secrets has implications for all of us.*

Relax, he messaged. *Sometimes our identities need to be disclosed. This should be Erik's decision. Sarah means a lot to him, and I'm guessing they have a future. As for Aug and Em, you and I both know if Erik tells Sarah, she'll tell Emily. And if Em knows…*

I nodded slowly in response, forgetting we'd been mind messaging. So this was it. Somehow I didn't expect the colonists' secrets to be revealed over a cup of hot chocolate on a snowy mountaintop.

Since it was mid-morning, the lodge wasn't too crowded. We found a table in the back. As we sat down, I remembered that Natalie and Rachel would be joining us soon. Thank goodness Sarah's incident had happened before they showed up.

The six of us huddled around a table, aliens on one side and earthlings on the other. My body began shaking with anticipation. Daniel touched my hand under the table, making me jump so violently I slammed my knee against the table top. I wondered if he could possibly be as nervous as I was. How would our friends react to aliens in their midst? Would they even believe us? Thankfully, I didn't have to be the one spilling the beans.

Erik started to speak, his voice hesitant but determined. "First of all, the colonists do have powers, as you've noticed. But we don't all have the particular power you recently observed, the ability to move people and objects. Some of us can do other things."

Augustine and Emily nodded, without speaking. Evidently, Erik's revelation was somewhat old news for them. But Sarah, never one to exercise patience, blurted out, "Like what kind of *other things*?"

"There are several gifts, but three main ones. As teenagers, we're not entirely certain which gifts we'll develop. Our abilities are still evolving, and we need to learn how to control them. Daniel has what you might call a sixth sense. He seems to know things before they happen, especially bad things. In fact, just before I called out to you, he warned me."

"Daniel didn't say anything," Augustine said.

"Well, actually he did, but you didn't hear it."

Augustine's usual mellow attitude slipped a notch. "Whoa. What are you saying? Last time I checked, my hearing was fine."

Erik took a deep breath. "What I'm saying is that we—the colonists—can communicate with our minds."

"You can't be serious," Augustine said.

"No way! You mean like telepathy? You talk to each other in your heads?" Emily asked.

"Awesome!" Sarah added. "But how? I mean, how do you manage that?" She turned to me with such a look of astonishment I nearly burst out laughing.

"Eve, you're a new member of The Colony," Sarah said. "Although you're not really new since Jarak is your grandfather, and of course, he is pretty much the leader of the pack and all. Did you always know how to do this, or did they have to teach you the telepathy stuff?"

All of this might have been funny, if what we had yet to reveal wasn't so earth-shattering. Literally. But so far, the conversation had proceeded better than I'd expected. My stomach lurched at the revelations still to come.

Emily grabbed my shoulder. "Maybe you can teach us telepathy?"

Thankfully, Erik answered for me. "Eve has only recently acquired the ability, but we can't teach telepathy to anyone. You sort of have to possess the right, uh, genetic material."

Emily appeared thoughtful. "That's what I thought, but I had to ask. So the big question is why do the colonists possess genetic material that's different from the rest of us?"

Erik expelled a huge breath. "Because the colonists aren't from here. The fact is our people are not from planet Earth."

Sarah and Emily stared at us in disbelief, but Augustine nodded enthusiastically. "Oh man, that's so cool. The Indian legends are true. It's unbelievable, but it all fits together. You guys are the Visitors. Misty's grandfather insisted the colonists came from—I can't believe I'm even saying this but—he said they came from the sky. He claimed the colonists were the Visitors he'd seen in his visions."

"Wait, wait, wait," Sarah said, backing away from Erik and glaring at Augustine. "You're buying this absurd story? So Erik and the colonists are *aliens*? What is this *The X-Files*? Seriously, if there was such a thing as aliens, why would they be in Ridgway?"

Augustine defended himself. "I don't know, why not? It's quiet and off the beaten path. Maybe you have a better explanation as to how you flew fifty feet through the air? If not superhuman powers, then what?"

Erik tried to calm Sarah down by putting his arm around her, but she recoiled. She was in no mood to listen. "No, Erik. It's not possible. I can accept the special gift thing, because I've witnessed weird stuff; besides, I believe most people are capable of more than they think. But there has to be a better explanation than the colonists being from another planet."

Erik looked defeated. "I'm sorry. There is no other explanation Sarah, because this is the truth. Why would I lie about something like this?"

Tears hovered in Sarah's eyes and her voice shook. "So, you guys aren't really *human*?"

"We're mortal beings like you. We simply have more advanced capabilities. Babe, please don't turn away from me. I'm the same person I was five minutes go."

Watching this painful scene made me uncomfortable. I totally understood how Sarah felt. If someone I cared deeply about revealed he was an alien, I'd freak out too. I studied Daniel, who hadn't said a word since the six of us had sat down.

What's up with you? I messaged him. *You're usually the problem solver. Can't you do something?*

She's Erik's girl. This is his deal. What do you want me to do?

As much as it pains me to admit it, you are the voice of reason. People listen to you.

Are you actually giving me a compliment, Miss Hunter?

I glared at him, imploring him to say something to help Erik.

Okay, but aren't you forgetting your particular gift? If you really want to help, try to calm her down while I explain about us.

Could I? I might have some healing skills but could I calm people like my grandmother? It was worth a shot. I focused my energy on Sarah, then got up to put my hands on her shoulders as Daniel began to speak. Immediately, I felt soothing warmth pass from my body to hers.

Daniel spoke up. "Sarah, get real. Like you said, you've known us since we were little kids. We're not much different than you. We eat, drink, and sleep every day. We break bones, get frustrated, and hate midterms. Most importantly, we do not sprout antennas from our heads, we don't eat people, and we have no desire to sleep in coffins."

My healing hands or his little spiel must've done the trick because Sarah giggled. The sound echoed around the table. I was floored by how quickly she'd returned to her usual self.

"Wow, this is like being in one of those teen sci-fi flicks, *My Boyfriend is an Alien.*

"Emily, you and Augustine are good with this?"

Emily shrugged, attempting to soften her grave expression. Augustine tried to justify his ready acceptance of our origin. "I've heard the Indian legends my whole life, and I've always hoped there was some truth to them. Erik has a point. Why would they lie about this?"

As if on cue, Misty Meyer, the Ute prophet's granddaughter, appeared at our table. Her long hair fell across her shoulders in multi-colored braids, but the necklaces and hoop earrings were gone. "What are you people doing inside on a day like this? Have you lost your minds? The snow is supreme!"

Guilty expressions lined the table, but we stared without uttering a word.

"Seriously, you guys look grim, like you've been assigned to save the planet. Care to share?" Misty glanced from face to face. "Oh my gosh, I'm so clueless. Something must be terribly wrong. Sorry but communing with nature puts me in la-la land. I totally ignored your vibes. Has Brad's condition worsened? Did his dad get caught?"

Misty stepped back as everyone started talking at once, eager to deny any bad news about Brad or his father. Erik's voice won out above the rest.

"No, we haven't heard anything about Mr. Spencer, and Brad feels as good as can be expected. We're bummed he's going to miss the whole season though."

Misty clearly didn't buy Erik's dismissal of our somber gathering. "That bites," she said slowly, evidently deciding to play along. "He must be miserable."

"You summed it up," Augustine said. "He laid a pretty heavy guilt trip on us when we took off for the mountain. Of course he's whining big time, but I do feel bad for the guy."

The rest of us nodded in unison, thankful to have a safe topic we could retreat to.

"Heard anything about his dad?" Misty asked.

"Nope. Still MIA, and the police won't let Brad go back to his house. He's staying with Ruth and her dad."

"Do you think I should send the tribe's healer over to see him? He's sort of a modern-day medicine man. His healing skills might be able to help Brad."

"Really?" The words popped out of my mouth without warning. Was it possible humans had healing powers too? "Can he actually *heal* people?"

Misty nodded. "Our people think he has a gift for healing, and I've heard some incredible stories throughout the years. Besides, there's a lot of stuff out there we don't understand. The universe always surprises you."

"I'll second that statement," Sarah muttered, sending Erik an ironic grin.

"I'll give Brad a call when I get home," Misty said. "Hey kids, if you've got things under control, I'm out of here. Don't want to waste that luscious powder. Let me know if you come up with any ideas to save the planet. And if you need some help, count me in."

We watched her walk out the door. Emily's next words echoed my thoughts exactly.

"Talk about coincidences. If I didn't know better, Augustine, I would think you summoned Misty here. Her appearance was positively surreal."

Augustine pulled Emily close. "Like Misty told us, there's much in the universe that we don't understand."

"Anybody up for taking on the trees?" Daniel challenged.

Erik groaned. "Are you trying to incapacitate the entire basketball team? Last time we took our boards down a tree run, I ended up with a shiner."

"It's all about focus, Erik. You're too easily distracted."

"Guilty as charged, but I'll head out with you. But first, speaking of focus, I need a minute to focus on my girl." Erik took Sarah's arm and led her to a private corner of the lodge. Although I tried not to watch, I couldn't help but notice the passionate kiss they shared.

"You up for some tree skiing, Eve?" Daniel asked, drawing my attention from the couple.

"I think I'll stick to the wide open spaces, especially until we get more snow. Bowls are my favorite." I smiled up at him, feeling the warmth emanating from his gorgeous green eyes envelop my whole body. I could feel his energy field pulse as our eyes connected.

Too bad. I'll miss you. I gasped as his whispered message invaded my mind.

Our brief moment of whatever it was ended abruptly with an enthusiastic exclamation from behind us. "There you are Danny! We saw Misty outside, and she told us you guys were holed up in the lodge. Is the hill too much for City Girl?"

Daniel yanked his gaze away from mine, and my body chilled instantly like I'd walked from sunlight into a cold storage locker. A breathless Natalie clad in a shiny silver and white parka and white pants ran over to Daniel and planted a kiss on his lips as if she hadn't seen him in years. To her credit, she made a lame attempt to smile in my direction. I made no effort whatsoever to return the gesture. Her friend Rachel ignored me, which saved me from feeling guilty about being rude to her too.

Suddenly I was angry at Daniel. How dare he flirt with me one minute and smooch with his bimbo girlfriend the next. I'd thought they were about to call it quits. I must've read too much into his actions. Obviously I was mistaken about his intentions.

I desperately needed to vent to Sarah, but she had other things on her mind. As she and Erik returned to the group, it was clear she was not going to leave his side. They had much to work out. I could definitely relate to her shock at the whole alien story. Within minutes, the group had split up, everyone heading out with Daniel for the trees except for Augustine and Emily who joined me in search of some groomed terrain.

As we buckled in, Daniel sent me a message. *Eve, I'm sorry. We need to talk.*

Skip it, Daniel. Looks like you've got your hands full, I replied, certain my fury was transmitted along with my words.

Despite the great snow and the picture-perfect weather, I couldn't pull myself out of the black mood I'd fallen into. Daniel's confusing behavior had turned me inside out. I had expected Augustine and Emily to pummel me with questions about the colonists, but they were uncharacteristically quiet. Finally, their silence became overwhelming, and I pleaded with them to ask me something, anything to distract me.

Emily studied my face. "Have you always known you were an alien?"

"No. My grandfather told me a couple weeks ago. It came as a complete shock."

"How did you know for sure he was telling the truth? Did you think he might be crazy?'

"I didn't get the chance. As he began telling me his story, he used his powers to fill my mind with beautiful images of the colonists' planet, Karillion. It has a gazillon trees, huge mountains, and three moons! There was no way I could deny what I saw in my head. Besides, the scenes all looked familiar."

"How's that even possible?" Augustine asked.

Unexpected tears sprang to my eyes. "I'm not sure exactly, but maybe my mom shared the images with me before she disappeared."

"Sorry, I forgot about your mom's disappearance. What a trip to discover she was an alien. But I can't stop thinking about the whole telepathy thing. Having that ability would be so cool! I'm totally jealous of you guys. Can the aliens adopt a protégée?"

For the first time since leaving the lodge I broke into a grin. "I'll have to check on that Augustine and get back to you."

We ran into the second half of our group as the mountain was closing and took the last chair up for a final run. Daniel mind messaged me a couple times insisting we had to talk, but I ignored him. I knew we'd have to communicate at some point, but I needed to calm down first.

To my immense relief, Daniel opted to ride back to Ridgway with Natalie and Rachel. Erik took the rest of us directly to the Andersens so we could bring Brad and Ruth up to speed. I figured those two wouldn't have a problem with our three friends being in the loop, but I warned Sarah, Augustine, and Emily to be wary of Tara and Mack. Poor Erik dreaded the next few hours. Telling Sarah he was an alien had been difficult, but now he had to confess to Tara that their secret was out.

Chapter 21

Brad and Ruth seemed relieved to find out our friends knew our secret. When we arrived at the Andersen's house, Brad appeared happier than I'd seen him since before the shooting. Ruth was good for him; and as it turned out, he was also good for her. Over the next couple weeks, I'd catch them chatting in the hallway or sharing a laugh in the cafeteria. It's funny how things work out.

I blocked my mind at school so neither Mack—or Daniel—could mind message me. I avoided Daniel at every turn, which proved to be much harder than I expected. After a few days he took the hint and left me alone. Brad let up on his heavy romantic pursuit and seemed content to be friends for the time being. Our make out session at Terra Dyne had been a mistake. I searched in vain for the right time to confess that I did not have romantic feelings for him. All my thoughts and emotions revolved around someone else.

The dreaded blowout I expected from Brad finding out I'd been in Daniel's arms at the gathering never materialized. Apparently Tara had decided to keep it to herself. I intercepted a few curious glances from Sarah, Augustine, and Emily, but aside from those odd looks, their behavior toward me didn't change after our alien revelations. However, I suspected they challenged Erik and Brad to levitate a few things.

The biggest surprise came from Mack. After his threat at the gathering, he slipped into the background. Day after day, he walked into Chemistry and headed straight for the back of the room, keeping his eyes averted. I experimented by reactivating my telepathic channels in class, but he made no further attempts to invade my mind. It was as if nothing had ever happened. Basically, our lives played out for the next couple weeks in a metaphorical suspended animation. We were biding our time until the ship came. As it turned out, we didn't have long to wait.

After our first Sunday in Ridgway, Dad and I began having dinner every weekend with my grandparents. Now that the secrets of The Colony were out in the open, I viewed Jarak and Lillian through different eyes and looked forward to our weekly gatherings. We spoke freely about the work at Terra Dyne, and the colonists' plans for the future.

Two weeks after Thanksgiving, my grandfather made a surprise announcement. "The Karillion ship will land at Lone Cone on December nineteenth—in four days."

My dad and I gasped. "Four days? Are you sure?" I demanded. "What makes you think they'll land out there? What should we do to prepare?"

Jarak smiled. "The answer to your first question is yes, I am certain they're coming on Thursday. As to the second question, they'll land at Lone Cone because our ship's landing left behind a trace of makar, a Karillion fuel source. Their sensors will pick up on it and detect our presence—the same way Zorak's crew found us ten years ago. As for what we need to do to prepare, nothing I suspect. They'll tell us what we need to do once they arrive."

I groaned with exasperation. "Grandfather, you're driving me crazy with this whole faith thing. How can you accept things so easily and manage to stay calm? We're talking about a ship from outer space. It's a big deal. You have no idea who or what might be on this ship. I realize these are your people, but aren't you a little apprehensive about what might happen?"

"My faith provides strength and minimizes fear. Despite the fact that I am ignorant of the occupants of this ship, I know they are not a threat to the colonists. However, my vision only extends so far. I have no inkling of what lies beyond the ship's arrival, although I must admit, I sense darkness on the horizon. Challenges lie ahead for all of us."

I flashed back to the chill I'd felt when Brad suggested the ship was coming to warn us enemies were headed our way. "That sounds like trouble to me. So you're still able to remain calm with danger ahead?"

"Eve, the exercise of faith sometimes dictates that we move beyond the edge of the lighted path and take a step into the dark, confident that we'll receive direction as needed."

"Well, I'm going to have to rely on your faith, because I don't have any myself."

My grandmother chuckled. "Of course you do, my dear. Your dad shared how you healed Quazimodo the day you left Denver. In order to exercise your healing gifts, you must have faith in your abilities."

"It wasn't so much faith in my abilities as it was sheer determination—a driving will for Quaz to live," I argued. "I wouldn't allow myself to consider any other outcome."

"Your experience was the beginning. Your abilities will expand beyond anything you can imagine. You have Khalaheem blood in your veins. Exceptional powers are your birthright."

I brushed off this descended-from-alien-royalty mumbo jumbo. I needed to formulate a plan for the next few days. Somehow I had to go through the motions until Thursday. There was no way I could hang out at school and act normal. Anticipating the landing of an alien spaceship made waiting for high school graduation look like a cake walk.

First, I asked Jarak how he planned to inform the others, because we'd been told us we were the first to hear the news. He said he'd already called a meeting for the following evening. Those who could not attend would be contacted immediately afterward.

Second, I wanted to know more precisely when and where the ship would arrive. We'd probably have to get ahold of a few snowcats since the snowy roads were impassable. I planned to head out to Lone Cone as soon as possible. After all, Jarak's psychic radar might be off a few degrees. And third, as much as I hated myself for my traitorous desires, I desperately wanted to talk to Daniel. Trouble was coming, and I needed him to help me prepare.

Thinking back to the eventful day on the mountain, I asked my grand-parents what they thought about Erik sharing the colonists' origins with our friends. My dad had taken the news well; after all, he'd been adopted into the alien family himself.

"Erik called us the evening you returned from Telluride," Jarak said. "He explained about Sarah's close call, and how your other friends witnessed the incident. Sometimes cases arise which involve extenuating circumstances. We're confident you've surrounded yourselves with trustworthy associates."

"Can we invite them to watch the spaceship land?" I asked, unable to keep the excitement out of my voice. Sarah would totally freak! How many people can invite their friends to an alien ship landing?

"I assumed Erik would make that request also because he'd want Sarah to be by his side. I'll discuss this with the Elders, but I don't anticipate any objections to their presence."

Before we left, I had one more thing I needed to discuss. Despite his recent indifference, I knew Mack meant what he'd said when he'd threatened me. The arrival of a Karillion ship might escalate his anger toward me and my grandparents. And yet I hesitated. When I told my dad about Mack, he brushed off my fears. I had no doubt the danger was real, but could I convince Jarak?

We finished dessert and everyone stood to begin clearing the plates. If I planned to tell my grandparents, it was now or never. "Mack Larsen threatened me," I blurted out, a bit louder than I'd intended.

"He threatened you?" Grandmother asked, as if she didn't understand what I'd said.

"Yes, he told me to leave town willingly, or he'd find a way to make me leave."

Jarak frowned. "What else did he say?"

"He claimed you were filling my head with bogus stories and phony revelations. He called you a control freak and said you enjoyed manipulating people." Sharing Mack's accusations was hard, but my grandfather had to know what he was up against. "I overheard him talking to Tara. They question your prophecies and your leadership. They resent the power you and the Elders have over The Colony."

My father grimaced. "We discussed Mack after the gathering. Why didn't you tell me all this?"

"You didn't seem to think he was much of a threat, so I dropped the subject. Besides, I didn't want to worry you."

Jarak sat back down, looking defeated. "I've sensed problems with the Larsens. Unfortunately, it looks like their attitudes have been transferred to their kids—or at least Mack. He has been troubled for a few years. As for Tara, her involvement disturbs me greatly. Loren and Raina Nielsen are exemplary parents. They would follow the Elders to the ends of the universe. Perhaps Tara is experiencing an uncharacteristic period of rebellion."

"Either way Grandfather, Mack has some kind of hold over her. She appears ready to do whatever he asks. Erik says she's no longer interested in snowboarding or spending time with any of her friends. She cornered me in the hall at school, blaming me for Brad being shot and saying people are going to get hurt because I moved back to Ridgway."

"I'll talk to the Nielsens about Tara, but Eve, you need to tread carefully around Mack."

"I've already shut down my telepathic channels at school because he threatened me via mind message."

Grandmother's face creased into a frown. "This sounds serious, Jarak. We need to make sure Eve is safe."

"She's surrounded by Daniel, Brad and Erik. What more protection does she need? In any case, I'll tell Daniel to increase his vigilance. Meanwhile Eve, I'm afraid you'll need to avoid any isolated places by yourself, at least until all this blows over. You're probably safe driving your car during the day, but any excursions after dark are too dangerous."

"But what about running or taking Quaz for a walk?"

"Unfortunately, the only young female colonist with the power to move objects is Tara, and since she seems to be part of the problem, you'll have to figure out a way to have one of the boys with you. Daniel likes to run, and he'd be happy to watch out for you."

I groaned to myself. I should've known Jarak would assign Daniel as my protection detail. Just when I was becoming accustomed to his absence, fate thrust us right back together.

Every colonist attended the Monday night meeting, except Daniel and Erik who had basketball practice. Since most of the adults had experienced their own journey through space, they remained calm like my grandparents, despite their enthusiasm for the new visitors. More than twenty five years had passed since they'd had any contact with their home planet. There was much speculation over the ship's purpose and occupants.

Brad arrived with Ruth and Jakob Andersen. His wound was healing quickly, thanks to my grandmother, but he still suffered from stiffness in his shoulder. He pulled me aside after the meeting broke up.

"This is incredibly cool! We are actually going to meet others from Karillion!"

I wanted to share in his excitement, but ever since dinner last night with my grandparents, I'd had a sense of doom that wouldn't go away.

All I could manage to say was something trivial. "I don't think I've processed it."

Brad didn't notice my misgivings but kept chattering at full speed. "I've missed you, Eve. Ever since Thanksgiving I feel like there's this huge distance between us. You should come over tonight. I know it's a little weird because I'm staying at Ruth's house, but she won't mind."

I knew we needed to talk, but I wasn't eager to hurt him. I begged off, saying I had a lot of homework which was true, but also an excuse. I hoped the ship's arrival would provide the boost he needed so I could exit his life quietly. I should win the award for coward of the year.

Brad gave me a questioning look but didn't push it, and I breathed a sigh of relief. He continued to lay out his plans. "We should head out early on Thursday. Jarak said the ship won't land till around midnight, but I'm thinking about ditching school and leaving while there's still daylight. I bet Ruth's dad would agree to take us out in his truck. The colonists own some land at the end of the road that's maintained all winter. Some of the families keep snowcats out there so they can access Lone Cone when the snow is too deep for four wheel drives."

"I had the same idea. I couldn't possibly sit through class on Thursday. I'll talk to Sarah, Emily, and Augustine. Jarak said we could take them out to Lone Cone for the ship's landing. They're going to be so excited. I trust them to keep our secret, but I'm glad I'm not the one who has to hide an alien landing from my parents."

Brad nodded, his eyes gleaming with maniacal fervor. He leaned close and whispered, "Eve, I haven't shared this with anyone else, but someone we know is on that ship. I can feel it with certainty. I think my mom is coming back."

"Brad, don't do this. You're setting yourself up for disappointment. It's fun to speculate, but this is not healthy. You don't need any more crap right now. It's better to assume she's not on board than suffer more agony when you find out you're wrong."

He disregarded my cautionary words. "You'll see. Someday you'll have a little more confidence in my judgment. I promise you someone on that ship is closely related to us."

Perhaps someday I would have more confidence in him, but today was not that day. Besides, only a week ago Brad had ignored Daniel's warning and confronted his father with news of the ship. I had faith in his abilities. I just thought they needed a little fine tuning.

Daniel called that night after he got home from basketball practice. His parents had filled him in on what happened at the meeting. When his name came up on my cell, I took several deep breaths before answering the phone.

"Hey," I said, attempting to slow my racing heart.

"How's it going?" he said, then "You've been avoiding me. I didn't think you'd pick up."

"Yeah, well, I had something I wanted to talk to you about." My voice broke.

Daniel waited for me to continue then filled in the silence. "Sure. Whatever you need." He paused again while I searched frantically for the right words to say. When nothing emerged from my mouth, Daniel resumed speaking, "Jarak told me I'm back on protection detail. Not that I ever really stopped exactly, but I thought you needed some space. He said you might need a running buddy."

I swallowed hard. "What about basketball?"

"I'm sure we can work something out. We can swap schedules and make a plan."

"What about your girlfriend?" I asked, not even trying to disguise my resentment.

"Natalie won't be a problem. She and I broke up."

My heart jumped into my throat. I'd been so busy ignoring him I hadn't noticed his voluptuous leech had vanished. I struggled to sound halfway intelligent. "That's good I guess. I mean if that's what you want."

"It was my choice. After that day at Telluride, I realized she and I didn't make sense anymore. I'm not sure we ever did. Our relationship was a lame attempt to fit in and be like everyone else, you know, just a typical American teenager. I guess I wanted to see what normal felt like. Anyway, it's over. One less obstacle."

Before I could decipher his last comment, he asked, "What else can I do for you, Eve?" All at once, he sounded peculiar, like he was forcing himself to perform a distasteful duty.

My irritation rose, and I snapped, "Look Daniel, if it's too much trouble…"

His annoyance matched mine. "I don't get you, Eve. You've spent the last two weeks ignoring me, treating me like some sort of disgusting insect. And now you expect me to overlook all that and jump to your rescue?"

"Forget it. I don't expect anything from you."

"What is it you want?"

"Nothing. Forget I said anything."

He sighed and his voice softened in resignation. "Could you please listen to me for a minute? I know you and Brad have a thing, and I'm not sure how serious it is. I've tried to stay out of the way, but I have to tell you how I feel. What I really want to know is not what can I do for you, but what do you want from me? You can't deny there's a powerful connection between us. When I'm around you, I feel…."

It was his turn to struggle for words. I waited, my cell phone clenched tightly in my hand, hardly daring to breathe and spoil the moment. The word he chose was perfect.

"Complete," he finally said. "I feel complete."

For once I knew exactly what to say. "Me too. I felt an immediate connection the first day we met. But then I saw you with Natalie, and the jealousy monster engulfed me. Every time I saw the two of you together I wanted to rip her face off. Sorry for being such a jerk."

"Wow, remind me not to get on your bad side. Seriously though, these last couple weeks have been awful. I've missed you." He exhaled dramatically. "I can't believe I'm telling you how I feel over the phone. I'd much rather take you in my arms and show you how I feel. Is it too late to come over?"

I groaned with frustration. "I'd love for you to come over, Daniel, but I'm buried. I have tons of homework plus our AP English paper to finish before Christmas break. I want to have everything done in case the ship's arrival, uh, changes things."

"Do you think your mom is aboard?"

"Jarak says it's unlikely, but he could be wrong. Brad has convinced himself his mom is coming. I hope he's right, for his sake."

"The last thing Brad needs is one more let down."

"Agreed," I said. "And speaking of Brad, he's been pushing for a serious relationship, while I've been waiting for the right opportunity to explain that I just want to be friends. After the shooting I couldn't bring myself to say anything. I don't want to hurt him. I think we should avoid any public displays of affection until I talk to him."

"No PDAs. I understand. Brad's one of my best friends. I'll try to keep my feelings under wraps. It's going to be nearly impossible to keep my hands off you though," he teased. "Are you sure I can't come over?"

I couldn't believe I was going to turn down his offer—twice. "Daniel, I really do have homework, and besides, it's almost eleven. My dad's already asleep, and he'd go ballistic if I snuck you in the house. Meet me at the cabin before school tomorrow." Part of me thought I must be dreaming. Was this really happening? Daniel actually wanted to be with me.

"Now I can relate to how the guys feel when I try to be the responsible one," he said. "It bites. Okay, you win. I'll be there by six-thirty, if that's not too early."

"I'll be waiting, but you're going to pay for making me get up so early."

"Oh yeah, what sort of payment do you have in mind?" he teased.

"How about you show up tomorrow, and we'll discuss it," I said, in the most seductive voice I could muster. Geesh, I could use some lessons on how to do this stuff.

"Hmm…that sounds promising enough to make me get out of a warm bed at an indecent hour so I can drive to the cabin in twenty-degree weather."

"Consider it protection detail."

Daniel laughed. "Yeah, I'm thinking surveillance duty with fringe benefits thrown in." Then remembering the beginning of our phone conversation, he asked, "Hey, you never said what you needed to talk to me about."

I took a deep breath before diving in. "How did you *really* know Brad was in danger? I mean, I need to know how the Seer thing works. You said everyone can receive revelation for themselves, and I've been getting these feelings—like something bad is going to happen. So how do you distinguish between actual revelations and normal thoughts and fears?"

"I guess with actual revelations, you're either being prompted to action, or you're being prepared for something. If you think trouble is coming, you should take extra precautions. We can't avoid all the bad stuff, but sometimes our choices can minimize painful experiences. Listen to the voices in your head, unless they're telling you to do something crazy."

"What if these warnings are just figments of my imagination?"

"The figments disappear, and you're no worse off than before. No harm, no foul."

"Thanks, Daniel. You make everything seem so simple."

"Better face it, Eve. You can't live without me."

"Oh my, how have I ever managed to survive this long?" I teased.

"That's one of life's great mysteries. Good night, Eve. Sweet dreams," Daniel whispered.

"Good night, Daniel."

I hung up, engulfed in a blaze of emotion. So this is what being in love felt like. A brief moment of panic intruded as I berated myself for telling him it was too late to come over. I probably wouldn't be able to study anyway, and I definitely wouldn't be able to sleep. Too bad because sleep might conjure up some pretty awesome dreams.

Chapter 22

Daniel arrived earlier than expected the next morning. Apparently he anticipated our rendezvous as much as I did. When I heard his Jeep drive up, I raced to answer the door before he could knock. I swung back the door then stood unmoving in the opening, overcome by a sudden case of shyness.

Daniel grinned. "Hello, Eve. It's a little cold. Are you going to let me in?"

"Oh, of course, come in," I stammered. He followed me inside, pulling the door closed behind him. After scanning the room, he wrapped his arms around me and cradled my head against his chest. We stood for several minutes locked in an embrace without speaking. Finally, he raised my lips to his and kissed me softly.

"What took you so long?" I murmured, snuggling closer. "I've been waiting all night for you." Quaz's tail thumped vigorously against the floor, anxious to be part of a group hug.

"Ditto," he said, rubbing the top of Quaz's head. "A couple times I almost jumped in the Jeep and drove over to camp outside your house, but then I figured your dad might think I was a stalker."

"Are you kidding? My dad and my grandparents worship you. They had you and I paired up before we even moved to Ridgway."

"Well, I guess they're smarter than we think." He kissed me again, and I responded eagerly. Heat coursed through my body as he pulled me closer to him. I couldn't help compare his kisses with Brad's. Daniel's were soft and inviting, whereas Brad's were hard and demanding. I could stay in Daniel's arms for hours. He interrupted my pleasurable trance abruptly by drawing back and looking around.

"Oh man, I almost forgot. Your dad's home isn't he?"

I giggled. "Yes, but don't worry, he's a heavy sleeper. I never see him before seven."

"Shouldn't we head to your room, just in case?"

"Daniel, you're such a worrier."

"Probably true. But I know how I'd feel if I stumbled out of bed and saw my daughter wrapped in some guy's arms before breakfast. Let's give him a break."

"Oh, so it's better for him to find us in my bedroom?" I teased.

"Nope, but at least we'll hear him coming."

I grabbed his hand, leading him to my room, our fingers laced together like we'd been holding hands for years. It was weird how everything felt so right. With Brad, I had to think about how to react to his romantic advances, but with Daniel, my body responded effortlessly.

We curled up together in a large overstuffed chair in the corner of my room. Although it was wide, I was mostly on Daniel's lap, but he didn't seem to mind. Promptly at seven, I heard my dad get up to make his coffee, and I hurried out to let him know Daniel was at the cabin.

He must've been tired because he merely grunted in acknowledgement. Under the glow of a new romance, I crossed the kitchen and planted a kiss on his cheek. He raised his eyebrow questioningly then with a sardonic grin suggested I return to my company. At that moment, my dad won the award hands down for best parent ever.

Dad left at seven thirty, and we were right behind him. I reminded Daniel that we needed to keep a low profile until I talked to Brad. We shared a passionate kiss outside while we warmed up our separate cars.

"Can't you talk to Brad today?" he grumbled. "I'm never going to be able to keep my hands off you."

"It's only a couple days till the ship lands. You'll survive, I promise. Seriously though, Daniel, even afterwards, we need to take it easy when Brad's around. I don't want him thinking I dumped him for you. It was never about that."

"Not even a little?" he asked, clearly fishing for flattery.

"Okay, I'll confess. It was hard to focus on having a relationship with him when all I could think about was you. Satisfied?"

"Maybe. I need to know I wasn't the only one dreaming of you and me together."

"There were times your *charming* personality became a bit tiresome," I said, kissing him again to soften my words.

He laughed. "Good thing you already know all my faults."

"Bye Daniel. Don't forget to keep your hands to yourself."

"See ya, Eve," he said, before getting into his Jeep and heading down the driveway.

As I drove to school, Brad sent me a text letting me know Mr. Andersen had agreed to drive us out to the snowcat sheds on Thursday. He didn't want to leave until noon though, so Brad suggested we hang out until then. I declined and made up another excuse, then scolded myself for being dishonest. Brad deserved better. We desperately needed to have a talk.

Brad met me in the school parking lot. "Two more days! Can you believe it? I feel like I'm about to spontaneously combust!"

"You better not, Brad," I teased. "You'll burn down the rest of the school."

He beamed. "No worries. But if I did burn it down, they'd never catch me. Besides, I don't plan to be here much longer anyway."

I frowned. "What do you mean?"

"Weren't you listening last night, Eve?" he said in frustration. "I told you, someone important is coming on that ship. If it's not my mom on board, I plan to figure out a way to take that ship back to Karillion and find her."

I gasped. "And then what? Geesh Brad, aren't you getting ahead of yourself a bit here? You'd actually go to Karillion?"

"Of course I would. Given the chance, wouldn't you?"

"I don't know. I hadn't thought about it, but I'm pretty happy on Earth."

He gave me a look of pure disgust. "Well, I'm not happy. A few weeks ago, my paranoid father shot me and became a hunted fugitive. I have no family, no home, and on top of it all, I can't even play basketball because of a bum shoulder. Why exactly would I want to stay here?"

My first thought was that he hadn't mentioned our relationship. I would've thought it meant something to him. My heart sunk as it occurred to me that our breakup would only add fuel to his desperation. Brad had a valid point though. The tenuous hold he'd had on his Earth life had disintegrated with a single gunshot. I couldn't contradict him.

We walked to Pre-Calculus in silence. Brad's initial good mood had evaporated. It was clear he viewed the Karillion ship as the solution to all his problems. He planned to hop on board and run away from everything. I had already learned that escaping problems wasn't that simple. They usually followed us no matter how far away we managed to run.

Most of the gang was clustered near the door when we got to class. We'd grown closer since the Telluride incident, especially Erik and Sarah. They sat against the wall as close as possible without being in the same seat. Their constant displays of affection usually annoyed me, but now that I could relate, their intimacy warmed my soul. The world seems a whole lot rosier when the one you love loves you back.

I decided to leave my telepathic channels open after meeting with Daniel this morning. I was flying high, and all my fears had disappeared. With him as my ally, I felt bulletproof. When Daniel entered class, a blast of energy nearly took my breath away.

Good morning to you too, Mr. Winter. You look tired. Up all night?

He started, but recovered quickly, flashing a brilliant smile. *Yep, some pesky wench invaded my valuable sleep time. Sorry about the intensity of that energy transmission. I wanted to get your attention, but came on a little strong. One look at you, and I lost all control.*

Keep talking that way, and I'll follow you anywhere.

He grinned at my coy remark, while simultaneously trying to respond to a comment from Augustine. When Mr. Ayers entered, he messaged me again. *Hey, I thought you kept your communication channels off at school.*

I usually do, but since we have to keep our hands to ourselves, I needed to find some way to reach out and touch you.

Works for me, but you sound an awful lot like a Hallmark commercial.

Watch it, mister. You don't want to get on my bad side.

And you're telling me something I don't already know?

Before I could think of a decent comeback, Mr. Ayers started the class, and I ended my conversation with Daniel. Even though the teacher couldn't hear us, it seemed rude to mind message while he was talking.

Brad's bad mood persisted. I was relieved when we headed in different directions after class. I walked to English with Sarah, Erik, and Daniel, trying to keep my distance from Daniel and act like nothing had changed between us. My fingers ached to clasp his hand in mine.

This is pure torture, I finally messaged him.

Tell me about it. He shot me a flirty wink. *Maybe you shouldn't stay so close.*

I gave him a dirty look and purposefully sat a couple chairs away when we got to English. A girl can only stand so much temptation before cracking under the pressure.

A surge of unsettling air washed over me, and I glanced up to see Tara's arrival. She glared at me and brushed passed the others without making eye contact. Apparently, I wasn't the only one on her avoidance list. Natalie followed close behind. She spotted Daniel, and then took a seat as far away from him as possible. Like I said before, we had lots of small town drama.

Mrs. Murphy reminded us our term papers were due in seven days and counted for a quarter of our semester grade. "No exceptions," she emphasized. "If a trip to the hospital or a kidnapping occurs, I want a signed note from the appropriate authorities.

Normally, I might have laughed at her joke, but after the last six weeks I hesitated. If I'd learned nothing else, I knew now anything was possible.

Daniel mind messaged me after English, promising me more mental torture at lunch. I allowed myself to enjoy the moment before I began building up my nerve to face Brad. Since Mrs. Murphy had ended class early, the hallways were quieter than usual. Suddenly a hand clutched my shoulder. I barely managed to hold back a scream.

"What the…?" I demanded. To my surprise it was Misty.

"Eve! Come with me. I've got something for you that will blow your mind."

Mystified, I followed her without asking questions. She skipped down the hall, stopping at her locker, her huge dark eyes dancing in her face. "Look what I found."

Misty opened her locker and pulled out a small leather pouch. She emptied its contents gently into her hand, and I leaned over to see what she held. I inhaled sharply.

Lying in the palm of her hand was a necklace—a silver chain threaded through a half-dollar sized medallion. In the center of the medallion was a small silver disc inlaid with blue-green stones. Hovering above the disc were three crescent shaped moons. I recognized it instantly. Karillion.

"Where did you get this?" I stammered. "Who does it belong to?"

"You'll never believe it," she paused dramatically. "Apparently, the necklace belongs to you." At my confused look, she explained, "My dad found a box of my grandparents stuff packed away in our garage. When we went through it, we found an envelope with the words 'Deliver to Evelyn Hunter' written on the outside. My grandmother made jewelry, and my dad insisted this was her work."

I reached for the necklace. "Can I—can I take a look?"

"Sure. After all, it's yours. The design totally rocks. Do you have any idea what this image represents? It reminds me of the planet Earth, except for the three moons of course."

I cringed in preparation for yet another lie. "Not a clue. Your grandmother's work is remarkable. She must've created many beautiful pieces."

"She was a master designer, and her jewelry sold all over the Southwest. Grandfather often helped her design pieces, but she had the artist's touch to bring ideas to life. Both of my grandparents were visionary people."

Tears sprang to my eyes, and I fumbled to hide them. Whatever force governed the universe had arranged for this connection to be made. The necklace symbolized this divine governing force. The message was loud and clear. I swallowed hard to pull myself together. "Misty, why do you think your grandparents wanted me to have this?"

Instead of answering, she studied my face thoughtfully. Last period's classes had ended and students brushed passed us, hurrying to their various destinations. But we stood apart, isolated as if stranded on an island in a sea of humans.

"I'm not sure why, but I'm getting the feeling you know exactly why my grandmother made the necklace and left directions that it be given to you."

I started to protest, but she held up her hand to stop me. "I like you Eve, so I'm going to be honest. You're a terrible liar. You recognized the medallion the minute you laid eyes on it. But that's impossible since it's been buried in a box for at least ten years. Okay, so maybe you've seen one like it before. That's more likely, but I'm guessing it's not the medallion you recognized but the image it represents."

I stared at Misty, caught off guard by her perceptiveness. Her grandparents were not the only visionary ones. I needed an explanation fast. In our solar system, Mars has two moons while all the planets beyond Mars have many moons. No known planets matched the image on the medallion. I considered telling her I'd seen pictures of a fictional planet with three moons, but how could I explain her grandparents' familiarity with those pictures? To my relief, Brad appeared in the hallway.

I caught his eye and sent him a mind message. *I have never been so glad to see you!*

He frowned. *I thought we agreed on no telepathy at school?*

Help me, for heaven's sake!

"What's up girls?" he said, glancing down at the small object I held in my hand.

"Brad, you've got to see this! Misty brought me this necklace her grandmother made. She says it belongs to me."

Brad picked up the necklace as carefully as I had. "Wow, this is incredible. The three moons are trick. You're grandmother had a vivid imagination."

"Have you ever seen anything like it?" Misty asked him.

He appeared to consider her question. "I think I'd remember if I had. What does Eve have to do with this?"

"My dad and I found the necklace buried in a box of my grandparents' things. It was in an envelope marked 'Deliver to Evelyn Hunter,'" Misty explained.

"Well, Ridgway is a small town so your grandparents probably knew Eve as a little girl. Maybe they really liked her and wanted to leave her a special gift." Brad was a much better liar than I was, but I could tell Misty was not convinced.

"Maybe. Anyway, I need to get to class, so I'll catch you two later."

I reached out to touch her arm. "Misty, I feel guilty taking this. Are you sure you want me to have it?"

"You're its rightful owner. Keep it close. Perhaps you'll remember where you saw this image before." She sent me a pointed look then wandered away.

"Thanks for rescuing me. She insisted I knew more than I was saying—that I recognized the planet with the three moons. I don't know what I would've done if you hadn't showed up."

"Oh, so now I'm your knight in shining armor?" he asked.

I rolled my eyes. "Getting a bit cocky aren't we?"

"The evidence speaks for itself," he quipped.

"How do you think she knew I recognized the image on the medallion?"

"You're not the best liar, Eve. I'm sure she picked up on your hesitation."

"Funny, she said the same thing. Is it a good thing to be a bad liar?" I asked.

His expression was inscrutable. "I guess that depends on what you're trying to hide." He reached for my hand, but I managed to avoid him by pretending to search in my purse.

Spanish passed quickly and lunch turned out okay too. Ruth joined us at our table, and she kept Brad occupied most of the time. I couldn't believe the change that had come over her in the past couple weeks. What I didn't know at the time was that she'd had her own epiphany. From the time Jarak announced a ship was coming, she'd been convinced her mom was on the way home.

Daniel behaved himself through lunch and our last two classes. I thought it might be awkward having the two boys together but Daniel handled it perfectly. I suppose like Brad he'd had lots of practice in deception. Other than a few flirtatious mind messages, we stayed apart and avoided suspicion.

I drove over to see my grandmother after school to show her the medallion. My grandparents had given me a key card to the main gate and the residences of The Colony. The vibrations welcomed me like the soothing sound of beach waves crashing against the shore. Grandmother exclaimed with delight upon seeing the necklace. "It's exquisite! What extraordinary workmanship."

"Misty Meyer said she found it packed away, in an envelope marked 'Deliver to Evelyn Hunter'."

Grandmother gasped. "Marvelous!" She watched me thoughtfully as I gazed at the medallion. "You've been given a sign illuminating your mission, my dear. Can you have any doubt of your place among our people?"

"I felt something today when Misty gave it to me. Like I was destined to be right here, right now, for some purpose I can't imagine. I don't know what I'm supposed to do."

Grandmother put her arm around my shoulder. "The knowledge will come in time. You will receive the guidance you need. I promise."

"Thank you, Grandmother. When you say things like that, it's impossible not to believe them. I hope to have faith as strong as yours someday."

Daniel stopped by again Wednesday morning, and we spent an amazing hour together. He examined the medallion with the same reverence Grandmother had shown, running his fingers across the three Karillion moons.

"This is incredible. Misty's grandmother created this for you. She must've known who you were, and where you came from. Think of it!" His eyes wandered over me. "This medallion symbolizes your role as a powerful presence among our people. Eve, you need to consider that you may in fact, be the Chosen One."

"Don't start that again. I'm not some deliverer of the Karillions, but I'm willing to concede that this is some sort of sign. The ruler of the universe has sent me a cosmic message. He knows who I am and wants me to do something. I have no idea what that is, but I'm fairly open to suggestions. Grandmother promised me they'd come."

Daniel responded by pulling me into his arms and kissing me. It occurred to me that for once, Daniel had allowed me to have the last word, well, sort of.

Wednesday's afternoon basketball practice was cut short, and Daniel surprised me by meeting me as I was leaving the grocery store.

"Nice to see you, Mr. Winter," I said.

"You also, Miss Hunter," he replied, standing behind me and nuzzling my neck. "Have you got time for an afternoon study session?"

"Daniel, please. We agreed no public affection. Someone might see us."

He sighed. "Yeah, yeah. I know. Off to the cabin then?"

"Sure. Let's hope Brad doesn't decide to stop by."

"Would he stop by unannounced?"

"Probably not. He's upset with me because I don't think his mom is on her way to Earth."

"Why is he so convinced she's coming on the ship?" Daniel said.

"Simple. Because that's what he wants to believe."

Daniel followed me to the cabin and hung out for several hours. While we nestled in each other's arms, Brad sent him a text asking for a ride to evening practice. After tapping out a reply, Daniel said, "I'll be glad when we're out in the open. I feel like I'm cheating on my best friend."

"Yeah, I feel the same way. I promise I'll say something this weekend."

As Daniel was leaving, I asked him how he'd found me at the grocery store. He grinned wickedly. "I refuse to reveal my surveillance secrets."

"Brad says I have this tremendous energy that sends signals a long distance. He said my vibrations could stop a train in its tracks." I blushed, embarrassed at the comparison. "Was he making all that up? Or is that how you knew where to find me?"

Daniel drew me close, gazing into my eyes. "Brad didn't make it up, but that's not the whole truth. I will always be able to find you, Eve, even without the aid of your riveting energy field that drives me insane. I've been waiting for you since the day I was born."

He kissed my lips with an intensity that bordered on desperation. I was confused but responded without asking what he meant. After all, how many times does someone tell you they've been waiting for you their whole life?

Dad and Jakob Andersen made arrangements to drive out to Lone Cone in Mr. Andersen's Ford Super Cab. The second row of seats gave Brad, Ruth, and I plenty of room. My grandparents decided to drive out with the Winters. Erik's family agreed to take Sarah, Augustine, and Emily, much to Tara's consternation. An event of great magnitude was about to occur, and everyone felt the need to draw strength and courage from one another.

We arrived at the storage sheds, pulled out the snowcats, and bundled up for a chilly ride to where the colonists' ship landed twenty-five years ago. I desperately wanted Daniel by my side as I settled in for a bumpy ride. Instead, I snuggled next to my dad and squeezed his hand, startling him once again with my sudden show of affection. Brad flashed me an odd smile that seemed to be part approval and part jealousy.

On arrival, we cleared a place in the snow in order to set up a makeshift camp and build a few fires for the large group. My grandfather told us the Karillion ship generated enough heat to enable it to land successfully despite the snow drifts. We gathered around the fires, greeting one another in low voices. Everyone was strangely quiet as if we occupied a sacred place, and I imagined for the colonists, Lone Cone was hallowed ground.

Brad reminded me to stay close especially after the sun went down. He expected Mack to use the element of surprise when making his move. I agreed, but was pretty sure this was neither the time nor the place. Besides, I felt completely safe surrounded by aliens with super powers.

We placed chairs around one fire with Dad and my grandparents on my left and Brad, Ruth, and Mr. Andersen on my right. Daniel and his family were seated next to my grandparents. Erik, Sarah, Augustine, and Emily sat across from us with Erik's parents and his sisters, Maddie and Sam, separating him from Tara. Mack and his family set up at another fire site.

Daniel mind messaged several times but was careful not to single me out when our gang congregated. As the sun began to set, I caught his eyes upon me and returned the emotion reflected there. *We're here. This is actually happening.*

How are you holding up? he asked

Good, but our earthling friends look petrified.

Daniel made a face. *I can totally relate because I'm petrified too.*

Not possible—the great and mighty Daniel afraid of aliens?

Not afraid of aliens so much as the unknown. Aren't you?

Not really. Usually the unknown doesn't bother me too much. I'm too busy being afraid of the stuff I already know.

That's what I love about you Eve. You've got it all figured out.

Was he kidding? I gave him a puzzled look, not sure how to respond. If that's what he really thought, he was sorely mistaken. I was as clueless as the next person. Whoever said love is blind knew what he was talking about. Erik wandered over to talk to Daniel, and we ended our telepathic conversation.

The sun sank behind the mountains, painting the twilight sky in shades of orange, purple and pink. A winter moon rose slowly, replacing the sun's light with a soft white glow. The temperature dropped immediately, and everyone huddled closer to the fires.

As the clock drew closer to midnight a hush descended. I felt like Cinderella except I was running toward the magical moment that would change my life instead of running away from it. We scoured the skies, searching for the first glimpse of an approaching spaceship. Brad finally stood up and began making laps around the campfire circle.

You okay, Brad? I mind messaged him.

I can't sit still. This waiting is killing me, he replied.

You're not the only one.

I watched as Ruth left her spot by the fire and joined Brad in his relentless pacing. They marched silently, eyes on the ground, creating a circular path in the snow. They made a nice couple, lifting each other's burdens and sharing the pain of loss. I breathed a sigh of relief, realizing Brad would be fine without me.

Thousands of stars blanketed the black sky, undiminished by the glowing moon. Suddenly we heard a gasp then a shout. "I see it! Look over toward the west, the three o'clock quadrant." Multiple sets of eyes followed the voice's directions, anxious to locate the target. And then we saw it. A brilliant light streaked through the sky, headed our direction. Abruptly, it vanished from sight, and groans erupted from the crowd.

"They must've activated the infamous Star Trek cloaking device to avoid detection," one of the colonists joked. A few nervous laughs were heard.

The comment reminded me of what my dad told me about the Karillion's invisibility cloak. I'd entered a new world where all sorts of objects of fantasy were coming to life before my eyes. My companions and I gazed skyward, waiting impatiently. Our reward came as the outlines of a ship slowly emerged out of the darkness.

I stared up at the cold December sky, unable to believe what I was seeing. The nearly full moon, poised directly over Lone Cone Peak, had disappeared behind some passing clouds. But I didn't need the light of the moon to see what was coming.

The huge, bullet-shaped object glowed with a brilliant white light illuminating the sloping, snow-covered hills and the nearly frozen waters of Disappointment Creek. It descended quickly, and then hovered overhead. I watched as the ship divided in half then mushroomed into a circular shape in preparation for landing. Filled with wonder, I questioned my sanity, despite the obvious visual proof.

I heard several exclamations of awe behind me. Most of those cries of astonishment came from those who had spent their entire lives on Earth. Like me, they had never laid eyes on a Karillion spaceship. Others were too young to remember the alien aircraft they'd disembarked from. Extraterrestrial beings were landing before my very eyes. My reality anchor drifted away.

I had the strange sensation of playacting on a movie set—perhaps one of the cast members standing next to Richard Dreyfuss in *Close Encounters of the Third Kind*. I half-expected the movie's musical score with its haunting tones and beeps to begin playing in the background. But this was no movie. The aliens were here, and I, Eve Hunter, welcomed them.

Chapter 23

I'm not sure what I expected, but the vessel before me was undoubtedly alien. The gun metal-colored exterior revealed evidence of interstellar collisions with space debris. Thick windows lined the sides, and I could make out shadowy movements inside. Gray smoke surrounded the craft accompanied by an unfamiliar burning odor. Upon contact with the frozen ground, the spaceship's immense heat had created a large puddle of water.

After some of the smoke dissipated, our group moved forward as one, much more orderly than I'd have guessed. My grandparents and some of the Elders led the way. We trudged through the melted snow in a trance, hardly noticing our drenched boots. Hanging toward the back of the crowd with Dad and my friends, I noticed that Mack and the Larsens pushed their way to the front. Brad started forward as if to follow suit, but then slowed to remain with us.

After several minutes, a large portal opened on one side of the craft, and three figures emerged. Instead of shiny metallic spacesuits, they wore tightfitting uniforms closely resembling wetsuits. All three removed their sleek headgear, and the smaller figure furthest to the right stepped forward, placing a hand on Jarak's right shoulder in greeting. Two of them were male but the smallest one was undeniably a female.

I heard a strangled cry behind me. "Anika? It couldn't possibly be…is it you?"

Jakob Andersen stumbled forward, splashing through the icy puddle. He stopped in front of the striking red-headed woman for an instant, and then threw his arms around her.

I heard a second cry. "Mom?" Ruth brushed past us into the arms of her parents. The overflowing joy of this sweet family reunion touched everyone, and we pressed forward, enthusiastically greeting the visitors. Dad squeezed my hand, and we exchanged hopeful smiles. Ruth's mom had returned, and our time would come. We would see Mom again.

Brad moved closer to me, his face crushed with despair. Tears coursed down my cheeks mirroring his own. I hoped he could find a way to share in the Andersen's happiness instead of focusing on his own disappointment. Anika's return gave us all hope.

A tall, muscular alien with olive skin, salt-and-pepper hair, and a closely-cropped beard addressed us in a deep voice. His language was unintelligible to many of us so Jarak translated. "This is Elikah. His companions are Rakar and Anika." He smiled, his eyes shining with tears. "Many of you are well acquainted with Anika, as she accompanied us to Earth many years ago. Elikah has an urgent message to share with us."

My grandfather's face fell as Elikah continued speaking. The faces of the original colonists darkened, and many dropped their heads. Whatever was being said was definitely bad. After a few minutes, Elikah broke off and stepped back for Jarak to address us.

"As pleased as we are to reunite with our fellow Karillions, this is not a joyous occasion. Elikah's group has travelled here to warn us. Zaran has sent Commander Zorak and his soldiers on a mission to Earth. They are not far behind—a week, maybe two."

His voice wavered as he continued. "Widespread disease and limits on childbearing instituted by The Source have decimated our planet's population. The planet needs more young and healthy individuals to serve the more menial needs of society. Zaran seeks an influx of Earth's citizens to cover Karillion's deficiencies. The goal of Commander Zorak's mission is twofold. He's been instructed to use any means at his disposal to bring the colonists back to Karillion. In addition, he intends to collect human prisoners. With these prisoners he intends to establish a servant class—in his words—a genetically inferior race, devoid of the special gifts our people possess."

"What should we do? Our only defenses are our powers and some inferior weapons. These are trained soldiers. How can we stop them?" Mr. Andersen asked.

"Elikah and his crew managed to escape with a weapon stockpile, primarily stunners. These stunners should allow us enough time to incapacitate and capture Zorak's soldiers. If we are unable to detain them, then we'll have to negotiate. The lives of the colonists are no longer the only lives at stake. "

"Capture or negotiate? Why don't we simply exterminate them?" Mack's dad suggested in a contemptuous tone, his eyes hard and defiant. "We can't risk showing weakness when our families are being threatened. Force is the only language Zorak understands. It's time to acquire more firepower and take action. Zorak must be killed."

My grandfather must have been crushed to hear his son spoken of in such a callous manner. I cringed at Mr. Larsen's ruthless attitude toward my uncle, even if he was dangerous. But then I remembered Zorak had kidnapped my mother and stolen ten years of our lives together. Instantly, cold anger invaded my body, and I silently added my support to this proposed plan. We must kill Zorak and all his soldiers.

Jarak's voice rang out with authority, "We do not intend to kill anyone unless absolutely necessary. However, we should be prepared to defend ourselves so I want all colonists to be fully armed. Carry at least two weapons. After the soldiers arrive, no one goes anywhere alone. Zorak's standard methodology was always to divide and conquer. Division creates chaos—an ideal situation for evil to prosper. I believe the ideal solution would be to gather everyone to Terra Dyne, because it offers the best security."

The Elders and the visitors conferred for a few minutes, while the remaining colonists contemplated what the future might hold. Although I trusted my grandfather, I had no doubt Zorak would find a way to get to us. We were sitting ducks.

Jarak dismissed us with sobering words. "Let's prepare for departure. We'll meet at Terra Dyne this evening at six o'clock to discuss our plan of action. If anyone objects to moving our families behind the gates, please inform us of opposing viewpoints and come prepared to offer alternative suggestions. We'll need to work together to survive."

The new arrivals reentered the ship to gather their belongings and set the cloaking device, while the rest of us extinguished the fires and dis-mantled the camp. After meeting Ruth's mom, I searched for my friends in the looming darkness. The four of them stood transfixed, staring at the spaceship. Erik had his arm possessively around Sarah's shoulder. Augustine and Emily moved as if joined at the hip. I watched them, curious about their thoughts.

Sarah and Emily approached me as Erik and Augustine moved to gather up tarps. As usual, Sarah spoke first. "Eve, the colonists will defeat the evil aliens. We will do anything you want us to do. Ridgway's not much, but it is our town and our people. Despite the bad news the aliens delivered, the spaceship landing was the most incredible thing I could ever have imag-ined. How can I possibly go back to normal life after all *this*?"

I struggled to suppress my anger at Zorak and tried to focus on the miraculous event that had occurred. Taking a deep breath, I produced a believable smile. "It was beautiful, wasn't it? Now we know the universe has limitless opportunity. But you are right, our lives will never again be normal. We've all been changed forever."

Emily added in a choked voice, "We'll help the colonists kick the bad guys butt in any way we can. We are so grateful you've trusted us with your secret. This experience has no equal. Erik said you convinced your grand-father to let us come."

"Well, I didn't exactly have to convince him. He anticipated a request from Erik before I ever said anything. Besides, Jarak thinks you're wonderful humans."

Despite my lighthearted tone, conflicting emotions battled for supremacy. Which person was I—the angry, vengeful person or the peace-loving, forgiving one? I desperately needed some of that faith my grandfather was always talking about. There had to be some way for the colonists to overcome what appeared to be an insurmountable catastrophe.

Sarah and Emily embraced me, and tears filled my eyes once again. Although I'd only known them a short time, these girls were willing to risk their lives for me, for all of us. Sharing this experience bonded us in a way that could never be broken. Finding out you're not alone in the universe changes everything.

Dad and I escorted my grandparents to the snowcat with the Winters and Elikah. Daniel and I managed to exchange a few messages before departing for our separate vehicles.

Can you believe this is happening? I messaged. *Looks like you'll have to protect me from something a lot worse than grizzly bears.*

I'm surprised Zorak waited this long to return. From what I've heard he's not one to let go of something he wants.

What does he want?

The colonists. All of them. He wants us to acknowledge that his side has all the power.

Do you think we'll survive? I asked.

One way or the other, we will survive, Eve. You may get to see those three Karillion moons sooner than you expected.

I shuddered. *It's too soon. I'm not ready.*

You're forgetting one very important thing. I'll be by your side no matter where your journey takes you. We can do anything together.

I nearly ran to him and threw my arms around his neck, but concern for Brad held me back. This softer side of Daniel continued to surprise me.

See you at school Miss Chosen One, he teased.

I told you not to call me that, I grumbled.

Not a chance I'm gonna obey those orders, especially since now I have two reasons for using that name. You are THE Chosen One and MY Chosen One.

I suppose you think you're cute.

Uh, yep. Actually, I do.

Goodbye Daniel. Hope you can fit that big head of yours in the snowcat.

Don't worry. There's lots of room. I'll miss you. He winked and climbed inside.

The rest of the group piled into the other snowcats. Ruth's mom climbed in the front with Mr. Andersen, and Ruth sandwiched herself between them, while Dad shared the back with Brad and I. Anika remembered most of the English she'd learned while on earth, so she filled us in on the situation on Karillion. I couldn't quite think of her as Mrs. Andersen because she seemed so—well, *alien.*

She recognized my dad immediately, and subsequently realized I was Kara's daughter. Her husband introduced Brad as Leka's son, stopping awkwardly after the introduction.

Brad supplied the missing information with undisguised bitterness. "My dad, Chris Spencer, is a fugitive, and I've been staying at your house."

Anika answered without skipping a beat. "Well, Brad, you're welcome to stay at our house as long as you like." My admiration grew at her impressive diplomatic skills. She continued, a frown creasing her forehead, "Although it sounds like all of us will be relocating to Terra Dyne."

She leaned into the back of the snowcat and focused her beautiful blue-green eyes on the three of us. "I want all of you to know that Kara and Leka are safe. They wanted so badly to come back to Earth. We often shared our grief over the loss of our families. They are amazing women and my dearest friends. In fact, Brad, if it weren't for your mother I wouldn't be alive. She saved my life."

She stunned us into silence. Mr. Andersen spoke first. "What happened ten years ago Anika? When the three of you disappeared we suspected Zorak, but we had no way of communicating with our planet…." His voice broke. "We've missed you so much."

Anika laid her hand on his shoulder. "Not as much as I've missed you," she said.

"To answer your question, Zorak kidnapped us. He came to Earth primarily to get his sister, but hoped to capture Leka and me too. As you know, Leka was taken from Visitor Canyon like Kara, and I nearly drowned fighting against the blinding waters by Meyer's cabin. John rushed out when he saw the water spout and witnessed the whole thing."

"I knew John Meyer moved out of Ridgway because something scared him," I said. "Dad and I are renting his cabin."

"Oh? What happened to your house?" Anika asked.

"We moved to Denver after Kara disappeared. I had to get out of Ridgway." Dad admitted. "We moved back a couple months ago."

"Why now?" At my dad's puzzled expression, Anika explained. "Don't you find it a strange coincidence that after ten years of exile you returned in time to greet our ship?"

"I wouldn't exactly call it exile," Dad said, ignoring the coincidence part of her comment. "We came back at Jarak's urging after Eve's sixteenth birthday."

"Oh, I see," Anika said, addressing me. "Your gifts began to emerge and Jarak wanted you back among your people. That seems logical. What gifts do you possess?"

Uh oh. Brad could not find out I was a Healer. I squirmed in my seat, desperately hoping my dad wouldn't say anything. "I don't really know yet," I blurted out.

Anika smiled. "I understand. Developing talents is a lifelong process."

My dad changed the subject. "Why did Zorak want the three of you specifically?"

Without one ounce of false modesty Anika replied, "Because Tom, we are daughters of the Khalaheem. We are some of the most powerful beings our planet has ever produced."

For a second time, we were stunned into silence. This time it was Brad who ended it.

"Why didn't my mom come with you?"

"Brad, I apologize for your mother's absence. I know you miss her. Elikah, Rakar, and I were chosen by the resistance to warn the colonists. Since we're Movers, we're assigned to relocate heavy equipment in the spacecraft hangars. When Kara relayed a message to the Khalaheem about Commander Zorak's mission, we immediately made plans to steal a ship. The three of us had government clearance for the hangars, so the task fell to us. Leka would've risked her life to come with us, but she's assigned to a military hospital under tight security. She is a gifted Healer and has made a huge difference through the horrible epidemics we've experienced."

Brad reached over and clasped my hand, bowing his head in acceptance. My dad frowned, sending me a look of consternation that made me feel ashamed. He'd seen Daniel kissing me at the cabin. Alien-human telepathy would've come in handy at that particular moment. I weighed my dad's disappointment with Brad's need for comfort. Compassion won out, and I ignored my dad's glare. There would be time to explain things to him later.

"Mom, can Zorak force us to go back to Karillion?" Ruth asked.

"He intends to complete his mission. It is our job to figure out how to derail his plans. We need to exercise faith in the colonists' abilities."

"Do you think he would kill us to accomplish his purpose?" Brad asked.

Anika hesitated before answering. "Commander Zorak is capable of anything. He prefers to persuade with flattering words—and he's proved to be very successful at doing so—but he is not opposed to violence. As Jarak said, it will take all of us working together to survive."

"What if we want to return with Zorak?" Brad asked.

"Brad!" Mr. Andersen admonished. "How can you say such a thing?

You have no idea what it's like on Karillion."

"I want to find my mom. And honestly, life doesn't sound so bad on your planet. Everyone has a job and a safe place to live. There is no hunger, no poverty, and no inequality. Plus, no guns are allowed in the general population, so people can't shoot each other over nothing. Sounds like a great place to me."

"But Brad," Anika argued, "Everything we do is orchestrated. Our power to choose is practically nonexistent. Do you actually want the government dictating where you work, where you live, and who you live with? Thank God Kara, Leka, and I were not forced to take another spouse on Karillion and produce offspring. I'm not sure I could've endured being forced to betray the family I already had on Earth. Can you imagine living under such a system?"

"Well, no. Not that last part, but the other things don't sound so bad."

I was dumbfounded. I'd always assumed Brad felt like everyone else. This was a side of him I'd never seen. I had to find a way to make him understand.

"Brad, the colonists escaped for a reason," I said. "This is your life we're talking about. Your ability to live the life you choose. You told me you hate working on your Jeep. On Karillion your desires would be irrelevant. If the government decided it needed mechanics, you could be forced to repair engines for the rest of your life. Day after day you'd be forced to live out a life someone else chose for you. It would be pure hell."

Brad addressed Anika. "It can't be so rigid for everyone. What about those in power, those who are in charge? They must be able to direct their own lives."

"Of course the directors of The Source along with our government and military leaders have much freedom to choose their own courses."

"Well then, it's simple. I'd have to find a way to become one of those people."

"Would you be willing to pay the necessary price? Willing to sacrifice family and friends who disagreed with you?" Anika questioned.

Brad didn't answer, but the burning passion in his eyes chilled me to my very core.

We switched out the snowcat for Mr. Andersen's truck and drove the long trip back to Ridgway, bombarding Anika with questions. By the time

Dad and I reached our cabin, it was almost four in the morning. We fell into bed, and sleep mercifully engulfed both of us.

Three hours later we met in the kitchen for breakfast. For the first time ever, I lamented the fact that I was not a coffee drinker. Opting for the second best option to bring my exhausted body to life, I made some hot chocolate while awaiting the lecture I knew was coming.

"Eve, please tell me you are not dating both of those boys?" Dad said quietly.

"No, Dad. Well, not exactly. I'm breaking up with Brad today, I promise. I mean we weren't even going out exactly. I told him I wasn't ready for a relationship, but he thinks we're a couple anyway. I've been meaning to set things straight, but then he got shot and I felt sorry for him. I decided to wait until after the ship landed, because I knew he'd be disappointed when his mom didn't show up. And then, a few nights ago Daniel called and things sort of escalated between us." I paused to take a breath. To my surprise, my dad started laughing.

I frowned. "Dad, this isn't funny. We've got huge problems with rogue aliens racing through space in order to kidnap us. Meanwhile, I'm preoccupied with finding a way to keep Brad's sanity intact while trying to salvage a little self-respect. I don't want to hurt him, and I'm afraid what he'll do when I break up with him. Not to mention what will happen when he discovers I'm dating Daniel."

Dad's expression turned sober. "You're in a sticky spot. But deceiving Brad is still wrong, and the sooner you rectify the situation the better. Honestly Eve, his tirade last night was disturbing. I'm afraid that young man will do whatever it takes to get what he wants. Heaven help the person who stands in his way."

I nodded my head in agreement, finished my breakfast, and gave Quaz some attention before Dad took him out for a quick walk. Exhaustion slowed me down to a crawl, but once I stepped outside, the cold jolted me into increasing my speed. I threw my backpack in the passenger seat of my Subaru, rehearsing the words I planned to say to Brad after school. As I turned the key in the ignition, an image flashed into my mind.

Brad and I stood in a dark, damp old building surrounded by people I didn't recognize. My heart hammered in fear. I turned sideways seeking reassurance from Brad, but his eyes stared directly forward. That's when I noticed his hand gripped around my arm like a vise.

My sight cleared as I tried to shake off my terror. The vision depicted an unfamiliar scene, definitely not a flashback. Great, I thought irritably. On top of everything else, sleep deprivation was producing hallucinations. How ridiculous. Brad would never hurt me.

Chapter 24

For the first time in weeks other than during his hospital stint, Brad didn't meet me in the parking lot. After my weird brain malfunction earlier, his absence seemed like an omen.

Opening up my backpack to check my phone, I found a text saying he'd be late for school.

I scolded myself for making up problems when I had enough to handle already.

Daniel met me in the hall. "Good morning, Miss Hunter. You look lovely as always." He leaned down to whisper, "Despite the all-nighter you pulled entertaining aliens."

Keeping my voice low, I responded, "Wow, such a charmer! You must've taken a few lessons from Erik. I like it. You're not looking so bad yourself, Mr. Winter—considering you were also a participant in last night's festivities. Walk me to class?"

His green eyes glowed warmly. "With pleasure." We trudged wearily to Pre-Calculus, drawing strength from each other.

"Aren't you afraid Brad will see us together?" he asked on the way.

"He texted me and said he's running late. This deception has gone on long enough. I've decided to break up with him this afternoon."

"Are you going to tell him about us?"

"I don't know. Maybe I'll hold off on that part. Either way, it's going to be ugly."

Brad showed up halfway through class, looking as exhausted as the rest of us. He took an open seat next to me and squeezed my shoulder in greeting. I flashed him a weak smile. Sarah kept nodding off, and Mr. Ayers actually had to wake her up when he asked her a question. If tests weren't coming up before Christmas break, most of us probably wouldn't have come to class. When the bell rang, I told Brad we needed to get together after school.

At the end of the day, I exited the school's front entrance and saw him leaning against my Subaru. He gave me a crooked smile, and my heart ached as I contemplated what was to come. I suggested we head out to the Reservoir, but when he offered to drive, I said I'd rather follow him in my own car.

His face tightened. "Fine. Have it your way."

Ridgway Reservoir sparkled in the bright sunlight, a brilliant jewel nestled amidst a forest of dark green pines. The blue sky shone picture perfect, contrasting sharply with the pure, white snow. I thought back to the first time we'd met there, not long ago although it seemed like another life time.

Brad pulled on his jacket and gloves as he exited the Jeep. "What's up, Eve? Why did you bring me all the way out here?" His voice had an unmistakable edge although he tried his best to sound casual, as if meeting out here was a regular occurrence. He was smarter than that.

I exhaled noisily. "It's not going to work between us Brad."

"That's it? 'It's not going to work?' Couldn't you have come up with something a little better?" His voice oozed with bitterness.

I struggled to explain. "I felt a connection to you from the beginning, even that first night at The Well when I thought you were crazy. You are so handsome and passionate. We have this strong attraction between us, but the more we're together, the more I realize we're two different people. I'm sorry. I care about you, but I don't feel the way you want me to feel."

"Why am I not surprised? My life's been on a crash course for a few weeks, so why should I expect anything different from our relationship?"

"Brad, please don't be angry."

He sat down on a snow-covered bench and put his head in his hands, oblivious to the cold, wet surface. "I'm not angry, Eve. I'm just tired—tired of nothing ever working out right."

I sat down beside him, wincing as moisture invaded the back of my jeans. We sat in silence watching the tranquil waters of the Reservoir. He leaned his head back wearily.

"Please don't say 'Can we still be friends?' or I think I'll barf."

I laughed. "Barf? Who uses that word?" Then I said gently, "I promise I won't say it."

"I've still got your back," he said.

"There's no doubt in my mind," I replied.

We stayed by the water until the sun began to set and the temperature dropped. We discussed Commander Zorak's mission and Jarak's plan to protect the colonists. Brad thought we should at least listen to what Zorak proposed, whereas I thought even being on the same planet with him was terrifying. He repeated his plans to travel to Karillion and find his mom, and I listened without judging, wondering why I no longer had the same desires. When I'd initially heard my mother was alive, I'd had an identical reaction. But things had changed. For now I knew my place was here on Earth. Someday, Mom and I would be reunited.

Sinking into the driver's seat of the Subaru, I breathed a sigh of relief. The dreaded blowup I'd envisioned had not materialized. Somehow we'd emerged still friends and virtually unscathed. Brad waved, threw his Jeep into reverse, and drove off.

I sent a quick text to Daniel saying I had talked to Brad. My stomach sunk when he asked if I'd told him about us. Not eager to defend my lack of courage, I texted back a terse 'No' and said I'd catch him at the game.

I followed the route Brad had taken up the winding road to Terra Dyne for the colonists' meeting. We entered the meeting hall together, and then parted with bittersweet smiles as he went to find the Andersens and I sought out my dad.

"Well, I broke it off," I said immediately upon seeing him.

"How did it go?"

"Not near as bad as I expected," I replied with a huge sigh of relief.

"You know, Eve, it's usually not the ordeals we anticipate that derail us, it's those unexpected ones."

I clasped his hand in mine. "My dad, the philosopher."

My grandfather stood at the same podium he'd occupied five days earlier. Grandmother, the Elders, and the newcomers shared the stage. I longed for Daniel to be there, but he and Erik had a basketball game. A bunch of us were headed over to the high school after the meeting. The room buzzed with conversation, some friendly, some hostile. It didn't take an abacus to figure out the colonists were not all on the same page.

"I will dispense with the formalities," Jarak began. "Elikah, Rakar, and Anika have informed us with regard to the current situation on our planet. As we disclosed early this morning, conditions have deteriorated, and the people of Earth have been targeted as potential Karillion slaves. Commander Zorak views humans as an inferior race. The circumstances for the colonists, as well as our friends and neighbors are grave. We will not be forced back to Karillion, and we cannot allow Earth's people to be harvested."

"After much discussion, we've decided we will listen to what Zorak has to say. We hope to discern his true intentions and devise a plan to stop him. If he insists on executing his mission to kidnap humans, we'll attempt to detain him and the soldiers who accompany him. Both sides will possess physical weapons and Movers; however, since the numbers of his associates are unknown, predicting the outcome is impossible."

"Meanwhile, Terra Dyne was designed to be a fortress. All quadrants will be sealed off from one another, and immobilizing gas canisters controlled by remote activators will be placed in every room. Colonists should familiarize themselves with the escape hatches. Everyone will be provided with a stunner, so make sure you know how to use one. As I suggested at Lone Cone, all families should make plans to move into this facility. Of course, you are free to choose otherwise, but if you remain outside the gates, we cannot protect you."

My grandfather ran his hand through his thick white hair. He looked ten years older than he had at Sunday dinner. Grandmother's elegant face was somber and lined with worry. The colonists next to me gripped each other's hands tightly—a scenario duplicated throughout the room. I braced myself for what Jarak planned to say next.

"Despite our best intentions, we expect casualties. Our families and our freedom are at risk, and we cannot stand idly by. We have no foreknowledge of the ship's date of arrival, so we expect everyone to remain vigilant. We'll stay in constant contact. Telepathic channels should remain accessible."

Jarak finished and opened the meeting up to questions. I surveyed the room, pleased to see the Andersens reunited and Brad by their side. Erik's family, the Nielsens, appeared calm, all except Tara who looked hostile. Mack slumped in a chair next to his family, feigning disinterest. If anyone decided to jump ship with Zorak's bunch, it would be Mack. Not surprisingly, Mr. Larsen was the first to speak.

"Many of us possess weapons—lethal weapons, not stunners. Are the Elders in agreement on the issue of deadly force?"

"Yes Daran, but only if necessary. We're trying to avoid a bloodbath; hence, stunners are the weapon of choice in addition to our individual gifts. We'll do what is necessary to protect our families and the citizens of Ridgway. As I said, we hope to convince Zorak to abandon his plan, so we can resolve this peacefully."

Although I didn't like violence, a part of me wanted Zorak to pay for what he'd taken from me, regardless of whether he ditched his mission and returned to Karillion.

Mr. Larsen laughed harshly. "Resolve this peacefully? Jarak, I'm afraid twenty-five years on Earth has addled your senses. This is Zorak we're discussing. The word 'peace' is not in his vocabulary." Gasps echoed throughout the room at his audacity.

My grandfather appeared unruffled. "You are entitled to your opinion, Daran. However, twenty-five years have also passed for Zorak; perhaps he is not the same person we remember." The conference hall erupted with loud voices of disbelief. Dad and I exchanged our own looks of skepticism. A trickle of doubt nagged at me. Could Jarak's love for his son be affecting his judgment?

"Quiet, please," Jarak said. "Elikah has informed us that Zorak's allegiance to Zaran and The Source may be weakening. He has sought input from many citizens on governing policies and has instituted lenient restrictions and more moderate punishments. Some of the Karillions believe he can be turned to our side."

I couldn't stop the words that shot from my mouth. "This is crazy! Have you forgotten that coming to Earth and kidnapping humans was Zorak's plan? He wants to force the colonists back to Karillion and turn earthlings into slaves. How can you believe he's changed? It's ludicrous to think of him as anything other than our mortal enemy."

Many of the colonists nodded in agreement. Brad sent a telepathic message of support. Even Mr. Larsen smiled in my direction. This last unexpected ally made me reconsider the rash words I'd spoken.

Jarak listened to my words with the same respect and patience he'd shown Mr. Larsen. When he responded, his manner was calm and a touch optimistic. "I understand our theories may seem implausible. Perhaps you are correct. We shall see." He stood, silent and majestic, seeming to increase in stature before my eyes as he concluded his remarks.

"Sometimes we embark on a course of action for a specific reason when in fact, the actual reason for that course of action is something entirely different from what we intended. Perhaps Zorak will discover something on Earth that changes his mind."

The faces around us were a mixture of comprehension and confusion. My face belonged to the second group. I pondered Jarak's words as he continued answering questions in his pleasant, composed voice. I didn't believe Zorak would listen to reason. Anyone who could tear a mother from her child was pure evil.

The meeting ended, and I rushed to my grandfather to apologize for my outburst. I felt ashamed for challenging him in front of everyone. He surprised me with a forgiving hug.

"Not a problem, dear one," he said. "You have good reason to distrust Zorak."

"Do you really think he could be persuaded to change his mind?" I asked.

"I do not know," he confessed. "Try to remember that few people are wholly evil. Even those who appear to be beyond redemption can often surprise us."

I was not convinced. I wandered over to say goodbye to Brad. Several families made plans to move into Terra Dyne over the next few days, the Andersens among them. Brad refused to relocate, and I could not persuade him otherwise. Moving was an easy option for Dad and I, especially since my grandparents would be with us. We'd have to figure out what to do about school; fortunately, Christmas break was two weeks away. No one had any idea how long we'd have to stay in the colonists' fortress.

I dropped Dad at the cabin and dashed to the gym to catch what was left of the basketball game. The second half had already started when I arrived. Finding Sarah and Emily in the crowd, I hurried over, taking a seat on the bleachers.

"Where's Brad?" Emily asked.'

"We broke up," I said, "Although technically we were never actually together."

Sarah guffawed. "You keep telling yourself that, sister. Everybody else sure thought you were an item."

"Yeah," I admitted. "Brad did too."

"Did you have a fight?" Emily asked.

"No. I really like Brad, but we're different people. It's like he wants out, and I just got in. He can't be happy with what he has, and he's always the victim."

"Seriously, Eve, if anyone's a victim, its Brad," Sarah said.

"And I feel bad for him, but like my dad always says 'just because you're a pig doesn't mean you have to wallow in the muck.'"

"Guess if you're a pig you probably like being in the muck," Emily giggled.

"Exactly. Sometimes I think Brad enjoys the muck a little too much."

"Sorry you guys didn't work out." Emily said.

"Things are good. Stay tuned for the latest developments."

"Such as?" Sarah raised her eyebrows, but I refused to say more. "Well, glad you made it. The meeting must've gone okay?" When I nodded, Sarah continued, "I feel like a total zombie. I don't know how the boys can run around the basketball court. I'm so tired I can hardly walk."

"Ditto that for me. This may go down as the longest day of my life."

"Augustine slept the entire trip from Norwood to Ridgway last night. That boy snores like a champ," Emily said.

Sarah and I laughed. "How could he possibly sleep after what happened?" Sarah asked.

Emily shook her head. "Augustine could sleep through an air raid. You should see me try to wake him up when my parents come home early."

Exhausted or not, the boys played well, and Ridgway was on top. Daniel, Erik, and Augustine orchestrated their moves smoothly, with little sign of fatigue. I noticed Brad come in and sit with the team on the bench. Ruth was nowhere in sight. I wondered how the Andersens planned to explain the reappearance of Ruth's mom since the townspeople thought she was dead. Erik's family had arrived before me, but Tara didn't show up until the fourth quarter, closely followed by Mack. I tried to focus on the court, but like Sarah, I was exhausted.

After the game, Daniel's eyes locked on mine, taking my breath away. *Hey gorgeous,* he messaged me.

I glowed with pleasure, returning his potent gaze with an equally admiring glance. Who knew a sweaty basketball uniform could be so sexy? I could stare at him all night.

You look magnificent, even if you are a sweaty jock. I've missed you, I messaged back.

Not as much as I've missed you, he replied with a grin, brushing his hair from his eyes. It took every ounce of willpower I possessed to drag my eyes away from him. Too late, I realized Brad had been watching us. His eyes narrowed, and he stalked from the gym.

Daniel! Brad knows! He was watching us! I messaged.

Oh man, this is not good. Do you want me to talk to him?

No, I should've told him earlier today. I feel awful. I'm going after him.

Eve, be careful, Daniel cautioned.

Don't be silly, this is Brad we're talking about.

I told the girls I needed to talk to Brad, and I'd be right back. Sarah and Emily were busy congratulating the team, so I figured they'd missed the exchange between Daniel and me along with Brad's reaction. I ran to the parking lot searching for Brad's Jeep.

I saw him as he started to back out.

"Brad, wait!" I cried.

"I have nothing to say to you," he said.

"Please listen to me. It's not what you think."

"Oh yeah? What is it then? You lied to me. You dumped me so you can lock lips with Daniel."

"I didn't lie to you. I mean this thing with Daniel started a few days ago. I knew you and I weren't going to work out before you got shot, before my grandfather told everyone about the ship. I should've said something then."

"Oh so now you're saying you felt sorry for me? Eve, you don't know what you want. All I know is you sure didn't act like you weren't interested during our little make out session at Terra Dyne."

"I know, and I thought maybe I could feel how you wanted me to, but I…."

Brad cut me off. "Save it, Eve. I'm tired of your lies. Why don't you go find Danny Boy and leave me alone."

I stumbled back into the gym. Sarah and Emily were gathering up their stuff. I sat down heavily on the bleachers, burying my head in my hands.

"I've made a mess of everything. Brad is furious and thinks I'm a two-timing uh—well, you know."

"It can't be that bad," Emily said. "Thirty minutes ago you told us you guys were good."

"We were good until he saw me, um—*communicating* with Daniel after the game."

"The green-eyed jealousy monster rears its ugly head."

"Exactly. What should I do?"

"Look, Eve, not to be callous," Sarah said, "but I think you've got bigger problems. Zorak and his compadres are coming to tear The Colony apart and kidnap a bunch of unsuspecting earthlings. Let Brad worry about Brad. Right now, you need to take care of yourself. Come on, let's go."

I nodded wearily. "I can't deal with the crowd at The Well tonight. Wait a minute while I tell Daniel I'm going home."

"So I take it you guys are more than just friends?" Emily said. Once again I nodded and headed over toward Daniel.

When I reached his side, he caressed my arm and pulled me toward him. I wanted to lay my head on his shoulder despite the curious looks we were getting from all directions, but I refrained. I couldn't take any more questions right now about my love life.

I spoke in a low whisper. "Brad took off. He thinks I dumped him for you. He hates me."

"I'm sure he doesn't hate you. Give him some time to cool off."

"We don't have time, Daniel. We'll need to be united when Zorak shows up."

"Brad is hurt. There's nothing you can say to make him feel better."

"Okay, well I'm going home. Want to join me?"

"I'd love to. Let me ditch the guys, and I'll see you soon. We only have a few days of freedom before we're imprisoned in Terra Dyne where everyone will be watching us."

I smiled. "At least we'll be together in prison. Don't be too long."

I joined the girls at the gym's exit, and we walked out to our cars. I couldn't get home fast enough.

Daniel was half an hour behind me. He stepped in the front door and enclosed me in his arms. His hands caressed my back as he touched my lips with his. I ran my fingers through his soft, silky hair urging his head toward mine. We kissed urgently, with a desperation drawn from forcing ourselves to be apart. Thank goodness we wouldn't have to hide any longer.

"This is the perfect ending to a very long day." I whispered.

"I can't believe the Karillion ship landed less than twenty-four hours ago. It seems like weeks. I don't know how everyone made it through the game."

"Pure adrenalin," I said. "I'm glad your family decided to move to Terra Dyne. I can't imagine being there without you. Brad said he didn't plan to relocate."

"I'm not surprised. Erik says he's not coming either. He doesn't want to leave Sarah and her family unprotected."

"Are his parents okay with his decision? I wouldn't let my son run loose with rogue aliens kidnapping whoever they can find."

"Erik's adamant about his decision. He will not leave Sarah. At least he's a Mover and a strong one too. He'll be okay."

"Daniel, how can we possibly keep everyone safe?"

He pulled me closer, stroking my hair. "I have no idea."

A couple hours later, Daniel left for home. The night stars glittered in the peaceful winter sky as we kissed goodnight. Unbeknownst to our friends and neighbors, an alien ship raced toward Earth, bringing danger to our unsuspecting little town. The good thing about having a Seer for a grandfather is finding out things will occur before they actually do. The bad thing is you have a tendency to become a little overconfident. Even a Seer can't see everything.

Saturday morning I had to drag myself out of bed so I could take Quaz for a final run before imprisonment. Dad was still sleeping, and I wanted to let him rest. I wasn't supposed to run alone but this would be my last opportunity for who knew how long. Daniel had given me courage, and I felt invincible.

The sun shone impossibly bright, reflecting off the blanket of white. Birds chirped noisily, oblivious to the chilly air. Snow crunched beneath my feet as I followed Quaz through the woods. Running through a mental list of everything I wanted to bring to Terra Dyne, I neglected to pay attention to my surroundings.

Suddenly a dark wave of energy engulfed me, and I came to an abrupt stop. "Quaz, hold up," I shouted. We were not alone. Quaz began barking furiously, and I scolded myself for not heeding my grandfather's warnings.

Mack stepped from behind some trees to our left. "Look who I found. Jarak's Chosen One out here all alone. I would've thought you had more sense."

"What do you want, Mack?" I demanded, not sure if I was more scared or angry.

"Must I repeat myself? Let me make it simple. This is your last chance. Go back to the cabin and convince your dad to leave. Today. Tell him you're scared; tell him you hate it here, whatever you have to do. I'm planning to get on that next ship, and I want you out of here so you can't screw everything up."

Quaz growled low in his throat, baring his teeth. I urged him to be quiet, afraid Mack would hurt him. "What are you talking about? I have no plans to go to Karillion. And why should you care if I do?"

I felt a surge of energy slam my body against a tree knocking the wind out of me. Mack advanced toward me, clamped his hands on my arms, and brought his cold eyes inches from mine. He practically spit his venomous words in my face.

"If Zorak finds out your Kara's daughter, he'll make you his primary target. My parents said he knows all that Khalaheem BS about a Chosen

One. I refuse to watch any Karillions drool over Jarak's little protégée. So actually, my naïve little friend, I'm helping you. Now get out!"

He released me, and Quaz and I ran.

I plowed through the cabin door, slammed it shut, and fell to my knees on the floor, sobbing. Dad rushed to my side from the kitchen.

"Eve, what is it? Where have you been? Are you all right?"

"We went for a run…Mack found us…He told me to come home, get you, and get out before it's too late. He means it this time." Quaz whimpered and laid his head on my lap.

"What is that boy's problem? Did he touch you?"

I took off my jacket and pulled up my sleeves. Bruises were already beginning to form where he'd gripped my arms.

"I swear I'll kill him. No one lays a hand on my daughter," Dad vowed.

"No Dad, he's too dangerous. Let's just pack our stuff and go to Terra Dyne."

Dad reluctantly agreed. "My gun should protect us. We should never have come back here. I am no match against the aliens' powers. You would've been safe in Denver. Do you know how frustrating it is to be unable to protect my own daughter?"

"I'm sorry you feel so helpless, but Dad we're exactly where we're supposed to be. I'm certain of it. Don't worry. We'll figure something out."

We packed in twenty minutes, gathering up computers, clothes, and books. Taking one last look around, my heart dropped. The cabin had become our home. I would miss this quirky little hideaway. Calling to Quaz, I locked the door and climbed into the Tahoe, on the move once again.

I texted Daniel on the drive, telling him we were on our way to Terra Dyne. I warned him to steer clear of Mack because he'd crossed the line, but I dodged his request to elaborate. I didn't want Daniel out there looking for blood like my dad wanted to do. My grandparents met us at the entrance to their ultramodern haven. The walls seemed to close in on me before I even stepped through the doors.

The day started out well enough with my grandparents surprising me by showing us the colonists' original spacecraft. I climbed inside and combed over every inch of it, thrilled to be so close to an actual object from outer space. Afterwards, we had a nice lunch in the company's cafeteria before everyone scattered to take care of various projects. Daniel had to help his family pack, and then had a basketball game in Ouray that night so I wouldn't see him until late.

I managed to entertain myself all afternoon by exploring Terra Dyne, at least the parts I could gain access to. It was even more massive than I'd imagined. Any time I wanted to take Quaz outside, I had to find a body-guard so long walks were out. I tried doing some homework but my mind kept creating disastrous scenarios, and I couldn't concentrate.

By the time we met for dinner, I was positively stir-crazy. Hopefully our lockdown would be of short duration. I had no clue how anyone endured a prison sentence. We were the first ones to arrive, so when my dad and grandparents disappeared after eating, I found myself alone once again. Quaz and I had just settled down in front of a huge television screen when my phone rang.

"Eve, it's Brad. Where are you?"

"I'm up at Terra Dyne with my dad. Mack confronted me while I was running this morning and told me to get out. This is as far as we made it."

"I thought you might be up there already," Brad said. Surprisingly, he didn't make any comments about Mack's threats. "I need you, Eve. Can you get away?"

"Last night, you called me a liar and said you were done talking to me."

There was a long pause on Brad's end. "I know, but…I don't know who else to turn to for help. Please, I need you. You said you had my back, re-member? It wasn't that long ago."

"Now you're trying to make me feel guilty. Tell me what's going on, or I'm going to hang up."

He responded after another long hesitation. "I found my dad, and he needs help. You have to come right away, and you can't say a word to anyone."

I gasped. "Is he hurt? Did someone shoot him?"

"That's all I'm going to say over the phone. Can you help me?"

"Of course, but I've got to figure out how to get out of here. It won't be easy."

"Okay I'll meet you at the front gate. Don't say a word to anyone."

I pulled on my heavy hooded jacket and snuck out of a side door, somehow managing to avoid the cameras which seemed to be everywhere. Alarms went off in my head warning me this was a bad idea, but I ignored them. Crouching next to the building, I peered through the darkness seeking the closest cluster of pines. I had no idea where the outdoor cameras were or if they were continuously monitored. Taking a deep breath, I ran for the cover of trees, more convinced with every step that I was making a huge mistake.

Brad was outside the gate as promised. I had to use my key card to get out and could only hope no alert sounded whenever the gate was opened. Brad's black Jeep camouflaged his shadowy form rendering him nearly invisible. I peered through the Jeep's tinted windows trying to see if his dad was inside. Although he'd sounded upset on the phone, Brad didn't seem to be in any hurry to get going. The darkness made it impossible to see his face.

"What's the emergency? Your dad's not in the Jeep, is he?"

He shook his head but didn't answer me. I persisted, my voice rising with frustration, "Tell me what's going on, or did you invite me out here for a little small talk?"

"That's unlikely," he finally said in an odd voice, "especially since you and I have nothing small to talk about."

"Look Brad, I get it. You're angry. Take me to your dad so we can figure out what to do. I need to get back before someone discovers I'm missing."

He shot me a strange look. "You're right. Get in. He's hiding out on Dallas Creek Pass."

Chapter 25

Brad pulled onto the highway. I waited a few minutes in silence, hoping he'd offer some information. Watching his profile as he kept his eyes glued to the road, I sensed something out of the ordinary. Although he'd always been a confident driver, he seemed to have lost his cool. His eyes darted from side to side, scouring the trees lining the road, as if he expected something to jump out into our path. Finding his dad must've messed him up.

"I can't imagine what you're going through, Brad, seeing your dad after what happened must be beyond tough. What can I do to help? Is he hurt?"

Brad jumped to his dad's defense. "He shot me because he was scared and confused. When he realized what he'd done, he had to run. People do a lot of things that surprise us." He looked at me accusingly.

I felt terrible. "I should've told you about Daniel while we were out at the Reservoir. I swear we've only been seeing each other a few days. I'm sorry. I never wanted to hurt you."

His voice shook with his reply. "You know the worst part is I allowed myself to dream we had a future. After I heard about the ship, I envisioned us traveling through space and building a new life together on Karillion."

"That was your dream, not mine. The only reason I wanted to go to Karillion was to find my mom and bring her back here. Earth is my home."

"Well, Eve, life doesn't always work out the way we planned."

I let his comment slide and turned the conversation back to his dad. "You still haven't told me if your dad is hurt, and what I can do to help."

Brad spoke slowly, mechanically, staring straight ahead. "He had a bad fall and ripped his leg up pretty bad. Rumor has it you saved your dog in Denver, so I thought maybe you could heal him."

"You knew about Quazimodo?"

"Surprised? You know it makes me sick to think you wouldn't even tell me about your powers. What did I do to turn you against me, Eve? Why couldn't you trust me?"

The conversation was taking a nasty turn. I hastened to defend myself. "I didn't turn against you. And I did, I mean I *do* trust you. I'm here, aren't I? I didn't tell you because I'm not sure I can heal anyone. When Quaz had his accident, I just reacted. Maybe he wasn't hurt as bad as we thought."

"Whatever."

"So you called me because you thought I could heal your dad? He doesn't even like me, remember?"

Brad shrugged. "Everyone else is at the game in Ouray."

"Great. Now there's a vote of confidence." I turned my face toward the window, not wanting to argue anymore. Maybe if I could help his dad he'd forgive me.

Ten minutes later we pulled off the highway onto a snow packed road near the top of Dallas Creek Pass. Brad shifted the Jeep into four wheel drive, and we bounced all over the road for about half a mile. The wind howled as we got out in front of a large storage barn that looked like no one had been there for years. I could see vehicle tracks in the snow disappearing behind the building. Brad drew a flashlight from his jacket pocket and opened the door, beckoning for me to enter. Again the warnings sounded in my head, but I proceeded.

I stepped inside struggling to see anything in the eerie blackness. "Mr. Spencer?" I called out as Brad swept his flashlight along the walls. A figure burst from the shadows seconds before a heavy thud slammed into my chest and shock waves spread through my body. I heard Brad yell something as I slumped to the floor and darkness descended.

The first thing I remember when I came to is how cold I felt. I shivered uncontrollably, and my hands and feet were frozen. Disoriented, I reached for something to cover myself up with and realized two things: my arms and legs were wrapped with duct tape, and I had a nasty bump on my head. The memory of a blow to the chest surfaced, and my shaking intensified. I had no idea where the shot had come from, or how long I'd been out. I could see the faint outline of a door but no other visible light, so I assumed it was still night.

Then I heard arguing outside the door. With horror, I recognized the voices of Brad and Tara. I couldn't believe they were my kidnappers.

"You should've told me what you planned," Brad said.

"What else were you going to do, convince her to let you tie her up?" Tara shot back.

"At least you could have warned me before you shot her so I could catch her before she fell. She probably has a concussion."

"Oh big deal. You weren't so worried about a little bump on her head when we devised this plan. I seem to remember you saying she needed to know what the pain of betrayal felt like."

"I meant emotionally, Tara. Mack insisted she would not be hurt. I should've known I couldn't trust you."

I cringed. Brad had aligned himself with Tara and Mack. He must really hate me.

Tara's voice dripped with animosity. "Listen Brad, sometimes things don't go as planned. You of all people should know that."

I could feel Brad's anger burn though the walls from my position on the floor. Was Tara trying to antagonize him? I didn't know whether a repeat performance of the cafeteria scene would be good or bad. Two Movers could probably do a lot of damage to each other.

Apparently Brad decided to ignore her baiting, at least for now. "I'm going in to check on her. If she's not awake soon, she's in trouble. That bump might have caused real problems."

The door swung open and Brad came through. I pretended to be asleep but the shaking gave me away.

"I'm sorry, Eve. I didn't mean for you to get hurt." He stroked my hair, and I winced as his hand brushed the knot on the back of my head. Tears ran down my cheeks.

"Why did you do this? I can't believe you hate me so much," I sobbed.

"I don't hate you. Everything will be okay. I'll get you a blanket from the Jeep."

"Okay?" I choked. "I'm tied up on the floor of some freezing cold barn with a horrible headache, and you're telling me everything's going to be okay? What's going to happen to me?"

Tara entered and Brad scowled at her, ignoring my question. "You can leave now. I told the Andersens I was going camping this weekend, so I'm staying with Eve."

"I'm covered too. My parents think I'm out for a last shopping spree with the girls before locking myself in Terra Dyne. Besides, I thought we decided to switch off watching our valuable prisoner," Tara smiled maliciously.

"Change of plans. I don't trust you to keep her safe."

"Well, you're stuck with me. I'm not leaving until Mack shows up."

Frustration overruled my fear. "Can anyone tell me what's going on? If you're taking me somewhere, let's get it over with."

"Gladly, Miss Chosen One. As soon as transport becomes available, you are taking a very long trip. Actually, all of us are taking a long trip—to Karillion," Tara said, smiling in triumph.

"What are you talking about? Are you planning to steal Elikah's ship?"

"No, we're not interested in his ship, although we did manage to steal a few of his stunners—highly effective weapons, I might add." She was enjoying this.

"Then how do you plan to get there?" I asked.

"Why, your Uncle Zorak, how else? He wants the same thing we want—the colonists return to Karillion."

"So you're going to keep me captive until he shows up?"

Tara's smile widened, and I was instantly reminded of the scene in which The Grinch has a wonderful, awful idea. She looked so pleased a twinge of terror broke through my wall of anger. "That is the plan. Fortunately for all parties considered, we don't have long to wait. Zorak's already here."

I shot a panicked looked at Brad, and he nodded to confirm Tara's words. "Mack's out at Lone Cone. He had a feeling Zorak would arrive sooner than expected. His parents taught all their children the Karillion language, so Mack can communicate directly with him. He contacted us as soon as their ship landed and told us to bring you up here."

"Why are you doing this to me, Brad?"

"Tara overheard our argument after the game and told Mack we'd broken up. He texted me and said he had a plan to get Zorak to take us back to Karillion. He must've figured I wanted out of here as much as he did. It's simple, Eve. We ally ourselves with Zorak by persuading your grandparents and the rest of the colonists to do what he wants. In return, he rewards us with positions of power on our home planet."

"How could you possibly convince Jarak to go back?"

"Actually, you're the one who is going to convince him, in a roundabout way."

I looked at him in confusion. He must know I'd never help him.

Brad's answer chilled me to the core. "Because you're the bait. There's no way he'd ever let us take you from him. He'd do anything to keep you safe."

Instantly, every ounce of optimism faded. My grandfather thought I was the great hope of his people, the long awaited Chosen One. He was committed not only to fulfilling his mission but to helping me fulfill mine. Would he abandon everything for me?

Eventually, I drifted off to sleep from sheer exhaustion but jolted awake when I heard some sort of large vehicle pull up outside. Mack entered the huge barn as the first strips of daylight began to appear. Behind him were three men dressed in the same wetsuit-type uniforms as Anika's group. I recognized Zorak instantly. His resemblance to my mother was startling. He had white blond hair and icy blue-green eyes that zeroed in on me.

"This must be our lovely captive, Miss Evelyn Hunter, my dear sister's daughter. I can't tell you how pleased I was when my new friend Mack informed us of your presence. By the way, I have your mother to thank for my command of the English language."

His perfect English surprised and horrified me. Despite the fear that engulfed me when he spoke my name, I forced myself to ignore Zorak, addressing my comments to Mack. Holding onto my anger helped me keep my fear under control. "I thought you wanted me out of here so I wouldn't wreck the alien party. Didn't you say I was the last person you wanted on Karillion?"

"Eve, you're so easily manipulated. That's what I wanted you to think so you'd run off to Jarak and he wouldn't suspect anything before it was too late. I planned to use you as a bargaining chip all along. But enough of that subject, we have guests and you're being rude. Say hello to your Uncle Zorak and his soldiers."

Communicating with Mack intensified my anger. I faced the aliens with barely concealed fury. "Welcome to Earth, Uncle Zorak," I said, "Or I should say, Welcome back to Earth. I seem to recall you kidnapped my mother on a previous visit."

Zorak touched my shoulder, and I recoiled as if I'd been burned. His hypnotic voice was low and unnerving. "I'm afraid you misunderstand what happened, Evelyn. I journeyed here to return three young women back to their home planet where they belonged. Their parents forced them to Earth before they were old enough to make decisions for themselves. I missed my dear sister and felt it was my duty to bring her home. Unfortunately, I only discovered later that she'd had a child. You would've been most welcome to come along."

"What took you so long to return to Earth?"

"Pressing concerns on Karillion kept us occupied. Civil wars, disease outbreaks, fuel shortages—numerous difficulties demanded all our attention. But now it's time to escort the rest of our exiled Karillions back to their planet. We also hope to persuade a few earthlings to join us for the trip of a lifetime. Humans will jump at the chance to journey to another planet."

He seemed confident of his ability to convince me of his lies. I glared at him, having the sudden insane urge to laugh at his audacity. How I longed to wipe the smug expression from his arrogant face. "Well, Uncle Zorak, I'm afraid you're not going to find the colonists quite as cooperative as you expect. They came to Earth in search of freedom, and I'm fairly certain they will fight to the death to keep it."

"I certainly hope you're mistaken. Between myself and the twelve soldiers who accompany me, I believe we can persuade Jarak and his Colony to come peacefully. After all, four of them are already here."

"You're conveniently forgetting that one of us is here against her will. Or did the fact that my hands and feet are tied up escape your notice?"

Zorak laughed harshly. "How delightfully amusing you are! You remind me so much of Kara, who you'll have the opportunity to reunite with very soon."

Zorak motioned to his two companions to step outside. Mack congratulated Brad on his role in executing the plan and asked Tara if she needed to get some rest. His voice softened as he spoke to her, and I couldn't help but notice that he cared for her. I hadn't thought him capable of caring for anyone other than himself. I wondered if she felt anything for him or merely saw him as a means to get what she wanted.

Brad brought me the blanket he promised along with water and some granola bars. I kept calm by reminding myself that someone must've realized I was missing. Mack and Tara spoke softly while Brad and I sat in silence. Like he'd said, there was nothing small for us to talk about.

Suddenly, the door swung open, and the shack filled with alien soldiers. My heart hammered in my chest as multiple pairs of eyes fastened upon my face. Brad pulled me to my feet, gripping my arm possessively. I looked to him for reassurance but he stared straight ahead. Instantly, I remembered the premonition I'd had Friday morning. Why hadn't I paid attention to the warning I'd received about Brad?

Zorak motioned for Mack to come forward. After several minutes of discussion, Mack told Brad to grab my cell phone. "Zorak needs to set up a meeting with Jarak. Using Eve's phone will prove that we're serious."

Suddenly it occurred to me to try to send a telepathic distress signal to Daniel and my grandparents. They had to be out looking for me by now. It was a long shot, but if they somehow got close enough maybe they'd pick up my signal. I concentrated all my energy on transmitting a cry for help, making sure to direct my plea only to its intended receivers. Between their superior powers and the weapons they possessed, I trusted the colonists wouldn't be led into an ambush.

Zorak contacted my grandfather, forcing me to listen to every word. He told Jarak he'd taken me prisoner to encourage the colonists to join his crew on the return voyage to Karillion. My spirits fell as I realized my grandparents would know I'd run away from Terra Dyne and walked right into a trap. After a short conversation, Zorak demanded a meeting at the Reservoir at noon and ended the call, refusing to be sidetracked by any other questions.

"Jarak will cooperate. He will not risk his granddaughter," he assured us after he hung up.

Zorak rounded up six soldiers then ordered Brad to ride along as their guide. When Brad started to protest, Zorak informed him in a quiet, deadly voice that his orders were not to be questioned. Brad was in way over his head. Would he blindly obey everything my uncle told him to do? My dad's words echoed in my head, *that young man will do whatever it takes to get what he wants.* I sure hoped Dad was wrong.

Zorak's group had been gone less than fifteen minutes when an urgent message burst into my mind.

Eve? Are you here? I'm outside an old barn on the Pass.

Daniel! Don't come any closer! Zorak's soldiers are everywhere! No sooner had I sent the message than I heard a commotion out front. Daniel's voice cried out, then silence. I screamed in terror. Please, I pleaded with the heavens, let Daniel be safe.

One of the soldiers in the barn shouted something I didn't understand and pointed his weapon in my direction, motioning me to move away from the entrance. Mack yanked me to my feet and pushed me down on some burlap sacks stacked at the back of the barn. He told me to shut up, warning me that Zorak's men were capable of anything.

Daniel? Are you okay? I messaged, but there was no answer.

Two of the soldiers who'd been on guard outside flung the door open, dragging a limp body between them. I stared at Daniel's motionless frame, too scared to move. Tara collapsed against a wall in shock.

"Is he dead?" she screeched.

Mack said something to the soldiers and received an answer in the choppy Karillion language.

"No, he's been stunned," he told Tara. "But the soldiers had their stunners on maximum when they made contact. He should come out of it in a few minutes." Mack knelt beside Daniel to bind his hands and feet with duct tape, clearly enjoying the task.

I felt sick. His capture was my fault. I had led Daniel into an ambush. Not only had my stupidity put my life at risk, but it had also endangered others. Tara checked Daniel's injuries, while Mack scowled and insisted he was fine.

Daniel regained consciousness slowly, looking around confused and disoriented. Suddenly, Mack took a swing at him, knocking him to the floor. I flinched as if I'd been hit myself. Mack leaned over him, and I scooted closer, struggling to hear.

"I will not have you screw this up, Winter," Mack said through clenched teeth. "I swear if you get in my way, I will kill you. Hell, I may get rid of you anyway; you've caused trouble for me my entire life."

"Mack, what are you saying?" Tara asked. "Leave him alone. Daniel is harmless. He's not even a Mover, so we could overpower him easily. He only came after us because of that stupid girl."

"Daniel is dangerous because he's one of Jarak's disciples. For some reason, people listen to what he says. We don't want him trying to derail our plans. I know he's a friend of your brother's, but I'm right about this. We'd be better off without him."

Daniel, I pleaded. *Please, don't do anything to set him off. He's unstable.*

I've known that for a long time. Glad to see you're safe. How'd you get here?

Brad made up a story, saying his dad needed help, so I snuck out of Terra Dyne and met him. Somehow he found out I was a Healer.

Where is he now?

With Zorak and six soldiers, meeting Jarak at the Reservoir.

So Zorak's already here. I thought those men looked foreign.

Definitely foreign—as in out of this world, I said. *How did you find me?*

I don't know exactly. I sensed you were in trouble, so I got in my Jeep and started driving, ending up here. It was almost as if someone else was driving.

That's bizarre voodoo magic.

Tell me about it. But now that I'm here, we've got to find a way to escape, Daniel said.

Zorak left six soldiers with us, four on guard outside and two inside. I'm sitting next to a small room but the door's closed, and I can't see if there's a way out. Right behind these burlap sacks are some broken boards leading to the outside. I'll see if I can loosen them.

The four of us sat and watched the two guards. Tara's face had gone deathly pale. It was obvious she didn't like how this was playing out. Her reaction when the guards had carried Daniel inside had revealed her feelings for him. Jarak must've been right about her crush.

Tara broke the silence with an unexpected request. "Mack, how long are we going to be stuck here? I am starving. If we hurried, we could grab some food and be back before Zorak."

Mack rolled his eyes. "No way. We can't leave these two alone. Anything could happen, even with the guards here."

Tara let out an exaggerated sigh. "Well, how about if I go then? I promise I'll hurry."

Mack's eyes narrowed. "Why are you so anxious to leave? Having second thoughts?"

She brushed off his suspicions. "No, I helped you come up with this plan, remember? Why would I back out now? I told you, I'm hungry, plus it's freezing in here."

Mack looked unconvinced but wanting to please Tara, he reluctantly agreed. "I guess we will need to have some supplies, because we may be here awhile. I'll go. Keep an eye on these two, and don't let them talk you into anything. Zorak will have our heads if anything happens to her," he said, tilting his head in my direction.

Tara rolled her eyes and flipped her hair with an exaggerated sense of superiority as if keeping the two of us in line was beneath her abilities. Mack exchanged words with the soldiers and exited.

Within minutes, I received a message from Daniel. *Tara is afraid Mack plans to kill me. She's going to disable the guards and get me out of here. I told her I wasn't leaving without you. Think you can get us through those loose boards so we can sneak out the back?*

I've almost pried one open. Give me a couple minutes. I worked feverishly, masking the squeaking boards by coughing. Tara glared at me, obviously not happy to take me along. I held my breath. One final yank, and the largest board would come loose.

Now! I messaged Tara as I ripped the board free. She discharged her stunner at one guard while simultaneously using her powers to slam the other against the wall. Both slumped to the floor. She untied Daniel, and then ran to bolt the door while Daniel severed my bonds. We pushed our way through the splintered boards without a backward glance. We had one chance. It had to work.

Tara suggested we split up to increase our chances of at least one of us escaping. Daniel argued but Tara was right. Success was more likely if we separated. A soldier spotted me immediately. For the second time in twenty four hours, I slumped to the ground stunned, but this time remained conscious. My bleary mind registered relief that this particular gun's stun level must've been lowered from maximum. The guard helped me to my feet, muttering something unintelligible. He dragged me around the side of the barn. It was then I saw Mack sitting in his truck, waiting. He'd never left.

He jumped out and raced toward Daniel's fleeing form. The other guards joined in the chase. Tara must've seen Mack head for Daniel, because she changed course, putting herself between the two of them. Everything happened so fast. Two guards aimed their weapons at Tara while a third raised his arm directing a surge of energy in her direction.

"No!" Mack yelled putting himself directly in front of Tara, shielding her from the impact of the stunners and the forceful blow of the Mover.

Mack's body slammed violently against the trunk of a towering pine, and his neck jerked sideways. He collapsed like a rag doll. Instantly, I knew he was dead. I remained frozen, my muscles paralyzed, my eyes taking in everything. The forest fell eerily silent as the soldiers gathered around Mack's body at the base of the tree. Our plan had gone horribly wrong.

Tara lay on the ground, apparently hit by one of the stunners, but Daniel managed to escape amidst the chaos. Two soldiers took off after him, while the other four carried Tara and I inside the barn. Miles of forest surrounded us, and Daniel had a good chance of evading capture.

Tara's sobbing echoed throughout the barn. "Mack is dead. What have I done? What have I done?" she wailed. I never thought I could pity Tara, but her sobs were heart wrenching. I loathed and feared Mack, but I didn't want him to be dead.

I said the only thing I could think of to say. "It's not your fault, Tara."

"Are you completely brainless? Did you *see* what happened? His death is my fault."

There was nothing to do but let her wallow in her misery. Maybe she had a point, but I shared the blame. If I hadn't listened to Brad and run away from Terra Dyne, Daniel would've never come in search of me, and Tara wouldn't have helped him escape. Mack died trying to protect her. What tangled webs we weave.

Sometime later, Zorak and Brad returned with the Karillion soldiers. Brad entered first, zeroing in on my condition before taking note of Tara's bonds. Her swollen eyes and bowed head added to his confusion. I observed his distress with a mixture of guilt, pity, and anger, not sure which emotion was stronger.

"Daniel came looking for me...." I started.

"How did he find you?" Brad interrupted.

I shook my head wearily. "It doesn't matter. Daniel found me and was captured. When Mack threatened to kill Daniel, Tara tried to help him escape. Mack was hit by a stunner and one of their Movers while trying to protect Tara. He slammed into a tree and broke his neck."

My words set off a new round of sobbing from Tara. Brad was too shaken to reply. Zorak entered the barn and offered his condolences. Apparently, his men had given him an update.

"I sincerely regret the death of your friend. He was a bold young man and would've made a powerful ally on Karillion. Let's hope no one else has to die in order for us to reach our objective." His face was grave, and his eyes troubled. He left to confer with his men, taking the guards who'd been stunned into the small room on the side of the barn.

Eve, this is not what I wanted. I didn't expect anyone to get killed, Brad messaged.

You knew how dangerous an alliance with Mack would be. Did you honestly think the colonists would drop everything and hop on board with Zorak? I was so angry I neglected to send my last words telepathically and screamed them out loud. "Now Mack is dead, and we're all responsible!"

I understand that now. We need to find a way out of here, he pleaded.

Oh yeah. That worked so well last time, I'm anxious to try to escape again.

Brad sank to the floor next to Tara and put his head in his hands. I turned my face away in disgust. I had nothing else to say to him.

I don't know how long we sat there buried in despair, but it seemed like an eternity. Zorak and his guards emerged from the side room and went outside. Zorak barked unintelligible orders at his men, followed by the sound of two vehicle engines starting up. He'd probably sent them to collect the colonists. Without Mack, we had no translator.

When he came back in, he watched me thoughtfully from across the room, as if trying to make a decision. Finally, he wandered over to us, his brow wrinkled in concentration.

"There's something about you that's so familiar," he said, rubbing his chin. "Besides the fact you resemble your mother…but there's something else, like I've seen you before." He seemed unsettled, as if he'd seen a ghost.

He addressed Brad but kept his eyes glued to my face. "Escort our friend, Evelyn, to that small room in the corner. I would like to talk to her."

Brad obeyed mechanically and helped me to my feet. All the fight had gone out of him. I walked slowly toward the side room, shuffling awkwardly with my duct taped ankles. Zorak motioned us in and closed the door behind us. Brad positioned himself in front of me.

Zorak's voice purred like a slithering snake. "I fear you're correct, dear Evelyn. My persuasive powers were woefully inadequate. The colonists will not go quietly. They will fight, and your loved ones will die. My soldiers are trained for combat. You need to convince the colonists that rebellion will only bring tragedy. We don't want anyone else to die, do we?"

Zorak walked behind me, pulling me away from Brad. He clenched his large hands around my neck, not quite choking me but squeezing hard enough to get my attention. "If you choose not to assist me, not only will you witness a massacre, but I'll take you to Karillion, and I'll see to it that you never see your mother again. Do we have an understanding?"

Before I could react, I heard a muffled pop and Zorak released his hold on me. I turned to see him fall to the floor with a gaping bloody hole in his back.

I gasped. "Brad, what have you done?"

"I'm protecting you. Now let's get out of here!"

"I thought the soldiers took your weapon."

"They did, but I brought a backup—with a silencer. Looks like I needed it."

I stared at him, unable to reconcile this person with the Brad I knew. I had to act fast.

"Quick, lock the door and rip off this duct tape! I have to do something or he'll die."

"So what if he dies? He threatened to kill us!"

Tears began streaming down my face. "Brad, I'm sorry, but I can't go along with murder. Please! I have to do what I can to save him. Lock the door and help me!"

Brad locked the door and pulled off my bindings, trying desperately to change my mind. "Don't you get it? Zorak is our enemy. We should be trying to escape." Finally realizing he wasn't getting anywhere, he muttered to himself, "I don't know why I'm listening to you. We're going to regret this. How many bad decisions can one person possibly make in a single day?"

Zorak mumbled as he began to lose consciousness, his breathing labored and his eyes unfocused. "So this is how my life will end—holed up in an old barn, shot by a boy, and stranded a million miles from Karillion."

His eyes took on a faraway look as if he viewed distant vistas.

"You are not going to die," I insisted. "I will remove the bullet and attempt to repair your organs and tissues."

Zorak tried to focus on me. "Ah—a Healer, I might have guessed. Why are you doing this? Why would you try to save me?"

"Don't waste your breath on stupid questions. I guess because you're a person, a living being. Besides, Jarak said not even you were beyond redemption."

Brad and I rolled Zorak from his side to his stomach. I pulled my jacket off, got on my knees, and placed my hands on Zorak's mangled back, concentrating on dislodging the bullet and weaving his damaged organs together. Blood seeped between my fingers and covered the front of my clothes.

I felt a surge of pure energy flow from my body into his. Keeping my eyes closed, I focused all of my will on his recovery. The deadly bullet slipped to the surface, and I tossed it across the room. Inexplicably, Zorak began to stir beneath my hands after a few moments, even as weakness descended upon me.

"Is it working?" Brad asked. His voice was fuzzy, like he was under water. When I didn't reply, he continued, his voice trembling with fear, "You better hope the soldiers don't get suspicious and try to get in here."

As if on cue, one of the soldiers pounded on the door, calling Zorak's name and shouting something in the alien language. Brad and I froze, searching frantically for a way out. We were trapped. If the soldiers came in, we had no chance.

Chapter 26

Zorak rolled onto his back and made a strangled sound, staring up at me in astonishment. My first thought was that he was overwhelmed by my healing ability. But then he reached up toward my neck and grabbed my necklace, cradling the medallion as if it were the rarest of gems. I jerked backward as the shouting outside the door resumed.

Zorak recovered enough to yell out a response without taking his eyes off the medallion. The relentless pounding stopped. Brad kept the gun trained on Zorak, shifting his weight from side to side nervously. But my uncle didn't notice. My necklace had his complete attention. "Karillion's moons," he whispered feverishly, running his finger over the crescent moons hovering above the glossy silver disc with the blue-green stones. "Where did you get this?"

"From a friend, Misty—a Native American friend," I said, rambling from fear and exhaustion. "Her grandparents made it years ago. I don't remember meeting them as a child, but when they died, they left a note saying the necklace belonged to me. Dad and I moved back to Ridgway a couple months ago, and Misty gave it to me."

"It is you," Zorak breathed. "Do you realize what this means?"

I shook my head slowly, my eyes locked on his face. The air around us thickened. I know this sounds crazy, but I had the sensation of the room filling with invisible beings. Brad lowered the gun, and let out a small cry. Something of monumental importance was occurring.

"The prophecy has been fulfilled," Zorak insisted. I tore my gaze away from my uncle and looked at Brad in bewilderment. Had Zorak's injuries damaged his mental faculties?

"As a young man, I dreamed of this medallion many times. Sometimes my dreams included a young woman leaning over me with this necklace dangling from her neck, and I would hear a voice saying, *You must protect the wearer of the medallion.* I wandered the streets for years, hoping to encounter this girl. As I got older, I convinced myself these visions were the imaginations of a youthful mind—and I stopped searching."

Zorak's eyes filled with tears, caught up in the turbulent emotions his memories created.

"So you believe I'm this young woman?" I said.

"Without a doubt. My dreams have come to life."

I didn't know what to do next, but I felt certain Zorak was not a threat. I motioned for Brad to put the gun away. "I don't think he plans to hurt us anymore."

Brad resisted, still uncertain of Zorak's intentions. "That's a great story but why should we trust you? Five minutes ago, your hands were around Eve's neck."

"Can't you see how these events have been orchestrated? Evelyn's medallion—the fact that it was created specifically for her and given to her shortly before my arrival—these circumstances mean my father has spoken the truth all along. Evelyn is the foretold Chosen One who will save Karillion and perhaps Earth as well. Maybe the Khalaheem are visionary guardians, as my father has always claimed."

Brad needed time to digest Zorak's information. He looked like he was barely keeping himself together. Sliding his gun slowly into his coat pocket, he leaned against the wall.

"Okay, say I'm buying your sudden change of heart. What happens now?" Brad asked.

"We have to abort the mission. We must leave immediately to prevent my soldiers and Jarak's colony from attacking each other. Now that I understand the truth of my father's teachings, I believe you are correct, Evelyn. The colonists will fight to the death to preserve their freedom, and Jarak will stop at nothing to protect you."

Zorak pulled my cell phone from his jacket and placed a frantic call to Jarak. Tears rolled down my cheeks as I listened to my uncle's words. "Jarak—father—my soldiers are on their way. I've spoken with Evelyn. I've seen her medallion, the medallion of my dreams. Father—forgive me for the terrible pain I've caused. We can work together to save Karillion and Earth. We are Khalaheem. It is our destiny."

Six months later at Lone Cone

It was midnight. We gathered around Zorak's ship, an assortment of colonists, Karillions, and earthlings. Zorak and his men had lived among us for six months. In that time, they'd witnessed the advantages of a society where men were at liberty to choose their own destiny. They were returning to Karillion to join the resistance and campaign for the freedom of their people.

Brad stood next to the Andersens, suited up in the uniform of space-flight. He had been granted his desire; he was going to find his mother. His dad had never returned. Ruth had blossomed under her mother's love, and her devotion to Brad had helped him move past the tragedies of his life.

Sarah and Erik had their arms wrapped around each other, watching the preparations for the ship's departure. Tara had mellowed somewhat in the past few months and had changed her mind about leaving the planet. She'd also begun to accept Sarah's place in her brother's life.

Augustine and Emily waited for takeoff, thankful Brad was the only one of their friends leaving for Karillion. We even had one unexpected guest with us—Misty. My grandfather had surprised me by inviting her to witness the spaceship's departure. He figured she deserved to know our secret since her role in delivering the medallion had altered the course of our lives.

Mack's family gazed upon the ship in silence, perhaps wondering if they'd regret their choice to remain on Earth with the colonists. They'd collected their son's body from the mountainside and had a simple funeral. The official story was that Mack had died from falling off a cliff. His broken neck and internal injuries substantiated that claim. No one blamed Tara or Brad for their role in his death.

Remembering the pain we'd endured brought tears to my eyes, but healing would come. My dad and my grandparents exchanged heartfelt farewells with Zorak, a testament to the progress we'd made and the bonds we'd formed since that awful day on Dallas Creek Pass. My uncle saved his last goodbye for me, the young woman of his boyhood dreams whom he'd been guided to find and protect.

"Goodbye, Evelyn. You have a vital mission before you and will undoubtedly succeed. You've already saved one lost soul. Be brave. I will find a way to send your mother back to Earth. We will meet again." Zorak hugged me tightly then headed for his ship.

The young man by my side gazed at me with so much love it took my breath away. Daniel had been my constant companion ever since the kidnapping, reluctant to let me out of his sight for fear I'd disappear again. Life held boundless opportunities for us. I clasped my hand in his, meeting his beautiful green eyes with love and hope for the future.

Acknowledgments

Ever since I read my first Nancy Drew book at seven years old, I've wanted to write a book. I am overwhelmed with gratitude that my dream has finally come to pass. I'd like to thank the many wonderful people who have helped me with my writing journey.

To the wonderful women of the American Night Writers' Association: Thank you for giving me essential guidance and the confidence to begin.

To my beta readers: Thank you for reading my manuscript, offering comments, and calming me down when I started doubting myself—which happened often. I'd like to send a special thank you to my first beta reader, Debbie Breese, and to an amazing, insightful young lady, Echo Gray.

To my friends and extended family: Thank you for listening patiently as I talked about my book, years before anything showed up in print. You continue to give me strength and courage.

And finally, to my husband and my sons: Thanks for enduring my tears, rages, and excuses. Your love and support mean the world to me.

About the Author

Wendy C. Jorgensen lives in Reno, Nevada, at least most of the time, with a wonderful husband who's a financial guru—thank goodness—and a golden retriever who's often mistaken for a sloth. She recently moved to Nevada from Colorado, where pieces of her heart are scattered all over the state. Wendy has two creative and brainy sons, and she's always struggling to keep up with their latest projects. She hopes to someday journey to the stars.

Made in the USA
San Bernardino, CA
08 August 2016